Whispers on the Water

She could not let him go believing he was unloved, unlovable. She had no idea what she had hoped for, perhaps in her naïvety that at the last moment he would relent, allow her to put her arms about him, let him see what his return to the trenches meant to her, what his return to *her* would mean to her. But he had spurned her advances, the love she had offered him, for the third time . . .

No man should go to war without the knowledge that he would be missed by some woman. That he was treasured . . .

About the author

Audrey Howard was born in Liverpool in 1929. Before she began to write she had a variety of jobs, among them hairdresser, model, shop assistant, cleaner and civil servant. In 1981, living in Australia, she wrote the first of her bestselling novels: this is the twenty-seventh. She lives in St Anne's on Sea, her childhood home.

Audrey Howard

WHISPERS ON
THE WATER

CORONET BOOKS
Hodder & Stoughton

Copyright © 2001 by Audrey Howard

First published in Great Britain in 2002 by Hodder and Stoughton
First published in Great Britain in paperback in 2002 by
Hodder and Stoughton
A division of Hodder Headline
A Coronet paperback

The right of Audrey Howard to be identified as the Author of the
Work has been asserted by her in accordance with the Copyright,
Designs and Patents Act 1988.

1 3 5 7 9 10 8 6 4 2

A CIP catalogue record for this title is available
from the British Library

ISBN 0 340 76933 5

Typeset in Sabon by Palimpsest Book Production Limited,
Polmont, Stirlingshire

Printed and bound in Great Britain by
Mackays of Chatham plc, Chatham, Kent

Hodder and Stoughton
A division of Hodder Headline
338 Euston Road
London NW1 3BH

I am dedicating this book to the memory of Aunty Dolly and Uncle Alf who were there with me during the bad times.

I

"You are not coming, George, and that's my last word on the matter. I can't think of anything worse than being lumbered with one's younger brother." The remark was made with the lofty disdain often assumed by the eldest in the family, which Arthur was. "I'm to meet Toby and Rupert and one or two other fellows from the university and the last thing we want is a crowd of kids—"

"I'm not a crowd of kids, you daft beggar," George said hotly. "There's only one of me and I'm sixteen. You're only a year older and you know that Pa likes us to go about together."

"I don't give a damn what Pa likes." There was a concerted gasp from the group of young people who were sprawled about the living-room as the last desperate words exploded from between the lips of the first speaker and he himself had the decency to look somewhat shamefaced.

"Sorry, Pa," he mumbled, though Pa wasn't present, and the rest of them sighed in relief. They all loved their father dearly and would not willingly upset him but it was very plain Arthur Tooley was quite resolute in his intention not to give way on this one. He was mad about anything mechanical in this era of the burgeoning growth of the motor car and the aeroplane, particularly the aeroplane which was why he was furiously determined to go and watch the spectacle of Mr Henry G. Melly, a member of a well-known Liverpool family, take off in his monoplane from a field on the outskirts of the city. And he didn't want the embarrassment of dragging his siblings with him. Even one brother was out of the question.

They were devoted to one another, the Tooleys, all seven of them, and would have fought to the death to protect one another from outside danger but that didn't mean they didn't have frequent disagreements, violent flare-ups among themselves which often led to hot words, since they were all quick-tempered and strong-willed. They were handsome, tall, with the warm colouring they had inherited from their father, glossy hair the colour of treacle toffee streaked with copper when the sun caught it, eyes glowing a rich honey brown, the amber of their skin seeming to speak of warmer climes than that of the north. Their mother, who was small, fair and blue-eyed, often remarked that had she not herself given birth to them she might have believed they were not related to her at all. At least one of them might have favoured her, she told them, as though it were some fault in them that they were the spit of their father. It was perhaps for this reason that she had borne seven of them before giving up hope that she might, if she was persistent and patient enough, hold in her arms a child who looked like her. John, who was eleven, was her last gasp, her husband whimsically remarked, and he was as dark as the others.

The seven of them lolled in various postures about the room, which was furnished comfortably, if in the slightly old-fashioned manner of the late Victorian era current when Edwin and Mary Tooley were married just eighteen years ago. Much of the furniture and furnishings had been inherited from their respective parents, all dead now, but the Victorians had built things, all kinds of things from piano stools to iron bridges, to last and last they had. The Victorian love of colour and ornament was more in evidence here than in any other room in the house. Rich drapes and hangings provided a background for plush furnishings, creating an opulent, if slightly shabby effect. The room had a highly polished wooden floor which Edwin often regretted when his seven children clattered in wearing their heavy, outdoor boots, making a din that could be heard at the Pier Head. From a rail hung dozens of pictures, some made from dried shells, needlework or tapestry panels, engravings and watercolours, so many of them the walls could hardly be seen. The woodwork was painted a rich brown. There was a cast-iron fire grate with a brass fender on which Arthur's boots rested and over it an elaborate mantelshelf whereon the ornaments beloved of Mary Tooley were carefully arranged. In the fireplace burned a bright fire piled high with glowing coals. Beside it a brass scuttle held more coals, black and shining and ready to be shovelled carelessly on to the blaze, for the Tooley family, though not enormously wealthy, were well placed in the order of things. The ceiling, painted white with distemper, was decorated with an ornate plaster centre rose of flowers and foliage and moulded cornices.

The centre table was covered with a maroon-coloured plush cloth under which many a shrieking game of Pirates, Lions and Tigers or Log cabins and Indians, all devised by Arthur, had once been played. The occasional tables and sideboard were solid, dark and intricately carved, a dark mahogany with a reddish tinge, and picking one's way round the crowded room in the long skirts of the day was no mean feat. Arranged on the tables and indeed on every available surface were glass and porcelain vases, a massive glass dome covering a display of stuffed birds and an array of boxes of all shapes and sizes. Mary Tooley had despaired as each new baby appeared and had finally decreed that until a child reached the age of five, when, presumably, it might be considered responsible enough to heed the warning, *don't touch*, it must be relegated to the family room or the kitchen, both of which were more plainly furnished. There was a deep sofa covered with a flowered shawl, an armchair in which only the rear portion of the master of the house was supposed to rest and several low, curved-back, armless button-backed chairs.

The only female in the room stood up and moved to the window. Pushing back the shrouding nets she leaned her elbows on the sill, cupping her chin in her hands, watching as a tramcar rattled by along Sheil Road. She was tall and thin, all arms and legs and sticking-out shoulder blades; coltish, her mother described her as, but there was a promise of a young beauty about her, a grace which would come as she matured. Her hair was plaited, the plait falling down her back to her buttocks where it was tied with a drab cotton ribbon. It was the thickness of a man's wrist and despite its rigid imprisonment inclined to be curly where tendrils escaped around her face and ears. Finding nothing to interest her in the view, which she had seen every day of her thirteen years, she turned to look round the room at its other occupants, two of whom were still arguing, the others staring moodily into space.

"Well, you can say what you like, Arthur Tooley, but I for one am going to see Mr Melly take off. I don't know what the rest of you are to do but if you imagine for one minute I'm going to miss this show then you're mistaken. Heavens, how often do we get to see a real live aviator—"

"He's not a *real* aviator, George. Just because he's got an aeroplane—"

"Didn't you tell us that he's one of only a couple of thousand men in the world to be awarded his Pilot's Certificate, Arthur?" his sister asked innocently, for George was not the only one who meant to see Mr Melly's aeroplane. She was dressed as young ladies of the day were dressed, at least in her station of life. She had just returned from school, the Clifton House School for Girls in Wavertree, and she still wore her drab brown drill-dress, or gym-tunic as they were being more frequently called. It had a belt just below the waistline and under it she wore a cream shantung blouse. The skirt reached to her knees and she wore dark brown woollen stockings.

"Yes, that's true, so I suppose you could call him an aviator . . ." Arthur still sounded dubious, for his idea of an aviator was someone like the Wright brothers, Henri Farman, or Charles Stewart Rolls who had been killed at the Bournemouth Aviation Week only last year.

The rest of them stirred restlessly, sighing and fidgeting, for this . . . this exchange, if it could be called that, between Arthur and Grace, in fact between any one of them and Grace, was a daily event. Grace had a quick mind and her father often remarked, almost sadly, for he loved her dearly, that it was a pity she had not been born a boy. In the verbal duels that took place among the children she always seemed to triumph as though, not being as physically strong as her brothers, even John, the youngest, her brain, her wit, her swift cleverness, her sharp intelligence had been given her in compensation. She was the only girl in a family of boys and it was not surprising, though her mother did her best to restrain it, that she thought as a boy, did her best to be included in what the boys did, to play the games boys played and was totally determined that when she grew up, which would be when she was sixteen, she declared, she meant to find employment as a man would. Not for her the tedious life of a woman like her mother who ran the household, her husband, and the rest of them with the military precision of an army general. Not that Grace could see this. She would not have believed it if anyone had told her that her mother was the real head of the family and, though she never went down to the shop in Lord Street, was the power behind the throne on which Edwin Tooley sat.

"We know what you're up to but you know Mother won't let you go, Gracie," Richard told her, crossing his ankles and lounging even lower in his mother's sewing chair. Richard was thirteen and Grace's twin. He was taller than she was, an amiable boy who, with a book in his pocket, was perfectly happy in his own company, perhaps the result of living cheek by jowl with five brothers and a sister. He was fond of poetry though he kept that pretty quiet and when he had had enough of the squabbles that are frequent in a large family, he would take himself off and wander along the marine parade where the quiet, patient presence of the great ships lay along the miles and miles of busy dockland and where he could hear himself think! He, George, who was sixteen, Robert, fifteen, Tom, fourteen and John who was eleven, all attended Blue Coat School which five years ago had moved out from the city and now occupied a site in Church Road, Wavertree. Edwin and Mary Tooley had chosen the prestigious seat of learning for their boys when Arthur, then five years old, was ready to begin his education. It had been famous ever since it was first opened in 1709, then a charity school, and through the ages there had been many a prominent Liverpool gentleman who had reason to thank its good offices for his own success. Close to Blue Coats further along Church Road was the Clifton House School for Girls and it was for this reason, as well as its reputation for educating girls to a good standard, that Grace had been enrolled there. Her brothers, in theory, were supposed to deposit her at the gates each morning and pick her up each afternoon, escorting her safely home but, as boys are boys and not awfully keen on being seen with their little sister, this seldom happened. Not that Grace cared, for like her brothers she had her own coterie of friends and God forbid the twain should ever meet!

Arthur, who was a brainy lad, the brainiest of them all, had moved on to the University of Liverpool on Brownlow Hill where he was to study engineering. They were all proud as punch, Mrs Tooley unable to stop herself from dropping into the conversation when she had friends for tea that her son was to be an engineer with a degree, for Arthur was only just seventeen and young to be already at university.

They sprawled, the attractive sons of Edwin and Mary Tooley, their hands in their trouser pockets, their long legs spread out before them, crossed at the ankle, and glumly surveyed their sister, for there was no doubt she would cause trouble. John lay on his stomach on the rug in front of the fire wrestling with a scruffy, rough-haired terrier by the name of Topsy, the dog growling in mock anger, the boy taking little interest in the conversation. It made little difference to him what they decided, for he meant to bicycle up to the take-off field the next day, a Saturday, and see the daring Mr Melly hurtle into the sky. Arthur at seventeen would be sure to go, but if Grace stirred up trouble with their little mother by demanding to be part of it, it was likely Ma would put her foot down and forbid the rest of them to go. Well, Ma would make it her business to see that Pa put his foot down. Pa was easy-going but Ma was a tinker when she was determined to have her own way and Grace was the one most likely to get her going.

"Well?" Grace demanded, looking from one to the other.

"Well what?" George wanted to know. He was closest to the fire and on his lap, because of it, was curled the family cat, Wally. Wally was a beautiful marmalade tom who must have wandered or been thrown out of his home and had been found shivering on their front doorstep on the day Henry Wallace gave a gift of £5,000 to the Liverpool Presbyterian Church of which their mother was a member. Wally, irreverently, had been named after the generous gentleman and though their mother had disapproved the name had stuck.

"Are we going to stand together on this?"

"Oh, for God's sake, Gracie, you know that whatever we decide if Mother says we're not to go, that's that."

"Not necessarily. We could just sneak off on our bicycles. In fact I don't think we should tell her." Grace warmed to her theme and Tom and Robert leaned forward eagerly, for they were always up for anything that smacked of excitement.

Arthur groaned and combed his hands through his abundant mop of dark, wavy hair.

"Hell's teeth!" Arthur was rather proud of the oaths he had learned from among his pals at the university and often flung them into the conversation to impress his brothers and sister, not, of course, in front of Ma and Pa. "I'm sorry I told you about it now. I could have just gone off with Toby and none of you the wiser. Now there's going to be ructions if you mention to Ma and Pa that you all want to go. Especially you, Gracie. The others might just get away with it."

"Damnation!" Grace swung away from the window and advanced into the centre of the room, her face bright with indignation, her eyes flashing like the beacon at the mouth of the river. "Why is it that you can all do things and I can't?"

"You know why, Gracie," Richard said resignedly. "You're a girl and Ma wants you to—"

"What? Become a young lady who marries well and produces a tribe of children like she did?"

"Something like that . . ."

"Well, she can go to the devil." Again there was a gasp of incredulity, for though their mother was strict she was fair and they all loved her. But then they were male and they had to admit that they were allowed far more freedom than their sister who, at thirteen, was expected to go about with Ma in the social sphere to which they belonged. They were far from gentry, like the Hemingways or the Osbornes, since the Tooleys were what was known as *trade*. Pa had a tobacconist's shop in Lord Street which he had started twenty years ago with the small inheritance his father had left him. It was a thriving business, being in a prime position, and anyone but Edwin Tooley would have been even more successful, perhaps expanding into other premises, but Edwin was an easy-going man. He was content with the income it brought him, an income that had allowed him and his family to live in comfort in Newsham Park. Sheil Road was bordered by Sheil Park at the front and Newsham Park at the rear, a very pleasant outlook, almost like living in the country. His boys went to a good school which would prepare them for the world of commerce he foresaw for them, and his daughter mixed with the better families where a decent, hardworking young man might be found as a suitable husband.

Arthur pushed himself out of his father's armchair, fastidiously smoothed down his jacket and trousers and straightened his tie, for Arthur was a bit of a dandy. He moved towards the door as though to say he washed his hands of the whole affair. *He* was going tomorrow and what the rest of them did was up to them. "I'm having nothing more to do with—"

As he reached for the doorknob the door opened inwards with great vigour and Mary Tooley entered the room, just in time to hear Arthur's words. She almost knocked him to the floor, for she was a bustling little woman and when she came into a room it was with the force of a whirlwind.

"You're having nothing to do with what, dear?" she asked, smiling, a smile they all knew well. It said that no matter how they wriggled she would have the truth out of them, and though she had no idea what they had been talking about she could tell by their guilty faces it was something they'd rather she didn't know about.

"Er . . . nothing, Ma."

"Now then, dear, you don't talk about nothing. It must have been something."

She arched her back and squared her shoulders and Grace's heart sank. She knew that no matter how long it took, her mother would do her utmost to have it out of them and though she might allow the boys to go tomorrow to see the marvellous Mr Melly take off into the skies, there was little hope of *her* being included. Unless the boys could be made to keep their mouths shut; if she could persuade them or bully them or bride them into keeping silent. If they said nothing about Mr Melly she might get out of the house on some pretext and cycle up there to watch the wonder of flight. She dearly wanted to see it, for though Arthur was an engineer, or would be when he had finished his studies, he was not the only member of the family to be passionate about the mechanical age.

She managed to throw a look of dreadful warning about the room as they all stood up slowly. The cat, screeching his displeasure, was dropped hastily to the rug where he fell on the dog who turned to growl at him. They tolerated one another but this was too much and as Wally spat and Topsy growled Arthur took advantage of the commotion and dashed from the room into the wide hallway that led to the stairs. He galloped up them two at a time, reaching the bedroom he shared with George, banging the door behind him, the echo of it telling them that whatever happened they were to leave him out of it.

The rest tried to do the same, uttering loud remarks about homework and jobs to be done which Pa had set them and Ma smiled as she moved into the room, opened her work basket which stood on a side table, withdrew a sock she was darning, sat down in her accustomed chair by the fire and began to ply her needle.

They ate in what was called the family room. It had a large rectangular table around which were nine plain, ladderbacked wooden chairs. Here the children gathered to do their homework, to play board games, to paint and draw and do all the things a growing family interests itself in. At mealtimes Pa sat at the head and Ma at the foot. Arthur, George and Robert were seated down one side, with Tom, Richard, Grace and John in strict order of age down the other. It saved a lot of squabbling, Ma had decided long ago, if her children were arranged in this way and always kept to the same seating at every meal. Pa would have allowed his children to sit where they pleased since he was a man of an agreeable, pliant nature, charming in his way, but this, in Ma's opinion, would only lead to disarray and constant quarrels over who was to sit where. As in most things Ma's will was law.

There was a shelved dresser against one wall stacked with the plain crockery the family used every day, as well as dishes of the best English stoneware in a pleasing design of blue birds perched on flowered branches, soup tureens to match, with gravy boats beside them. There were copper pots and copper soup ladles, jelly moulds and a bowl of fruit, and to one side a pile of ironing just completed by their maid. The Tooleys' nature, every last one of them, was not to be scrupulously tidy, and there was an air of homeliness, of comfort and warmth about the room. It looked out over the strip of garden at the back of the house, which nurtured a few apple trees, and at the long windows hung curtains of rich red wool to keep out the cold east wind that blew across the Pennine range. The tablecloth was snowy and in the centre was placed a beautifully arranged vase of spring flowers bought that morning from St John's Market. Ma did all her own marketing, having most of it delivered to the back kitchen door.

Number 10 Sheil Road was a large, semi-detached, three-storeyed family house. There was the living-room at the front, a dining-room behind the living-room, which was used only on special occasions, and behind that the family room which led into the kitchen and scullery. On the first floor lay three bedrooms. The front bedroom which overlooked the long strip of garden and Sheil Road was occupied by Ma and Pa, the second was Grace's and the third had been transformed into that wonder of wonders, a bathroom with running water.

The third floor was the boys' territory, Arthur and George sharing one room, Robert and Tom the second and Richard and John in the third. Above them were the attics where a room with a window in the roof had been partitioned off and was the private sanctum of

Nora, the family's elderly, outspoken maid of all work. Let any one of them, including Grace, wander up there and Nora, who was Irish with a temper to match, would box their ears. Only the mistress of the house ventured up to Nora's room now and again. Nora was a treasure who worked for next to nothing and had been with Mary ever since her marriage and not one of them dared to cross her. There was a daily cleaning woman, Mrs Dutton, who came in to help with the heavy work and do the family's laundry and so the household was made up.

Nora could be seen through the arched doorway that led from the family room into the kitchen, which had white, lime-washed walls, stirring a pan of Mary Tooley's delicious gravy on the top of the big, cast-iron range. The range was hopelessly old-fashioned but if it did its job, which it did, why change it, Mary declared. Nora agreed with her. The gravy would be served with the neck of lamb, the spring cabbage, the roast potatoes and the mint sauce which Mary herself had prepared, all waiting on the scrupulously scrubbed and enormous pine table where most of the work was performed. She was an excellent cook. Let into one wall was a door which led to the walk-in pantry. Another, which stood open, led to the scullery with its own stone sink, draining-board and wooden draining-racks.

They tucked in with the appetites of the young which even a family upheaval could not destroy and it was not until the last portion of apple sponge pudding and rich creamy custard, over which Tom and John had fought, was eaten that Ma spoke, continuing the conversation that had been interrupted in the living-room, just as though there had been no time between.

"So, my dear, what was it that you were to have nothing to do with then?" she enquired sweetly of Arthur.

Arthur, primed by the quick-witted mind of his sister who had cornered him in his bedroom after George had gone down, coloured to the easy blush of the boy just growing into a man. He took a deep breath and prepared to lie for her, or suffer the consequences. Arthur was "sweet" on the pretty daughter of the recently moved-in family next door, a wine merchant of prosperous means, and was of an age when any mention of a member of the opposite sex plunged him into a dithering state of imbecility. None of his brothers knew of his passion for Josie, but Grace, being of the female sex, had noticed immediately and unless Arthur backed her up she would spread it to the four winds, she had told him, smiling sweetly as she watched him fling himself about the bedroom. He had blustered and almost been driven to strike her but he had given in.

"It's the school sports day next week, Ma, at Grace's school" – which was true – "and I absolutely refuse to go. I'll only be roped in to run in the three-legged race or something . . ."

His brothers stared at him in bewildered amazement, since this was the first they had heard of it.

"What is wrong with that, son?" Pa asked mildly, sipping an after-dinner glass of port, one that his new neighbour had recommended.

This last remark released them from their open-mouthed wonder and let off such an uproar of objections among his sons who swore they wouldn't be seen dead in a *girls'* race that Mary Tooley was quite distracted and did not notice her daughter's quiet smile of satisfaction.

2

Grace waited until she heard her mother close the front door firmly behind her before darting furtively into Ma and Pa's bedroom and peeping out from behind the snowy nets at the window. Ma was halfway down the narrow garden path where she stopped to study the progress of the antirrhinums that Pa had planted in readiness for the summer. She and Pa were keen gardeners, spending hours each Sunday when the weather permitted weeding this and pruning that, putting in the bulbs, crocus, daffodils and hyacinth, earlier in the year and which now were over, and lately the bedding plants such as begonias, busy Lizzies, aubretia and allysum which bordered the lawn, long and thin, but nevertheless Pa's pride. Like a billiard table, it was, and if any of them should dare walk on it, it would be the worse for them. As for that dog which would dig a hole in the most unlikely places to bury her bone, she would be out of the house and down at the lost dogs' home before you could say Jack Robinson, a favourite saying of Pa's!

Ma had her shopping basket on her arm and was dressed for a visit to town in her good dove-grey three-quarter coat and ankle-length skirt, her wide-brimmed pale grey hat decorated with a profusion of pink silk roses, grey kid gloves and a long, furled umbrella and she looked what she was, the well-turned-out wife of a successful tradesman. She wore grey kid boots buttoned down each side, with a two-inch Louis heel, smart but comfortable.

There was a tramcar just turning the corner out of West Derby Road and as it stopped outside the house, Ma crossed the road to the tramlines in the middle, nodding graciously at a cyclist who halted to let her pass in front of him. The conductor, recognising a lady when he saw one, took her elbow as she boarded the tramcar and after seeing her seated inside, rang the bell for the driver to proceed. Ma had this effect on people. Mostly men. She was so dainty, so pretty, so agreeable and at the same time gave the impression that she was in need of male protection, which was not true as the Tooley family all knew. She was the daughter of a master cutler, a man of means, and was well brought up but without the pedigree to make the marriage her father wished for her. Instead she had married Edwin Tooley, the son of a ships' chandler in Water Street, a prosperous little business but not one, to his father's disappointment, Edwin felt he could put his life into. Why he had chosen to become a tobacconist was never quite explained, either to his wife or to his children, who were not, of course, consulted, nor, if they had been, would they have been unduly interested anyway. He was an outgoing man, he liked people, he had an easy, pleasant way of chatting to his many customers who came from all walks of life, from the man who bought five Wild Woodbines in a paper packet to the gentleman who purchased his very best cigars, and it was perhaps this that made his business so successful and himself so content. He had made a happy marriage and if his children had been brought up in the slightly unorthodox, some would say *lax*, way that was not an example of the times – the Victorian era had ended only ten years ago – they had emerged unscathed, well-mannered, good-natured, wilful at times but controllable. Mary was the ruler of their lives, the arbiter whose last word was law and they loved and respected her for it. And if she had known the intentions of her daughter on this day she would not have blithely boarded a tram and gone off to town for a morning's shopping.

Grace let the nets fall and dashed from the room, galloping down the stairs two at a time, leaping the last into the wide, hushed hallway which was lit only by the fanlight over the front door, skidding on the bright rug that covered the black and white tiled floor and almost crashing into the hallstand. The tall grandfather clock that stood under the stairs ticked the minutes away solemnly and Grace muttered under her breath, for the boys would be waiting for her in the lane at the side of the house. Ma knew that Arthur and George were to go to see Mr Melly and his aeroplane, though the reason for it was a mystery to her. But then boys would be boys, violently excited about anything new and so she had shrugged as they discussed it at breakfast. The others had held their breath just in case Ma took it into her head to question them on what they might be doing this Saturday morning but she and Pa had been conferring on the likelihood of the strikes and riots that threatened Liverpool and how, if they took place, they might affect the tobacco business. If the strikers gained the upper hand at the tobacco factory in Boundary Lane, where might the tobacco, so essential to Pa's business, be obtained? they asked one another. The flight of Mr Melly was far from their minds.

Mrs Dutton was on her knees scrubbing the rosy flags of the kitchen floor, her back bent into the effort and as Grace exploded into the kitchen she gave a great start and almost knocked the bucket she had just filled with hot water from the boiler on to its side.

"'Ere, young lady, wha' d'yer think yer up to?" She reared up on her knees and wiped a red, wrinkled hand across her dripping nose. "Yer nearly 'ad me bucket over." She turned to Nora who had whipped round, just as confounded, and stood, one hand on her hip, at the table where she had been rolling out a nice bit of pastry for a steak and kidney pie of which the master was very fond. On the rug before the glowing range Wally lifted a disdainful head and contemplated Grace with feline indifference but Topsy, who had only minutes before been rebuffed by the boys when she had indicated she wanted to go with them, bounded across to Grace and looked up at her hopefully, her head on one side.

"Yer see tha', Nora?" Mrs Dutton continued in high dudgeon. "Nearly 'ad me bucket over, she did, an' wharr I'd like ter know is where she's goin' dressed like tha', an' more ter't point does 'er Ma know about it?" Both she and Nora were well aware of Mrs Tooley's uphill tussle to bring her daughter up as a young lady should be in a house full of lads, and she'd not be best pleased to hear that she had been roaring up and down on them dratted machines with her brothers which it seemed she was about to do. It was a mystery to them why the lass had been bought one in the first place but then it was known Mr Tooley was soft-hearted where his daughter was concerned. Mrs Dutton surveyed Grace from head to foot disapprovingly. Mrs Dutton and her family had never in their lives been further than the Pier Head, let alone over the water to New Brighton on the ferry which this lot did frequently, and the way the "gentry", as she was apt to name the Tooley family, ripped about the countryside, and beyond, was a bloomin' wonder to her.

"Aye, I'd like ter know that an' all, Grace Tooley," Nora said with the outspokenness of the old and life-long servant. She spoke as she found and she found young Grace's "get-up" and her obvious determination to leave the house stealthily by the back door decidedly suspicious. Her ma hadn't said anything about her daughter going out. Them lads had vanished ten minutes since and now, two minutes after the mistress went off to town here was the lass slipping out the back door in a very secretive manner, *and* dressed for cycling. Oh yes, Nora recognised cycling gear even if she herself had never been near one of them infernal things, and never would neither.

"Oh, Nora, dear Nora, please don't try to stop me," Grace pleaded, getting ready to leap Mrs Dutton's bucket and be off through the door, just as though the two women would forcibly try to restrain her.

"Would it do any good if I did?"

"No, I'm afraid it wouldn't. I'm to go to see Mr Melly fly his aeroplane from a field in Old Swan—"

Nora screeched in horror and threw up her hands. "Why in the name of God would yer wanner do tha'? 'Tisn't natural. Birds 'as wings an' man don't an' if this 'ere Mr What's-his-name was ter fall outer't sky on ter yer 'ead yer ma'd never fergive me."

"He won't do that, Nora. Men have been up in their flying machines for years now and one day I shall go up, I promise you."

Nora, being a devout Catholic, crossed herself hastily and so did Mrs Dutton before plunging her red hands back in her bucket where they belonged. The world today was a mystery to her.

"Well, don't say I didn't warn yer," Nora pronounced gloomily, looking as though she were convinced this was the last time she and Grace would ever clap eyes on each other.

Arthur, naturally, had been the first in the family to possess a bicycle. At the age of twelve when he had been deemed old enough to take a responsible view of the ever increasing motorised traffic on the roads, traffic brought about by the fascination of the wealthy – who were the only ones who could afford them – his father had taken him to the Rover Bicycle Shop in Lord Street, almost opposite his own business, and bought him the latest safety bicycle. It had a sprung saddle, a plunger brake, curved front forks, a chain guard and, an added bonus when it was Grace's turn, a dress cord to protect a lady's clothing from the spokes.

Each of Edwin's children on reaching their twelfth birthday was given a bicycle and though he was only just eleven Edwin had relented in the case of John, since it meant without a bicycle he could not go about on the family outings of which his brothers and sister were so fond. Round and round the bicycle track at Sefton Park was one, along the road beside the river was another; and out into the country beyond the outskirts of Liverpool was a particular favourite. It was a full day's trip taking a picnic in the basket on the front of Grace's machine, the food Nora put up eaten in a field waist-high with grass and wild flowers and where Arthur took "snapshots" with his hand-held Brownie; it had cost him a whole five shillings, which had taken him a month to save up! Pa considered that Arthur was conscientious enough to look out for his brothers and sister, especially young John and so, on the day that Mr Melly was to take to the skies, their bicycles were wheeled out from the building at the back of the house, once a stable, and in a great state of breathless excitement were pushed into the lane, Arthur balancing Grace's machine with his own as they waited impatiently for their sister.

They were all dressed in what was the cycling fashion of the day, the boys in tweed knickerbockers tied below the knee, checked woollen waistcoats and Norfolk jackets, thick woollen socks, flat-heeled shoes, a flannel shirt with a collar and tie and a cloth cap. It was the customary outfit of the middle-class cyclist in direct contrast to that of the working man who had to make do with wearing his ordinary clothes, his trousers fastened with cycle clips. Grace, whose mother was violently opposed to the "rationals" or knickerbockers which Grace longed to wear and in which the more daring – *fast*, Mary called them – lady cyclists dressed, wore an ankle-length skirt of a sensible navy blue. It would not show the mud that would be bound to fly up from the wheels, her mother insisted, sturdy boots, a warm woollen jacket of vivid scarlet which had been her choice – against her mother's wishes – and a straw boater with a scarlet ribbon about the crown.

Prescot Road was a bustling, hustling stream of motor cars, the occupants bundled up as though they were off to the North Pole. Special protective clothing was essential, for most of the motor cars were open to the elements, the passengers sitting high above the road where every splash of rain, every speck of dust, every stray breeze hit them straight in the face. They all wore goggles, the women donning hideous hats around which veils were draped, with heavy tweed overcoats which, when the weather became warmer, would be changed for ones of alpaca or holland.

The Tooleys, peddling furiously lest they miss one moment of this momentous day, watched them go by with envious glances, for though they loved their bicycles their dream was that one day Pa would consent to purchasing a motor car, though at the moment there was not much chance of that since he was among those who believed the motor car was just a nine days' wonder. There were small traps, gigs, a brougham or two, hansom-cabs pulled by a horse, motorised cabs, motorcycles and crowds of pedestrians, all hurrying in the direction of Old Swan, such a turmoil of traffic the Tooleys were forced to ride one behind the other.

"I had no idea so many people were interested in aeroplanes," Grace shouted to Arthur's back as they leaped from their machines and trundled them into the field which lay between the Black Horse Inn and Knotty Ash Station.

"My God, I've never seen such a crowd," Arthur gasped after they had been directed to stow their bicycles in the yard of the inn, whose owner was run off his feet doing more business in an hour than he did in a week. "Where in hell's name have they all come from? Half of Liverpool must be here. Keep an eye out for Rupert and Toby, won't you?"

"Since none of us knows what they look like . . ."

"George has met Toby," Arthur bellowed, doing his best to keep his brothers from dashing enthusiastically on to the field where the aeroplane could just be seen surrounded by a phalanx of supporters.

"We just want to get a closer look, Arty," Tom yelled, darting under the arm of a policeman but the constable caught him by the scruff of his neck and dragged him back, telling Arthur in a stern voice that any person found to be "hinterfering" with the "hairyplane" would be severely dealt with.

The field was ringed with spectators who seemed to be holding their collective breath, kept well back by attendants, for there at the edge of the field was the aeroplane, the flying machine which, to most of them, was one of the wonders of this modern age and one they had never seen on the ground, let alone in the air. How was it done? How did it work? What was it that got the flimsy little thing off the ground, and when it did, what held it up? Many of them, those who revelled in dramas in which they were not involved, had come with the precise hope that they might see it fall from the sky, but they were curiously silent, those who stood to stare, for they felt they were in the presence of something not quite of this world.

With great difficulty Arthur kept his brothers and sister together, moving in a little group on the edge of the crowd looking for the best vantage point, never taking their eyes off the aeroplane in case it should suddenly dart into the air when they were not looking. There were dozens of men around it doing mysterious things to its wings, its wheels which were strangely like those on their bicycles, to struts and wires and other bits and pieces unknown to the awed spectators. It looked like nothing less than a wooden crate on which someone had stuck two wings yet this was the marvellous piece of machinery that was to change the world, or so Grace and Arthur firmly believed, though she knew they were not in the majority. Even the motor car would not last, many declared, so what chance had the flying machine in the eyes of those who were blind?

"Tooley, there you are, old chap," a voice behind them said. "We've been looking for you but I must admit the crowds were beyond us. Who would believe that so many would gather to see Mr Melly take to the skies. I swear I laboured under the belief that the great British public had no interest in such things and yet here they are in their thousands from every class, come to watch."

George and the younger boys were so enraptured and so afraid of missing the take-off which seemed imminent they didn't even turn as the young man who addressed Arthur strolled towards them but he and Grace both twisted to look in his direction. He was a tall, gangling youth, probably about the same age as Arthur, somewhat affected in his manner and elegantly dressed but pleasant enough as he swept off his well-brushed bowler hat and bowed in Grace's direction.

"Toby, glad to see you," Arthur called out. "And you too, Rupert. Have you found somewhere to get the best view of the take-off?"

Grace nodded and smiled at Toby as they were

introduced. He held her hand for a moment but her whole attention was riveted on the young man Arthur had addressed as Rupert. A tall, dark-haired young man, slightly older than her brother, she had time to think before, at the age of not quite fourteen, she fell into love, a love which, even then, in her childlike bewilderment, she believed would last a lifetime. She didn't know how she knew, for she was still a girl, a child she supposed her mother would call her, but in that moment of hushed breathlessness her life as she had known it changed for ever. Her heart dipped sickeningly in her breast then rose again and she felt the blush, the bugbear of the young and inexperienced girl, flood her face. But though she was not quite fourteen her body was already maturing. Her budding breasts pressed against the fabric of her shirt which was revealed beneath the jacket she had unbuttoned and the proud curve of her shoulders gave her a posture that was almost queenly. She was still awkward though, barely across the threshold between childhood and young womanhood, but she did her best to compose herself as the young man, his rich brown eyes warmly admiring, moved behind Toby towards her. She overdid it in her attempt to hide her exploding feelings so that she appeared grim and she noticed from the corner of her eye that Arthur was frowning at her.

"This is my sister Grace, Rupert," he was saying. "And my brothers are over there," indicating the animated group who had pushed their way to the front of the crowd. Rupert had not the slightest interest in his brothers, only the exceptionally pretty but unsmiling young lady who offered him her limp hand.

"Good morning, Grace. I had no idea young ladies were interested in the flying machine," were the first words he said to her. "I know my sisters aren't." He spoke with the lazy accent of privilege, the privilege of an education at one of England's public schools.

'Oh . . ." she answered him. It was all she could do to speak at all, she who was without nerves, without a young girl's shyness, a girl who had never in all her life been at a loss for words. Afterwards she was incensed with her own gaucherie but her mouth was so dry and her heart continued to leap about like the frog Tom had captured last weekend in a jar. He was so handsome, so tall, a whole head taller than she was and his smile was quite brilliant, his teeth white and impossibly even in his sun-darkened face. Where had he been, she remembered wondering, to be so tanned? He was long-boned, hard-muscled, like an athlete, and she was not surprised when she learned later that he played not only rugby and soccer, but was champion of the university on the track and field. He had a narrow waist and long legs and everything about him was exactly in proportion. He glowed with health and the pleasure he found in life, and about his mouth there seemed to be a constant curl of humour.

He offered her his arm, to Arthur's astonishment, and to her own, she took it. "I do believe Mr Melly is about to take off," he told her, "and I'm sure you haven't a good view from here." He led her through the crowd by the simple expedient of putting his shoulder to those who stood in front of him, sweeping them to either side, despite their protests, and leading her behind him.

"Can you see all right?" he asked her softly, bending

his head a little over her shoulder and she managed to nod. He had stood her in front of him, his hands on her shoulders, his body so close to her back she could feel the warmth of him. His chin almost rested on her boater and she knew that she would never be capable of watching the take-off and flight of Mr Melly with any degree of interest, and what's more, she didn't care. The sounds around them were merely the lazy buzzing of bees, the movement of the crowd no more than the lazy circling of them about the hive, and when the small aircraft finally lifted itself into the air, its bicycle wheels hovering for a terrifying second as though reluctant to leave the ground, even the dramatic gasp of the crowd barely reached her.

It was not until the aeroplane had gained just under a thousand thrilling feet and had turned to head in the direction of the city and the river, that she came from the trance into which Rupert's hands, his closeness, the fragrance of his sweet breath on her cheek had thrown her.

They were all around her then, her brothers, Toby, Rupert, cheering and waving with the rest, telling each other what a splendid sight it had been; had they noticed his scarf which had seemed in danger of becoming wrapped around the propellor, and they could hardly wait for his return which was promised in about forty minutes. If the take-off had been thrilling what would his landing be like? The crowds, Grace suddenly discovered, just as though she had been captured under the glass dome in her mother's sitting-room, seen but unseeing, were wild with excitement, her brothers included, which was just as well or they would have been mystified by her own behaviour. They were exhilarated by it all and had no time to wonder at the unusual silence and sudden and inexplicable beauty of their sister, lit not by the sunlight as they might have thought but by her entrance into the world of a young woman. Her eyes were a golden glinted brown, her hair, slipping from her long plait, was polished to the sheen of a chestnut, her skin as fine and flawless as bone china. Her lips were full and pouting as though waiting for a kiss, a deep carnation pink. She was, in fact, exactly as she had set out that morning but with the added sheen that blooms in a woman in love.

He was watching her as the drone of the aeroplane whispered on the faint breeze, becoming louder and louder as it approached the field. It was exactly forty-one minutes since it had taken off. As it approached, with an almost cheeky movement the wings wobbled from side to side as though Mr Melly were waving to them and the whole of the vast crowd was silent, so silent a bird, impervious to the importance of this moment, could be heard warbling in the trees on the side of the field. Down it came, that fragile parcel of what seemed to be bits of paper and wood glued carelessly together, and, with a lightness that could not have been copied by the bird in the wood, landed on the grass at the far side of the field.

There was a roar that could have been heard, *must* have been heard at the Pier Head where a similar crowd had watched the aeroplane swing across the Mersey. Men threw their hats into the air which fell to earth to be trampled underfoot. Women shrieked in a most unladylike way and children did cartwheels across the crushed grass. Arthur and Toby jumped up and down then hugged one another in a great demonstration of shared delight, for they were intent on being engineers and would, when they had finished their schooling, both be in on the designing of aircraft. George and the boys had escaped the restraining arm of the constable who was doing his best to hold back the hysterical crowd and with great howls of ecstasy dashed with hundreds of others towards the airman who was doing his best to climb from his aeroplane.

"Are you not going to join them, Grace?" Rupert asked her smilingly, then was amazed when he perceived that she was weeping. At once he bent down to her, taking her upper arms with gentle hands, for suddenly he had realised that she was younger than he had earlier believed.

"Grace, what is it? Tell me," he beseeched her, still somewhat bewitched and more than a little bewildered by his reaction to her young beauty. He didn't know her at all. He was acquainted, no more, with her brother who had played in the same rugby team as himself during the winter and was to try for the cricket team in a few weeks' time. Arthur was a good chap, reliable, pleasant but not one of his friends. Toby, who was distantly related to him in some obscure way, had persuaded him to come today and now here he was with a crying female, a young girl no less, on his hands and he didn't know why she was crying or what he should do with her. Her brothers had gone haring off across the field towards the flying machine, which he would have liked to do but, being a gentleman, he could hardly leave the girl here in a state of extreme distress.

"Grace, may I fetch your brother?" he asked desperately, but to his consternation she shook her head, turned on her heel and ran like the wind, her boater flopping about on her back, in the direction of the gate that led from the field.

Two months later Mr Melly flew in his monoplane to Manchester in a startling forty-nine minutes, and back again in sixty-five since he had what was known as a "head wind", on the return journey, Arthur explained.

Surprisingly, though her brothers cycled up to the field to see him, Grace Tooley did not.

3

In the weeks that followed she found herself gazing
blindly at nothing, her unfocused eyes seeing nothing
but a face, a smiling, humorous face, a curling mouth
from which she waited breathlessly for words to come.
She didn't know what. She didn't really know what was
the matter with her, for she was too young for the
turmoil and sweetness of adult love; she only knew that
something tremendous had happened that day and it
had upset the happy equilibrium of her life. She would
come from her trance when her name was called from
some other part of the house, to find herself standing
at her bedroom window, her mother's nets pushed
back, her hand on the window frame, watching Mrs
Dutton hanging out the washing in the blue air and
sunshine of the summer's day, clothes pegs in her
mouth with Topsy frisking about her feet. Well, not
watching exactly but Mrs Dutton was there and so was
Topsy so she supposed her eyes were on them, or was
it the herb garden Ma and Pa had put in with which
she was apparently so absorbed? Drifts of parsley and
chives, coriander and dill, lemon verbena, lovage six
feet tall against the high brick wall which separated
their garden from the Allens'. At the far end of the long
narrow garden was Robert, his bicycle upside down on
the flags, mending a puncture.

All there for her to see but she had not seen them, only the face of Rupert . . . Rupert . . . whose surname she didn't even know and was afraid to ask in case the family should turn to her in amazement as she revealed her feelings. They *must* show, surely? They must see a difference in her, but it seemed boys were remarkably obtuse when it came to their family and what was taking place right under their noses. Its members were there where they had always been, their brothers and sister, their mother and father and as long as their meals were on the table and they had a clean shirt for school – though that didn't rate very high! – the goings-on, the day-to-day happenings of the house went unnoticed. Grace might be a bit quiet, disappearing from time to time to her room or the den the children had made above the stable years ago but then she was a girl and it was well known that girls were not like boys in their interests and concerns. Not that Grace had been like other chaps' sisters but they supposed, if they noticed at all, which was unlikely, that she was growing up and therefore away from the rest of them. She still joined their frequent expeditions during the long summer days but she seemed disinclined to be enthusiastic about climbing trees or paddling in the stream which flowed through the bit of woodland in the old quarry on Black Horse Lane and where sticklebacks and tadpoles abounded.

Only Mary, and she said nothing, even to her husband, was aware of the change in her daughter. Grace had, three months ago, begun that time in her life which many women described as the "curse" and though Mary, being a sensible woman with somewhat radical views on the upbringing of children, had acquainted her child with what were known as the facts of life, or, foolishly, the "birds and the bees", it had still come as something of a shock to the growing girl when she began to bleed for the first time. Her mother had comforted her, told her exactly what to do and though Grace had been faintly disgusted with the whole thing, saying it was not fair that she and not her brothers should be so afflicted, she had grown accustomed to the monthly palaver. It was enough to make any young girl alter her ways, or so Mary believed, and so Grace's episodes of distraction, her sudden inclination to disappear instead of playing squabbling games with her brothers round the family room table, were not, in Mary's opinion, something about which, as a mother, she should be worried.

On this particular day Ma was upstairs getting ready to make her usual Saturday visit to town and Pa had already left for the shop. The children had just finished breakfast, the good breakfast that Nora and their mother liked to get inside them every day, for weren't they growing youngsters, when Robert, lounging with his elbows on the table in a way that would not have pleased Mary, spoke up. John, who had successfully dammed his porridge with crumbled toast to his sister's disgust before furtively placing the bowl on the floor for the eager Topsy to finish, picked it up and innocently stacked it with the others. George was at the window staring down the garden at something that had caught his attention and Tom and Richard were arm wrestling, wrinkling the tablecloth and scattering cutlery.

"We haven't been anywhere exciting for ages," Robert was saying. "Here it is the middle of August and all we seem to have done this summer is ride up to Sefton Park or the old quarry. I think it's high time we should go for a long ride somewhere today."

"Where?" Grace asked languidly, studying her nails and wondering if she should use the manicure set given to her at Christmas by her mother and which had been received with little enthusiasm at the time. Young ladies *did* buff their nails and do whatever the tools in the set were meant to do but until recently it had not concerned her. Francie Allen, who lived next door and had taken to accompanying her to school since they were the same age and in the same class, manicured her nails once a week, she told Grace, so perhaps she might do the same now that she . . . now that she . . . what? . . . now that she . . . And for the life of her she didn't know how to finish the sentence.

"How about Peel Hall? We haven't been there for ages. We could take a picnic."

"Well, I for one have been too busy studying for such pastimes," Arthur replied loftily, poking his nose over the top of *The Times*, which Pa brought into the house since he thought its contents were of a more instructive nature than the Liverpool *Echo* or the *Courier*. He liked his children to be aware of national and international affairs and insisted that each of them, with perhaps the exception of John, read some small item of news, which they often did not understand, out to him each day. The older ones were expected to remember and repeat to him important events that had taken place, like the current period of unrest that was taking place in Liverpool and other parts of the country. There had been a proclamation by the Lord Mayor of Liverpool warning the railway strikers that if necessary he would call out the military and exercise full powers under the Riot Act if they continued in this disruptive way. They had not heeded his warning and the Riot Act was read only last week and a mass meeting of strikers on St George's Hall plateau had been dispersed quite violently by the police. Twelve policemen and over a hundred strikers had been injured. A mob had erected barricades in Christian Street and the military again were summoned. Rising prices and stationary wages were blamed. There had been a four-day railway strike in Newcastle which had led to "sympathy strikes" in other parts of the country, Liverpool being one, but the children of Edwin and Mary Tooley were not unduly interested since their standard of living was of the best and had not suffered because of it.

"Hey, look at this, will you?" George spluttered from the window, his nose pressed against the glass. "It looks like that friend of yours from the university."

"Who? Toby?" Arthur rose to his feet and joined his brother at the window but the rest stayed where they were, for the rather supercilious Toby had not impressed them. Drifting on the air, getting louder as it drew nearer, was a kind of chugging noise, like that of a motor of sorts coming through the open window, and when Arthur yelled in amazement it brought them all to their feet to press behind their brothers. All except Grace who knew before she looked who it was. How did she know? She was often to wonder but whatever it was it caused the blood to drain from her face and her heart to stop so that she thought she might faint and the best place to be in a faint was sitting down.

"By God, it's Rupert, and will you look what he's riding, the lucky blighter. I'd heard from Toby he was thinking of getting one before he leaves but I didn't know he'd actually done it."

"What make is it? Can you see from here?" George said excitedly. "Come on, let's go out and see."

There was a mad stampede for the door.

"It looks like an AJS racing machine to me . . ."

"No, it's got an overhead camshaft . . ."

"The AJS came fourth in the Junior TT . . ."

"Reckon it's an American Indian twin . . ."

Their high, excited voices trailed after them as they jostled each other to get to the front door, and from the kitchen Nora appeared, wiping round a dish she had just washed with a tea cloth.

"What's all't fuss? Sounds like bloomin' army's stampeding up the 'all. See, damn dog's at it an' all," as Topsy raced between her legs, diving through the front door which the boys had left open. It must be something exciting, for the dog never left any place where there might be the chance of a tit-bit.

Nora stared suspiciously at Grace, for never since the lass was born had she allowed herself to be left out of anything that involved her brothers.

"What's up wi' you?"

"Nothing. There's nothing wrong with me. It's just the boys getting excited over nothing," Grace answered airily, getting to her feet and sauntering from the room. When she gained the hallway she leaped up the stairs two at a time and banged her bedroom door behind her before collapsing on to her bed in a fit of what she could only call dithering. Her heart was banging alarmingly so that she felt she might choke and little quivers ran along her limbs. She didn't dare look out of the window, for if she saw him she would undo all the good and calming work she had forced on herself during the last three months. He had been at the last event when Mr Melly had flown to Manchester, Richard had told her, as mystified as the rest as to why she had, for the first time in her life, detached herself from an expedition, but she had held herself tightly in hand, thankful when her mother had intervened.

"Grace doesn't have to go everywhere you boys do," Ma had said coolly, totally ignorant of the real reason for Grace's refusal to join them, thinking that her daughter's recent entry into the world of womanhood was excuse enough.

Wally, who had been lying on her bed in a patch of sunshine, raised his head in vast irritation, then, with that strange sense animals have, settled himself close to Grace's side as though to comfort. He purred and wriggled, inviting Grace's hand but for once Grace was unaware of the animal.

It was no use. She couldn't stop herself. Pushing Wally unceremoniously to one side, she crept from her bed and peeped through the nets to the gate at the front of the house. Her brothers, and even James and Norman, Francie and Josie's brothers from next door, were gathered round the splendid motorcycle which Rupert had ridden over. It gleamed in the brilliant sunshine. It looked strangely like an ordinary pedal bicycle with thin cycle tyres, a leather saddle, down-turned handlebars with a horn attached and the word *INDIAN* painted just above the engine.

But it was not on the motorcycle that her attention was fixed, but the man – for he was that in comparison to the boys gathered about him – who lounged against the gatepost. He was tall, supremely confident and yet not arrogant, with a light boyish air about him, beautiful, well bred, well polished, intriguing and she recognised that those strange feelings he had awoken in her in May were just as they had been then. There was a link, a bond, something in him that whispered to her, which only *she* could hear and of which he was unaware and she was too young to understand. It was a thread tying her to him, invisible, gossamer-like but as strong as one of the hawsers down at the docks which kept the huge liners tied to the shore. He drew her like a candle flame and yet she must resist it, for though she was still in her girlhood she was mature enough in her youthfulness to know that this man was not for her. He was grinning at something Johnny had said, a sudden radiance of good humour at an eleven-year-old boy who most men of his age would have ignored and she longed to rush down and scream at him, "Look at me . . . look at me, not at him, or *anybody*," but she was a schoolgirl, a child to this glorious male who surely must have half the young women of Liverpool in love with him.

She skulked, there was no other word for it, in her bedroom until the "putt-putt-putt" of the motorcycle told her that Rupert was leaving. From behind the nets she watched him as he climbed easily into the saddle, pulled his cap firmly down over his thickly waving, windblown hair, raised his hand in a farewell salute and roared off up Sheil Road in the direction of West Derby Road. Had he asked about her? Enquired where she might be? Was she well, perhaps? She would never know, for she would never ask. They might wonder at her lack of interest, she who had been in the thick of any adventure going, but their total absorption with the machine would keep them occupied. They watched him go, the little band of awestruck, admiring youths, then, when he disappeared round the corner towards Knotty Ash, they turned, all talking at once, and sauntered up the path, round the side of the house, making towards the building where their own mundane bicycles were stacked and where they would discuss for hours the finer points of Rupert's machine.

"Rupert was here this morning, Pa," Arthur said as they sat down to their evening meal, "on his new motorcycle."

"Rupert?" Pa poured gravy over his pork chop.

"Yes, you remember we told you about him when we went to see Mr Melly take off in his monoplane in May. And again in July. He's related in some round-about way to Toby."

"Toby . . . ?" Pa asked vaguely, turning his attention back to his plate.

Arthur, exasperated, leaned forward the better to make his point.

"Take your elbows off the table, dear," his mother admonished.

Arthur straightened his back and picked up his knife and fork, sighing. He cut into his chop and put a piece into his mouth. "Yes, Pa, the chap I'm at university with—"

"Don't speak with your mouth full, dear," his mother told him.

Grace sat quite still, willing her hands to pick up her knife and fork and begin the task of eating the food in front of her. Resounding in her head were the words "before he goes away" which Arthur had uttered earlier and which, though she had heard them and had even assimilated them into her senses, had not really made a great impression on her. She had been too worked up over Rupert's sudden appearance and her absolute determination not to go down to the gate with the others where she was sure she would have made an absolute fool of herself. But now, as Arthur did his best to interest Pa, who surely he must know hadn't the slightest enthusiasm for anything mechanical, the words came back at her again and again. "Before he leaves, before he leaves," which meant, devastatingly, or perhaps *thankfully*, Rupert was going away somewhere and she would never see him again. The thought of it ripped painfully through her and at the same time filled her with a great tide of relief. Resolutely she cut up her pork chop and put a portion in her mouth and began to chew. It was like trying to eat a piece of leather and when, at last, she swallowed it, it stuck halfway down her throat and she had to grab for her glass of water, drinking it in great gulps to help the meat down.

"Where's he going then?" John asked obligingly before Pa did. Pa was doing his best to show interest in his sons' friends but they had such strange, weird even, hobbies these days, hobbies to do with this mechanical age which was not his cup of tea at all.

"Oh, he's off to that military academy to learn to be a soldier . . . Where is it? It's called Sandhurst and it turns out officers."

"Lucky beggar. There's nothing I'd rather be than a soldier," George remarked.

"No, you wouldn't, dear. All those nasty guns," Ma murmured serenely.

"I'd rather be a sailor," Richard added. "See a bit

of the world. When I was down at the docks the other day they were launching a torpedo-boat destroyer at Cammell Laird's across the water. They're going to call it *Wolverine*. I'm going to—"

"Richard, dear, please try not to talk with your mouth full. It is most ill-mannered."

"Sorry, Ma, but you should have seen the crowd."

"Yes, dear, I'm sure it was very exciting. Now eat your cabbage up."

"I don't like cabbage, Ma."

"It's good for you."

It was no good. She just couldn't sit here listening to the usual family drivel, doing her best to appear normal, to eat her dinner as though nothing out of the ordinary was happening when all she wanted to do was hear what Rupert was going to do and where he was going to do it. And when? When was he to leave? Was this a sudden decision since it had been understood, at least by her, that he was taking a degree in some subject at Liverpool University. That in itself was strange since a gentleman of his class and education might have been expected to go to Cambridge or somewhere but now it seemed he was to do neither but was to learn to be an officer in the army. Oh, why had Ma interrupted with her silly attempt to instil manners in the boys and thrown Arthur off the track?

She would not, of course, say a word. She would not question Arthur. She would sit here quietly and eat her meal, for it was nothing to her where Rupert went, or what he did. Or if it was she didn't mean to let her family know it.

"Where's he going?" she heard herself say sharply.

So sharply even she was astounded. They all turned to look at her and Ma, for some reason, frowned.

"Who?" Tom forked the last of his cabbage into his mouth as he spoke and Ma's frown deepened.

"Will you please empty your mouth before speaking," she said sternly.

"Ma, please, can someone at this table at least try to keep to the conversation in hand. We were talking of . . . of . . . what's his name?" – doing her best to appear casual – "Rupert and where he was to go to. Arty, you were saying . . . ?" She turned her unfathomable gaze – at least she hoped it was unfathomable to her mother – on Arthur.

"Rupert? You mean Rupert Bradley?"

"Dear God, how many Ruperts do you know?"

"Grace, what *is* the matter with you, child? Arthur was . . ."

She was tempted to rise from the table and storm out of the room. Run like some mad demented thing from the house and down the length of the back garden to the den, lock the door and cry and cry and cry, not only for the loss of her childhood which she knew quite definitely had come to an end today, but for the loss of her love and the man who had awakened it in her.

Arthur saved her, not intentionally but because he admired Rupert Bradley who was, without a doubt, one of the most popular young men at the university. If he hadn't been firmly fixed in his determination to be an engineer, something to do with the motor car or the aeroplane, he would have liked nothing better than to go into the army. He had always enjoyed school, the company of other boys in their vigorous and manly games, the camaraderie, the shared interests, that special bonding which the female sex lacked – though he did admit to himself that Josie Allen, the first girl who had ever captured his interest, might be good fun – and the idea of continuing it in a career in the army was very tempting. Besides which he was nearly eighteen and his mother's rather cloying protectiveness, which stretched from the baby John, who was not a baby really, to himself, was becoming too much. He had a great affection for his brothers and sister but it would be grand to be an individual, himself, Arthur Tooley, instead of part of a group. Sometimes he was sorry he had chosen to go to Liverpool University and not to one away from home where he might have gained some independence. As soon as he had his degree he meant to apply for a job at one of the growing manufacturers of the motor car such as Daimler in Coventry or the Birmingham Small Arms Company who had taken them over. Get away from home and make his way in the world as a man of invention.

"Apparently his family are army. There's been a soldier in every generation going back to Waterloo, so he told me. It should have been his older brother but for some reason . . . medical, I believe, they turned him down so Rupert's to go instead. Sandhurst . . ."

"Where's that then?" Nora, who had just placed a creamy rice pudding in front of Mrs Tooley, asked with the familiarity of long service. They were all used to it. She listened in to every conversation and even, as now, interjected a remark or two if she felt so inclined.

"It's . . . well, to be honest, I don't know where it is. Down south somewhere but apparently he goes there for two terms to train as an officer then he's to join the

2nd Battalion . . . I think he said the 2nd, the King's Liverpool Regiment where all his family went."

"When?" Again all heads turned to Grace. It was not that they thought it odd that she should be interested but it was the way she asked the question. Strangulated was how her twin would have described it and, after all, they had shared the same womb for nine months and as if that had bound them together despite not being identical he seemed to have imbibed, along with the nourishment come from their mother, an intuition about her, and the sense not to air it in public.

"When's he going . . . to this Sandhurst?" she managed to say almost naturally.

"Daft, I calls it," Nora muttered. Nora had lost her young soldier sweetheart at some God-forsaken place in the Sudan in one of the terrible wars which soldiers would keep on bothering with and she didn't hold with it. "There's too much fightin' in this world, if yer ask me."

No one took any notice. "Well, he's finished at the university. He's off to see an elderly aunt up in the Lake District on that motorbike of his. Try her out on some of those winding country lanes and hill climbs. He's even talking of taking part in the Isle of Man TT—"

"What's that, dear?" Ma asked with little interest.

"It's a race for motorcyclists, a thirty-seven-and-three-quarter-mile mountain course. First time in the Isle of Man."

"Really, dear. Now who would like some more pudding? Edwin . . ." smiling lovingly down the table at her husband whose own smile had wandered amiably from face to face as his children kept up their lively conversation.

"But when is he going . . . to Sandhurst?" Grace asked desperately, knowing full well that she was drawing unwanted attention to herself, for what difference would Rupert Bradley's departure make to her life, or indeed to anyone's in this family? He was of a different class. His family had a large house set in extensive gardens and a bit of parkland out beyond Old Swan. It was rumoured that his mother was related in some way to a baronet and his father, though not of the gentry class, was a fabulously wealthy shipowner who was the son or the grandson, Arthur wasn't awfully sure, could even be the great-grandson of the Hemingway family, one of Liverpool's greatest shipowners of all time. So why the dickens should Grace give a damn about the departure of this acquaintance of Arthur's?

"Grace, for God's sake – sorry, Ma – does it matter? Within the next week or so, Toby told me, but I tell you what, as soon as I've saved enough I'm going to have a motorbike just like his. Even if I have to get a job to earn the money—"

"Over my dead body, Arthur," Ma protested. "No son of mine will take some low job just to earn a few shillings to buy one of those nasty, smelly things—"

"I'll employ you on a Saturday, my boy," Pa interrupted quietly and at once he and Ma were at it hammer and tongs with Nora joining in as was her right, since she had put the first nappy on Arthur when he was born right here in this house.

Unnoticed, Grace slipped from her chair and let herself out of the back kitchen door. Topsy frisked along beside her and pretending to be totally unconcerned. Wally followed, his tail high, his back quarters swaying. She was weeping even before she reached the stable door.

4

She knew something was disastrously wrong even before she had shut the front door behind her. She could hear Pa's voice raised and over it the almost hysterical shrieks of Ma who seemed to be doing her best to be heard over Pa. Arthur's voice rose and fell, first in a kind of logical manner as though he were arguing something quite rational then beginning to peak in a way that was ready to outdo Ma. The shouting came from the family room, the door of which was firmly closed.

There was a lovely aroma of baking drifting through the hallway, almonds, she thought, or was it coconut, probably both, for Ma and Nora were never happy unless they were turning out something tasty, and not only tasty but artistic to tempt the children's appetites which didn't need tempting anyway. There was a delicious smell of a meal being cooked, stew with dumplings and on the table which she could just see through the open kitchen door was a tray of biscuits newly taken from the oven: a multitude of shapes on which Nora had iced pretty figures of children and animals and flowers with which once, when they were younger, they had all been delighted. Nora still did it even though they had outgrown such things. Sitting on the stairs were her brothers: John and Richard on the bottom step, elbows on knees, chin in hands, above them George and Tom and on his own above them was Robert, all of them in exactly the same anxious pose. Each one was munching on a biscuit and at the foot of the stairs sat Topsy, watching every mouthful, her ears pricked, her stubby tail swishing in eager anticipation.

They all, except Topsy, turned to look at her and Richard shrugged and raised his eyebrows. From the kitchen doorway where she leaned her shoulder against the frame, Nora's florid face peered out and Grace wondered why she was not hanging about between the double doors of the family room as was her wont, doing her best to put forward her opinion, which was, after all, worth having, to Ma and Pa.

"What is it?" Grace whispered to the five faces, something in their attitude and the unusual circumstances causing her to keep her voice lowered. Pa *never* shouted and Ma was on the whole a calm person who believed in the power of reasoning, *her* reason which usually overrode theirs.

"Tha's wharr I'd like ter know," Nora retorted sharply, giving the small milk pan in her hand a vigorous swipe with a tea cloth. "Shut t'door in me face they did. Me what's guided this fambly through many a rough ride an' all I sed was 'what's up?' like I always do. Well, that's t'last time, I can tell yer." She swung round and crashed the inoffensive pan on the kitchen table but no one took any notice, for they had heard the same words a hundred times and she still offered her advice and her opinions on everything under the sun whether it was asked for or not.

Grace crept across the black and white tiles and

squashed in beside John and Richard. "What are they shouting about? What's Arty done, for goodness sake? They sound as if they're coming to blows."

"I wouldn't be surprised." Richard sighed dramatically. He had eaten his biscuit but he was still famished after playing a rousing game of rugby football at school, and it looked as though their evening meal would be late, that's if it materialised at all.

"But what . . . ?"

Behind them Robert shifted his position to allow Topsy to climb into his lap, absently stroking her scruffy brown fur and she licked his face in the hope of picking up a crumb or two. "He wants to leave university." He said it so casually Arthur might have professed a desire to take a walk down to the docks.

"What!"

"You heard."

"Leave university? But all he's ever wanted to do was get a degree in engineering."

"Precisely."

"Tell the whole tale, old chap," George intervened from below him. "He—"

Robert gave his brother a hearty push which nearly unseated the lot of them in a domino effect. John yelled at them to "put a sock in it" and Topsy began to bark. Nora jerked into the hall ready to give the lot of them a piece of her mind when the family room door opened and Ma's angry face glared out at them. It was clear her normal unruffled calmness had been discarded and in its place was not only anger but a sort of *lost* look.

"What's all this commotion? Oh, it's you," she spluttered as though they were the last people she had expected to see in her hallway. "Well, you'd better come in and hear the mad scheme your brother has come home with but let me tell you that I mean to put a stop to it at once. After all the economies your father and I have made in order that he, and you, might have the best education possible it seems your brother doesn't give a fig for it. Oh no, he wants to go gallivanting off on some capricious jaunt. Come in, come in for heaven's sake and listen to this."

She ushered them in and they all took up lounging positions round the room, leaning on any handy piece of furniture. The room was warm, a good fire leaping in the blackleaded grate and the table was already set for their meal. The curtains were not yet drawn though a misty grey dusk was already falling. A sighing wind moved the branches of a denuded forsythia bush outside the window. It tapped against the glass and Topsy wandered over to investigate. Reassured that it was not an intruder she sauntered back and settled herself with a sigh on the mat before the fire. The double doors between the two rooms opened explosively and standing there was Nora, her arms folded over her bosom, the tea cloth still in her hand. Her face dared any of them to order her away. They were *her* family and she had as much right as any of them to be included in any drama, which it appeared this was. Ma sat down, her face as tight as a prune, but Grace could see something in her eyes that said there was more to this than Arty giving up university. Ma was frightened. "Go on then," she said acidly to her eldest son.

"Ma, this is a chance not to be missed, surely you can see that," he pleaded.

"I can see nothing of the sort. Speak to him, Edwin, tell him it's ridiculous."

"Son, what your mother says is right. You've been at the university less than a year and you were lucky to get in at your age."

"I had the qualifications, Pa," Arthur said stubbornly.

"I know that and we're very proud of you, aren't we, Mother, but you're a year at least younger than—"

"Which means I've time to do this. It's only for a few weeks, a couple of months at the most and then the dean says I can go back, catch up and—"

"Only a week or two back it was aeroplanes or the motor car, now it seems you're mad to go to sea."

"Go to sea?" George's mouth fell open and the rest of them copied him, staring at their brother in stupefaction. Grace sank down on to one of the chairs about the table and watched her eldest brother's eager expression, then turned to Ma, suddenly understanding her look of fear. Ma was a woman who liked all her chicks about her, to care for, to love, to cherish, to boss about, to scold, to protect and the idea that one of them, even for a short time and even if he was to all intents and purposes a man, was to leave her sheltering wing filled her with terror.

"Ma, can't you see what an experience this will be for me—"

"A ship is slightly different to an aeroplane, Arthur," she said tartly.

"I know that but it's *engineering*, don't you see. It's to do with engines. When I get back I promise I'll return to university and work like the devil to catch up. Please, Pa," appealing to the one who was most likely to accede. "Toby's relative is on the board at Harland and Wolff's and when he heard that Toby was interested in becoming an engineer, a *marine* engineer, he invited him to be in on it and Toby asked if I could come along since we're friends. The ship's already launched, funnily enough the day after Mr Melly went up, d'you remember, Grace" – turning eagerly to his sister – "which seems like some sort of sign. It's the biggest liner to be built, so big they had to build special piers to accommodate her. She reached a speed of twelve knots and it took six anchor chains and two piles of cable drag to stop her—"

"I don't see—" his mother began.

"There were one hundred thousand people to see her go to the fitting-out basin though there was no christening—"

"Christening?" Ma said faintly.

"Mmm. White Star don't do it apparently but Toby is to be involved with the fitting-out . . . experience, you see, and his people have said he can take a friend so . . . Oh, Ma . . ." His young face was lit with a sort of reverent hopefulness which surely Ma would find hard to resist, Grace thought. He was so intense, so hungry, so filled with a fire which she found irresistible and she prayed that Ma and Pa would be unable to resist it too.

"I wish I could go," John mumbled in the sort of voice that said he didn't really expect anyone to take any notice. No one did.

"I'm going in the navy when I'm old enough," Tom remarked grandly. "I shall—"

"Be quiet, Thomas, this doesn't concern you."

"I was only saying."

"Well, don't." Ma straightened her back even further and folded her hands in her lap as though doing her best to keep their trembling out of sight. It was as if she knew she had lost, lost the first of her children to the outside world and was attempting, in her Ma-like way, to come to terms with it. She had always been strong, had Ma, Grace thought, and for a moment she was overwhelmed with a sense of someone else's pain instead of her own which plagued her from time to time.

She had just come in from spending an hour in what she and her brothers called the "den", driven in by the intense cold. The den was fine and dandy in the summer months but at this time of year, no matter how you wrapped up, you couldn't stick it for long. It had been Arthur who had started it when he was about eight years old and George seven, probably to escape the five babies who had come after them and who hindered their boyish games. George was all right but Robert, Tom, Richard and Grace were a nuisance and John still a babe in arms.

The den was in the hayloft above the old stable, used by the previous owner at the end of the last century when horses and the carriage they pulled were the only way of getting about. There was a door in the wall that led to a crumbling stone staircase and the floor above the stable where hay had been stored in the loft. When the two small boys had decided it was to be their den, the place where they could escape Nora's and their mother's sharp eye and their little brothers' and sister's attention, they had furnished it with a few disgusting horse blankets which had been left behind by the previous owner; with all the paraphernalia of their boyhood, boxes of interesting nuts and bolts, tattered books, seashells picked up on the beach at Bootle, a stub of a candle which might have alarmed their mother had she known of it. It was not until Grace came to be included in their all-male club that the place took on a look of comfort. She brought in an old sofa she had bribed the boys to smuggle down from the attic when Nora and Ma were out, several cushions and rugs, since there was no way she was about to lie on the horrible old horse blankets, she told them. Over the years had been added a cupboard or two, a couple of rickety tables, vases in which she arranged dried flowers, some watercolours Ma had not cared for to hang on the wall, a badly worn Turkey carpet and a violently coloured Chinese folding screen. They had all been discarded by Ma and Pa and stored in the attic "in case", which was Ma's way of saying she could not bear to throw anything away that might, some day, be of use!

And it was to here that Grace often escaped, especially since the day she had met Rupert, for it was here she had a chance to be alone with her thoughts and . . . yes . . . her dreams without the fear of Ma or Nora roping her in for some domestic task. The boys, as they grew and became more concerned with their bicycles, their eternal games of football or cricket or just wandering off with other boys to get into mischief in Sefton Park, had gradually discarded their hiding place. But she, and recently Francie from next door, went there to exchange their views on the boredom of school, the nuisance of parents and the unfairness of being a female in a male world. They had found a shared interest in the subject of female suffragism and had decided when they were older they would definitely join the struggle to procure the vote for women. They had gone together to watch the Women's Coronation procession last June on the day their new King and Queen had been crowned and slavishly followed the progress of Emmeline Pankhurst, Mrs Emmeline Pethick-Lawrence and, of course, Christabel Pankhurst, who was their idol.

Francie had turned out to be quite a decent sort of a girl, the same age as herself, but there was one thing Grace did not share with her and that was Rupert Bradley. He was locked securely in her heart and no matter how Francie tried to draw her out on the subject of *boys* which she and the girls of their age were beginning to find inordinately interesting, Grace would not break her silence. Rupert was not a boy. He was a man. A soldier and he had vanished from her life as surely as if he were dead, which he was to her. Arthur had mentioned casually that Toby had attended a farewell party at Rupert's home when Rupert went off to the Royal Military Academy at Sandhurst but that had been last autumn and since then his name had never been spoken. Except in the dark of her room and then in a whisper as she tried to put the meeting with him in its proper place. It had been no more than a dream, she whispered to herself in the silence, one that she was reluctant to wake up from but knew she must, for she had her real life to get on with.

Nora shifted her weight from one foot to the other, clearing her throat, and as though on cue they all turned to look at her.

"Well, I can't see any 'arm in it," she told them. "After all, lad's eighteen now an' no longer a babby."

"This has nothing to do with you, Nora," Ma said coldly.

"Oh really. Tell me 'oo it was gorrim through the mumps that time an' 'ow about when 'e fell outer that tree an'—"

"We are not talking about that."

"No, burr I am. Wharr I'm sayin' is I'm as concerned as you when it comes ter't lad's welfare so don't you go tellin' me ter mind me own business. This *is* my business."

"Oh, for goodness sake," Arthur burst out irritably. "Am I to go or not? I've to let Toby know. She's to be in dry dock by the 3rd."

"What, the 3rd February?" Ma was clearly horrified, for it was already halfway through January.

"Yes. Toby's to book us passage over to Belfast."

"Oh, Edwin, please, don't let him go," Ma wailed and Pa stood up and moved to sit beside her, putting his arm about her shoulder.

"Dearest, I know you'll miss him. We all will, but, really, it will only be for a few weeks and then he'll come home and return to university. It will do him good, widen his horizons."

"I don't want them widened and ten minutes ago you were as against it as I am."

"It was a shock, I grant you, but I've had a moment or two to consider and I believe it will do him good."

"Ma, listen, please." The rest of them waited in hushed silence, even Nora. "Do you remember when we all went down to the Pier Head last June to see *Olympic* come in? Do you remember what a magnificent sight it was as she sailed up the river and the crowds that were there? A luxury liner. Well, this is her sister ship along with the *Britannic*. Think what prestige it will give you to be able to say that your son has been instrumental in helping to fit her out."

Arthur paused and the rest of them could see the change in Ma and silently applauded Arthur, for it was exactly the right approach to bring her round. She would love to boast of her son, the one who was to be an engineer, being involved in such an undertaking and not only that but of his friendship with a young man whose relative was connected with the building of such a wonder.

"Please, Ma, say it's all right. I promise to behave and look after myself. I'll wear my winter vests and change my socks every day."

Ma began to smile and they knew he had won. She wouldn't let it go, of course, during the next few days, scolding him one minute and ready to weep over him the next as she prepared him for his trip to Belfast. She would be hard to live with when he had gone, worrying over whether he had aired his underwear and should she send on his hot-water bottle, for it would be bound to be cold in Ireland but she would be brave for that was her way.

It was George who suggested they go for a ride, take some sandwiches and cycle out to . . . well, wherever they fancied since it would be the last time until Arthur returned in April, at least for Arthur. It was damn cold, still being January, but the sun shone out of one of those ice-blue skies that only come in the winter. The sun was a misty pink circle catching the frost which had, during the night, painted the branches of the trees with a light dusting of silvery white diamonds. They were etched like lace above their heads as they wheeled their cycles from the stable, harried by Ma and Nora who begged them to keep well wrapped up and not to sit on the frosted grass and to be home well before dark.

"No, we won't take sandwiches," Arthur had declared, wildly excited by this adventure he was about to set out on, and just a little bit apprehensive, Grace knew, though she said nothing. It was the first time he had ever been away from home. The first time in his life he was to sleep under a roof that did not contain his family, and he wanted this trip to be a memorable one.

"We'll have our lunch at that pub, you know the one on the other side of Lower Hargrave at the top of Merrydown Hill. What was it called? I know, the Hawthorn Tree. Best food for miles."

"How would you know?"

"Toby told me. He's sweet on the landlady. A real looker, so he says."

"That's a long way, Arthur, especially in the winter when the days are so short."

"Rubbish," John said stoutly from the lofty age of twelve which could see no difficulties in anything he wanted to do. It had taken the concerted efforts of Ma and Pa and Nora to persuade him not to take Topsy along who, he declared stoutly, could sit in Grace's basket and would love the treat!

Because they had decided only that morning to ride as far as the Hawthorn Tree since it was such a grand day, they were late in leaving. Ma had implored them not to go at first, not at this time of the year but, riding in pairs with young John leading the way, pedalling so fast they had a job to keep up with him, they took a short cut through Newsham Park, along Lister Drive, Moscow Road and into Black Horse Lane.

She saw him first even though she was behind the others. George and Robert had already passed the handsome wrought-iron gate from which he had emerged and she and Arthur were the last in the group. Perhaps it was because for the past six or seven months he had rarely been far from her conscious thoughts it seemed quite natural for him suddenly to be there, in the flesh instead of a shadowy image she conjured up. His motorcycle was propped up against the gatepost and he was fiddling with something on it, his back towards them so that, had Arthur not recognised him, or perhaps it was the motorcycle for Arthur was better at recognising machines than people, they would have passed by unnoticed.

"Hey, it's Rupert," Arthur shouted, scattering a flock of crows from their nests and at once the others turned, almost running into one another as they jammed on their brakes.

Rupert lifted his head to see who was calling his name. His face had a streak of oil on it and his hands were filthy. He wore a pair of very old breeches, ones that men wore to ride a horse, Grace had time to think, and a tattered old jumper under an equally tattered check jacket. He was hatless and his hair, cut shorter than the last time she had seen him, fell in unruly waves above his eyebrows. He looked quite glorious and her heart settled dismally into the truth that no matter what happened to her in the future, no matter who she met or which way her life went this man would always have her heart. She would be fifteen in May but for the past eight months she had loved this man and at the same time told herself that she did *not* love this man. She had lied.

"Arthur, this is a pleasant surprise." Rupert's face crinkled into that boyish, endearing smile she remembered so well and when he turned politely towards her she was as startled as he by the instantaneous magnetic force that passed between them, by the breathless sensation of recognition of how it was, or could be, with them. She was not to know that not only did he look glorious but so did she. As soon as she was out of sight of the house she had discarded her boater, jamming it into the basket at the front of her bicycle. Her hair, which had begun the day in a neat plait, had come undone and the rich brown gloss of it tumbled about her head and down her back to the saddle of her machine where it curled profusely and where the sunlight caught it turning it to a rich chestnut. Her face was rosy with the cold and the exertion of pedalling and her eyes shone like golden guineas. They were set in lashes so thick and dark they almost touched her eyebrow and spread a fan nearly to her cheekbone. Her skin was without blemish, smooth and amber-tinted and the full coral pink of her mouth was startling against it. Her lips were parted in a soundless exclamation of surprise and had they been alone Rupert Bradley believed he might have kissed her. She had grown since he had last seen her, upwards and outwards and had the figure of a woman. She *was* a woman and yet he knew she was . . . well, still at school, a child, and he felt a deep flood of shame as the desire a man feels for a woman swept over him and which he could no more stop than he could stop the birds overhead from circling and croaking their displeasure at being disturbed.

They looked at one another while Arthur and the rest clustered round his motorcycle. They were both lost in a silent world of contemplation, contemplation of each other and what it might mean, if anything.

". . . home on leave?" he heard Arthur ask while questions seemed to come at him from all sides from the other boys and he knew that if he didn't snap himself out of the trance he had fallen into they would begin to show surprise and embarrassment.

He dragged his gaze away from hers, feeling as he did so that he had somehow torn a part of himself. He made a great effort not to look at her again, to keep his eyes on her brothers, or on the motorcycle which they all admired, determined, as soon as possible, to get himself back inside the gates of his home where he would be safe from her innocent gaze. He had meant to take a spin on the machine but some noise he had not quite liked the sound of in the engine had stopped him and now he was captured, not by her – even though he was! – but by the enthusiasm of her brothers for his motorcycle.

It was quite ten minutes before he felt able to escape. "Well . . ." he said tentatively, letting them know that he had things to do, when a voice, a female voice from behind him made itself heard over the babble of the boys.

"Rupert, is that you, dear? I was just going to . . . Oh, I see you have company. Goodness, where are your manners, leaving them standing about at the gate in this cold. Ask them in, dear, and I'll get Cook to make us all some coffee. Come along, all of you. Now, I'm Rupert's mother and you must be . . . now *who* must you be? Well, it doesn't matter. Do bring your bicycles in. My husband has just gone . . . d'you know I can't remember where he's gone, I'm getting so forgetful. Now, dear, what is your name?" she asked Grace, taking her arm and drawing her up the curving driveway towards a splendid stone-built house.

"Grace Tooley, ma'am." Grace had no choice but to go with her, the others, including Rupert, tagging along behind. It seemed their day out was to end here at Garlands, the name she had noticed carved in the gatepost against which Rupert's motorcycle had been propped.

"Grace Tooley, and where are you from, Grace?" Mrs Bradley asked and without waiting for an answer continued, "And do go and change into something decent, Rupert. You look absolutely dreadful."

Grace heard John sigh, loudly and disconsolately, as he trailed up the steps behind her.

5

"That silly old woman spoiled our day," John raged as they headed back in the direction of Sheil Road. "It was Arthur's last ride and I was looking forward to having a good lunch in that pub and seeing the woman Toby's sweet on and now it's too late. As if anyone was interested in her stupid conservatory and that—"

"Oh, do shut up. There'll be other days."

"But not with Arthur, at least not until he comes home in April."

"Well, that's not so long off."

"It's *ages*," John moaned in the depth of the despair with which children view anything more than an hour hence as for ever.

He and Grace were cycling side by side in the lowering dusk. It was not even the time for dusk to fall, being only just gone two in the afternoon, but the beautiful winter's day in which they had set off had clouded over, with, Mrs Bradley warned them, a promise of snow. It was nothing to do with her, John had muttered as they set off down the drive after spending absolutely *hours* being bored to death, but Arthur had been inclined to agree with Rupert's mother and so that was the end of it.

Grace could not think of another day that she had enjoyed more though she had to admit to herself that it was Rupert who had made it so. As they had entered through the front door of the lovely old house he had murmured politely something about getting changed, dashing away up the wide staircase, taking them two at a time as though there weren't a moment to spare, or waste, and hardly had Mrs Bradley steered the silently awed Tooleys through a cheerfully overcrowded room towards the double glass doors into what she called *her* conservatory, than he was back again. He was still dressed casually but in a well-cut tweed sports jacket under which he wore a woollen polo-neck jumper, grey flannel trousers and polished brown brogues. His hair had been brushed and he brought a faint aroma of cologne with him.

The conservatory was a revelation, at least to Grace though the younger boys were inclined to fidget, particularly John. Richard caught her eye and pulled a comical face but Mrs Bradley didn't seem to notice. The room through which they had sidled, walking in such a tight group that they were in danger of bumping into one another, was filled with all the impedimenta of the Victorian age with which they were familar, though there were several objects that disconcerted them. There was a vast expanse of deep pile carpet to start with in shades of pale pink and cream and on it stood dozens of small tables and solid chairs, whatnots, glass-fronted cupboards, tall sideboards and rosewood sofas and on every surface that was flat enough, hundreds of ornaments, bric-à-brac, ivory, sandalwood, soapstone, and in the middle of all the clutter what looked like, to John's open-mouthed fascination, an elephant's foot. Had they just cut it off and was the elephant hobbling round all lopsided in some faraway forest, he wondered wildly, or perhaps it wasn't real? Just made from a bit of old leather. He would have liked to examine it more closely for signs of blood but George pushed him from behind and he had no option but to enter the glass room.

Grace was enchanted. She had heard of such things, of course, and seen pictures of them in Ma's gardening book which came monthly but actually to step into one was like stepping into a beautiful garden. A warm garden in foreign parts where the sun shone all year round. There were exotic plants she had never seen, come, she supposed, from lands where such things grew in the open but which would never survive in this harsh land of the north. She recognised ferns and a trailing plant which had flowers – were they orchids? – positively dripping from it, while the rest, white and red, purple and pink, and one of the palest blue, hung round the glass walls in profusion. There was even a plant, a vine, she supposed, on which in time grapes would cluster. The floor was tiled in pale terracotta, the ceiling high domed, exquisite with wrought-iron moulding, and all about were pots of different sizes and colours with more plants spilling over their sides. There were white painted wrought-iron tables and white wicker chairs heaped with bright cushions, fluted pedestals sporting small statuettes, some of them hardly clothed, and among the hanging baskets were singing birds in cages.

Mrs Bradley twittered about the conservatory in much the same way as the birds in their cages, arranging the Tooleys and her son in chairs to her own satisfaction, ringing a small bell, and when a neatly dressed maidservant appeared, bobbing a curtsey, ordered coffee and "something for these great boys to eat, Sara" at which John perked up enormously. She never stopped talking, which was a relief to Grace, telling them how lovely it was to see Rupert after so long though it seemed to Grace he had been gone no more than three or four months. He was on leave for a day or two and why hadn't he put on his uniform, she demanded of him, since she did so like to see him in his uniform and did they know that he was to be gazetted an ensign in the 2nd Battalion, the King's Liverpool Regiment when he had completed his training at Sandhurst. Now where had the others got to? she asked vaguely, fixing her eye on John which caused him to choke on the enormous piece of chocolate cake the maid had put on his plate – winking at him as she did so. As if *he* knew! He didn't even know who she was talking about, he complained later to Grace, and when it turned out to be her other children, "Alan, Eve, Caroline and Louise" she twinkled, Rupert reminded her that they had gone riding. Why hadn't he gone with them? she questioned and the others listened in fascinated silence as he explained.

"You know I wanted to give the motorcycle a bit of a run, Mother," he said patiently.

"Oh, that thing!" Her tone was disparaging and she shook her head and it was then that Arthur spoke up for the first time, actually the first one of them to do so.

"I wouldn't mind having a look at . . ." he said.

At once they all sprang up, all except Grace, babbling that they would also like to see Rupert's machine, which they knew was on Arthur's mind, and though

Rupert protested that it would not be polite to leave their sister he was overridden by the boys' assurances that old Grace wouldn't mind.

"Perhaps Grace might like to . . ."

"Of course she wouldn't, dear. Not that smelly old thing. She's quite happy staying with me, aren't you, dear? We shall have a nice talk until you come back."

Though she would dearly love to have gone *anywhere* that Rupert went, Grace found that "having a nice talk" with Mrs Bradley was no hardship. Mrs Bradley was kind and gracious, with a great capacity for chattering, moving smoothly from one subject to another so that Grace had little to do but listen and nod and smile and accept innumerable cups of coffee. All the while she was talking Mrs Bradley kept getting to her feet and darting about the conservatory, snipping at this and that with a pair of scissors she produced from the pocket of her skirt.

It turned out that she had no chance of any sort of conversation with Rupert which, at one and the same time, disappointed her and filled her with relief. She would have had no idea what to say to him and had she known it, he was in the same quandary. He was a handsome young man accustomed to the admiration of young women. He was not without experience of the delights of the flesh, flirtations and dalliance but this young girl, though he had met her no more than a couple of times, seemed to appeal to something inside him that he hadn't even been aware was there, nor did he know what it was. Desire, the needs of the flesh were far from his mind, since she was too young for them, even if he wasn't. It confounded his senses and threw him into a strange and unwanted confusion which he didn't care for. She was tall, long-limbed, with a womanly figure and yet she had the sweet, defenceless air of a child. She had been brought up to be polite, well-mannered; her attitude towards his mother showed that. She was perhaps fourteen or fifteen, still at school, for God's sake, and he felt it was a damn good job that he was to return to Sandhurst the next day, for God knows what bloody silly thing he might get up to. His eyes turned constantly to her where she sat next to his mother and now and again their gaze met and held and he hoped to God no one noticed it.

Not until he had managed to pry his guests from his motorcycle and his mother, reminding her that the Tooleys were set on a ride out, did he speak to her. He walked them down to the gate, trundling their bicycles and turning to wave to Mrs Bradley who had begged them to come again, just as though they were old friends. As the boys leaped on their cycles and prepared to pedal off he managed to snatch a word alone with her and then it was only to apologise for appropriating their last day with their brother before he went to Belfast.

"My mother is the kindest person, really, but she is not very . . . perceptive."

"Please, it's been lovely. I enjoyed the . . . the conservatory and your mother was . . . was lovely."

"Your youngest brother wasn't best pleased." He smiled to take the sting out of the remark.

She laughed. "John is still a boy . . ." from her lofty height of fourteen, nearly fifteen, as she liked to think. His nearness was disconcerting. She watched his face, the rich, soft brown of his eyes and saw them darken as he caught her looking at him. He blinked, a long slow drooping of his lashes and her heart moved in her chest. She looked away hastily, roses flagging at her cheeks and he was bewitched, then decided he was a bloody idiot, for she was no more than a pretty girl who had caught his eye. A pretty girl, but not to be trifled with, certainly, for she was the sister of a friend, a good girl, a *nice* girl!

Again he apologised for monopolising them, hoped politely that they might enjoy their ride, lifted his right hand to his forehead in what might have been a salute and turned away, striding back up the drive as though he hadn't a moment to spare.

They got no further than the outskirts of Much Woolton when the skies began to assume the appearance of the inside of a lead container. It was intensely cold and though the boys all wore a good overcoat and Grace a voluminous, wool-lined cloak it was beginning to look as though their outing was doomed.

It was then that John made his bitter remark about Mrs Bradley spoiling their day, and Grace felt obliged to point out to him . . . well, to *yell* at him over her shoulder as they headed back the way they had come, that even if they hadn't stopped at Garlands—

"Garlands?"

"You know where I mean."

"It's the daftest name for a house I've ever heard."

"Well, that's just like you. I think it's a lovely name and it's a good job we did stop or we'd have been in Lower Hargrave by now—"

"Exactly."

"And marooned in a snowdrift."

"It's not snowing."

"It soon will be, you fool."

They would have continued their bitter argument if Arthur had not stepped in. "For God's sake, the pair of you. Will you cut it out. This is supposed to be a good day out and as far as I'm concerned it has been—"

"I don't know how you can say that, Arty," John growled. "I was—"

"You saw the motorcycle, didn't you?"

"Will the lot of you shut up," George bellowed into the snapping wind which had just started to make itself felt. "Save your damn breath for the ride home."

"Hear bloody hear," Richard snapped and though they were all slightly shocked at the "language" they could not help but laugh.

Ma and Nora welcomed them as though they had been to the Arctic and had never been expected to be seen again. The fire in the kitchen was halfway up the chimney and the seven of them sprawled in a semi-circle round it, their bare feet to the blaze, drinking hot chocolate and eating toasted teacakes, since it was over three hours since they had gorged themselves on Mrs Bradley's cook's chocolate cake. Ma and Nora were entranced with Grace's description of the inside of the Bradley house, particularly the conservatory, one of which it was Ma's dearest wish to own, though less concerned with the boys' excited squabbling over what they had liked best about Rupert's motorcycle. The elephant's foot was greeted with disbelief and the pink and cream carpet with some scorn since how on earth would you keep it clean, said Nora. Pa sauntered in, his pipe in his mouth, a fine Meerschaum which had aged to the colour of amber, the bowl carved into the shape of a man's head with a profuse beard. He had a dozen pipes, briars and porcelain and clay, kept in a wooden rack and fixed to the wall in the family room. Below it was a short shelf on which he kept his tobacco boxes with tightly fitted, hinged lids engraved with country scenes. The fragrant aroma of the tobacco lingered in the house and though Ma sometimes complained about it they all knew, Ma included, that Pa would not be Pa without his pipe.

"What's all the fuss about?" he asked mildly and so it had all to be gone over again while Topsy scrounged among them for titbits and Wally purred ecstatically under Arthur's hand, and for an aching moment, just as though the encounter with Rupert had honed her senses to a sharpness she had not known before, Grace felt something break inside her. The expression on her face must have changed and been noticed, for Pa sat down in the chair beside the fire, the one Nora rocked in at the end of the day, and his hand fell on Grace's head. He stroked her tumbled hair, saying nothing, and at once the feeling of uncertainty vanished. There was laughter and warmth and the familiarity of the people she loved about her. Rupert Bradley, for she put the strange feeling down to him, was gone from her once more and though she had felt the curious pull of his masculinity drawing her towards him again today, the tightening of some bond between them, she told herself it was nothing but her imagination. She was not unaware of the effect her looks – she supposed she was pretty for she had been told so – had on the opposite sex. She had seen the admiration in their eyes and something else she was not sure she recognised, or even wanted to. There was an instinct in her, a female instinct that did not trust this soft, honeyed drowning his presence triggered in her, though at the same time she did not believe he was the sort of man who went out of his way to trap an unwary female into his clutches. Dear God, would you listen to her, her mind whispered. She was like some writer of Victorian melodrama! Clutches, indeed, what a way to describe the . . . the . . . she didn't know what to call it. Oh, for goodness sake, her young and practical mind jeered, stop it. Stop dwelling on Rupert Bradley and get on with life as it is. She had a wonderful life, she told herself. She loved her parents, especially her pa and though her brothers were a damned nuisance – a thought that would not have occurred to her six months ago – she thought the world of them.

She leaned her cheek against Pa's knee and stared blindly into the fire, wondering as she did so why she couldn't quite believe what she had told herself. Not about her family, who were so dear to her, but about forgetting Rupert Bradley.

Arthur caused his mother a great deal of upset by doing his best to persuade them not to see him off, even *her* and she was not to know that he was afraid that she might show him up in front of Toby by clinging to him and showering him with farewell kisses. He and his friend had decided when their plans had been finalised that as two young men of the world who were off on an adventure before settling down to their studies, and as they would only be away for eight or nine weeks anyway, there was no need of fuss, of making a great to-do of it, but his mother thought otherwise. Her eldest son was going off to unknown parts, which they were to her even if it was only Belfast, where she could not keep an eye on him and she was determined to exercise her authority over him right up to the very last minute. They all wanted to come down to the docks, even Nora, to see him off and so he might as well accept it, Ma told him calmly.

"But Toby's people aren't to come, Ma," Arthur protested.

"Ever since he started knocking about with that Toby he's done nothing but put on airs and graces," George snorted. "Toby's 'people'! What's wrong with saying Toby's family like anyone—"

Arthur rounded on his brother. "Oh, do shut up, our kid."

"Really, where do you pick up such sayings?" Ma lifted her chin, for she believed her family to be above such Liverpool vernacular. "Our kid, indeed. You'll be calling your sister 'Mrs Woman' next." She continued calmly and neatly to pack her son's suitcase, putting in half a dozen pairs of newly knitted socks which she and Nora had worked over during the past fortnight.

Arthur pushed a hand exasperatedly through his dark, wavy hair, groaning dramatically, for they were all there except Pa, of course, even Nora, lounging about the bedroom he shared with George, getting in the way, fiddling about with his books and maps, asking did he want to take this or that.

"Ma, I can pack my own stuff. Won't you—"

"I know you can, dear, but I just want to make sure you don't forget anything. Now pass me those vests, Nora."

"Ma, you've already packed half a dozen vests, and shirts *and* jumpers which I won't need."

"It'll be cold in Ireland, dear."

"And we wouldn't want you to catch a chill, Arty dear," jeered Tom who would have liked to go too.

"That will do, Tom," Ma said firmly.

Arthur gave up. He had argued that he and Toby were to share a cab, a motor cab, naturally, down to the Pier Head and the landing stage from where the ferry to Ireland sailed and there would be no room for all of them.

His mother was unfazed.

"Then we'll follow in another. Your brothers and sister want to see you safely away."

"Make sure you've gone so that I can spread out in the bedroom."

"*George*, that's not nice, really it isn't."

"Sorry, Ma." And George winked conspiratorially at Arthur.

They all went, of course they did, and in the end Arthur was glad because Toby's "people" were there too, though not in such great numbers as the Tooleys. Ma clutched him to her in panic at the last moment and Pa had to detach her clinging hands and draw her into his own arms to prevent her following Arthur up the gangway. As George remarked in an aside to Robert, anyone would have thought Arthur was off on one of those immigrant ships that lined the docks, those taking the thousands upon thousands of hopeful souls, three and three-quarter million in the last decade, to a new life in the United States of America. But just the same, being a close family, they all hugged him warmly and bugger Toby's family who were more restrained. They watched him, Grace and Ma, with tears in their eyes, as he eagerly climbed the gangway, turning to wave energetically when he reached the top.

For a second they stood, Arthur, his five brothers, his sister, Ma and Pa, and Nora, dressed for the occasion in her best black, in a silent bubble of distress at this, their first parting, then he grinned and waved again before disappearing with Toby in the direction of the first-class cabin, compliments of Harland and Wolff, they were to share.

"At least he'll have a proper bed tonight," his mother comforted herself, just as though for the next eight weeks her son was to sleep on hard bricks and straw.

"He'll be home before you know it," Pa told her, his arm about her shoulder. Grace noticed that Toby's family, probably afraid they might be forced to share a moment with the Tooleys who, in their superior opinion, were not quite the thing, had already started to walk up Princes Parade away from the landing stage, but she and her brothers, with Ma and Pa and Nora behind, followed the departure of the Irish ferry as it edged away from its mooring and began to make its way up the river. They walked as far as they could along the parade, separated from the water by stanchions linked with heavy chains, and just as the ship disappeared in the winter mists the one o'clock gun at Birkenhead was fired, as it was every day.

Ma sighed. "Well, he's gone, God bless him. I hope he remembers to change his socks every day."

"You told him often enough, Ma." John put his arm through his mother's and kissed her cheek. She smiled.

Pa had promised Grace and her older brothers that while Arthur was away they could take it in turn to do his job at the shop on the corner of Lord Street and Whitechapel. Just on a Saturday, of course, as Arthur had done, and earn half a crown a week on top of their usual pocket money. The boys, particularly, were thrilled at the idea, for it meant they could save the extra cash towards the motorcycles they were all mad about. There were loud and enthusiastic discussions every week on the make of cycle each boy would have, ranging from the Sopwith-made ABC 398cc twin-engine gearbox unit in a spring frame, to the AJS Model K7, a racing machine with a chain-driven overhead camshaft engine of 350cc capacity, whatever that all meant, Ma was to say to Grace as they sprawled in front of the fire, *supposed* to be doing their homework.

Grace and Francie had discovered the thrill, not of motorcycles, but of the cinema and with the extra half-crown in her pocket, which was a *lot* of money, they were able to indulge their passion for George Robey, Lupino Lane and Chrissie White. They saw *Tilly and the Fire Engine* and *David Copperfield* at the newly built cinema in town which was devoted entirely to showing films instead of at the music hall where they had previously been screened.

Grace loved the shop. It was situated on a corner and so had two shop windows, one in Lord Street, the other in Whitechapel with the entrance on the corner.

She felt a shiver of pride and anticipation each time she got off the tram in Church Street and walked across the road towards its smart façade. Above the shop window was a sign on which was painted – hopefully – *Edwin Tooley and Son* and across the front window in fancy lettering was the message *Tobacco*

Specialist. The wide window was tastefully arranged with pipes of all sorts, briar, which was a hard root wood brought from France, meerschaum, which was German for *sea foam*, Pa had told her, packets of cigarettes from the cheapest Gold Flake and Wild Woodbine to the most expensive, which might be scented or coloured, some even with edible, telescopic and wooden ends for the converted pipe smokers to bite on. There was more to smoking than met the eye, Pa was fond of saying and the great range of goods in the window proved it. Matches, of course, and cigarette lighters, airtight tobacco jars in beautiful designs, pipe racks, velvet-lined leather pipe cases and a dozen variety of cigars.

Inside there was a counter which went round two sides; on the top of one, glass cases in which were more accessories needed by the smoker and at the back of the counter shelves, a dozen of them from the floor to the ceiling, which were again crammed, tastefully, of course, with smoking necessities. Pa wore a plum-coloured velvet smoking jacket and Mr Hynes, who had worked for Pa for as long as Grace could remember, a cream linen jacket.

She loved it and though Pa did not say it in so many words she knew she was popular with the gentlemen customers.

On Monday, 15 April the Clifton School for Girls was closed in order that a leak which had mysteriously sprung in the lavatories could be repaired, and Grace was in the shop when the news that was to rip her family to shreds was received.

6

Ma had been bewildered and Pa furiously angry on Friday morning when a postcard bearing the White Star emblem on the front was delivered at number 10 Sheil Road, postmarked Queenstown, Ireland and dated the day before, 11 April 1912. They had had numerous letters and cards from Belfast where Arthur had been, in his words, in seventh heaven to be working in the fitting out of the world's largest liner and had eulogised over things none of them could make head nor tail of, concerning the "workings" of the ship, the only word they understood being "propellors". On 3 April, when Arthur and Toby had been away from home seven or eight weeks, the ship had left Belfast and had begun her sea trials and, wonder of wonders, the two young men, no doubt with the help of a few strings pulled by Toby's relative, had sailed with her and only ten days ago had arrived in Southampton, the ship dressed in flags, a vivid description of which Arthur had sent them. They were to have left the ship at this point and travelled back to Liverpool by train but the little devil, with Toby, had apparently persuaded someone to let them sail to New York, and, presumably back, on the ship's maiden voyage. Arthur hadn't had room on the card from Queenstown to go into detail and so they would have to wait until his return but

Grace and the boys, driven to silence by Pa's rage, wouldn't like to be in his shoes when he came home.

Later John commented sagely, "Ah, but he will have done it by then, and that's all that matters. If he's prepared for the punishment then what he's done won't matter to him. That's how I'd look at it anyway."

"The little bugger," Pa had exploded. Pa was not given to swearing which showed how angry he was with his eldest son. They all stared at him, dumb-struck.

"But what does it mean?" wailed Ma, turning the card over and over in her hands as though to extract some meaning from it. Nora and Mrs Dutton, who had been intending to scrub out the pantry, appeared in the doorway, Nora with the frying pan in her hand and Mrs Dutton swinging the bucket which she was about to fill with hot water.

They were at breakfast, a Friday, Grace was to remember for ever since she had not done her science homework and science would be the first subject of the morning. Miss Derham would not be best pleased and would, no doubt, give her detention to make up her deficiencies, but the postcard from Arthur, who was expected home this very day, wiped all thoughts of her science homework from her mind.

The postcard was brief but though it was no more than a piece of thick paper it seemed still to retain the essence of Arthur's excitement, filling the room with it so that they all became somewhat infected by it though they didn't let Pa see.

Dear Ma and Pa,
    *We were offered a trip to New York. Couldn't
miss it, could we. Letter following.*
    Yr loving son,
    Arthur

"Couldn't miss it! And what about his studies? He
can miss those, can't he? The young puppy! And after
we gave our permission for him to go what does he do
but take advantage. Talk about give him an inch and he
takes a mile. Mary, we have been too lenient with our
children, I have decided, and things must change." But
they all knew that Pa didn't mean it. He was upset that
his son had taken it upon himself, without consulting
his parents, to go sailing off to the other side of the
Atlantic and probably wouldn't be home for weeks
now. They had all been looking forward to Arthur's
return and all the tales he would have to tell them,
being the only member of the family who had, so to
speak, been *abroad*, which Ireland was to them.

They had spent the weekend speculating on the
wondrous luck of Arthur – not in Pa's presence, of
course – who had not only sailed across the Irish
Sea to spend time on what was, after all, no more
or less than a holiday, probably drinking gallons of
Guinness – John's morose description, for he would
love to taste Guinness – but was now on the high seas
on his way to New York. New York! The Statue of
Liberty and . . . and . . . they could not actually think
what else of interest New York contained, certainly
not the cowboys and Indians John had read about
and longed to meet, but things of splendid excitement
which *they* were not experiencing. It just wasn't fair

and when was life going to start for *them*? the boys complained bitterly.

They were surprised to get word the following Monday morning that as the Clifton School for Girls was closed that day all pupils were not to attend.

"Lucky beggar," grumbled Tom when he heard. "I wish our prison would close for even an hour, never mind a whole day."

"It'll be Easter soon, old chap," George comforted him, "and then we can do that trip to Lower Hargrave we promised ourselves. Arthur'll be back by then."

The five boys set off in various stages of disgruntlement, allowed to ride their cycles as Grace was not to go.

"What will you do, dear?" Ma asked mildly. She had got over the shock of Arthur's card and though she was somewhat nervous of the idea of her first-born getting further and further away from her across that vast ocean, he was having a wonderful experience, she had told herself, and, best of all, mixing with such a nice class of person, taking it for granted, since Toby was related to a member of the board of directors of the White Star Line, that her son would be travelling first class. Mr Bruce Ismay was a passenger, she had read somewhere, so was one of the wealthiest men in the world, John Jacob Astor, Sir Cosmo Duff and Lady Cosmo Duff and many other prominent people from all spheres of life, and who knew what advantages her boy might gather in the way of advancement. Toby was a nice young man, a proper sort of friend for Arthur to have and it appeared to her, dreaming her mother's dreams, as mothers do for their offspring, that their friendship could lead anywhere, not just for Arthur but for his sister. Young gentlemen of the sort she hoped Grace might one day meet and marry would be found more easily in Toby's circle. This trip, which had been such a shock initially, might turn out to everyone's advantage.

"I think I'll go down to the shop and see if Pa needs any help," Grace answered, for if she stayed at home who knew what boring job her mother might find for her.

She was wrapping up a box of Half Coronas for Mr Wright, who was a regular customer and who always tried to flirt with her a little bit whenever he came in, when she was distracted by the sound of shouting coming from the street. The door to the shop was closed, for the weather was still cold, but the shouting, the raised voices, the clamour of some sort became louder and louder and she and Mr Wright exchanged bemused glances. Pa often said that an open door persuaded customers to come inside and browse around and very often they bought something, even if it was only a packet of Gold Flake, but the nippy wind which was blowing straight up Lord Street had made closing the shop door imperative today, despite being almost halfway through April.

As she had passed St John's Garden on William Brown Street this morning she had noticed that the neat beds were full of large trumpet daffodils and narcissi, nodding cheerfully in the wind, and surrounding them in a ribbon of colour were bright red tulips, the variety known as "parrot" with ragged petals, the soft purple of violets, and edging the beds the delicate yellow of primrose. The grass verge had been recently cut and the green was quite brilliant in its new spring colours. How beautiful it had all been, how peaceful and forward-looking to the year to come on that morning when her life changed so drastically.

Automatically her hands continued to wrap Mr Wright's cigars, tying the string in a neat bow as Pa had taught her, but she found herself craning her neck over the display in the window in order to see what was happening in Lord Street.

"What the dickens is going on?" Mr Wright murmured, moving towards the door and opening it to peer out. Even Pa, in the back of the shop where he and Mr Hynes had been blending pipe tobacco, had left his bench, Mr Hynes at his heels. Grace came round from behind the counter and the four of them crowded in the doorway, on their faces that expression of bewilderment which does not know whether to turn to one of disbelief, gladness or horror, depending on the circumstances. People were running, others stood stock-still as though frozen to the pavement and to their utter amazement women were crying into their handkerchiefs.

"What the . . ." Mr Wright said, moving hesitantly out on to the pavement and Grace followed him, her head filled with images of dead kings, train derailments, massacres, epidemics in which thousands were dead so that when she heard the actual words being passed from one man to the next she shook her head in total, scornful, unbelieving derision.

TITANIC! That was the word on everyone's lips. *Titanic.* But what the dickens were they saying? It was as though she heard the sounds of voices, of shouting, the cries of denial, from beneath water, which irony she later could not get out of her head. Hollow, echoing words she did not really understand and though she stared and stared and listened desperately to make sense of it all, it *made* no sense. They were saying, these milling shop workers and factory hands, the draymen and policemen and lady shoppers and business gentlemen, the hansom-cab driver who had started it all off having just come from the docks, that the largest ocean vessel ever launched, the most splendid, the safest, the *unsinkable Titanic* had sunk! That she had gone down off the coast of Nova Scotia. Voices were tossed hither and yon, speaking of icebergs and lifeboats and really where had they got such a foolish story from? Arthur was on the *Titanic* and he was her brother, her big brother and he wasn't about to drown, was he. Good God, they'd had a card from him on Friday so how could . . . could . . . Please . . . it could not be . . . Were they all *mad*?

Slowly she turned to Pa and was afraid, as she had been afraid in the night as a child but had been comforted by him, to see his old, old face, grey and sunken, his shaking hands at his mouth, his eyes staring in terror into hers. There was no comfort there, no smiling words telling her there was nothing to be afraid of. She put out her hand to him, longing to feel the strength and protection she had known all her life but his head had begun to shake and, horror of horrors, there were tears trickling down his cheeks, running in the sudden wrinkles that creased his cheeks.

"Pa . . . Pa, it can't be true, can it?" she begged while behind Pa Mr Hynes, who had been told about Arthur's escapade on Saturday, and had had to smile, he said, for wasn't that lads all over, put a hand on his employer's arm.

"See, come inside, Mr Tooley. Let me go and find out wharr it's all about. The *Titanic* . . . God bless me, biggest ship in't world . . . it *can't* be true. See, Miss Grace, come inside wi' yer pa and we'll put kettle on . . ."

Mr Wright's face was as mushroom-coloured as Pa's, for he had a son who was purser on the White Star Line; indeed there would be many Liverpool families whose sons or brothers were crew members, and if it was true – which he couldn't believe – there would be bound to be lists of survivors down at the White Star Line offices.

His box of Half Coronas forgotten, he darted off in the direction of the docks, Mr Hynes at his back and, it seemed, half the population of Liverpool went with them.

They sat in the back recesses of the shop, Grace and her pa, holding hands, not speaking, for each was waiting for the other to offer reassurance, but it seemed their thoughts were frozen in their shocked minds, afraid to be let loose in case they should be overwhelmed. They waited for Mr Hynes to come back from wherever he had gone to tell them it had all been a big mistake, that it wasn't the *Titanic*, but another ship, perhaps the *Olympic* which they had seen sail so majestically up the Mersey last May, that someone else's son and brother was lying at the bottom of the Atlantic Ocean, or that the passengers, if it was the *Titanic*, were all safe. Grace could think no further than this. It was as if all her life she had been waiting for Mr Hynes to come back, and when he did she knew, not only by his expression but by the tears that streamed down his face, that the impossible, the unthinkable had happened. Mr Hynes had worked for Pa ever since the shop had opened before Arthur was born. He was a sort of uncle, despite the fact that Pa always called him Mr Hynes, as they all did. He had watched Arthur grow up, a toddler, inquisitive and a bit shy in the shop where he had come to see his pa, a young boy who never stopped asking questions, a youth, mad on machines and intent on telling everyone who would listen what he meant to do about them. Now, what was he, Jack Hynes to say, how was he to speak through his own sorrow and tell the lad's father and his sister that the *Titanic* had hit an iceberg and that she had gone down in four hours taking so many of the people on board with her it didn't bear thinking about. They were still searching for survivors, the message that had come from the White Star Line in New York reported and perhaps Arthur was among them. They must be positive, he told them as he wept for young Arthur. Just keep it in their minds, he reiterated, that there *were* survivors and Arthur, who was young and strong and a good swimmer would most likely be among them. They must not give up hope, he said into their blank and uncomprehending faces. They must pray but they were not a praying sort of a family really, only Ma going regularly to the Liverpool Presbyterian Church and then her family suspected it was more a social occasion than a religious one.

"You get on home," he said kindly. "I'll see ter't shop. I doubt there'll be many customers today . . ." And then could have bitten his tongue since the remark only served to remind them, as if they needed reminding, of what had happened.

"Yes," Pa said vaguely, rising to his feet, still clinging to his daughter's hand, as they were all to cling
to Grace in the next few months. Even on the tram
which was filled with people, excited as some people
are at others' disasters, some silent, others tearful,
but everyone talking of the catastrophe which had,
or would prove to have taken so many lives. No one
knew exactly how many yet but one passenger on the
tram had had it on good authority, though from where
he did not say, that there had been two thousand two
hundred souls aboard, and how many of them had
survived, he added ghoulishly.

Ma was in the front garden as they walked hesitantly,
still hand in hand, blank-faced, blank-eyed, towards
the gate. She was inspecting the colourful bed of
wallflowers she and Pa had put in. Brilliant velvety
orange, yellow, bronze and lilac, loved by butterflies,
she had said, and even as they passed through the
gate she was bending over to sniff their lovely scent.
The gate clicked and she turned to see who it was
and her face began to smile at the sight of them
until she realised that they should not be there, not
halfway through a Monday morning, and the smile
slid away like wavelets from a beach. Grace watched
it, her mind up to that moment quite frozen in its own
mould of disbelief, saw it crumple, dissolve somehow
and just like her pa, Ma became old and grey before
her eyes.

Even before she spoke, or they spoke, she began to
back away, keeping them from her, keeping whatever
it was they had to tell her at bay. As long as she didn't
know, it hadn't happened, whatever it was. She shook
her head in denial and put both her hands to her

mouth which opened wide like a child's in a wail of silent terror.

"Mary . . . dear," Pa quavered, holding out his hand, the one that was not holding Grace's.

"No . . . no . . . no," she said sternly.

"Dearest . . ."

"No, Edwin . . . no . . . I absolutely forbid it."

The front door, which stood open, was suddenly filled with the robust form of Nora, and behind her was Mrs Dutton. None of the three women had the slightest idea what Pa was going to tell them, they only knew it was appalling, otherwise he would not be here. But their fertile minds were busy before the merciful shock came to take over, with the disaster which had surely shattered someone they loved. One of the boys, it must be . . . dead: an accident at school . . . a tram . . . those damn cycles . . .

Nora came slowly down the steps, moving towards Ma who had begun to moan in the back of her throat.

"Lass . . ." Her voice was quiet, rough but filled with a depth of loving tenderness that wrapped about them all, and for a blessed second Grace thanked the fates that had brought Nora into their lives, for, really, she couldn't do it on her own. Not Ma and Pa as well. Her brothers . . .

"Mr Tooley?" Nora asked, bracing herself for the worst, her arms ready to catch the swaying, suddenly frail figure of her mistress.

Pa turned to Grace and passed his hand over his eyes. He looked at her imploringly with an expression that said he hadn't the words nor the strength to tell his beloved wife that her eldest, her first-born, might be at the bottom of the ocean in the ship which he had loved, lying among the machinery which had been his life and now, had caused his death.

"Grace . . ."

Grace swallowed then led him forward as if she were the parent and he the child. She bowed her head for a moment as though in shame then lifted it to look into her mother's eyes. She did not know that her face flowed with tears.

"Ma . . ." Her voice was no more than a croak.

"Go on, lass," Nora begged her.

"The ship . . ."

"The ship . . . ?"

"The *Titanic* . . ."

Ma began to scream then, to fling herself about, striking at Nora who did her best to hold her. Pa just stood there, passive, waiting for someone to tell him what to do, whatever that might be, deep in the shock that had shattered his normal judgement. Mrs Allen from next door came hesitantly down her own front steps, then began to hurry along the length of her garden and up the length of theirs.

"What . . . tell us, Gracie," Nora demanded.

"It's sunk . . . sunk . . . last night and . . ."

"Arthur . . . ?"

"We don't know . . . we don't know . . . we don't know . . ."

She remembered little of the next few hours, or even days. Mrs Allen had pulled her into her arms, she recalled that, and held her, prevented her from falling to the grass, and, presumably, brought her inside the house along with Pa. She had vague memories of swimming languidly through water, or that was how it seemed, breaking to the surface now and again where she caught glimpses of a face she knew, usually awash with tears or contorted in grief. At times she ate something, whatever was put in front of her though she could not have told you what it was, and wondered vaguely why she felt no pain, no sorrow, nothing, not realising that she was deep in shock which would eventually wear off and that that was when the pain would begin. Sometimes when she rose to the surface from the warm, comforting depths of the water, it was dark and she was in her bed. Someone was with her and when she turned over the solid, reassuring bulk of Nora sat up in a chair and murmured to her so that she fell back into sleep as the draught the doctor had given her dragged her under again.

The house was filled with people; she didn't know who they were half the time, except for Nora and Mrs Allen. She didn't know Mrs Allen very well except as the mother of Francie, but she seemed to take over, quietly pulling a protective blanket about the shivering, suffering, silent Tooley family.

Her first really coherent moment was four days later. She had noticed that the people around her were becoming less blurred, more pressing on her awareness though she didn't want it. She wanted to stay in her protected cocoon for ever, for here nothing much bothered her, but someone was crying, someone quite overcome with sorrow and it jerked her back to reality, to the comfortable chair she sat in, the warmth of the cheerful fire blazing on the hearth, to the almost overpowering scent of flowers which filled the room. Vases everywhere, spring flowers like the ones she had seen in St John's Gardens, vivid colours which hurt the eye and the heart.

She sighed, as though something deep inside her was telling her she had spent enough time cowering in her hidey-hole. That she was needed elsewhere and though it tormented her, bent her almost double in agony, she had other and more powerful obligations than her own misery.

John was crouched on the rug at her feet, his arms about his knees, his head bowed. He was weeping blindly, hopelessly, his thin boy's back shuddering with each sob that racked him. Beside him Topsy watched him, her ears quivering, her nose almost in his ear, her distress so evident her coat rippled with each shudder. She kept shoving her nose a little nearer, doing her best to comfort the boy, now and again her tongue giving his cheek a tentative lick.

Grace cleared her throat, for it was days since she had spoken a word.

"Johnny," she whispered and at once he and the dog turned to her. Her brother's face was swollen, his eyes puffy in his young face. It was as though he had been bearing his sorrow alone and now, suddenly, here was someone who understood how badly he was missing his brother who, though they had quarrelled and bickered and done all the things brothers do to one another, he had idolised.

"Oh, Grace . . ." he blubbered, wiping the back of his hand across his nose, and at once she held out her arms and, big as he was, he flung himself on her lap. His arms rose round her neck in a stranglehold and they rocked together, comforting one another in the only way humans know, and that was with closeness.

"Oh, Grace . . . Ma is locked in her bedroom." He hiccupped. "And Pa is with her and Mrs Allen has had to go home, she said; and Nora . . ."

"Where is Nora, darling?"

"She's gone with Mr Allen to the White Star Line office to . . . to . . . I don't know . . . something about Arty."

His sobs rose to a peak of pain and Topsy did her best to climb on to Grace's lap with him.

"Where are the others? George . . . and . . . ?"

"George has gone to school. How can he?"

"I don't know, sweetheart. Perhaps it made him feel better."

"You won't leave me, will you, Grace."

She hugged him to her and the pain overwhelmed them both in a rigour of something she could only call agony. "No, love, I won't leave you, but what about Robert and Tom and Richard – where are they?"

"Robert's gone to the shop with Mr Hynes."

"With Mr Hynes . . . ?"

"He said – Mr Hynes – that it might take his mind off things, though how anybody can have their mind taken off their brother being drowned just by serving in a shop is beyond me, Gracie, it really is."

"And the others?"

"They've taken their bicycles somewhere." He was beginning to relax against her, his weeping had abated and his hand, to Topsy's vast relief and pleasure, fell on her head and he pulled her ears.

It was at that moment that the front doorbell rang.

"Oh, God . . . not another." John's voice was stronger, less inclined to wobble in tears. "The bell's never stopped ringing."

"Is there no one to answer it?"

"No, Mrs Allen's gone home and Mrs Dutton, too. She said she'd be back soon to give Nora a hand with dinner but nobody seems to want to eat, though I must admit a toasted teacake might be nice." His voice was wistful, for he had a boy's voracious appetite and it had not been catered to during the last few horrific days. Not that he had wanted to eat but now, with Grace showing signs of being herself again, which made him feel better, he thought he might just force something down.

"I'd better answer it," Grace said doubtfully, though she couldn't bear the thought of listening to some well-meaning person offering their sympathy. But it might be something to do with . . . with . . . Arty; if he was a survivor . . . or . . .

"Don't go, Gracie," John pleaded.

"I must, Johnny. Just wait here with Topsy and I'll come straight back."

She opened the door tentatively, no more than a crack, ready, should it be needed, to spring back to safety in the hall. Standing on the doorstep, his back to her, splendid in his uniform, was Rupert Bradley. He turned as the door opened and in his eyes and on his face was an expression of such compassion, such a need to be anything she wanted of him, she moved without thought into the arms he lifted to her.

Standing at the gate was the shining splendour of a motor car!

7

It was the strangest thing but from that moment, as she stood with her head beneath his chin, her arms clasped at his back and his wrapped tightly about her, she began to feel her strength seep slowly back. She had not been aware that she had been weakened, since she had not really been aware of anything at all during the last few days, but though he said nothing, and neither did she, she was eased.

John broke the spell. He was confounded, she could see that, to find his sister in the arms of a soldier he did not at first recognise, but with the resilience and acceptance of youth, more important things came to claim him, like the smart officer's uniform the soldier was wearing, his first sight of the motor car that stood at his gate and the excuse – a visitor – to offer refreshments.

"Ay, I say, this is wonderful. It's Rupert, isn't it?"

"John," Rupert murmured, giving the boy the sort of nod one chap gives to another.

"What a grand surprise, isn't it, Gracie?" John continued excitedly. "And what a marvellous cap," taking Rupert's cap from him. "And will you look at the badge on it . . . mind if I try it on?" And when Rupert signified his permission he plonked it on his head and postured in front of the mirror in the hallstand.

Grace moved reluctantly from the circle of Rupert's arms but he still held her hand, his own warm, hard, slender and yet strong, comforting, and again she felt that balm enter her wounded heart. She was conscious that it wouldn't last, this feeling of relief, for she seemed to know, even if the others should not accept it, that they would never see Arthur again. Nevertheless she felt that she would survive to bear the pain, and the pain of the others of her family, with the strength this man had incredibly given her. His eyes were not on the boy but looking deeply into hers as though to gauge the depth of her grieving and to let her know that she had only to lean on him and he would support her. She chanced a small smile.

"I only just heard. I arrived home not an hour since and when Mother told me . . ."

"We had a card from her. She is kind . . ."

"Yes, she is. She wants me to bring you round. Not today, of course," he added hastily, "but when you feel more able. She felt unable to intrude on your mother and father . . . your family's . . . but I had to come. To check that . . ."

"I'm glad you did. We don't know yet whether . . ."

"He has not been found?"

"No."

"Grace, how hard it must be for you."

He was touched by her fragile young beauty which was emphasised by the black of her mourning dress. He had not previously thought of her as fragile, for she was tall, full-breasted, long-limbed, but her brown eyes were sheened with gold, translucent with tears shed recently and beneath them were pale grey shadows.

She felt a strange sense of loss as he was forced to turn away. John was taking his arm and drawing him, not to the family room or the sitting-room where visitors had gathered lately, but back towards the door, flinging it open to gaze in silent wonder at the motor car.

"What make is it?" he asked, awestruck.

Rupert looked back at her and tried to smile as though to say what was he to do, but just at that moment the gate opened and Nora, dressed from head to foot in the deepest black, as they all were, at least Grace was – she didn't know about Ma and Pa – the boys in the grey suits they wore for school with black armbands and ties. Nora, quite regal in her sorrow, accompanied by Mr Allen, also wearing a respectful black armband and tie, walked up the path. Though Mr Allen stared curiously at the handsome motor car at the gate, Nora did not even give it a glance. On the Tuesday, the 16th, a report in the *Daily Mirror* had raised wild hopes that the *Titanic* had not sunk at all, that she was actually steaming towards Halifax, Nova Scotia with all passengers safe. Other conflicting messages told the world that many ships had gone to her aid and that all the passengers had been taken aboard, that every man, woman and child on the great liner was safe. It had, of course turned out not to be true.

"Now then, John, what're you doin' hangin' about at front door?" she said kindly but firmly, for this was a house of mourning. Catching sight of the tall figure of the handsome young soldier who was a stranger to her, her face grew hard, for her family were not to be trifled with at a time like this, or indeed at any time if she had anything to do with it, so who was he and what was he doing here?

"Grace . . . ?" Her voice had a query in it. She was not feeling at all well, for the lad's death had hit her hard. The total collapse of both Mr and Mrs Tooley, the responsibility for the children, who were lost without the guidance of their parents and heartbroken into the bargain, had put a tremendous strain on her. Mrs Allen next door had been a steady support, dependable and kind, and what she would have done this morning at the White Star offices without the masculine bombast of Mr Allen, who was used to dealing with bureaucracy, she shuddered to think. She was not a woman to be intimidated by anything but she was not herself at the moment, doing her best to steer the Tooleys through this disaster, and the Allens had proved to be more than good neighbours but good friends to them all. It had been chaos down at the offices of the White Star Line but they had ascertained that survivors had been picked up from the stricken ship but, because he had been on no passenger list, Arthur's name had not been among them. He would surely have sent a cable by now, the harassed official had told them, which made sense, of course, but did nothing to ease Nora's desperately low spirits.

"This is Rupert Bradley, Nora. A . . . a friend of Arthur's." His hand reached for hers again, for it seemed to him this young girl needed *somebody* to sustain her, and she managed to say Arthur's name without a tremble in her voice. "He has come to offer his . . ." She had meant to say "condolences" which was the word most visitors to the house used but it seemed too trite so she let her voice trail away, then, "Rupert, this is our dear friend, Nora McNee, who lives with us."

"Miss McNee." Rupert bowed his head politely but did not take her hand since he was aware she was a servant. In his class one did not shake hands with a servant.

Mr Allen took his leave, but hopping about at the edge of this polite exchange John could not be ignored. He was dying to get out and inspect the wonderful machine that stood in front of his house and with the arrival of his brothers, George presumably from school, that's if he had *been* there, the others from wherever they had spent their time away from the bleakness of the house, and who were clustered round the vehicle, he could not be prevented from leaping down the steps and going like a bullet from a gun down the path, Topsy barking at his heels.

"Will you take tea, sir?" Nora eyed the insignia on the young soldier's uniform but could not make top nor tail of it. He was an officer, that was obvious, but since she did not know of what rank she plumped for "sir".

"Please, Rupert." Hastily Grace let go of Rupert's hand which had seemed an extension of her own arm, aware of Nora's disapproving look.

"Well . . ." He was watching the boys who were doing everything but drive the vehicle. The motor was not his but his older brother's, who had loaned it to him on the understanding that he would return it within the hour.

"I've got some crumpets, Gracie. 'Appen if the young gentleman'll try one you might get summat . . ."

At once Rupert swung round anxiously, startling Nora. "Has she not been eating, Miss McNee?"

"No, sir, and it's understandable but I'm desperate to gerr a bit o' summat—"

"Come, Grace, while the boys are occupied you and I will drink tea and eat crumpets and then I shall take you and them for a ride in the motor."

Grace began to smile but Nora was somewhat shocked.

"Eeh, sir, I'm not sure 'tis proper, in the circumstances, like."

"Miss McNee, it will do her good, and the boys, of course, to be taken out of themselves for half an hour and then, perhaps when I get back I might pay my respects to Mr and Mrs Tooley."

He was so perfect. He was miraculous. She loved him and the people she loved, which included Nora, seemed disposed to feel the same way. Well, not exactly, of course, for her love was something she couldn't describe. She loved her ma and pa. She loved her brothers. She loved Topsy and Wally. All different kinds of love. What a muddle it all was, these feelings she had for different members of her family, but then he was not a member of her family and what was in her heart for him, buried deep in her heart, was precious and unique. But he was liked. She could see that Nora, who did not give her approval easily, liked him. He was polite, generous, kind, a gentleman in every way and one day . . . one day . . . She got no further than that. At fourteen her character was not yet fully formed. She had not completely left girlhood nor had she yet become a woman. She had known a sheltered childhood and nothing in it had led her to believe that things were not always what they appeared to be; and what she saw in Rupert Bradley's eyes, the expression of tenderness on his face told her that this man was true, that the feelings he displayed for her, *for her*, were real. Because she was young, innocent, inexperienced in the ways of men she did not look at them more closely. He was here. He had held her in his arms, taken her hand and her dreams ran away with her.

They ate crumpets and drank the tea Nora brought in on a tray, using Mary Tooley's best china, her silver cutlery, her finest drawn lace tray cloth. He told her of his training, what filled his days at Sandhurst, the fun he and his fellow officers got up to, at least what was suitable for a young girl's ears. He described the countryside about the academy then moved on to his mother's conservatory, the herb garden she was planting, his brother Alan who was about to become engaged to be married, his sisters and their love of horses and for half an hour she was lifted out of the black depth of her family's loss and was later to feel ashamed that he had made her laugh.

"Well, I suppose I had better rescue Alan's motor from those hooligans . . . oh, I beg your pardon."

"No, they really are hooligans most of the time but your visit . . . the motor . . . has given them a respite for a few minutes from their sadness."

They stood up and again he took her hand, his eyes filled with that gentle compassion she found so soothing. His hair, which had been smoothly brushed when he arrived had, with his habit of running his right hand through it as he talked, become a tumble of glossy waves over his forehead and she had a great deal of trouble keeping her free hand from brushing it back. What a glorious creature he was. His cheeks and chin were recently shaved and she could smell the sharp, clean fragrance of what seemed to be lemon. He was frowning slightly as her grief saddened him and his eyebrows, dark and silken, dipped over the tobacco brown of his eyes. She could see her own reflection in them and when he blinked she was sorry when she disappeared.

She had nothing to put on but a three-quarter coat of black wool, plain, its drabness taking what colour she had from her cheeks. Recently Ma had begun to allow her to wear the pretty fashions of the day, mostly white muslin, with pintucked bodices, high-necked ruching, tight-sleeved and tight-waisted with sashes of blue or pink velvet, ankle-length skirts which revealed dainty kid boots to match, hats with wide brims, the crown a flower garden of roses or daisies. Now her hat was black, like an upturned mushroom, unadorned, swamping her loveliness, hiding her youth.

The boys were ready to whoop with joy, quickly subsiding when Nora, who had come to the gate with her charge, rounded on them with a sibilant hiss to remember where they were, *who* they were and the circumstances in which they found themselves. They might go for a ride with . . . with Mr Bradley, his rank again baffling her, but they were to behave circumspectly, though she did not use this exact word.

Grace sat in the front with Rupert. The vehicle was black, highly polished, with red leather seats. There seemed to be an inordinate amount of brass fittings, lamps and other objects she could not name, a spare tyre next to the driver with a motor horn handily attached. There was a windshield which was a great boon since Rupert had the hood folded back and, after George had turned a handle at the front of the bonnet which prompted the engine to spring into life, and leaped into the back with the other four boys, they were off with a thunderous roar which frightened the life out of her. Even the boys were silent for a full five minutes, since none of them had ever been in a motor car before. The silence did not last long when they all began to shout questions at Rupert at one and the same time.

"It's a Darracq, isn't it?"

"What year?"

". . . horsepower . . ."

". . . fast can it go? Do try her out . . ."

"I'm seventeen, Rupert. Can I have a go?"

"Isn't the factory turning to mass production?"

She found she had nothing to say. She was filled with a sense of peace which would not last but at that moment was very welcome. The sun shone brilliantly, washing a field covered in wild daffodils to a patchwork of gold and pale green. In the ditches at the side of the road marsh marigolds made a bold splash of butter yellow and the blackthorn hedges were in blossom, a drift of starry white. Primroses were thick in the grass and they rattled past an orchard beside a farm where the plum and damson trees were an enchantment of blossom, like lace against the azure blue of the sky. She felt she could speed on like this for ever with Rupert by her side, but sadly she knew that this was just a small stitch in the repair of the torn fabric of her family's life.

They were speeding along Prescot Road towards

Knotty Ash. Rupert was the only one to wear goggles and the rest of them had tears streaming down their cheeks but for the first time since they had heard about the *Titanic* they were tears of joy, of excitement caused by the wind and the forward movement of the motor car. The boys jostled one another to shout in Rupert's ear, almost falling over the side and into the road. A man sitting on a horse-drawn milk float turned to stare after them as he was swallowed up in a cloud of dust, and a couple sedately coming in their direction on what Tom shouted was a Royal Enfield tandem, the back made specially to accommodate a lady, had to stop, wobbling into the ditch at the side of the road.

It all ended too soon but Grace was comforted by Rupert's suggestion that if he could beg the machine from Alan in a day or two, would she accompany him to Garlands where his mother would like to give her tea. Now she was not to think of this as a light-hearted invitation of the sort ladies extended to one another. It was nothing of the sort. Had she and Grace's mother known one another she would have called but it was not correct to intrude on a family at a time like this. Now if Grace did not feel like it she would understand but his mother had really taken to her and . . . well, it was up to her. Might he telephone her tomorrow?

Grace had to admit that the Tooleys had no such instrument in their house. She stood, a forlorn creature in her drab black, her hat drowning her and Rupert felt a ridiculous urge to whip it off her head. He had thought her so lovely, so fraily lovely when he had first seen her but now she looked . . . well, not at all as he remembered her last year. Still, he had promised his mother, and Grace herself, so he smiled, lifting her chin with his gloved hand to look into her eyes which was like looking into a glass of sherry. They were transparent, the pupils a sable pinpoint in the centre, the lashes surrounding them a tangled, moist tracery of black. Her mouth quivered and her lips were moist too, though this time a pinky apricot.

"Dear Lord, you're so lovely," he said without thinking, then turned away abruptly, for he knew it was not the sort of thing a man of twenty says to a fourteen-year-old girl.

He leaped into the motor, nodding at George who was standing ready to crank it, then he and the machine were away up the road, turning to wave at the group of youngsters who watched him admiringly.

The children of Edwin and Mary Tooley ate the meal Nora put in front of them, alone as they had been for the last four days. They had enjoyed the release from grief Rupert and the motor car had provided for them, but now they were back with the reality of the loss of Arthur and the effect it had had on their parents.

"Are Ma and Pa never to come down again?" Tom asked angrily, spearing his fork savagely into the sausage on his plate. He was not really angry, just a frightened boy of fifteen whose world had fallen apart and whose parents, who had been there for him since the day of his birth, had hidden themselves away from everybody. He had spent the day with Richard down at the docks and the vast quayside of Liverpool which stretched for six and a half miles along the shore of the River Mersey. There had been ships of all kinds, even some sailing ships, their denuded rigging a lacework against the deep blue of the spring sky. They had wandered in almost total silence, for they did not know what to talk about in this terrible moment of their young lives which had been turned upside down by events. Two great Cunarders, the *Mauretania* and the *Lusitania* were berthed in Canada Dock basin and they had stood for an hour watching the busy gangways, listening to the porters' shouts and the strident, cheerful whistle of the dockers, so much in contrast with the awfulness of home. They had breathed in the smell peculiar to dockland, a mixture of tobacco, the sea, of tar and timber, coffee beans and spices.

"I feel like stowing away," he had mumbled to Richard. "It's so bloody awful at home."

"I know. Where d'you fancy? America or Australia?"

For a while they had entertained one another with the theme of where in the world they would sail if they could. There had been a ferryboat going across the water to New Brighton when they got back to the Pier Head and without consulting one another they had run across the moving gangway and jumped lightly on board, narrowly missing a dip in the cold, grey waters as it was lifted clear. A man shouted obscenities at them and another chased them round the decks since they had neglected to purchase a ticket, but they had eluded him and for a while had felt almost themselves again.

The sight of the splendid Darracq parked outside *their* gate had again lifted their despairing spirits and they had set about investigating every inch of her – motor cars were always female they had discovered from Arty who knew about such things – until Rupert had come out and taken them for a spin. It had been a good day, despite . . . But now they were back home, eating sausages and again their ma and pa were missing and really, it was too bad. They all slumped their elbows on the table in defiance of Ma's repeated admonishments, which, of course, were missing, and no one seemed to care, neither Grace nor Nora, which seemed even worse, another crumbling in the solid foundations of their ordered world.

Grace was too busy with her own secret thoughts, enchanted and at the same time ashamed that she could think of such things at a time like this. Only this morning she had been floating beneath the surface of her misery, aware that things weren't as they had been, aware that they would never be again. She supposed she had been in what she had heard Nora and Mrs Allen call, thinking she wasn't listening, "nature's way of dealing with shock". It had worn away, that welcome unawareness, and there were bad times to come, but Rupert had brought something with him that would sustain her in the weeks and months ahead.

He came the next day and, thankfully, at least he thought so, the boys were off somewhere, she didn't know where, and though she supposed she should be concerned she had not as yet reached that point where the mantle of responsibility draped itself across her vulnerable shoulders.

He was not dressed in his uniform today. He wore the sports jacket and grey flannels he had had on when they saw him at Garlands, with a snowy white shirt over which was a rather fancy knitted waistcoat the colour of pale sand. His tie was the only jarring note, a peacock tie of blues and greens and yellows which matched nothing he wore. Over this he had put on what was known as a "dustcoat", borrowed from his brother, and had even brought one for her, to protect her clothing from the dust, he explained, and a pair of goggles! He laughed, holding her arms out from her sides to get a better look at her, but Nora, who supervised the whole thing since it seemed to her to be inappropriate at this sad time, snorted her disapproval.

"I don't think yer ma'd like it, Grace," she said sharply, but the sight of the lass's face which in that comical moment had eased and become the face Nora was used to, shut off the words she meant to utter. Poor lass, poor little lass, for in Nora's opinion she had a hard row to hoe in the future. Nora had seen the state of Mr and Mrs Tooley and what was to become of these bairns who were wandering around rudderless?

He didn't take her to his mother. It was as though he knew she was not up to chatting, or even listening to his mother chatting. His mother was the soul of kindness but his sisters were not at all sure they approved of their brother taking an interest in this family, despite the tragedy of their circumstances. Eve particularly was inclined to be shrewish at times as she waited for some member of the aristocracy to come along, preferably on a white charger, and carry her off to the life she considered her due.

He manoeuvred skilfully through the thick and bustling traffic of William Brown Street, Whitechapel, past Pa's shop and on down to the Pier Head. It was an exhilarating way to travel, she decided, dangerous at times as they weaved through waggons and drays, horse-drawn and motor cabs and bicycles. Liverpool was a dynamic city made up of peoples from all parts of the world, a flourishing city whose folk were not about to be left behind in this modern, ever growing, mechanised world.

He left the motor parked outside the Dock Board offices where they discarded their dustcoats and goggles. He took her arm and even through the drab thickness of her black coat she could feel the warmth of it run through her to reach her heart which beat fast with love.

The river was wind-ruffled as they took the ferry, and overhead the cries of the gulls as they hung on the air waiting for the scraps that were flung over the sides of the ships were harsh and yet musical. The sun touched Grace's cheek and reached her eyes and when she looked up at Rupert he felt a sharp tug of his emotions as their incredible tawny gold, sunk in the pallor of her face, caught him unawares. His feelings for her and about her were so bloody mixed. The white smoothness of her skin, the pulse beating in the soft curve of her neck, the parted moistness of her rosy mouth, so plump and child like, moved him to a tenderness he didn't want to feel.

When they reached Rock Ferry since he was, after all, a gentleman, he tucked her hand in the crook of his arm and began to walk. The sky was again a blue arc above their heads and a lark which swept the curve of it sang its heart out. The scent of the newly growing grass, away from the smells of the river, was sweet in their nostrils.

There were cottages with gardens filled with spring flowers, somewhat wild but appropriate and Grace felt her sorrowing senses quicken with life. They came to an inn where she drank cider and ate pork pie and pickle, and though Rupert had nothing much to say and neither did she, he was healing her, just with his quiet, understanding presence.

The boys were at the gate when they arrived home, wild with envy and erupting with angry denunciations. Why hadn't Rupert waited for them? Where had they been? Really, it was most unfair of Gracie to hog the motor car when she knew nothing about it, and cared less. They had only been a ride on their bicycles up to Knotty Ash, they told him accusingly, passing his gate, not saying so but obviously hoping to catch sight of him and the marvel of the Darracq.

He smiled good-naturedly as Grace divested herself of the unflattering dustcoat and goggles, the scarf which held the hideous hat to her head, handing her down as though she were an elderly lady. She did not look elderly as she took off her hat with the veil, holding it carelessly in her hand. Her hair gleamed in the sunshine, a coppery brown, slipping over her ears and falling in loose wispy curls. A bit of colour had returned to her cheeks and her eyes glowed. She smiled at him, a smile just *for* him, her teeth white and even between the full rosiness of her lips. He wanted to kiss her but instead he shook his head and tore his gaze away from her to her brothers.

"Lads, I'm off tomorrow and I must spend some time with my mother or she'll cast me off without a shilling," making a joke of it so that as he climbed behind the wheel, waving to them all as he drove off, she was still smiling.

8

The discreet knocking at the front door of number 10 the following Sunday was not at first heard by the occupants. It was as though the visitor wished to announce his presence but at the same time could not bear to cause distress or inconvenience to those inside.

Breakfast had been at the usual time, a hearty breakfast, for though three of the members of the family might be said to be off their food, the other five weren't.

"I could eat a bloody horse," John announced, obviously for effect, daring anyone to criticise his use of "language", as his mother called it, or at least *used* to call it before she vanished from his young life. Grace was fast in her dreaming memories of the day she had spent alone with Rupert, and the others didn't much care since no one seemed to care a lot about them. Or what they said or did.

But Nora heard it and the boy was surprised and infuriated when she boxed his ears. "Don't let me hear yer speak like that again, yer wicked boy. Just because yer ma an' pa aren't about don't mean yer can use such words. I've a good mind ter wash yer mouth out wi' soap an' if I catch—"

John swung round in his chair and glared at her and the others watched in horror. "You've no right to hit me, you . . . you bloody woman. And I'll say what I like. Nobody gives a damn what happens to me in this house and *I've* a good mind to pack my bags and go and . . ."

"Yes?" said Nora threateningly, though inside she was as horrified as the rest. She knew what was wrong with the little lad, of course, and though she hadn't said anything to the grieving parents she felt that they should spare a thought for their children, who were just as sad and bewildered. They needed their mother and father at a time like this and though she and Mrs Allen, bless her, did what they could, it was not the same as taking your troubles to your own ma and pa, was it?

The knock at the door saved John from answering, which he couldn't have done anyway, for where would he go to get away from this adversity that had come into his young life and quite devastated it? He couldn't cope with it and so he hit out at it, at them, and at life itself.

"Who can that be?" Nora muttered, hoping to God it wasn't another well-wisher though those had thinned out during the last few days. The world and his wife had seemed to be on her doorstep at the beginning of the week, the doorbell driving her to distraction as neighbours and acquaintances came to pay their respects. So who was this, and on a Sunday as well?

"It's Mr Hynes," she whispered as she came back into the family room. "Him from't shop."

Grace, who had been half-heartedly spreading marmalade on a piece of toast hoping that it might go down more easily, looked up in astonishment.

"Mr Hynes?"

"Aye, he wants ter see yer pa."

"Pa?"

"Aye, what shall I do with him?" Meaning she was not sure what to do about Mr Tooley who had not left his wife's side, except for necessary personal attentions, since she had been carried up to her bed last Monday.

The five boys looked at Grace expectantly and at the same time with little interest since what was it to do with them? They had shuffled through the past week with the freedom that, under ordinary circumstances, would have delighted them, even Nora, who usually had eyes in the back of her head for any wrongdoing, paying them little heed. They had none of them been to school and even Robert, who had thought he might pass the time in the shop, had soon made his escape. He didn't want to be stuck behind a counter, even for a few days or until his pa returned to normal, he had told Grace in the breaking voice of an adolescent boy. At the time it had not unduly concerned her, since she had still been drifting in a pool of mindless misery. The only high spot in the week had been the drive in Rupert's motor car. Today they supposed they would get on their cycles and go off to wherever they pleased, which, when it was not frowned upon, seemed to lose its flavour.

Grace rose to her feet and faltered beside the table, biting her lip and frowning, while Nora, out of her depth with this situation, waited for Grace to tell her what to do. Dear God, this family were in a terrible turmoil, she thought when she, Nora McNee, who had once been its backbone, should be waiting for a little lass to give her an order.

"I'd better go and see what he wants." Grace's tone and manner were hesitant, looking round the table for one of them to make a suggestion. George was the oldest now, almost eighteen, but he was calmly forking bacon into his mouth as though the whole thing was the concern of anybody but him. He would leave school at the end of term and he knew exactly what he was going to do then; in fact he might do it before the end of term it was so bloody miserable here. These, naturally, were private thoughts so let Grace sort it out, whatever it was, or go and fetch his father.

"Shall I come with you?" Richard stood up reluctantly and Robert had the grace to look somewhat sheepish but she shook her head, then lifted it courageously as she moved towards the hallway.

Mr Hynes sprang to his feet as she entered the living-room. A fire had not been lit since nobody was expected and the room felt chilly. He still wore his overcoat, his bowler hat twirling round and round in his hands as though he had come on an awkward errand. Beside him on the occasional table was a small attaché case.

"Mr Hynes?"

"Good morning, Miss Grace. I'm that sorry ter bother yer at a time like this burrit's yer pa I wanted ter see. It's a bit . . . well, if yer could ask 'im ter spare me a minute I'd be grateful." He didn't know whether to smile or not, for this was a house of mourning, so he did his best to look pleasant but sorrowful at the same time.

"Well . . ."

"Is it . . . will it be inconvenient fer yer pa to . . ."

"No, not at all; but you see . . ."

"I can't come at any other time, yer see, what with the shop an' all. Sunday's the only day it's closed, as I'm sure yer know an' . . . well, if yer could ask Mr Tooley I'm sure we could make arrangements."

"Arrangements?"

Mr Hynes was horribly embarrassed. "Well, it's cash, yer see, Miss Grace. Accounts comin' in an' that." He did not add that his wages had not been paid for the week just gone and he and his family were not the kind who had money in the bank to tide them over. Mr Hynes had married late in life. He had four young children and the money went out as soon as it had come in and how was his Martha to manage with no wage in her hand this week?

Grace stood irresolutely for a moment or two while Mr Hynes watched her anxiously, then her face cleared and so did Mr Hynes's. He straightened his bowed shoulders. He didn't know why but he felt this lass, just a slip of a girl, would sort it all out somehow. She gave you a feeling of confidence, trust, the reassurance that she was quite capable of making it all right. He let out his breath on a long sigh of relief.

"Sit down, Mr Hynes, please." He sat. "Nora will bring you tea . . . coffee . . . while I go and talk to Pa." If the thought of knocking on that firmly closed door daunted her she did not show it.

"Tea, please, Miss Grace, 'd be very hacceptable."

"Mr Hynes wants to see Pa," she told the assembled company as she re-entered the family room, "and will you take him a cup of tea, Nora."

"Oh, Lord," Nora whispered, for no one had knocked on Mr and Mrs Tooley's door in the past week except her and that was only to pass in a tray of something or other tempting, most of it not eaten. Mr Tooley's hands had appeared in the half-opened doorway and that had been that. Really, these poor children, it was too bad, but perhaps now something would be done to winkle them out, meaning Edwin and Mary Tooley, and get this family back on its feet.

There was no sound behind the closed door of her parents' room and the tentative knock she applied to it sounded loud and intrusive. For several moments there was no response then Pa's voice said quietly from the other side, "Yes?" Just that. No more, and for some unaccountable reason, for after all Ma and Pa had suffered a terrible loss, in a terrible manner, Grace felt something that might be called anger run through her.

Her voice was firm, loud, she thought, but perhaps that was what was needed. "Pa, it's Grace, I must see you. It's important."

"Not now, Grace. Your mother is sleeping and—"

"*Yes*, now, Pa. Mr Hynes is downstairs and needs to speak to you." As we all do, she said under her breath.

"Grace, dear, I cannot. Ask him to come back when—"

"When, Pa? He can only get away from the shop on a Sunday, as you must know and he has things to—"

"*Grace*, I said not now."

She thought she was beaten and was about to turn away, since she could not drag her father forcibly from his hiding place but instead she put her hand on the doorknob, turned it and was surprised to find the door opening. She stepped inside her parents' room and for a moment could make out nothing but the vague shapes of the furniture. The curtains were drawn and the lamps turned off.

"Pa," she quavered nervously, then was startled when her father's voice sounded from the far side of the bed. He rose from the chair, confused, she thought, by the sight of her and in the bed lay her mother, asleep, as he had said, so deeply asleep she did not move as Grace spoke.

"Pa, please come downstairs and speak to Mr Hynes. The poor man is quite desperate and—"

"Desperate?"

"It's about money, Pa. Bills, I think and he—"

"Grace dear, please, I cannot concern myself at the moment with—"

"But, Pa . . ."

"Your mother is not at all well." In the dark she saw him pass his hand across his face and heard the rasp of stubble against it.

"I will sit with Ma, or Nora can come up but you must see that . . . that even now . . . with Arty . . ."

"Ah, don't, Grace . . . don't. It's not being able to have a funeral, you see, that's what's wrong with her; and I can't seem able to help her. That's what's wrong with me."

"Pa." She made her voice stern and yet inside her a great bubble of compassion filled her chest and made her want to say to her pa, "It's all right, don't bother, stay with Ma," but she knew somehow that she couldn't. She had seen the way her parents' desertion had affected her brothers this last week. They should do their grieving together, as a family, with Ma and Pa, the adults, acting as a lifeline to its younger members. The boys had nobody but Nora, and herself. She had Rupert!

"Pa." Her voice was sharp. "You must come and see Mr Hynes."

"Ssh." Pa put his finger to his lips and gazed in agony at the still, silent figure on the bed. "She has only just gone to sleep and I—"

"Pa, I'll call Nora to sit with her and then you must come downstairs."

Suddenly he capitulated and with Nora, hastily brought up, tiptoeing past the open-mouthed group of boys who had gathered at the bottom of the stairs, their pa crept down them for the first time in almost a week.

He looked at them as though he were not awfully sure who they were and they certainly gaped at him, for they scarcely recognised him. He was their pa but twenty years older. He had not changed the clothes he had worn that day. He had not shaved, barely slept or eaten since the moment the bottom had dropped out of his world, or so it seemed, when he was told his eldest son, the son of whom he had been so proud, was at the bottom of the Atlantic Ocean along with 1,658 other souls, or so the latest figures estimated. He had not, it seemed, for a minute held out any hope that Arthur might be one of the survivors.

"Pa . . . ?" His youngest boy, only a baby really, who desperately wanted his mother, as all children wanted their mothers, no matter how old they were, at moments of crisis, held out his hand and his pa took it.

"John . . . oh, John," he said sadly, knowing his own deficiency, frightening the boy badly, but unable, it seemed to do anything about it, then walked past him and into the sitting-room. Mr Hynes, cup of tea still in his hand, rose eagerly to his feet, then, seeing his employer swaying in the doorway, put the cup and saucer carefully on the table. He walked towards Edwin Tooley, smiled at the children, then closed the door.

Ten minutes later Pa was seen to walk past the open door of the family room, eyes front, and on up the stairs. Grace came to the door and watched him go and those who might have been looking at her and not at Pa would have seen the expression on her young face change from one of hopelessness to one of determination. When Pa had vanished she whirled about and to the astonishment of the rest strode, they could describe it in no other way, into the sitting-room, closing the door firmly behind her.

The drama continued. Nora had cleared the breakfast table and the boys were dithering about trying to decide what to do with this day that stretched before them. There was a game of football kicking off at ten on the recreation ground attached to the Technical Instruction Centre on Prescot Road in which a couple of boys from their school were playing. Should they take their bicycles and ride out to the Delamere Forest which was a full day's expedition? New Brighton's fairground was open but they needed money for the ferry and the attractions to be found there and Pa couldn't be asked, could he? There were a hundred and one things to do in this great city of theirs but somehow they seemed to have lost their flavour.

They forgot their indecision as they pushed into one another in an effort to watch as Grace suddenly erupted from the sitting-room, raced up the stairs and after knocking, first quietly, and then with more force on their parents' bedroom door, several minutes later came down again with Pa in tow, a very reluctant Pa, certainly, shambling along like one of those homeless itinerants who were often seen being moved on by a constable in town. He did Grace's bidding just the same.

He and Grace and Mr Hynes had been shut up in the sitting-room for twenty minutes or so when Pa came out and returned to his and Ma's bedroom, his face expressionless. Mr Hynes shook hands hesitantly with Grace at the front door and Grace came slowly back to the family room, where she sat down abruptly in one of the chairs at the table.

"Well," said Nora, hovering at the connecting door, "what the dickens was tha' all about? Is yer ma ter come down or wha'? Yer pa looked none too clever but is he ter go ter't shop termorrer? That Mr Hynes is a nice chap but I reckon he couldn't run fer a tram let alone't shop."

Grace sighed, putting her head in her hands for a moment, then lifted it to look round at the bewildered circle of faces. They were all waiting for her to tell them what had gone on in the sitting-room and why she had been included. The expressions on their faces were more or less the same and yet their separate characters altered them slightly. George had a wary look about him. He would be eighteen next birthday and though it had not been spoken of out loud it had been taken for granted that when he left school he would go into the business with Pa. Arthur, of course, had been set on his course from an early age so the next in line was George, the logical choice, or so it would seem. Robert had another year at school but seemed to have no particular idea what he would do with his life and Tom was the same. A bit of a handful was Tom, somewhat secretive, and of them all inclined to dig his heels in, to argue over where they should go, or what they should do, often causing disruption over nothing at all. Her own twin, Richard, was easily led, easy-going, happy to let the others have their way, and John was still a baby, defiant if he thought he could get away with it, showing off, as boys of his age did but basically sweet-natured. She loved them all. They were her brothers, but she was aware, after the second interview with Pa, that she must do something about them, for it had been made clear to her that Pa never would and if left alone they would get out of hand. Ma, who had been the strength of the family was temporarily – Grace hoped – weakened and until she gathered herself together Grace must take over.

"George," she said abruptly, "would you like to work in the shop with Mr Hynes?"

George looked horrified. "Bloody hell, no. What-ever gave you that daft notion?"

"Now then, lad . . ." Nora began but she was ignored.

"I thought not." Grace stood up and walked to the window, pulling aside the nets as though looking outside for inspiration. Wally rubbed himself against her leg, purring loudly and she bent to pick him up.

"You realise that Pa is . . . is not himself."

"That's pretty obvious," Tom sneered.

"Now listen 'ere, young man . . ." Nora began but again nobody took any notice and Grace became increasingly aware of what the tragedy of Arthur's death had done to this family. Nora, usually staunch, opinionated, supportive, wise and never one to hide her light under a bushel, had become uncertain, made that way by the crisis which she seemed unable to cope with. She supposed that some people were like that. Those who you thought would be a pillar of strength fell apart and those who were quiet, mild-mannered, unassuming, proved themselves to be capable of taking control. Was she like that? Only time would prove one way or the other.

"Then you are to go back to school tomorrow and get on with your lives as they were before . . . before . . ."

"And who are you to order us about, I'd like to know?" Tom again.

"Pa has put me in charge of this house and of you."

"Oh, come on!"

"Go upstairs and ask him if you don't believe me." Which was a risk but how else was she to get them in order?

"Well . . ."

"Go on, Tom. Go and knock on the door and ask him what you are to do. If you're so sure you are old enough and confident enough to do as you like go and ask Pa. He'll only confirm what I've just said. I am in charge."

"But George is the oldest now that . . ."

"I've just asked George if he wants to earn his living in the shop and he says not. Someone has to help Mr Hynes."

"So who's that to be then, Gracie?" Richard asked mildly.

"Me."

There was total silence for perhaps ten seconds then they all began to bluster at once, including Nora, telling her that if she thought they were going to take orders from her, a *girl* and one not yet fifteen then she must be mad. Anyroad, this from Nora, how could she take her pa's place since she knew absolutely nowt about working in a shop? John shouted that he wouldn't mind taking Pa's place; what kind of wage would he get and it would be a damn sight better than school, and he thought he might buy a motor car. Robert stamped about and declared nonchalantly that if Grace was to leave school then so was he. He'd always fancied working down at the docks; there must be plenty of jobs for someone strong like him and if there weren't he might try for a place on a steamer and see a bit of the world. Only George was silent, staring off at some place only he knew about, his face empty, his eyes unfocused.

"So how are you to help Mr Hynes, Grace?" Richard asked her, and she wondered how it was that she and Richard, who were after all twins and perhaps might have been expected to share their characteristics, should be so totally opposite. It seemed that when resolution of mind was given out while they were still in the womb, she had got the lion's share. He was quite content to do as he was told, to go along with whatever was decided upon as long as life continued, or *returned* to what it had been before Arthur's death.

"I've just been . . . with Pa, naturally" – though Pa

had just sat there and nodded, eager to get back to Ma – "and we've been going through the books."

"Books . . . what books?"

"Account books . . . er, order books . . . things like that" – trying desperately to remember some of the things Mr Hynes had told her she must learn – "and he is going to teach me the business until Pa is able to return. When Ma's better, I mean," she added hastily. "There are things that will need Pa's signature – cheques and things – but I shall bring them home and Pa has promised to check them and . . . and sign them and . . . and things will go on just as before. I shall serve behind the counter and go to the . . . the tobacco factory and . . . well, learn the business like Pa did."

They stared at her in wonder, Nora shaking her head in disbelief. Wally struggled in her arms and she realised she had the cat in a stranglehold. Letting out her breath slowly she allowed the animal to jump to the floor, doing her best to look as though there were nothing strange in the mad, mad plan she had devised to keep her family afloat. They had a thriving little business, a shop that was well placed and with a good supply of regular customers; she had heard Pa say so hundreds of times so all she had to do was keep it going. They might have to employ a boy, Mr Hynes had told her, whom he would train but she was to learn to be her pa and he, who knew the business like he knew his own front room, would teach her.

George took a step towards the fireplace and picked up the shovel ready to throw some coal on the fire. "But . . . but you're only fourteen. What? Why?"

"I'm nearly fifteen and, besides, there are thousands

of girls all over the city who leave school at fourteen
and start work."

"Yes, but they're—"

"What?"

"They're not like you."

"What does that mean?"

"Well, their money's needed at home. They don't
go to a school like yours."

"George, all of you, please help me on this. Ma . . .
Ma has been struck down by Arthur's death and Pa
can't leave her yet. Someone has to see that the shop
doesn't go under. You, George, and you, Robert,
don't want to take over and I think that's right since
your education is important to you. Tom's . . . well,
he's better at school" – meaning more under control
– "and John's too young. Believe me this is the only
way for now. Now, go and do whatever you were to
do and leave me to go over these books Mr Hynes
left with me. I shall probably bring Pa down again to
help me." Which was not true. "Nora will make you
up something to eat so stay out all day. Tomorrow it's
back to school and you'll need to be strong for . . .
well, off you go."

She lay in her bed that night, her head filled with
figures, with whirling thoughts of what tomorrow
would bring, of her frantic hope that her brothers
would do her bidding and return to their proper lives.
She felt so *old* and yet far too young to be taking on
this terrifying task of keeping her family together. She
prayed, again to those faceless gods, that her brothers
would not turn against her. She was afraid that they
might defy her and just go to the devil, for what would

she do then? Ma *must* recover soon and when she did Pa would be there, as he had always been, to take over from her but until then she must grit her teeth and pit her will against those of her brothers. And what of poor Arty? In all this dreadful day, which had almost brought her to her knees and in which she had found the strength from somewhere to stay upright, she, and she supposed the others, had not given a thought to their brother whose death had caused all this. They should all be together mourning him, not torn apart by the anxiety of what they should do next.

She tossed restlessly, her heart sorely tried by memories of her brother and as though he had come, as he had come this week, to comfort her, Rupert's face imprinted itself on her closed eyelids and she drew it into herself and was at peace. She slept.

9

She decided she would not wear the black since it was so unbecoming, so dismal, not the sort of thing customers wished to see in the shop assistant who served them their Gold Flake or Havana cigars. Not that she wished to appear disrespectful towards her dead brother but she had decided when she and Mr Hynes worked out what should be done that she would make an impression, a good impression, and one way was to look as becoming as possible. She had a plain, rather severely cut mid-grey skirt of alpaca, tightly waisted and with a small flare about her ankles which she thought would be appropriate, and with it she wore a succession of crisp white blouses, high-necked with a full sleeve, tight at the wrist but all prettily pintucked. A wide belt of black leather and high black boots completed the outfit. On her fourteenth birthday Ma and Pa had given her a beautiful silver locket, oval, engraved and hanging on a long silver chain. She put it on, promising herself that one day she would have a photograph of Rupert in it. She looked attractive but discreet, she and Nora decided, though Nora, of course, had been almost out of her mind with worry over the whole thing. Even Mrs Allen had tried to intervene but Grace was quietly firm.

"There is no one else to take over, Mrs Allen.

Someone has to keep the business going until Ma recovers and Pa can go back to work."

"Your brothers, dear. Surely George, as the eldest—"

"George does not care to work in a shop, Mrs Allen. Besides, the boys' education is more important than mine. Pa has given me—"

She stopped speaking abruptly. She could not tell this woman, kind as she was, but a comparative stranger, that she thought her father had lost his mind, even if it was temporary, and that he had told her and Mr Hynes to do what they liked with the shop, he didn't give a damn about it now. It was quite extraordinary the way he had folded up and gone in on himself. She had always known that Ma was the strong one and so she supposed with her mother out of action – she prayed to some god or other, she didn't know which, that it would not be for long – Pa had lost his bearings.

Mrs Allen, who had come in just as Grace was about to run for the tram to town, took in Grace's outfit, her expression disapproving. She had said to her Fred last night that she thought the whole idea was absolutely mad, letting that child, the same age as their Francie, go to work in the tobacconist's shop. She felt intensely sorry for the girl, for all of them who had suffered such a blow, but surely there was some other way to keep the business going, didn't Fred think so?

"I'm sure you're right, dear," Fred had answered from behind his Sunday newspaper, which was his usual response, but now, with the child in front of her, looking *years* older than she really was, she felt bound to say something. The girl had even put her hair up, for heaven's sake, something she would not allow her girls to do until they were sixteen. She looked quite . . . quite . . . well, glorious was the word that came to mind, in her neat waisted blouse and skirt and her hair like a burnished conker, those that her sons, James and Norman, brought home from beneath the trees in Newsham Park. With it piled on top of her head in a sort of loose bun, she would be bound to attract attention.

Nora thought so too. She had just come from the kitchen to make sure the lass was well wrapped up in the black, three-quarter coat and the shapeless hat that she had worn for the past week. She was infuriated to find her with her hair uncovered, fastened on top of her head and with loose curls drifting about her ears in a most alluring way.

"Yer not goin' out like that, Grace Tooley," she said sternly. "I said nowt about the blouse an' skirt since they're decent but yer hair should be properly plaited as befits a lass o' your age. Get upstairs an' purrit right."

"That's just what I was thinking, Nora," Mrs Allen remarked kindly. "Really, dear, you're not old enough to have your hair done like that."

"Mrs Allen, Nora, I am to work in a shop, not as I did as a schoolgirl on a Saturday to earn extra pocket money, but as an employee of my father. I am to do adult work and I must look like an adult."

"Them men what come in t'ert shop'll get wrong idea, child, an' yer ma wouldn't like it."

"Ma and Pa have . . . have elected to remain apart from . . . they have . . . Pa has given me free rein to act as I see fit in the shop, with the help and guidance of Mr Hynes and I believe that means I may dress in a way I think is appropriate. You approved of what I was to put on, Nora, so why should you object to my hair?"

Nora, and Mrs Allen was the same, didn't quite know how to put into words the startling picture this young girl made and what an effect it might have on the males who were the main customers in her pa's shop. She was no longer the young girl who had careered about the place with her brothers; who had ridden her bicycle at top speed to keep up with them; who had climbed trees, skinned her knees, made holes in her stockings, played cricket and even tried football on the park at the back of the house; who had scrapped and argued and fought to be included in every activity they enjoyed. She had become a woman, quiet, mature, self-possessed, or so she appeared as she buttoned up her coat and pulled on her gloves.

"Well, put yer hat on then, love," Nora wheedled.

For a moment she was a child again in a grown-up world. "Oh, Nora, I daren't. It will make it look a sight and I'm afraid I won't be able to do my hair again without my triple mirror. Now, I must run or I'll miss the tram."

Mr Hynes insisted that for the first week she did nothing but serve in the shop, which she was used to. She was to learn by heart where every cigar, cigarette, pipe, tobacco pouch, pipe rack, indeed every single commodity sold in the shop was kept, and the price of each, so that when she served a customer there would be no hesitation on her part. There were men who liked to roll their own cigarettes, working men, and in a drawer were what Mr Hynes called "the

makings". There were long, coloured spills for taking
a light from a fire and even something called "smokers
tongs" which were used to lift an ember from the
coals to light a cigarette. Matches, cigarette lighters,
ashtrays, cigarette boxes of silver, ebony, ivory and
carved wood, short cigarette holders and long ones
for those who liked a "cool" smoke, not to mention
the enormous range of cigars and cigarettes.

That first day was very confusing since she was
aware that she was not just some schoolgirl helping her
pa out on a part-time basis, "playing" at it in a sense,
but a working woman who meant to keep this small
business of her pa's ticking over until he returned. Mr
Hynes was mostly in the back of the shop, blending
tobacco for the hand-made cigarettes that were popular with his better-off customers: individual gentlemen
liked the kudos of having their own individual cigarettes. But it was not long before she found she had
no need to keep running into the back to ask where this
was, or that, or how much was a particular item. Mr
Hynes had put an advertisement in the Liverpool *Echo*
for a "lad", one who would do deliveries, run errands,
who would polish the mahogany cabinets, clean the
windows, sweep up the shreds of tobacco that fell to
the floor when Mr Hynes was blending, and before the
end of the week they had had two dozen applicants.
Mr Hynes had done her the honour of helping him
to consider which lad would suit and so Archie Watts,
fourteen years old, as big and willing as a carthorse and
as bright as a new-minted sixpence, was hired.

At the end of the first day she took home with her
three letters that needed her pa's signature and which
he signed without even glancing at them, and a book

of cheques, on every one of which he put his name.
As Mr Hynes said, they could have run off with Mr
Tooley's entire savings, had they a mind, winking at
her to let her know he was making one of the little
jokes he thought might make her smile. He was so
relieved to have his wages put in his hand, a day
or two late, but there just the same, he could have
kissed her, in a fatherly way, of course. She had run
to the bank on the Tuesday and drawn out the cash
they needed for the day and Grace was made aware
of the honesty and loyalty of this man who, during
the past week, could have helped himself to the cash
in the till and no one the wiser. He accounted for every
penny, taken and spent, all put down in the ledger in
his neat hand and, when they'd a minute, he would
reveal to her its mysteries. And if they couldn't find
that minute he would come round to Sheil Road next
Sunday and go through it all with her. He admired her
spunk enormously, though naturally he wouldn't have
had the temerity to say so; and her loveliness, which
he treated as something almost unearthly, bowled
him over at times. She had what was known as an
"hour-glass figure" and her only a lass of fourteen,
nearly fifteen, as she was fond of saying.

The days ran into weeks and the weeks into months
and at the beginning of September Rupert Bradley
strolled into the shop. He was in his officer's uniform
and looked so sublimely handsome, so exactly as she
remembered him, so exactly as she had dreamed about
him every night, her heart plunged, then rose again
into her throat so that she knew she would not be able
to answer him when he spoke. He was the quintessence
of the image all young girls dream of in a lover, a

beautiful young male and yet absolutely masculine with a certain toughness about him learned in his training to be a soldier. He was broad-shouldered, narrow-waisted and his breeches and exquisitely polished knee boots showed off the length of his well-shaped legs to perfection. She had heard nothing of him, nor *from* him since the day he had taken her out alone for a ride in his brother's motor car and though she had admitted it to no one, not even herself, she had half hoped he might have sent her a note, or perhaps visited when he was on leave. Not that she knew anything about the army or how often its soldiers were allowed home but what did it matter? Here he was, his deep brown eyes glowing with health and humour, his strong, uncompromising young mouth stretched in a wide grin of delight at the sight of her.

She was dusting the lower shelf behind her. She had removed the colourful packets of Turkish cigarettes, expensive at tenpence for five, the Gold Flake, threepence halfpenny for five and the Wild Woodbines at a penny for five, and stacked them on the counter, and after she had dusted the shelf she would arrange them tastefully again and then start on the next one.

She turned, the duster still in her hand when the doorbell pinged and there he was. He whipped off his peaked cap; she put a hand to her hair as women do when they are caught unawares by a good-looking man, forgetting the duster, and for a moment had a hysterical desire to scream with laughter, for it must have looked as though she were dusting her own hair. He seemed not to notice in his surprise at seeing her.

"Grace, what are you doing here? I only came in to

buy a few fags, expecting perhaps to see your father –
I knew this was his business, of course – and here you
are as pretty as a picture and looking very efficient."

Efficient didn't sound very *feminine* but he had
said she looked pretty so perhaps efficient wasn't
so bad. She was deeply flustered, conscious that she
was blushing and totally speechless in the face of
this bombshell which had exploded and for several
moments she could do nothing but stare like – as she
said afterwards to herself – some soppy schoolgirl! She
would have given her year's wages to have been able to
smile in a natural manner, to move to the counter as
though he were no more than a friend of her brother,
someone who had done them all a kindness at that
terrible time.

But she couldn't. She could only stand and stare,
her eyes wide, deep as clear golden pools, the pupils
coal black, her rosy lips parted as if she might speak.

"How are you?" he asked her, his eyes twinkling
with good humour and admiration, for she was an
exceptionally pretty girl. She had grown up since last
he saw her, no longer in the drab of mourning, her
crisp white cotton blouse inclined to strain somewhat
over her full breasts so that the peaks of her nipples
stood disturbingly proud! Her hair gleamed as though
it had been polished, drawn up into a knot at the crown
of her head and from her hairline wisps floated, one
caught across her mouth, and for a breathless moment
he wanted to lean across the counter and detach it then
smooth it gently behind her ear.

Rupert Bradley was a man not unfamiliar with the
admiration of women, for not only was he attractive
but he had a wit, a certain masculine charm which

appealed to them, young and not so young. But this girl, child she was really, awoke some emotion in him that he had not felt before, a feeling of wanting to protect, to shield from the darker side of life, though he was not certain what he meant by that. He wished, he supposed, to befriend her. The way in which she was looking at him reminded him of a shy doe, dazzled by the sunlight as it steps from a leafy glade which, he told himself ruefully, was sheer bloody nonsense. But even so, though she was so . . . so lovely he could not, as he might with some other young woman, treat her in any way that might be considered . . . flirtatious. The way in which he would treat any attractive member of the opposite sex.

When she did not speak his grin widened, for he was not unaccustomed to having this effect on females.

"What are you doing here?" he went on. "School holidays, is it? I'm sure your father is glad of your help." His expression became serious then as that week in April came back to him. "How is your father, and your mother, of course? Are you . . ." He was about to say "getting over the loss of your brother" which, he realised, was not at all the thing, for one did not "get over" such a tragedy in a few months. "Are you feeling . . ." Then his voice tapered off before he began again.

"Forgive me, I am being insensitive. How can anyone . . ."

"No." She found her voice at last. "You were kind to us then and I'm sure you meant no . . ."

"You know I didn't, but won't you tell me why you are here in the middle of the week when I'm sure you should be at school?" His eyes had begun to twinkle again and his mouth curved in his humorous smile.

"I've . . . I no longer go to school. I work here now, full-time. I help Pa to run the shop. He and Ma were . . . not at all well after Arthur so I took over."

"You took over!" His jaw dropped and she began to smile. "But you're so young. How in hell – I beg your pardon – how the dickens did you manage that?"

She was beginning to recover from the shock of seeing him and her confidence rose a little. "It seems I have a head for business." She said it simply with no wish to boast. "Mr Hynes, who has worked for Pa for many years, is a good teacher and between us, with Archie – he's our assistant," she added hastily, "we are managing very well. Pa comes in now and again when Ma is . . . has a good day. I'm sorry, you will have to excuse me for a moment," as a man in a muffler and a flat cap entered the shop.

Rupert stepped back, still slack-jawed with consternation, and some other emotion which was telling him that this girl, this young woman was really quite amazing. He remembered her stoicism at the time of her eldest brother's death and the way she had rallied her brothers, the way she had coped without the support of her parents, in fact who had supported them!

"Yes, Mr Atkinson," she was saying to the working chap. "What can I do for you?" Giving him a smile which clearly took his breath away.

"I'll 'ave five Wills, queen."

"And shall I wrap them for you, Mr Atkinson?"

The man, pocketing his small pack, was tickled pink, laughing as he left the shop.

There was movement at the back of the shop where

a door opened into another part of the premises and Edwin Tooley hovered in the doorway. At his back was another man wearing a green apron and behind him an enormous lad with a plain but engaging face. They all three seemed taken aback at the sight of a young soldier hanging about, not at the counter but towards the back where the glass-fronted cabinets were arrayed. Soldiers were not a common sight in Liverpool. Sailors, yes, but men in khaki were rare.

"Pa, you remember Rupert, don't you?" Grace said, moving to take her father's hand in hers as though to reassure him that all was well. That there was nothing to be alarmed at and yet again Rupert felt astonishment wash over him. "He was a friend of . . . of Arthur's." It was evident that Arthur's name was not spoken of very often, for Mr Tooley's face twitched painfully though he did his best to control it.

"Of course," though Rupert knew he didn't. "Er, is it" – he was looking at the insignia on Rupert's shoulder – "er, I'm not sure . . ."

"Second lieutenant, sir, but please, call me Rupert." He held out his strong young hand and Edwin Tooley put his trembling one in it and Rupert was made aware of the disastrous results his son's death had had on Grace's father.

"I was wondering," amazingly he heard himself say, "as it is nearly lunchtime whether you could spare your daughter for an hour. I'm sure she is invaluable in the shop but with your permission . . . the Adelphi is just a stone's throw." He smiled winningly and even Edwin Tooley found his face relaxing into a matching smile.

It had been a lovely summer, warm blue days shot

through with gold as the sun shone day after day and even now, though entering autumn the warmth and benevolence lingered on. There was no need of a coat so Grace merely pinned her straw boater to the soft tumble of her hair and drifted out of the shop to take Rupert's arm which he gallantly offered her. She was in a daze of wonder, a dream, one of those she had indulged in in her bed at night but now, this one had come true. The strong feel of the muscles in his arm sent a thrill of quivering excitement through her, starting in her chest where she felt barely able to draw breath, moving along her limbs until she thought her legs would not support her all the way up Church Street to Ranelagh Place where the Adelphi lay. The flowers in the gardens surrounding the Cathedral Church of St Peter were still blooming, beds of marigold in slashes of vivid yellow and orange, "pompom" dahlias, a delicate pink, the petals edged in white, blood red and yellow, zinnias and rich, purple night-scented stock.

She could not have described to Josie, with whom she had become friendly recently, the hour she spent in the smart dining-room of the Adelphi where Rupert ordered their lunch as though he frequented such places every day of the week, which he probably did. She had a vague memory of floating in a sort of tranced enchantment in which there was soft music and lighting, pretty women in fashionable gowns, attentive waiters gliding about in black and white elegance, flowers and heady perfume. She ate fish that melted on her tongue and something in a tall glass that seemed to contain whipped cream, thinly sliced fruit and nuts. Rupert drank wine but he would only allow her a glass of fruit juice since as he said, laughingly, she was a working girl and it would not do for her to be tipsy in the shop. He did not mention that she was far too young, for he sensed she thought of herself now as a grown woman. She *looked* like one. The covert glances of admiration from the other male diners were evidence of that.

"And how is your mother now, Grace?" he asked her in his kind and what she recognised, despite her youth, as a sensitive way. He himself had never lost anyone close to him, knew nothing of grief nor the awful despair of recognising that he would never again see someone he loved, but beneath his smiling charm, his confident vitality was a heart that was susceptible to the pain of others.

"She's improving. She kept to her room for several weeks after . . . after the . . . and, of course, Pa wouldn't leave her so that is why I volunteered for the shop."

"Your courage amazes me."

"Does it really?" She positively glowed beneath his admiration.

"But you must have missed your mother."

"We did, especially John. He's the youngest, but one day she just came downstairs and though she's not yet as she should be she's *there*. This summer has been so glorious, the weather, I mean, and she loves gardening so that has helped enormously. She spends all her time planting and weeding and dead-heading her roses and it seems to have eased her pain. At first people used to stop and try to commiserate with her and she used to cry but then . . . people are so kind, Rupert, they realised and said nothing except good morning, isn't it a lovely day, that kind of thing and gradually she began to respond, to talk to neighbours. So Pa is back in the shop which is a great help. Not full-time, for he worries about Ma."

"And the boys, your brothers?"

"Oh, they were awkward at first; they didn't know how to act, you see. Boys are taught from an early age not to cry and so they try not to but . . . Anyway, they are all back at school except George who finished last term and is waiting to hear from a firm of lawyers."

"He wants to be a lawyer?"

"No, I don't think he does. He is very restless."

He watched her gravely. He had lit a cigarette, one of the expensive kind her pa and Mr Hynes hand-made in the back of the shop, not with a handsome cigarette lighter but with a match from a plain box of matches. When she spoke her face became alive with expressions that changed with her feelings. It was sad, wistful when she spoke of her lost brother. Hopeful, ready to smile at the mention of her mother's slow recovery, eager, lighting up immediately, rosy as a child's as she spoke of her enthusiasm, and plans, she said, for the shop, woefully frowning over her brother's unsettled future. He found himself focusing on her mouth, the long upper lip, the short lower lip which was full, curving up at the corners. She had a slight indent to the left of it; he hesitated to call it a dimple which it wasn't, but it flashed in and out as she talked. She leaned towards him, her elbows on the table, her eyes wide with marvelling wonder as he described his own mother's success with several new exotic plants in her conservatory, then leaned back shyly when he said she really must come and see them.

"Mother still talks of you," he told her, finding himself longing to put out a finger and push back a wayward curl which fell from beneath her boater. He felt so at ease with this child, so at peace, and yet filled with a kind of joy, for she delighted him so.

But it all had to end. She had taken longer than her allotted hour for lunch but somehow it didn't seem to matter. They strolled back in the sunshine, she with her arm through his, not speaking a lot, their steps matching, for she was tall and used to walking with her brothers.

He took off his cap and held out his hand when they reached the shop, smiling, not knowing quite how to end this delightful episode. Passers-by streamed on either side of them, eyeing the handsome young officer and the lovely, serious young woman who seemed unable to tear their eyes from one another.

He returned his cap to his head, settling it comfortably, then saluted her with his swagger-stick and without another word turned on his heel and strode off in the direction of the motor cab rank at Central Station.

10

There were very few male heads that did not turn to look at Grace Tooley and Josie Allen as they strolled arm-in-arm along Hood Street in the direction of Whitechapel. Dusk was falling and the gas lamps had been lit, casting a pleasing golden glow over the busy street and placing healthy colour in cheeks that by day might have been pale and often gaunt, for there were many poor and hungry in this great city. The girls were so accustomed to their fellow citizens, without meaning to be thoughtless, they scarcely noticed. Grace was tall, long-limbed, graceful with a sway to her hips which the men coming out of the tobacco manufactory found mesmerising. She hated wearing a hat and, as usual when Ma was not about, had discarded it, swinging it by its ribbon in her hand. Her dark, burnished hair, now that it was no longer plaited, tumbled about her head, held perilously to the crown by a vivid scarlet ribbon to match her jacket. Her cheeks were flushed and her eyes glowed with the excitement of this excursion. Bronze and rose and honey was how Josie described her, which was much better than peaches and cream, which it seemed *she* was, much to her disgust. This had made Grace laugh but then many of the things Josie said made Grace laugh which was why she enjoyed her company so much. Josie was not as tall as Grace and she had a delicate prettiness which contrasted sharply with Grace's vivid looks, pale silvery hair, the deepest of blue eyes and a rosy, pouting mouth. A look of wide-eyed innocence and naïvety which was far from the truth, for Josie Allen had the sharp intelligence of her father whose successful business brain, hard head and shrewd acumen in the world of commerce had made him a "bob or two", in his own modest words.

Like Grace, Josie worked in her father's business in Water Street, in the office of the wine and spirit merchants he had begun twenty years ago, the coincidence of which had drawn her and Grace together despite the difference in their age. They were both "career" girls, or so they liked to think, not realising that had it not been for the fact that it was their fathers who employed them, without qualifications, which neither had, they would have found it almost impossible to find such good posts.

Francie, when she and Grace were thirteen, had been her friend as they had been at school together, but since then the world had altered beyond all recognition for Grace. Francie was still a schoolgirl and Grace was a working woman.

She felt a certain guilt when it came to remembering those days just after the *Titanic* had gone down, taking Arthur with her, for it had not occurred to her that she and her family were not the only ones to miss him and to mourn his loss. That day when she had crept to the den, simply to get away from the general air of doom and to have a good cry all on her own was one she would never forget. The sound of quiet weeping had crept down to her as she climbed the stone steps, the sound instantly stilled as her shoes clicked on the worn stone. She had hesitated, for the person who was crying – not one of the boys, surely – had come here for privacy, as she had. Nevertheless she had peeped over the rim of the steps and been confounded when she saw Josie from next door crouched in a corner with her fair hair all over the place and her eyes wet with tears. Even then she had felt a certain envy that Josie, who she scarcely knew up to that moment, could weep so beautifully with none of the blotchy redness she herself acquired after a few minutes of tears and blowing her nose, which turned red with the rest of her face.

"Josie . . . ?" she said hesitantly, wondering whether to leave Francie's sister to her grief, whatever it might be, then, with a sudden intuition, and remembrance, she knew why Josie was here. Grace had teased Arthur about his shy interest in the pretty girl next door but had not for a moment imagined that his feelings might be reciprocated.

"I'm sorry," watching sympathetically as Josie scrambled to her feet.

"No, really, you are . . . were his sister and your loss is so much greater; he and I . . ."

"He . . . you were in love?" There was astonishment in Grace's voice.

"Oh, no . . . no, nothing like that but . . . we might have been, given the chance. I knew he liked me and . . . well, it is all so desperately sad . . . he was too young. I had nowhere to go to get away from the family to . . . mourn him, if you like, without someone asking me . . . He told me about this place, offered to show me. Oh, dear, I'm sorry but I'm going to start again."

For perhaps ten minutes the two girls clung together and wept for the bright enthusiasm, the good-natured sweetness, the cheerful patience of the young man who had died, and it had begun then. Josie was two years older than Grace but it didn't seem to matter. They shared not only a common interest in their working lives but in their sadness for Arthur, and from that day they had become friends, going about together, even though Francie moaned that Grace was *her* friend and Josie had stolen her. This was, to Grace and Josie from the lofty heights of their businesslike world, an indication of Francie's immaturity.

Their parents were at first surprised at their closeness, again because of the difference in their ages, which didn't matter to *them*, but after all a female of fifteen was so much younger, not only in years but in her level of womanhood, than one of seventeen. Still, they were good for one another, they admitted, and it gave each set of parents a feeling of security to know that their girl was in the company of one of whom they approved.

In January the two families, as a mark of respect, along with many other families, had attended a service at St Faith's Church, Great Crosby, at which a memorial had been unveiled to Mr Joseph Bell who had been chief engineer on the ill-fated White Star ship *Titanic*. It had been a sad occasion, but in a way it had eased their anguish, especially Ma's. She had grieved desperately that she had not been allowed the formal dignity and release of a funeral. A funeral was an ending, a saying goodbye to the loved one with respect and honour, and the circumstances of Arthur's death had denied them that, but to stand with hundreds of others in the church, among them Mr Bell's family, and mourn those who had gone was a comfort to her.

It had been several weeks before Grace could bring herself to read the reports of the sinking of the great ship and in a way, though she had needed to see the complete picture, she had wished that she had left them unread. The description of the women of Southampton, wives and mothers and sweethearts of the crew members, who had waited patiently for days and days around the notice-board at the White Star offices, desperately scanning each new list of the survivors as they came in. The wonder of wireless transmission had brought those lists but at the same time mistakes had been made in the names so that Adlerson became Anderson, Demneder became Domander and others had a question mark after them so that their grieving relatives were still in the dark. They continued to wait and hope with increasing despair to hear if further lifeboats had been picked up, the lack of which seemed to be the prime reason for the tragic loss of life. Those saved had been mainly women and children, and Grace knew that Arthur would have been one of those helping them into the lifeboats, bravely standing back, as *some*, apparently, had not, three Italians, it was said, being shot as they rushed to save themselves. The bald statements of the ice field through which the *Titanic* had, for some unaccountable reason, despite warnings, blindly ploughed. Mr Hynes, who took the *Daily Mirror* and had saved a copy for her in case she wanted to read the accounts of the tragedy, patted her shoulder gently as she crouched in the back of the shop, weeping, not just for herself but for the thousands like her, handing her his own snowy handkerchief, saying nothing but speaking sharply to Archie when he put his head round the door enquiringly. Mr Hynes had agreed with her that it would be kinder not to show the newspaper to Ma and Pa.

She had been working at the shop for about six months when Mr Hynes, who had always gone on his own before, asked her if she would care to accompany him to the tobacco factory off West Derby Road where the tobacco for the hand-made cigarettes was purchased. It had been Pa's practice to do the buying but naturally Mr Hynes, who had been with Pa for all these years, was capable of continuing with this part of the business when Pa was "unwell", as his present condition was euphemistically called. Pa was doing a stint at the shop by now, not himself by any means, but capable, in a vague sort of way, of dealing with customers while Grace and Mr Hynes were absent.

They had begun their tour in the room where the tobacco was unpacked from the hogshead which had come from the bonded warehouse at Stanley Dock. She watched the "hands" as they were called, being unpacked, loosened and piled in such a way that the air could circulate to remove moisture. Stemming the tobacco was the next procedure – the removal of the thick, woody midrib or stem – and then the tobacco was blended, since some leaf had more aroma and strength than others.

It was too complicated a process from the hogshead to the finished cigarette for her to remember it all but the sight of the endless rods of cigarettes passing by on trays almost faster than the eye could follow, then on to the packing machines was mesmerising. The packing machines were the most up to date of their kind and could take five, ten or twenty cigarettes, arrange them in one, two or three rows in foil and tissue, then feed them into individual cartons, hundreds of thousands an hour. It was something she tried hard to describe at the table that night.

They listened with various degrees of politeness and yawning boredom.

She sighed. "Oh, I know it's all very boring for those not interested but I was fascinated and so would you be" – to the older boys who pulled a face – "and I found it engrossing," she finished defiantly. Pa leaned over and squeezed her hand.

"I want to go," John said. "Can I go, Pa, can I?" turning enthusiastically to his father. Edwin Tooley had been going to the factory virtually every week for the past twenty years and had never once considered describing it to his family, since it had not occurred to him that they might be interested. Time enough when one of his sons came into the business, he had thought, imagining George, or perhaps Robert – not Arthur, of course since his course was set on engineering – and now, in the way of fate which eludes us all, it was his daughter who was slowly gaining a grasp of what he had done for most of his working life. And yet surely, one day, his little girl, as he still thought of her, would marry and have her own family. But there was still Tom, Richard and now John, who seemed sincerely interested.

"I don't see why not," Pa said slowly. "Mr Hynes could take you when next he goes."

John was thirteen and still had years at school but

he was no scholar, not like Arthur, none of them was, but if just one of his sons followed him into the business it was enough. The strange thing was, and Grace sensed it, he did not really grasp how well she was fitting into the routine of the shop. She was even asking if she might go on a bookkeeping course in order to bring the accounting more into line with the twentieth century, as she put it, doing away with the rather laborious and, she decided, old-fashioned way the books were done now.

It could not be said that they had recovered from Arthur's death, for it was not something from which, like illness, one got better, but they learned to live with it, to adapt slowly, to creep back painfully into a life that was acceptable, even enjoyable at times. Ma spent a good deal of her day in the garden, and, since she had no grave to visit, she had made a small . . . Grace supposed it might be called a shrine for Arthur. Pa had a piece of marble, no bigger than a dinner plate, carved with Arthur's name, no dates, which Ma placed in a small bed in the corner by the house and in the bed was a cushion of flowers, dainty pink cyclamen four inches high surrounded by cream pansies flushed with pink. Behind this, in the corner now called "Arthur's garden" was a white climbing rose which Ma trained up a trellis against the wall and though perhaps it might seem somewhat morbid, like having a grave in one's garden, it gave Ma a great deal of comfort and who could deny her that.

In the spring, practically a year from the day the *Titanic* was lost, the Allen children began to plague their parents for bicycles like the Tooleys. The boys, who all went to the same school, had become friends and, also like the Tooleys, longed to join the Cyclists Touring Club of Great Britain whose membership was increasing annually by ten thousand. The annual subscription was five shillings and its song could be heard wherever a group of cyclists moved at the universal pace of eight miles an hour.

"Ta-ra-ra-boom-de-ay," they sang and the Allens longed to be in on it.

"Really, dear, I can see no harm in it," Fred Allen said to his wife, who in theory had no objection to it either. The Tooleys were a respectable family and the friendship which had grown since poor Arthur was drowned was pleasing to her, but she still hesitated. She was thinking of Henry, who, at six – an unexpected latecomer to the family – would kick up such a fuss if he wasn't allowed to go she was not sure she could stand it. She was over forty and found him a difficult child at her age, but was it fair to hold back the others just because of a spoiled, arrogant and wilful little boy? She sometimes wished she had plucked up enough courage to attend the discreet little clinic in town, begun by a certain Doctor Marie Stopes, who advocated birth control. She knew her Fred would not have approved, since most husbands felt that a woman's job was to provide him with children but Henry was so trying at times. Not that she didn't love him but he really was a scamp!

Fred had his way and bicycles were bought for Josie and Francie, of the kind Grace rode, and for James and Norman with cross bars and horns, splendid battery-run lamps and packs on the back to carry picnics and the cycling maps which were so essential. Cycling had become so popular in the last decade the railways had introduced special rates for carrying not only people, but their bicycles as well, and in the company of other members of the club they went to places they had never dreamed of years ago. They took the train from Lime Street Station up into the hills between Lancashire and Yorkshire, cycling, with other members of the club, through miles of pine wood and oak forest, across vast tracts of purple, heathery moorland, freewheeling breathlessly at great speed to grassy downs where they would stop to eat their picnics before urging one another onwards. The ladies exclaimed over the masses of flowers that burgeoned, purple vetch in the hedgerows, meadowsweet and honeysuckle rambling in an explosion of colour and fragrance, stellaria, traveller's joy, bright scarlet poppies in the gold of a wheat field, bedstraw, white campion, ragged robin and brambles. Where they went the traffic consisted of nothing more than a milk chariot rattling by, a fruiterer's van and horse, a man on horseback, a sluggish cartload of bricks. Ladies, who in the past had been forced to stay at home, were now free to move about unchaperoned and often, as the Allen and the Tooley parents became used to it, Grace and Josie, sometimes just the two of them, now and again with Francie in tow, as Josie put it, crossed the water by ferry to Woodside. They would cycle to Bidston Hill, climbing up to the lighthouse from which, on a clear day, they admired the views westwards to the Welsh mountains, south to the line of the country of Cheshire, east to the river and Liverpool where smoke hung thick as a curtain, and north to Liverpool Bay. The village of Bidston had a church and a house built in the reign of Elizabeth and at the side of the road, greatly daring, they ate ham and eggs at a public house, ignoring the sidelong glances of the eager young working lads who had never seen anything like them in their lives!

She had not seen Rupert Bradley since last September, not since the day he had come in to the shop and taken her for lunch at the Adelphi, and if she thought of him, dreamed of him, stared into the darkness of her room at night trying to picture his face, she kept it to herself.

In July the whole family accompanied by the Allens had stood among the milling, excited crowds at the Pier Head on the occasion of the opening of Gladstone Dock in Bootle. Their Majesties King George and Queen Mary, who were to do the honours, as Mr Allen described it, passed them by in their carriage in the procession along Princes Parade, so close, Mrs Allen remarked to Mrs Tooley, as they still called one another, that she could see in every detail the colour and style of Her Majesty's outfit and the close brimless toque of which she was so fond. The five boys, with the Allens' two, darted about like monkeys, here, there and everywhere so that Ma was constantly alarmed when she couldn't see them, which was how she had been since Arthur went. Mrs Allen's Henry wanted to be with the older boys, so between them Ma and Mrs Allen were torn to tatters, they said, by the activities of their spirited sons but they all agreed it had been well worth the effort. They had watched their Majesties go aboard the Mersey Docks and Harbour Boards tender *Galatea* in which they were to proceed up the river, and then with the squirming protesting Henry held by the hands of the two ladies, wandered up the esplanade among the good-natured crowd. Mrs Allen was wonderful with Ma and Ma seemed to find Mrs Allen's placid equanimity, along with Henry's determined activity, a great support on which to lean her weakened spirit just when she most needed it.

They couldn't end the day here, Mr Allen said jovially, gently prodding Ma and Pa into enjoying themselves. They must go up to Sefton Park for tea in the Palm House, he insisted, arranging everyone and everything, as was his genial way, to his own satisfaction. His motor car was parked outside the Custom House, a gleaming Vauxhall Prince Henry, surrounded by an admiring crowd of men and small boys, all shining silver paintwork, brightly polished lamps and beautifully smelling black leather seats, which showed how well he was doing in his business, Pa said, on the quiet, of course, to his overwhelmed wife. The two ladies, with the wriggling Henry on his mother's knee, sat in the front and the three girls with Pa, squashed together like sardines in a can, were at the back. The boys, George and Robert, Tom, Richard and John, James and Norman, flew along behind on their bicycles, watched by an anxious Ma who turned round constantly to look for them, hanging on to her hat lest she lose it, as far as Sefton Park where an exquisitely grown floral display in the shape of a crown and the words "Welcome to our King and Queen" was on show.

It was no more than a week later that, as though he had been waiting for the moment when, in his opinion, his ma would be able to stand it, George announced that he was off the next day to join the navy! It was no good Pa making a fuss, he told the slack-jawed occupants of the dinner table, he had decided a long time ago, last year, in fact, and if it hadn't been for . . . for Arthur he would have done it then. He was to take the train to Portsmouth, and when his ma began to cry, silently, which was even worse than a noisy outbreak, he hung his head as though in abject shame. He was eighteen years old, a young man with his way to make and could he be blamed for wanting something that he knew would upset his mother, Grace could see that, but it was unfortunate that his heart's desire was to go to the sea which had already taken one of her brothers. It had been a terrible blow and a terrible time for them all to get through but they had and he had been home on leave only last week, his young face doing its best not to show his enthusiastic fervour for his new life. He was a naval rating and so far had been no further than the English Channel so Ma had got used to it. After all, they were not at war so he would hardly be engaged in any fighting, Pa soothed her and the year drifted on towards 1914.

Today, a Saturday afternoon, which Pa allowed Grace to take off once a fortnight, she and Josie had been to the recently opened cinema to see the film *Hamlet* starring Sir Johnston Forbes-Robertson which had been wonderfully acted, they both agreed, but they had decided that they weren't really keen on Shakespeare, even at school. They had much preferred the film *London by Night* which they felt their parents would not have approved of, making it all the more exciting, since it portrayed the city as full of danger, fallen women and temptation for a young man who had come down from Oxford to study law. It had been thrilling, a little bit risqué but they had loved it. But best of all was *East Lynne*! They had cried absolutely buckets, again Josie showing not a sign of it while Grace came out of the cinema looking as though she had been in a punch-up, she complained.

She and Josie strolled along Whitechapel, turning towards Church Street and Bold Street, drawn to the shops as girls of their age usually are. They were both from well-placed families and, since they were what they liked to call "working girls" had a wage of their own to spend. They were aware, as young, attractive women always are, of the appreciative male glances that came their way but, arm-in-arm, smiling at one another, took no notice. It was almost Christmas and the shop windows were glorious with coloured lights, with banked arrays of every conceivable Christmas gift those with cash in their pocket might care to buy, depending on how much was there, from the magnificent furs in the window of Irelands in Bold Street, to the trinkets in Woolworths.

"Dismore's Silversmith and Jewellers" caught their eye and for several minutes they stood with their noses pressed to the glass, admiring jewellery cases from which spilled a platinum and diamond choker, brooches of rubies and diamonds, a butterfly exquisitely crafted in emeralds with rubies for its eyes, pearl dog-collars and long gold and pearl chains of featherweight delicacy, cobwebs of sapphires, coils of silver encrusted with tiny moonstones and all tastefully arranged on black velvet. There were half a dozen magnificent diamond rings set in gold, all with no price, of course, and as they watched, holding their breath, the back of the window opened and an elderly,

immaculately dressed gentleman took out the tray of
rings and, leaving the small door to the window open,
moved behind the counter and placed the tray on
it. There was a soldier, an officer, with his back to
them and even as she watched, she and Josie, with
bated breath, for what young woman does not relish
romance, Grace could feel the cold begin somewhere
inside her, just as though a small sliver of ice had
slipped down her throat and into her chest. The
soldier was accompanied by a beautiful young woman
wrapped around in magnificent furs, sable she thought
with that part of her brain not struggling to reject the
picture before her.

The soldier turned and bent over the velvet pad on
the counter, revealing his profile, then, after picking
out a ring, slipped it on to the left hand of the beautiful
woman, smiling down into her delighted face. She
thought he was about to kiss her and the shop assistant
evidently thought so too for he turned away discreetly.

She wanted to run and run, to scream out that it
wasn't happening but she was trapped, trapped by the
frozen weight of her legs and by Josie's arm through
hers and by Josie's excited murmuring on what was
happening in the shop.

". . . getting engaged at Christmas. How wonderful
and what a gorgeous-looking female. I wish he'd
turn round so that we could get a good look at
him. Don't men look good in uniform, especially
officers. Look at that Sam Browne," referring to the
leather belt-like contraption that was placed diagonally
across his shoulder and back. "Which one d'you think
she'll choose? I'm not sure I like diamonds myself . . .
ostentatious . . . birthday stones . . ."

Suddenly aware that her friend was not responding to the delightful contemplation of the scene taking place inside the jeweller's Josie turned and looked enquiringly into Grace's face and was quite appalled by what she saw.

"Grace . . . Dear God, Grace, what's the matter? You look awful. Shall we . . . Is it that stuff we had in the cinema?"

Grace moaned. She couldn't help herself and at once Josie put her arms round her, conscious of the concerned glances of passers-by, some of whom, especially the gentlemen, hesitated, longing to help.

"Josie . . . get me home, Josie," Grace was whispering, shivering in Josie's arms, leaning against her so heavily Josie thought they both might fall to the ground.

"Miss, can I help?" A gentleman removed his bowler and seemed ready to put his arm about them.

"A cab, please. My friend is not well."

"Of course." And not only did the gentleman procure a cab within thirty seconds, Josie wondering why it was that cabbies responded at once to *men*, he climbed in beside them and escorted them home.

When she had installed Grace into the arms of her fretting mother, Josie was surprised to find him still on the pavement outside the house, his face anxious, his eyes admiring, his manner that of a gentleman, repectful. She asked him in for tea!

II

The next day she was huddled like a wounded animal – that was how she felt, as though she had been shot in some vital part of her – under her eiderdown when there was a soft tap on her bedroom door and, when she listlessly answered from her bed, Josie's smiling face peeped round the door.

"Nora said I could come up." She approached the bed and the smile slipped from her face. "She said you weren't too good so I thought you might feel like a bit of cheering up." Her lovely hyacinth eyes clouded over to become a sort of slaty blue, a sure sign she was troubled. "What's up, our kid?" she added in a fair imitation of the Liverpool idiom.

Grace struggled to sit up. She had fooled her mother and Nora into believing that it might be something she had eaten the previous day that had struck her down but Josie had been there, had seen her change from a shared and delighted contemplation of the scene in the jeweller's shop to a state of collapse in a matter of seconds and there was no way she could deceive her.

Josie fell to her knees and leaned her elbows on the bed, her chin in her hands studying the face of the girl who had become such a good friend since Arthur's death. They were like sisters; no, that was not strictly true since she felt only a dutiful fondness for her own sister. It was a bond that could not be described, perhaps caused by their shared sadness over Arthur's death, but it had grown, warmed to a strong affection and they had been glad of it in the past months.

"What's the matter, Gracie?" she asked quietly, her pretty face creased with concern. "What happened outside Dismore's yesterday? It was something that upset you dreadfully, anyone could see that, even Mr Booth was genuinely troubled." A faint flush tinted her smooth cheek and she lowered her gaze somewhat shyly so that even Grace, deep in her wretchedness, could not help but notice it.

"Who's Mr Booth?" Her attention caught for a moment.

"Don't you remember he brought us home in a cab?"

"Did he? It was all such a blur, Josie, but if you say so."

Josie leaned closer to her, then took her hand which was plucking restlessly at the raised embroidery on the eiderdown.

"That's what I mean. You were in some sort of a faint. One minute you were fine and then you kind of fell down or you would have done if I hadn't had hold of you and it seems to me that it was when you recognised the officer and his fiancée."

Grace snatched her hand from Josie's and flung herself away, turning her face to the fireplace where a rosy fire burned.

"Don't . . . don't for God's sake say that. Fiancée indeed! He might just have been buying her a ring . . . a Christmas present; she might have been trying it on for one of his sisters or . . . or . . ."

Josie's face was tender with compassion. "Gracie, he was putting it on her left hand, the third finger of her left hand, the finger where an engagement ring goes—"

"That proves nothing," Gracie wailed, stubbornly interrupting Josie's soft voice and all of a sudden tears spurted from her eyes, washing her cheeks. Bowing her head, she wept beyond consolation. "Oh, Josie, what am I to do?"

Josie's voice was careful. "About what?"

"Him."

"Who's him?"

"Rupert."

"Rupert?"

"Oh, for heaven's sake stop repeating everything I say. I'm so . . . miserable. I thought he liked me, you see. He was at the field when Henry Melly took his monoplane up, over two years ago now, nearly three. I was not quite fourteen but the moment I saw him I . . . oh, Lord, why am I telling you all this? I've kept it to myself because he was older but I thought . . . And then when Arthur was lost he was so kind to us all, to me and then he took me out to lunch at the Adelphi so I sort of got the idea that he thought I was special." Her voice dropped. "Josie, he *did* think I was special. I saw it in his eyes. I don't understand how but you can tell a thing like that. Even so young I was woman enough to recognise . . . but he went away and I haven't seen him since. And now . . ." Her voice trailed away and she turned her face into her pillow.

"Now he's engaged to someone else."

Her voice was muffled. "I can't bear it, Josie. I've thought of nothing else all this time. There have been plenty of chances to . . . to become involved with other chaps. Nice, respectable chaps, you know what I mean. They come in the shop but I'm not the slightest bit interested. I've been waiting for . . ."

"For Rupert to come home?"

She turned her face eagerly to Josie. "Yes. When I persuaded Pa to have a telephone put in at the shop *and* one at home, which wasn't easy, I thought . . . I thought . . ."

"That he might get in touch?"

"Oh, Josie, I've spent the last two and a half years waiting for him. It was all I did. It was all I am. The girl who waited for Rupert and now . . ."

She wept inconsolably in Josie's arms, wringing herself dry of tears but not the feelings she had held inside her all this time. They remained and she had a tragic feeling that they always would.

At last the storm was over and she mopped her face with the towel Josie brought her from the old washstand, glad that her friend had not mouthed all the usual platitudes about "getting over it", "time heals", "you'll meet someone else", "plenty more fish in the sea," and all the nonsense some might have thrown at her. Josie sat beside her quietly, holding her hand, waiting, just there should she be needed, a willing ear and a pair of comforting arms, for she knew her friend well enough by now to understand that she would never tell anyone else of this heartache.

"Anyway," Grace mumbled, making a great effort to perk up, giving her nose a last swipe, "who's this Mr Booth and why does he make you blush?"

"He doesn't make me blush and he's not anybody in particular."

"I can see that. You've gone all soppy with your eyes."

"Grace, you're talking nonsense."

"Tell me just the same." For anything, *anything* that would take her mind off the appalling scene yesterday and what it meant to her life, was welcome.

"He was kind. So concerned and anxious that you were all right. I . . . I liked him and—"

"Of course, he liked you."

"Well, I don't know about that," Josie said primly.

"Don't be daft. How could he help but like you and there you go again, blushing and simpering."

Josie reared up indignantly. "I am *not* simpering. He was very kind to you – to us – when we needed him. When you had gone inside, there he was still waiting by the gate to enquire after you so . . . well, I couldn't just ignore him so I asked him in."

"And what did your mother have to say about that?"

Josie smiled at the memory. "She was considerably startled but he seemed to make a good impression. He is exceedingly polite. She seemed to like him."

"And so do you."

Josie blushed and avoided Grace's eyes. "Don't talk nonsense. I only met him yesterday."

"That's time enough, Josie. Believe me, I know."

Josie pressed her hand compassionately then impulsively planted a kiss on her pale cheek.

"I'm that sorry, Grace."

"I know."

That had been at Christmas and now it was the end of July 1914 and in October, when she would be nineteen, Josie was to marry Mr Booth, Philip Booth who was a gentleman and articled to a solicitor in Queen Square, and Grace and Francie were to be bridesmaids.

Grace never could understand why they were to go to war with Germany as it seemed they were and when Mr Hynes, who read not only the *Daily Mirror* but yesterday's copy of *The Times* which a regular customer passed on to him when he came into the shop to buy his Double Coronas, explained to her the official thinking on the subject she could not understand that either. She felt that if she only knew *why* she might accept it more easily. Mr Hynes said it had been coming for a decade and he was not at all surprised, since it was needed to sort out the simmering quarrels and rivalries that were bubbling to the boil in Europe, and though he went on to explain about Germany and France, Russia and Austria, Alsace and Lorraine, she felt so . . . well, she could only call it mystified she scarcely listened. She hadn't been aware that there had been any simmering quarrels and rivalries, but then she had been too engrossed with her own and her family's troubles for the past two years or more to take much notice. Besides, ever since Arthur's death for some reason Pa had refused to have a newspaper in the house so she often browsed through *The Times* as she ate her lunchtime sandwiches in the back of the shop.

This day at the end of July she was at the bench and had been about to blend the pipe tobacco favoured by another regular customer. The newspaper was propped up on the bench while she worked and at the same time did her best to make sense of the reports that indicated that war between the two countries was inevitable. She flipped over another page and though she had been expecting something, something she dared not put into words, not even thoughts in her own head since the day she had seen him in Dismore's choosing what must have been an engagement ring, the words that struck out at her from the page in the newspaper blurred her vision and whirled in her head like starlings breaking from the trees. They told her baldly that the marriage had taken place between *Captain* Rupert Bradley and Miss Jessica Curtis at the Church of St Margaret's in London.

The blow to her heart as she read the words hurt her so agonisingly she was forced to clutch at the bench on which she had been working lest she went crashing to the floor. The sight of his name in black and white, coupled with that of Miss Jessica Curtis who, it was reported, was the youngest daughter of Colonel Anthony Curtis – a colonel on the general staff – plus a flowery report of what was described as a society wedding, was like walking into an unseen brick wall. Though she had steeled herself for it, knowing full well that an engagement invariably led to marriage, the actual fact and her own reaction to it frightened her badly. Surely one person could not have this deep and enduring feeling for another and nothing come of it? She supposed that some small part of her which had no logic, no rationality, no sense really, had still clung to the hope that something would happen to prevent it. Her longing for him would never leave her, she knew that. From the first moment years ago on the day Mr Melly had taken to the air in his flimsy machine, so had her heart, flying swiftly towards Rupert Bradley.

His smile had closed like a fist about it making it, and her, totally his and the pain of knowing irrevocably – after all it was printed in the newspaper – that he loved this Jessica, was ready to destroy her. She was driven by the compulsion of her love to this one man, drawn like a magnet to the source of the deepest pain anybody could endure, ready, it seemed, to go on suffering it and she was agonisingly aware that she must let it go if only she knew how.

But at this moment, which she recognised as the worst in her young life, even overwhelming the death of her brother, the words crippled her and somehow she could not seem to move her legs. She reached out blindly for the stool that stood at the side of the bench and eased herself slowly on to it, afraid that any abrupt movement might topple her into an abyss, a black abyss so deep it terrified her, for if she fell into it would she ever be able to claw her way out? The final loss of him was like a cold tide that threatened to engulf her, to sweep her away as it retreated back to the open sea, where, if she didn't take great care, she would be left to drown. And the strange thing was, she didn't really understand why she should feel like this since he had never been *hers* to lose. She had known in her heart of hearts that his feelings for her were no more than the affection a man feels for a young girl, a child really, the sister of a friend who had died and therefore needed his sympathy. She did her best to comfort herself with the thought that perhaps this wealth of emotion was really no more than a girlish crush on an older, attractive man who had paid her some attention, but if that was the case why did she hurt so much?

She could hear Mr Hynes talking to someone in the shop and whoever it was laughed. The doorbell pinged and Mr Hynes's footsteps sounded as he moved round the counter to open the door which the customer had closed. The day was warm and following Pa's instructions the door was left open to entice customers inside. She wanted to scream at these ordinary things, just as she had wanted to scream outside the jeweller's last Christmas but she managed somehow to keep the sound deep in her throat. In the weeks and months since then she had done her best to appear the same, which had been a hardship in itself and she admitted to herself, and to Josie, that had she not had her friend to hold on to, to talk to, weep with, she might have gone under. Sometimes in the night when the house slept she would put her face in her pillow and actually moan into it, the sound heard only by Topsy who scratched at her door to be allowed in. The dog had lain beside her, and licked the tears on her face, her eyes bright and curious in her scruffy face and Grace wrapped her arms about the devoted animal for comfort. She could not bring herself to believe that she would never see Rupert again but now, with the announcement in black and white in front of her, she knew that it was so. Like a child she had believed that she had only to wait a few years and he would come home and recognise what was between them. Now she was a woman and she must accept that the man she loved was married to another.

Though she had perused the newspapers from cover to cover and had done her best to understand what was happening in Europe she had been blind and deaf to the implications, despite Mr Hynes's efforts to educate her. She had not really understood what it was to mean to her and her family and to a million other families with sons. It was not until the eye-catching advertisement first appeared, not just in the newspapers but on every hoarding in town that it finally penetrated her dazed brain.

YOUR KING AND COUNTRY NEED YOU
A CALL TO ARMS

An addition of 100,000 men to His Majesty's Regular Army are immediately necessary in the present grave National Emergency

Lord Kitchener is confident that this appeal will be at once responded to by all those who have the safety of our Empire at heart

GOD SAVE THE KING

She was deeply ashamed that while she had been brooding on her own unhappiness, *wallowing* she supposed it might have been described as, her world as she and her family knew it was on the verge of disaster. That her country was in terrible danger and, even then, as she dwelled on these things she did not fully realise what it would mean.

"I feel I want to do something, Josie," she said to her friend the following weekend as they strolled in the sunshine along Dean Road towards Wavertree Park which was a pleasant walk from Sheil Road. "I just can't stand tamely behind the counter of Pa's shop selling cigarettes and tobacco when there must be *something* women can do. What d'you think? Will there

be some part for women to play in this war? Nobody
seems to know quite what is to happen, everybody
rushing about looking for something patriotic to do
and that Phyllis Dare singing about the lads who
should go. Go to the 'front' wherever that is, I suppose
she means. Ma has already started rolling bandages,
would you believe, and Nora's off to the shops to
buy in enough food to last for the duration of the war
though how long that—"

"Philip's going." Josie interrupted her, her voice
almost a whisper.

"Going? Going where?"

"To join up, of course."

"To . . . oh, darling, not—"

"Yes. He is to go to Aldershot on Monday."

Grace stopped and turned to Josie, taking both
her hands in hers. They were almost at the gates
of Wavertree Park where the Botanic Gardens were
a picture at this time of the year. They could hear
the birds raising their voices from the aviary and
she had time to wonder at the strange *sameness* of
the day when the next few days would probably
see their world change as the men marched away
and the women stayed behind to weep. It was a
lovely August day and again her thoughts marvelled
at how the sun could shine so serenely when armies
would soon be facing one another in battle, not quite
sure how or when this would take place, imagining
something like the pictures she had seen of the charge
of the Light Brigade in the Crimean War. The park,
strangely enough, was almost empty as though people
could not quite bring themselves to leave the safety
and familiarity of their homes when this threat hung

over them, and when Josie and Grace entered the Tea House, the waitresses were standing in little groups talking in excited whispers, for how was this to affect them? They stopped to watch the two young women, one in a muslin dress the colour of bluebells, the other in saffron yellow, both with wide-brimmed flower gardens to match on their heads. One waitress hurried over and they ordered tea and cakes though neither of them felt like eating.

"What about your wedding?" Grace asked hesitantly.

"Philip wants to wait until the war's over," Josie said tonelessly. "Christmas, he says. They all say that but when I argued with him he wouldn't listen. He won't speak the words out loud but he doesn't want to leave me a widow, perhaps with a child but I would rather that than nothing."

"Tell him, Josie." Grace's voice was urgent, for she knew how *she* would feel about it. "Insist on it. I know I would."

As she spoke the smiling features of Rupert Bradley imprinted themselves on her eyelids, for she had found, as she knew she would, that the heart does not stop loving because the loved one is married to another woman. He was in her thoughts whenever her thoughts were free of the day-to-day routine she followed in the shop. He was the last thing she thought of when she fell asleep at night and the first thing she thought of when she woke and she waited patiently, doggedly enduring the pain, for this to end as surely it would. He had gone for ever from her life and she must not only accept it but find an alternative which, she supposed, was another man to whom she might give her affections. She didn't want to go through life an empty shell without love in it. She wanted children, a home of her own, though it looked as if this goal might be further out of reach than ever now with all the young men dashing off to the nearest recruitment office.

She wanted to help in some way, to bring the war to an end. She didn't know how but as she had said to Josie, there must be something for a strong, healthy young woman like herself to be engaged in during the coming conflict. Already there were men marching through the streets of Liverpool, at their head a band thumping out triumphant, martial music, people spilling out of shops to watch them go by, excited, chattering, waving, whistling as though the lads were off on a holiday. Men throwing on their caps and following at the tail end in their eagerness to join up. There had been a queue over two miles long at the recruiting office as he walked by on his way to work, Mr Hynes had told her. Even Archie had tried his best to get in on it but his mother, alerted by Mr Hynes, had sworn that she'd stop his gallop, dragging him by the ear from the very arms of the burly recruiting sergeant who, she told forcibly, had no right to be leading a lad of sixteen astray. Mr Hynes, as a man of over forty with children, was exempt and so was Pa. He was not himself again, even yet, and never would be she was inclined to think, but at least he was able to work in the shop if she left.

But in the dark of her bedroom where she often paced the night away, nursing her grieving heart, she was well aware that the first to go would be the regular soldiers, one of whom would be Rupert. It was not this precisely which made her long to help in some

way to shorten this war but the feeling that if she
and every other able-bodied woman did their bit,
whatever that might be, then the quicker it would be
over. Christmas! Dear God, she hoped so, for though
Rupert would not be marching home to her, at least
he might march *home*!

"I've decided to go nursing, Gracie." Josie's quiet
voice cut through her thoughts. "With Philip gone I
can't sit on my behind and twiddle my thumbs until
he comes home."

"But I read somewhere that you have to be twenty-
one before they'll take you."

"I know, but that's to France. Nurses will be needed
in this country to nurse the wounded and until I can
get to France that's what I shall do."

"But where will you go?"

"I have an idea and I'm going as soon as Philip
leaves."

"When is—"

"He's to go to an officers' training camp so it won't
be right away but Kitchener's Army, as they're beginning to call it, won't be far behind the Expeditionary
Force." Only a few days ago they had never even *heard*
of the British Expeditionary Force!

"You're so brave. I wouldn't know where to begin."

Josie leaned eagerly across the table, scattering cutlery as she grasped Grace's hands. Her eyes were
a bright, translucent blue as though she were close
to tears.

"Come with me, Gracie. I've been told the London
Hospital in Whitechapel is taking on probationers.
Nurses are being called up, the hospitals are short-
staffed already and there is . . . worse is to come.

It will be for three months at first. I was talking to Angela Watson, at school. She was head girl, d'you remember?"

Grace nodded slowly while a great swell of something throbbed through her, a fervour that told her this was what she had been waiting for.

"Well, a relative of hers is a Sister there and she told me to apply at once. Angela is twenty-one so if we say we were at school with her who's to know we're not the same age as her."

"You don't look twenty-one, Josie, nothing like," Grace told her absently. "And look at the size of you. Small and dainty, not a great lanky thing like me."

"Nevertheless I'm as strong as you any day of the week," Josie answered belligerently, giving the impression she was about to challenge Grace to an arm-wrestling match to prove it. "Anyway, I can but try. If they turn me down I'll have a go somewhere else." Her grip on Grace's hands tightened. "Come with me, Gracie. I'd feel so much better if you were with me. We could try and stay together."

"I'd give anything to do it."

"Well, do it. Just pack a case and come."

"There's . . . there's Ma and Pa."

"Your mother's got Nora and my mother would stand by her. Besides, Mother would feel so much better if she knew we were going together."

"Doesn't she mind? Your going, I mean."

Josie sighed. "Yes, she does, but she knows she can't stop me. Well, legally she could because I'm still under age, but if Philip goes then so must I. She knows that. Oh, Grace, please say you'll come."

"The shop . . ." Grace said feebly.

"Mr Hynes will hold it together and your pa is so much better. Archie is still there . . ." Smiling as they all had at Archie's attempt to get into the army and his sad failure. Sad in his eyes at least.

Grace took a deep breath then looked into Josie's eyes, her own glowing with tawny stars.

"Will you, then?" Josie breathed.

Grace nodded her head and the waitresses were momentarily entertained by the sight of the two pretty and beautifully dressed young ladies jumping to their feet and doing a little jig between the tables.

12

The telephone was making its jangling voice heard as she ran lightly up the steps and let herself in with her own front door key, a concession allowed her since she had become a "career woman". The instrument stood on what was grandly called the telephone table which was taller than the normal occasional table. The telephone was known as a "skeleton" telephone, rather elegant, black, of course, as all telephones were. It was decorative which was what had persuaded Ma to allow such a thing in her hallway, the handset resting across it which, when lifted, allowed the caller, after turning the handle to the side, to get in touch with the operator. Next to it was a chair so that the caller or the recipient of a call might be comfortable for its duration. Not that Pa encouraged lengthy calls, or indeed any calls at all unless they were to do with business. As it happened not many of the family *received* calls, for the telephone was a rare luxury in most homes, owned by very few. Grace sometimes rang Josie, her Pa rang Mr Hynes at the shop or vice versa and now and again, when he was in port and could gain access to an instrument, George rang Ma which she thought was a miracle and well worth the danger of handling it. Both Ma and Pa were somewhat nervous of the machine and Nora wouldn't touch it with a ten-foot bargepole, she announced stoutly when it was installed, edging round it as she moved from the kitchen to the front door as though, should she drop her guard, it might shoot out some fearsome spark! It was a wonder they didn't all get "electromocuted" in their beds, she announced. It had been bad enough, several years ago, when Mr Tooley had decided to put in the electricity so that, with a flick of a switch, light flooded the rooms. Not that she liked to bother with the perilous stuff. Give her a decent lamp any day of the week. You knew where you were with a lamp. She had only just got used to *gas* lamps never mind electricity.

Grace herself dusted the telephone!

"Isn't anybody interested in answering this telephone?" Grace shouted towards the back of the house, for usually the boys raced one another to be the first to get to it. Even as the words echoed along the hallway she realised that no one could possibly hear it, or her, since there was the most horrendous commotion coming from the family room. Ignoring the clamour of the instrument, she stood in the middle of the hallway, gaping foolishly at the closed door from behind which the commotion came. Topsy was barking and a voice, a voice so livid with anger she scarcely recognised it, told her savagely to shut up.

Dragging herself from her mazed trance, she moved across the hall and flung the door open with a vigour that caused it to hit the piano that stood behind it and it almost bounced back in her face. She wavered in the doorway, gazing with astonishment and dread at the incredible scene before her. Her family were all there, Ma, Pa, Robert, Tom, Richard and John, plus Nora and Mrs Allen, and what with Topsy still barking her head off, despite being ordered to be quiet, and Wally dashing like a marmalade blur for the sanctuary of the kitchen, it seemed like a madhouse. She couldn't make top nor tail of what was happening or what they were all shouting about.

Pa stood with his back to her at the window, staring out at something, she didn't know what. His shoulders were slumped and he seemed to be trembling, for the papers in his hand shook like leaves on a branch in a high wind. Ma was crouched, wild-eyed, white-faced, in the chair beside the fire, her normally neat hair dragged about her head, looking into what appeared to be the pits of hell from the expression on her face. Before her knelt Nora, doing her best to pull her back from the edge, or so it seemed, while Mrs Allen hovered at the back of the chair, patting her shoulder and telling her to be brave, or that's what it sounded like over all the din. Richard and John were at the table which was set for the family's evening meal and from the kitchen came the familiar delicious smells of cooking.

And round and round the table, waving their arms, jerking backwards and forwards, meeting each other with what appeared to be muttered oaths and "tuts" of irritation and shaking of their heads, were Robert and Tom. Their young faces were flushed and their eyes livid with excitement, and Grace's heart lurched, for though it had not been spoken of out loud exactly, inside she knew what this was all about.

"We've all got to accept it, Mrs Tooley dear," Mrs Allen was murmuring somewhat ineffectually. "It's the lot of women all over the country. In every home it's happening . . ."

"Not in yours, Mrs Allen," Nora said tartly.

"No, I agree, but—"

Grace sprang to life. "Would someone like to tell me what's going on?" Even though she knew.

Every head in the room turned towards her and Topsy, who was badly frightened by the loud voices and the tension in the room, barked even louder. With an oath borrowed from her brothers and one which, in normal times, Ma would have objected to most strenuously, she picked up the small dog and deposited her in the kitchen, shutting the door on her.

"Now then, what is it?"

"Grace . . . oh, Grace, I can't stand it," Ma wailed.

". . . norr 'avin' it. Once is enough fer . . ." from Nora.

". . . dear, now that you're home I'll go," Mrs Allen said apologetically.

"These, Grace, these have come for the boys," Pa moaned, waving what was in his hand.

"Everybody's going, Gracie, and after all . . ." A shout of defiance from Robert.

"If anybody tries to stop me I shall just go to another," added Tom.

". . . not fair," cried John.

". . . be eighteen soon and then . . ." Richard exaggerated wildly. He stood up and almost knocked his chair backwards in his determination to be heard. Only John who, at fourteen, big as he was, like them all, said nothing beyond the unfairness of it, since he knew he hadn't a chance of going. Going where? her bruised heart asked, lagging behind the sharpness of her mind which knew exactly where they were off to and what was causing this tornado to race through her home.

She watched Mrs Allen slip from the room with a murmured remark that she would be back later, then walked over to Pa and gently took the envelopes from his hand. Each was marked with the dreaded – dreaded by mothers of sons, that is – OHMS stamp and she was aware that Lord Kitchener was calling his two latest recruits to their duty. She looked round sadly, sad not only for her ma and pa who would, before the day was out, revert to the dreadful state Arthur's death had flung them in, but for herself. She could tell by her parents' attitude that though they were shocked, frightened, angered by what they saw as their sons' irresponsibility to them, who had already lost one son, they did not *really* believe that they would go. Ever since Arthur's death they had lived in a small, protected vacuum where the outside world was kept firmly at bay and their children had been careful to keep them there. They could not bear another loss, another blow to their happiness which they had taken for granted all their lives, so they sheltered themselves from the world, but now the world had broken in, knocked down their carefully built, fragile defences and forced its way in. Tom could be held back, for he was not yet eighteen but Robert would eventually be conscripted if he did not volunteer, which, it seemed, he had.

She cleared her throat, feeling something inside her shrivel hopelessly, for she was well aware that this was the death of her own hopes, hers and Josie's. Josie would still go but Grace wouldn't, couldn't.

"Robert . . ."

"Now it's no use you going on at me, Gracie," her brother said hotly. "We've volunteered."

"When?"

"Last week and we're—"

"And you didn't think to say anything?"

He hung his head for a moment since he was an honest lad, then he lifted it proudly, a young warrior off to defend his King and country, and his family, as young warriors did. "We knew you'd try to stop us so—"

"Tom can't go."

"Who says?" Tom's defiant spirit would not allow him to be spoken to like this. He was off to be a soldier and that was that. As he had tried to tell them, if Pa went down to the recruiting office and told them Tom Tooley was too young at only just eighteen he would merely go to another in Manchester or Preston and join up there. He wanted to go in the "Pals" Brigade with his brother and other Liverpool lads but he was prepared to do anything to get in. If you're big enough you're old enough, was his argument.

"Please, Grace . . . please, dear, don't let them go." Her mother's agonised voice whispered about the room and her two oldest boys winced, for they loved her and didn't want to hurt her but this was their sacred duty, their *patriotic* duty, surely she could see that. They were sorry about Arthur but they could not let his death stand in the way of what they, as brand-new soldiers, must do. They could not stand back and let others do the fighting for them, could they? It wouldn't be right. It wouldn't be honourable. They must prove to themselves and to others that they weren't cowards. They must march away with the other Liverpool "Pals" as they had seen young men do this last week. Their orders had come. They had their railway warrants and were to take the train tomorrow morning.

"When are you to go?" she asked at last, knowing that there was absolutely nothing that she could do or say that would keep them from their purpose. She had been out and about in town this last week and had seen the almost hysterical fervour, heard the songs, listened to the excited young men begging to know how soon they could get to the front. They longed to fight, even die for "Honour, Justice, Truth and Right" as the slogan had it, so why should her brothers feel any different? They were young men, weren't they and she was proud of them.

But Ma and Pa and Nora did not agree with her.

"No, they're not going," Ma screamed and Pa jerked towards her while Nora cowered back against the chair opposite, unable to contain Mary Tooley's dementia. "They're not going to be taken from me like Arthur was. I won't allow it, Edwin. Tell them. Tell them. My heart cannot stand being broken again. Not again."

"Ring for Doctor Prentiss, Robby," Grace told her brother quietly, "and then go next door, and take the others with you. Stay there until I come for you."

"This's knocked stuffin' outer me, Edna, I don't mind tellin' yer. Them two lads is nowt but babbies an' after what 'appened ter Arthur it don't bear thinkin' about. Mrs Tooley's gone ter pieces an' master's not much better."

Nora sipped her tea tearfully. She and Mrs Dutton were seated at the kitchen table, their elbows on its scrubbed surface, each holding a mug of hot, strong, sweet tea – which was how they both liked it – between their cupped hands.

"Aye, I know, burr a lot's gone just same, Miss McNee." Edna Dutton shook her head sadly. She was unconscious of the irony that though they were both servants Nora called her by her christian name while she still addressed Nora as Miss McNee. There was, naturally, a difference between a "daily" and a "housekeeper" as Nora liked to call herself.

"Them next ter me they've three lads only just outer school," she continued, "and they was off yesterday. Their mam's out've 'er mind wi' it. All I can say is thank God mine's too young."

"When I think o' that Tom, only just eighteen." Nora was unconcerned with Edna's neighbour or even Edna's relief over her own young brood. "I can still see 'im, an' not so long ago, neither, wi' 'is tie allus undone an' 'is socks allus comin' down an' 'is boot laces undone an' now 'e's off ter be a soldier. An' them two what's left. What's ter be done wi' 'em wi'out their ma an' pa ter see to 'em? Just when they was gerrin' over Arthur, an' all. It's that lass I'm sorry for. Eeh, I wish I were more 'elp to 'er but it's fair knocked me fer six, this 'as."

"They say there's already fightin' in France an' lads gerrin' theirselves killed."

"Eeh, don't, Edna. I can't bear't thought, really I can't. An' who's ter do their washin' an' ironin', tell me that? Never lifted a 'and all their lives, neither of 'em. Eeh, I dunno."

"See, 'ave another cuppa tea, Miss McNee."

"Mekk a fresh pot, Edna, will yer. Push that damn cat outer't road. Damn thing's allus under yer feet an' dog's as bad. Yappin' out there in't yard all day long."

"It's not used ter bein' shut outside, Miss McNee."

"Aye, them lads ruined it an' now . . ." Nora began to cry again, reaching into her apron pocket for her handkerchief and holding it to her face, her distress so great Edna felt compelled to put a sturdy arm round her shoulders which shook violently.

"All they could think on were them infernal machines afore they set off. Must be purrup on't stable wall or't tyres'd rot, they said. Like them bicycles were more important than their ma's 'ealth. An' it's that quiet, yer see," she sobbed. "'Ouse is like a grave wi'out 'em. Arthur dead an' three lads gone off fightin' fer their country. Eeh, if I see that there Lord Kitchener's face on a poster once more I swear I'll throw summat at it. 'Your Country Needs You' and that finger pointin'. It's not right ter tekk young lads from their famblies. I tell yer I'll never sleep sound in me bed until they're all 'ome again, Edna. See, fetch that pot over 'ere an' pour me a fresh cup."

"You do understand, don't you, Josie. I feel so badly after I promised you I'd go with you but with Ma and Pa in such a state and even Nora falling apart, there's no one to take over. I know your mother's been a brick but I can't expect her to run our household as well as her own."

"Grace, you must have known that the boys would go, at least Robert and later Tom but I can see that you are bound to stay, at least for a while, with your parents. Are you sure Nora . . . ?"

"Positive. She loves the boys as though they were her own and is as upset as Ma and Pa over this. Oh, she'll recover and become her old self when she gets used to it, but just for now I'm the only one holding it all together. Richard's not much help. I can see he'll not be far behind the others. They are all such big chaps and look older than they are."

"Well, I don't mind saying I think it's most unfair that you have to take it over, Gracie. Lord, you're only just seventeen yourself. What will you do about the shop?"

"Oh, I shall still go to the shop until Pa recovers and as long as I'm coming home of an evening I think Ma will be all right, but if I were to leave at this moment for London, as you are, God knows how Nora would manage, especially the boys."

Grace and Josie were sprawled on the sofa in the den. Grace had brought out a tray with a jug of Nora's lemonade, two glasses and a plate of biscuits which Nora had insisted on baking, for it gave her a feeling of familiarity to bake a batch of this and that in these dreadful times, even if half those for whom she baked were no longer eating them. Topsy had escaped from the back yard and had followed Grace up the stairs, and Wally, sensing a bit of peace in this strained household, had wandered casually at their heels. Both animals lay on the worn rug together, the tension in their family joining them for the moment in a strange amity.

"So, it's tomorrow then," Grace said, doing her best to be casual.

"Yes, first thing."

"Can I come and see you off?"

"What about your ma?"

"Oh, Nora will cope for an hour. And I'm going to make it plain to both Ma and Pa that I shall still go to work."

Josie shook her head sadly. She had been looking forward with eager anticipation to this great adventure she and Grace were to share. Not that she treated it lightly. Already there were rumours that great hordes of wounded were being ferried out from France, the Channel alive with boats taking replacements for those who were coming home. But with Grace beside her she had felt, since it was the first time either had been away from their families, they would have been a great support for one another.

"If . . . if things improve will you see if you can join me? I know you're too young but if Tom can persuade them to allow it, then so can you."

"I'll try, Josie, but Ma's still sedated and Pa won't leave her." She sipped her lemonade and absently fed Topsy with a piece of biscuit. "Have you heard from Philip?"

Josie's young face softened. "A letter last week." Grace's aching heart murmured silently that she would have given half her life to have been able to have what Josie had. Even with things as they were, with men in horrible danger and their women waiting mindlessly at home for them, she yearned to be one of them. Rupert's sun-darkened face smiling whimsically into hers, his rich brown eyes conveying his message of love as they said their parting farewells. Josie might know fear and loneliness, a longing to have this all over and her love back home with her, but at least she *had* it. She had Philip and the tender knowledge that he loved her and, when it was over, would come home to her.

"There is something that might interest you," Josie continued slowly, her hands busy pleating the hem of her skirt, her eyes cast down watching them. "I wasn't going to tell you because selfishly I wanted you to come with me but . . ."

"Yes?" Grace leaned forward.

"Angela Watson told me there was a rumour that several landowners have offered their homes. For nursing the sick and wounded, or whatever is needed. Childwall was mentioned and Old Nook Hall so if you were still of the same mind, when your parents are recovered, you might be able to get in at one of them and yet still be close should they need you."

Grace shrugged and, leaning forward, pulled at Topsy's ears which sent the dog into ecstasies. "It wouldn't be the same without you, Josie, but I'll think about it."

"Only you did say you wanted to do something for the war effort and I'm offering it to you."

"I know, and thank you, but at the moment I don't know whether I'm coming or going. When Ma comes out of the sleep the doctor put her in she's got to be told the boys are gone and I'm not looking forward to that. And Richard and John, who, by the way, are nothing short of minor heroes at school since they have *three* brothers serving, need a sharp reminder that with things as they are *I* am in charge. Dear God, Josie, I'm not looking forward to it. I would have thought Nora might . . . but it seems I'm all I have."

"Dear Grace, I shall miss you."

"You'll write, won't you?"

"At least once a week."

"Hey, don't make promises you might not be able to keep. Philip will expect a letter or two wherever he is."

"In France by now."

Grace looked shocked and her hand clutched at Josie's in loving compassion. "Already!"

"Yes, they don't get much training by the sound of it. It's pretty horrendous . . . what's happening to the regulars and the volunteers are being rushed through and over the Channel."

"The . . . the regulars? You mean . . . men like Rupert?" Grace's face had lost all vestige of colour and the hand that had held Josie's so gently had it now in a grip of iron.

"I'm afraid so, dear Grace. Have you not read the newspapers lately?"

"I knew they had gone; the British Expeditionary Force, they called it but . . ."

"I'm that sorry, Grace, but that means the men who are regular soldiers."

She was to read many conflicting reports in the next few months, not only in *The Times* which still was handed in faithfully by the same regular customer, but in the letters they received from Tom and Robert, mainly Robert for Tom was not much of a hand with a pen. The gentleman who was so generous with his newspaper had a son, an officer in the Lancashire Fusiliers, who had gone across with the first batch halfway through August, arriving at Le Havre where, it seemed, they had received a rapturous welcome from the French. They had been showered with bouquets, chocolate, fruit and wine, he told his father. From there they had marched to some place Mr Davenport – for that was the customer's name – could not quite decipher but where they had been joined by a squadron of French cavalry. It was on the following day that they had seen some fighting at what was later to be recognised as the Battle of Mons but Lieutenant Davenport had not gone into details except to say he was well and to send love to Mother.

It was shortly afterwards that the great retreat of the British Expeditionary Force began. The Germans outnumbered them, overwhelmed the little army and as they fell back reinforcements were urgently called for. Men were needed and needed now.

In September the long retreat was over and the army had turned about once more and were advancing with the French, pushing the Germans back across the River Marne and finally to the River Aisne and in nine days had regained a strip of France about fifty miles wide.

"This'll finish them off," Mr Davenport told her jubilantly. "This is the decisive battle of the war." But it seemed Mr Davenport was wrong, for in a few short weeks, having raced to the sea, the British were taking part in the defence of Ypres, or Wipers as the soldiers called it, but again the British were literally at their last gasp, reduced by huge casualties, one of them Mr Davenport's son, outgunned and outnumbered by more than ten to one. Ypres was saved, just the start of the struggle, though none of them knew it yet.

The following month the two sons of Mary and Edwin Tooley, having finished their training and been ferried across the Channel – guarded, though they were not aware of it, by the battle-cruiser on which their brother George was serving – marched side by side into a village by the name of Ploegsteert, which the troops instantly christened Plugstreet.

"We're billeted in an old farmhouse, with the animals rooting about outside and a pile of manure in the centre of the farmyard. You can imagine the smell . . ." Robert wrote cheerfully, making it sound as safely rural as Fir Grove Farm on Black Horse Lane where Mr Melly had once taken off in his monoplane, which was his intention. He did not want to frighten Ma and Pa with tales of trenches filled with water in which rats swam, with views over fields that were nothing but seas of mud and holes of water, of "bomb-proof" shelters and continuous rifle fire by snipers from both sides.

Kitchener's Army, who now were trained and wearing the uniform of the King, were pouring in their thousands across the Channel, filling the empty places of those killed at the front, but in Whitehall a new strategic plan was being mooted. If the Dardanelles could be forced, if Constantinople could be captured, Germany would be stabbed in the back. With this in mind a contingent of regular, territorials and naval reservists was quickly cobbled together and sent to the Mediterranean to join the Australian volunteers who had finished their training in Egypt, and towards the end of April they sailed in convoy for the island of Mudros.

Among them was Captain Rupert Bradley.

13

Charlie Davenport lay flat on his back with one leg suspended from a pulley and stared at the ceiling, which seemed a long way off from his bed. He was watching the lines of soldiers forming and re-forming, the patterns he saw created by the stains in the cracked plaster, the pictures etched in his mind transforming themselves into the scenes that he studied for the most part of every day since he had been here. Scenes that he did his best to erase but when you could not sit up, let alone get out of bed, played themselves out over and over again until he thought he might simply go mad. The pain and the drugs he was regularly given did battle with one another inside him but it was not this that distressed him but the charging lines of infantry that would keep moving across the ceiling. He had come to terms with the pain, the small darting flames that seared the nerves in his leg, but the advancing troops on the ceiling, the officers' whistle signalling the advance, the smoke, the bursting shells, the cries of frightened men and the screams of the wounded would not let him be.

It was only when *she* came that he was allowed a tiny island of peace, a moment of calm, of release from the chaos that invaded his mind. It had been so since he had fought in the first Battle of Ypres. He and one hundred and sixty thousand soldiers of the regular army had been involved, if such an ordinary word could be used to describe the horror of war, in the Battle of Mons in August, in the first Battle of the Marne in September, where the first trenches were dug and then the race to the sea at the end of October to defend Ypres which was so vital to hinder the Germans' advance. He had seen his first man killed at Mons, a German trooper who had somehow lost his way in the wood where he, Lieutenant Davenport, had been out visiting his sentries. One of his men had, without a moment's hesitation, picked up his rifle and fired, killing the German instantly and all the time the sun had continued to shine through the glorious autumn colours of the trees, the bells were ringing and the Belgian peasants could be seen walking placidly to church. It had affected him deeply, for the contrast between one and the other was so ghastly. He could hardly believe that they were at war and yet one of his men had shot another in what seemed like cold blood.

But that was soon to change. He had fired his pistol a hundred times since then as the enemy advanced in a mass and had been mown down so that you couldn't see the ground for bodies. Time after time he had given the order "Rapid Fire" and been jubilant to see them fall, advancing and retreating, advancing and retreating and all about him men fell, his own men, until the regular army was seriously reduced in numbers, most of them killed by shrapnel. Some died instantly, and others didn't. He had seen men hang, like Christ crucified, on the barbed-wire where they were entangled and heard them weep to die, or calling for their mothers. He had seen men separated from their limbs which flew over their heads before they fell, and it was these, lying at his feet in agony staring at their arm before their puzzled eyes, or with their stomachs held in with their own hands, who haunted him as they marched backwards and forwards on the ceiling of his hospital room while he lay and waited for them to tell him whether they were to cut his leg off. He had already undergone two operations, one in a hospital at the front and one here, wherever that was, for he had lost track, not only of time, but of place. And yet his wound had been clean when compared to the horrors he had witnessed in three months of fighting. A bullet had entered his leg just below his knee-cap and had been removed but the filth that clung to a soldier's clothing, including officers', for there was very little soap and water available in the trenches, had entered his flesh with the bullet and it seemed certain that the leg, if gangrene was confirmed, would have to be amputated.

That had been in November and now it was May, an unseasonably warm May, more like August, he had heard one of the nurses say in that determinedly cheerful voice they deemed necessary to address the wounded. His bed was next to a French window which stood open, giving him a view of wide sloping lawns where rows of beds and wheelchairs held those men considered well enough to sit in the sunshine. He could see a park sloping down to a field in which cows browsed and a farm waggon crawled along a track. The hedgerows that divided the field from the park were a dazzle of white and at the base were meadow buttercups and bugle, red campion and wild hyacinth. Beyond the field was a line of woods and drifting above the elm trees were flimsy clouds. So peaceful, so quiet and yet in his head he could still hear the barrage of the guns and the crack of rifles, the whimpers of breathless men, the screams of the wounded. *Where was she?*

The door at the end of the ward stood wide open and when he turned his head he could see out into the corridor, the strip of shining polished floor, the corner of a chest of drawers on which a vase of flowers stood, peonies in a profusion of white, yellow, pink and red, put there by *her*, brought from her mother's garden, she had told him, and a chair or two for waiting visitors. He could hear the clack of heels and the familiar squeak of a wheel on one of the trolleys and his heart began to beat a little faster. Sister Randall appeared, moving to the first bed in the ward, the bed that was surrounded by a screen which he knew meant bad news for the man who lay there. Then, the miracle happened and the trolley appeared and pushing it was the person for whom he had waited since last night when she had brought him a cup of cocoa. He watched her, unaware that he was holding his breath, drinking in, like water that revives a thirsty man, the gentle loveliness of her as she spoke to the man in the second bed. He heard her voice and knew a sudden violent need to kill the man, who was already halfway there and who was keeping her from him.

"Did you sleep well, Sam?" she said, then, glancing at Sister Randall who had just appeared from behind the screen, put her hand to her mouth and grimaced. "I mean, Captain," she added, for she knew, they all knew, that it was frowned upon to call a soldier by his Christian name. It bred familiarity and who knew where that might lead in the close contact of soldier

and nurse. She kept forgetting and was always being
ticked off but they all loved her for it, waiting for her,
if Sister was about, to whisper their Christian names
as she bent over them. "I've brought your milk. Can
you mangage with your straw?"

"Thank you, Nurse, I did sleep well," the captain
answered, giving her a wink. "And if you'll just put
the glass in my hand . . ." She patted his hand, the
one he had left, and placed the glass of milk in it.
She rearranged his pillows and smoothed the space
where his legs would have been, before moving on to
the next bed. There were four more before she would
reach him.

His eyes never left her. Though her hair was covered
by the white, close-fitting cap, with a fluted frill at
the back, her dark hair seemed to have a mind of
its own, determined on escape, and several wisping
tendrils curled on to her forehead and over her ears.
If Matron saw her she'd get the rounds of the kitchen,
as his mother's cook used to say. She wore a mauve
check dress with a high starched collar, the skirt of
which reached her ankle bone. Over it she wore an
immaculate bibbed apron, a red cross on her breast.
Her neat waist was cinched in with a wide petersham
belt. Thick black stockings and flat black laced boots
completed the uniform. It was the most hideous outfit
in which to put any woman but she looked beautiful.
Her eyes blazed with a golden light which reminded
him of the candles his mother liked to have on the table
when they dined and her honey-coloured skin was as
soft and smooth and perfect as silk. Her eyelashes
swept her cheek when she looked down into the face
of a soldier and her rosy mouth parted on a smile that

he swore kept many a man alive, for to die meant
he would never see it again. She was graceful and
her name, which he knew to be Grace, suited her to
perfection.

At last she reached him and though the thought of
drinking milk was repulsive to him he would take it
from her hand and drink it, even had it contained
hemlock, for as the glass changed hands their flesh
would touch and it was the moment that he lived
for.

"Charlie," she whispered, smiling, as a child does
at some innocent wrongdoing. "Can I interest you in
a nourishing glass of milk, Lieutenant?" This time
out loud.

"Lovely," he answered and he did not mean the
milk. "But I'm not sure I can hold it myself, Nurse."
He smiled, the smile becoming a wide, boyish grin as
the pain that rode him galloped off and left him as
he had been in the summer of last year. An engaging,
cheerful young man without a care in the world except
the determination to get to the Western Front before
the war ended without him.

A couple of years before that he remembered
hearing his father, who was manager in a bank in
Whitechapel, speak of the sad family of the tobacconist
where he bought his cigars and whose son had gone
down on the *Titanic*.

"A lovely girl," Father had said, though none of
them had taken more than a polite interest since none
of them knew her, and he himself was just about to get
his commission in the Lancashire Fusiliers and was full
of himself and nothing else. "And what a heavy burden
she has to bear," his father had added.

"Oh, and why is that, dear?" Mother had asked him kindly.

"Oh, it seems her parents have gone to pieces and the girl has had to leave school and take charge not only of the shop but of her five remaining brothers."

"How sad," they had all murmured and now, here she was, giving Charlie Davenport the will to live, to recover, and to make this beautiful girl love him as he loved her. They all loved her, of course. The officers in his ward were ready to fall in love with the first halfway pretty girl who was nice to them but not in the way he loved Grace Tooley.

"Now then, Lieutenant, let's not have any foolishness this morning." But her eyes twinkled and she continued to smile down at him. "I have a lot to do before the visitors arrive and, besides, it's my half day and I promised my mother I would be home for lunch."

"I wish I could come with you, Grace," he whispered as she bent over him. The long wisping tendril of dark curling hair escaped further from her cap and the end of it touched his cheek. Without conscious thought his hand rose and tucked it tenderly behind her ear and she turned a faint pink, then glanced about hastily to see if anyone had noticed. No one had except the chap in the next bed who winked.

The fragrance of something – was it a perfume she wore or just the sweet natural smell of woman? – washed over him and he was quite amazed, and somewhat ashamed when he felt a stirring in the pit of his stomach which swiftly moved to his "private parts" as they were described by the medical profession. By God, it was a long time since this had happened to him and he felt a wave of relief, for a man worries about such things when he has been badly wounded. He had had his share of pretty women even at his young age. He was popular with them, for he liked women as well as lusted after them which was, after all, what a man did. He knew himself to be attractive to the opposite sex. He was slender as yet, particularly since he had been wounded and then so ill, waiting for maturity to put bulk on him, for he was just twenty-one. He had an engaging, cheerful disposition which had stood him in good stead recently, with a teasing smile, vivid blue eyes and crisply curling fair hair. He was six feet in height, when he stood up, that is, which he hadn't done for many months now, with a loosely knit frame.

"Who knows, Lieutenant," she whispered back, "if you behave yourself."

"And what does that entail, Grace?"

"Stop calling me Grace for a start. You'll have me sacked."

At once he became serious, for the worst thing that could happen to him would be to lose her.

"What's happened to my milk?" the chap in the next bed complained though, like Charlie Davenport, he didn't give a toss for the milk, only for the nurse who was to bring it to him.

"Wait your bloody turn," Charlie murmured, but lay back, for he could see Sister Randall looking enquiringly at this end of the ward. "Go on, Nurse, I'll see you when you get back."

The pain seared him as she turned away.

The ride from Childwall to Sheil Road took no more than twenty minutes. As she did every time she came out of the gates of Old Nook Hall and turned on to

Allerton Road she glanced across the fields towards
the house where once she had sat with Mrs Bradley
in her enchanted conservatory. Arthur had been alive
then and he and Rupert had escaped, as young men
do, the tedium of adult conversation, taking her eager
brothers with them to get a closer look at Rupert's
motorcycle. What wonderful times they had been,
the young men filled with the enthusiasm of youth
for anything new and she herself daydreaming over
the handsome son of her hostess.

They were all gone now, Arthur dead, his death
breaking her mother's heart. George was part of the
British Grand Fleet on reconnaissance sweeps of the
North Sea, serving on the battle-cruiser *Indefatigable*,
and though he wrote frequently he said nothing of
what he did or of the skirmishes the British fleet had
with the German. Both Robert and Tom were at the
front with what was left of the "Pals" Brigade, writing
as often as they could thanking Ma for the frequent
parcels she sent them, short letters only and then
censored, written in pencil and with what looked
like mud on them. They had been home on leave
in March and between them had devised a "dot"
code with which they could let Grace know where
they were, which meant which battle they were in,
which she was not sure was a good thing since to
know where they were was even more frightening.
The papers had reported on the Battle of Neuve
Chapelle, the second Battle of Ypres and from what
the dots would tell them it seemed she would then
know where and when they were fighting. On their
leave they had had their photograph taken, Robert
standing with one hand on the back of the chair where

Tom sat. Two serious-faced young warriors in their khaki service caps with the badge of their Liverpool regiment pinned at the front. A standard tunic above pantaloons and puttees, their buttons gleaming with polish, which was not how they had been when they arrived at Lime Street Station. Still with the mud of the trenches on them and other stains which no one cared to ask about and the boys did not volunteer. They had been in battle and had seen many of their comrades killed and wounded. The change in them, even after seven months, had been heartbreaking.

And, as she had expected, Richard, her twin, and the dearest to her heart, had enlisted in April, two weeks before his eighteenth birthday. He was determined to become a flyer and had been accepted into the newly formed Royal Flying Corps. He was still in some secret place in England, learning to fly, and though Ma was stronger now, finding some comfort in the church where she spent a great deal of her time with other mothers of sons at the front, she clung to John and Grace with a fervour that irritated John and aroused great compassion in her daughter. She remembered when Ma had attended church every Sunday, a respected member of a decent Liverpool middle-class family, her thoughts going no further than the knitting bees, the sewing circle, her desire to become a member of the choir along with other comfortable matrons with whom she was acquainted. The religious side, though she attended to it regularly, had taken second place, but since her boys had marched away she had discovered that actually to pray in the Lord's house gave her more certainty that her prayers would be listened to and answered.

All she asked was that her sons would come home to her. She had lost one and felt it was incumbent on the Lord not to meddle with the others. So far her prayers had been answered and in return she threw herself into every organisation that might help the boys at the front. The soldiers, sailors and now airmen, who would benefit from *her* personal war effort.

And as they always did at least once every day, though she was concentrating on the narrow lane and its dusty tracks, cycling past fields springing with new grass, alongside orchards exploding with blossom, fields newly ploughed into curving furrows as black as coal, Grace's thoughts turned to Rupert. She had no one now to tell her where he might be, on which front he might be fighting. It was almost a year since he had married and perhaps even now was the father of a son or a daughter. The thought was agony to her who had wanted to be the mother of his children, to be his lover, his wife, his friend and anything else he desired of her, and she knew quietly inside her, that should he ask, she still would. He had dropped out of her life as swiftly as he had appeared in it that day at the field when Henry Melly had flown above them and her own heart had flown away on the wings of the small monoplane. It was still with him, with Rupert, wherever he was and when she looked across the farmlands towards Garlands she often thought she might visit Mrs Bradley and enquire after him and . . . and his bride. Mrs Bradley had been kind to her and had written when Arthur had died. She had told Rupert to bring her, Grace, to Garlands but the visit had never taken place. She knew, sadly, that it never would now.

It never once occurred to her that Rupert might

have been one of the multitude of casualties that were flooding hospitals all over the country. She received regular letters from Josie, telling her of the fleets of ambulances which came with dreadful regularity from the hospital trains bringing the wounded just as they left the battlefields. She told of the silent lines of people who watched in appalled silence as each hospital train came in and deposited its mangled victims, khaki-clad, unidentifiable bundles of filthy bandages, dried blood and ghastly faces, lying sometimes two to a stretcher, and each with a label giving their condition and therefore their turn in the order of things. She had not been able to cope with it, she told Grace, but she had. She had not been able to stand looking into each agony-twisted or vacantly blank face in case it should be that of Philip, but she had. She could not manage the sights and the smells which made her vomit, but she had. The moans, the screams as bandages were changed, the babbling voices begging her not to hurt them, and her certainty that she could not do it, but she had.

Grace knew that Josie was the bravest woman she had ever met, as were all the nurses who were the first to take in these poor, mutilated bodies, for the London hospitals were as much in the front line as the men who filled them. It was only when they were cleaned up and beginning to heal that they were transferred to places like Old Nook Hall where they were more or less convalescent. Many of those she nursed would be ready to go back to the trenches as soon as the doctor passed them as fit for service and as she swerved slightly to avoid a horse-drawn milk van, the driver shouting after her to "watch yerself, Nurse," she wondered if Lieutenant Charlie Davenport would be one of them.

It was his being wounded in the action at the Battle of Mons that had finally stiffened her resolve to do as Josie was doing and become a Voluntary Aid Detachment Nurse. She had been behind the counter as usual serving a packet of Gold Flake to the lad who worked as a telegram boy for the post office and who was convinced, he said, that the war would never last long enough for him to get "over there".

"I don't know why you should want to do that, Lenny," she had told him tartly. "You of all people know how many of our men are being wounded, are missing in action, or getting killed. How many telegrams have you got in that pouch?" indicating the leather bag at his waist. "Just in Liverpool alone."

"Aye, there's a lorra them, miss, burr I'm a man" – he was fifteen – "an' a man's gorr 'is duty ter do, 'asn't 'e?"

"That's true, Lenny, but at your age I'm sure—"

"I'm goin' as soon as—"

The door of the shop opened and the familar figure of Mr Davenport crept, she could describe it in no other way, over the threshold. His face was as grey as the skies which hung heavy, matching the mood of the nation, over the river and he seemed to shiver as Lenny's last words reached his ears.

"Lad, don't . . . don't break your mother's heart," he blurted out to Lenny, who gaped at him then sidled out after grimacing in astonishment at Grace.

"Mr Davenport, what . . ." But, of course she knew, for what else but one of the dreaded telegrams could have reduced the jovial banker to this sad state.

"Charlie . . ." was all he could say. He held out his

hand and she put his box of cigars in it and when he left she shouted into the back that she was going out for half an hour.

"Where you off then, lass?" Mr Hynes asked her, popping his head round the door.

"To join up," was her reply.

It had been First-Aid classes to begin with and what was known as a Practical Nursing Class. She learned bandage rolling, attended lectures given by doctors on the prevention of infection and contagion, and had been granted an interview at the newly opened Hospital for Wounded Officers which had been converted from Old Nook Hall at Childwall.

The scene that had been played out in the family room at home had been reminiscent of the ones her brothers had suffered when they left to serve their country and she had felt as they did, she was sure. She could see them now, young men not yet matured, young warriors setting off to find the Holy Grail in the high-charged atmosphere of patriotism and sacrifice and it was the same with her. She must, *must* do something and though she could not leave her family as Josie had done – after all Josie's brothers were far too young even to think of going to the front – she could nurse here in her own home town. The doctor who had given the lectures had told her, when she shyly asked, to apply to Old Nook Hall, to ask for Matron Holbrook and to mention his name, and she had done so and here she was, a probationer. Not a nurse by any means, but at times she was asked to help with injections, with changing dressings and holding the stumps of amputees and Matron had asked her particularly if she would care to go to London, or even apply for France, since her nursing skills were what was needed near the line.

But her mother's hysteria, her fainting, her cries of terror, her promise that if one more of her children was to leave she would throw herself in the Mersey, had put a stop to that. Even Doctor Prentiss had warned her of her mother's weakened heart and mind and what affected her mother also attacked her father. She was needed at home, he told her sternly and if she tried to carry on with it, meaning her intention to go to London, he would personally speak to Matron Holbrook about it. He had even managed to persuade Matron that "Nurse" Tooley needed to sleep in her own home at night and not in the nurses' home at the hall. She had forced herself to make it enough. Pa was back in the shop. Her mother was occupied with what she called her "war work" and at least she was doing something useful.

As she cycled furiously past the Clifton School for Girls there was a vigorous game of hockey being played on the sports field and she spotted some of the girls with whom she had once been educated. Younger than her, most of them, but among them was Francie Allen who played for the "Old Girls". How long ago that had been. In years no more than four but it seemed like centuries when she had been a careless child, playing in the golden sunshine that had warmed them then, every day, it seemed now, when she looked back on it.

She turned into Sheil Road and was just in time to see Lenny climb on his bicycle which had been propped against the gate of number 10, and cycle towards her and Boaler Street. He waved sadly as he passed her.

14

"Nora, I cannot and will not give up my nursing. Now more than ever I feel the need to go on. I know it sounds . . . well, I'm not quite sure what it sounds like but surely you can see that the sooner we get this bloody . . . yes, there is no need to look shocked, I mean *bloody* war over, the sooner they will come home . . . No, not . . . not poor . . . but the others. Oh, Nora, surely you can see it. We should all be striving to get it over and bring them back and if I can help in only the smallest way I must do it. I'm sure if I stayed at home as you and Pa think I should, it would make not the slightest difference to the outcome, or the length of it but if every soldier or nurse or anyone fighting in it gave up where would it end? Nora, you must see that."

"I do, lamb, but Grace, yer ma's absolutely . . ." The word she was looking for was "prostrate" but it was not one in Nora's vocabulary. "She's not 'erself, queen, norr after losin' . . . two sons."

Grace made her voice deliberately brutal. "She's not the only mother to lose . . . to lose a son . . . sons."

"Don't, don't, Grace. That little lad, 'e were nowt burra babby an she an' yer pa 'ave tekken it 'ard."

"We've all taken it hard, Nora, but I must get back to the hospital. There are men there who need looking after. I want to help them. Mr Davenport's son,

Charlie, he might lose his leg and there are many more, in a worse way than he is."

"But that little lad, that's wharr 'e was, a little lad."

"He was a soldier, Nora . . . oh, please, don't cry."

"Nay, I can't 'elp it, lass. It were me what purr 'is first napkin on 'is little bum."

"Please, please, Nora, don't, don't. I loved him, too."

"'E should never've bin allowed ter go. Only eighteen an' 'is young life snuffed out."

Nora put her head on her crossed arms which rested on the table and wept broken-heartedly. Topsy crept up to her, her ears down, her tail moving hesitantly in an attempt to placate as though the tears were her doing. Even Wally raised his head from the rug and stared in what seemed a sympathetic manner at the weeping woman. Edna, who had come as usual to give the rooms a good "bottoming", which she did every Monday, stood at the back of Nora, twisting her hands ineffectually in her apron, wondering whether she should go or stay. She had also meant to clean the windows this afternoon but she could hardly go about her work as though nothing had happened, could she. Eeh, this poor family, what next were they to suffer? Whatever it was it seemed Miss Grace was going to put up a bloody good fight, poor lass.

Grace moved about the kitchen, picking up a dish, a spoon, then putting them down again, twisting from here to there as though in an attempt to lose the pain. She could still see Lenny's almost apologetic wave, for he had known he was delivering an appalling message to her family, as he delivered appalling messages to so many families. The words in the telegram ran clearly across her vision:

REGRET TO INFORM YOU THAT PRIVATE THOMAS TOOLEY 2ND BATTALION KING'S LIVERPOOL REGIMENT DIED OF WOUNDS APRIL 28TH. LORD KITCHENER SENDS HIS SYMPATHY.

That was all. No details of how he had died which was a mystery in itself for there had been no battle reported since the Battle of Neuve Chapelle on 10 March and if he had been wounded then he would have been sent home to be nursed. Or if not then certainly to one of the hospitals behind the line, depending on the seriousness of his wounds. They had waited and waited for the past week perhaps to have some word from Robby but nothing had come and as the week progressed Ma became convinced that he was dead as well. Ma still held the telegram in her hand as she had done for the past week as if it was the only link she had with her dead son but this time Grace meant to speak out. Though it might appear cruel, hard-hearted to brave that closed door and encroach upon her mother's devastated grief she knew it was the only way. The hospital had given her a week's compassionate leave but they expected her back tomorrow. After all Ma had Pa, she had Nora, she had Mrs Allen who had been kindness itself to the bereaved family and though John, her last son, could not be said to be much comfort to his mother, at least he was still at home. Mind you, Grace had said privately to Mrs Allen, it was plain to see that it was his intention to avoid the terrible atmosphere at home as much as he could. Though he grieved for Tom, it gave him a certain status at school to have a war hero, a *dead* war hero for a brother. He would be fifteen soon, a tall, well-built lad, as all the Tooley boys were, and there was a certain glint in his eye when battles such as Mons, Ypres, Neuve Chapelle were mentioned, which frightened Grace. There was the story of that lad from Scotland Road reported in the Liverpool *Echo* who had landed in France when still aged fifteen and had been wounded at the beginning of May just after his sixteenth birthday. John had bought a copy of the newspaper when he was in town and shown it to Francie who in turn had told Grace that John had taken a great deal of interest in the report.

She had at last forced her way past her father who stood guarding the door of the bedroom he shared with Ma. He was her father. She loved and respected him, for though she had lost the man he had once been before Arthur died, as they all had, he was still her father, her beloved father. Weakened terribly by the loss of his sons and by the collapse of her mother she could not help but feel compassion for him as he did his best to stop her entering the bedroom. In his way he was only protecting his wife.

"She is sleeping, Grace. After all she has been through . . ."

"Pa, I'm sorry, but I must."

"Grace, dearest, don't . . . please don't . . ." Please don't make it harder for me, he was telling her and she longed to put her arms, her strong, young arms round his frail shoulders and tell him not to worry, she wouldn't leave him but she knew it was out of the question. This was her war, the war of the young, men and women, and she must be allowed to take part in it.

Even as she put him gently to one side and moved across the darkened room to her mother's bedside she was suddenly startled by what she could only describe as an exploding light in her eyes. It lit the room to garish brightness, outlining every piece of furniture, to be followed by instant darkness in which she could see nothing. A nothingness that badly frightened her, and for some strange reason, though he had not been on her mind at that precise moment, Rupert's face swam across her vision. Laughing he was, as she had seen him laugh on that day she and her brothers had visited Garlands, a happy face showing nothing but the certainty of the young that this happiness will simply last for ever. Then the room became visible again, dim but with enough light to make out the window, the dressing-table, a chest of drawers, the wardrobe and the bed on which her mother lay. Her mother with a face like that of a ghost, blending into the whiteness of the pillow, only the black holes in which her eyes were buried plainly visible. Her hair, which had been turning grey for several years now, was in a snow-white tangle on the pillow.

The feeling of disorientation, of being not here but in some strange and terrible place, persisted for several moments. Grace stood still, the blood in her veins slowing to an icy coldness, a sluggishness that seemed to tell her that it was about to stop moving altogether and that she would fall to the carpet in a faint but her pa's voice begging her to leave Ma alone caught her before she fell.

She took a deep breath, putting the strange experience to one side. She was obsessed with death and disaster, she told herself, with wounded and dead soldiers, with terrible worms of thought wriggling in her mind warning her of what might be happening to all the men she loved who were in constant danger, and was it any wonder? But she must put *all* aside and speak firmly to her mother, make her see the unfairness of her clinging to Pa who in turn clung to Grace who was needed to look after the men who came back damaged from the front line.

"Ma, I must . . . speak to you, darling. They need me at the hospital."

Her mother's blank eyes looked at her without expression. She was like a lost child who has somehow got separated from a comforting hand and doesn't know how to find it, but Grace knew she must not let her mother's pain and loss keep her, Grace, from moving on. Her mother, without speaking, was asking how *she* was to go on without her lost sons but Grace was about to tell her that that was what she must do. Manage without her lost sons!

"Gracie, leave her. You don't understand. I know you're grieving for Tom. He was your brother but there is no pain greater than outliving your own child. Twice now we . . . can you blame her for being as she is?" Her pa's voice was firmer.

"I've come to tell her that I must go back to the hospital tomorrow, Pa." Her own voice was firm, clipped because she knew it must be said and the only way was quickly. She must not weaken. In a way she felt angry with Ma for being as she was, and angry with Pa for allowing it, but why should she, Grace, feel guilty?

Guilty that she was to abandon her mother – that was how Ma made her feel and it wasn't fair – and return to what was not only her duty, which sounded pompous, but was what she wanted and needed to do.

Her mother began to cry weakly and Pa shuffled over to the bedside, doing his best to push Grace out of the way.

"No," he was saying, "no, dearest, don't upset yourself again. Grace won't go if—"

"Stop it, Pa, stop it." Grace's voice was thin and harsh and the pain she felt, the pain she was inflicting ripped her to shreds but she must be firm. There was Rupert, Robert, Richard, George and there was Charlie and in a way they all called to her and one woman's grief, even if she was her own mother, could not be weighed against them. "I am returning to the hospital in the morning. I have telephoned Matron and told her and I have also promised I would take my turn of night duty."

"Grace, you must do what you think best. I understand but your mother doesn't. She wants to cling to those she has left. Nora—"

"Nora will run the house, Pa, she has promised me and I want you to help her. Make it easy for her, or as easy as possible. She loved Tom and Arthur. They were sons to her who had no children and she is grieving but she has promised to look after you all."

"I can't leave your ma. The shop . . ."

"Mr Hynes is capable of running the shop. I have promised that I will go in on my afternoon off and look over the accounts with him until you get back."

"I'll not be back for a long time, Grace, you know that."

"I know nothing of the sort, Pa." Her voice softened and she took her father's hands between her own. They trembled but she held them steady. "Pa, there are thousands of mothers and fathers all over the country sharing the same . . . unhappiness you and Ma are suffering but they are getting on, proud that their sons have . . . well, you know what I mean. You and Ma must be strong and proud of your children, all of them. Don't . . . don't brood. Make Ma go to the church, to the many things women like her are doing for their boys and you get to the shop. Take your place among the men and women who are struggling to get on with life no matter what it throws at them."

"Grace, my dear, if only I had your courage."

She curled herself into a ball and buried her head beneath the eiderdown to muffle the sound of her weeping. She wept for Tom who had died of his wounds, a young man, no . . . a boy, for he had gone straight from school to the front. He had learned about death there and death had searched him out and taken him and though she knew it wasn't fair, what *was* fair about this war? Absolutely nothing. Robert was still, presumably, in the greatest danger though he had made nothing of it in his letters.

Dear Ma and Pa,
    We dug trenches today. We marched here yester-
day and sang as we marched. Ted Walker played
a mouth organ and Jimmy Dean a penny whistle
and the rest of us sang. The sun is shining and we
rested by the side of the road. I heard a blackbird
sing. The parcel was wonderful and tell Nora the

*cake went down a treat. Not to worry, Ma, we
are fine.*

    Your loving son,
    Robert

That was an example of the letters they had received
from both Tom and Robert but she, who had spoken to
men who had been in the battles, knew that the almost
idyllic tone of her brothers' letters, almost as though
they were on a bit of a holiday, was totally false. Tom
was gone. Her rebellious little brother, for though he
had been a year older and twice as big as her she had
always, for some strange reason, thought of him as that,
was dead. She could see him now, pedalling like the
wind along the path at Sefton Park, weaving in and
out of folk walking in the sunshine, oblivious to their
shouts of indignation. Always in trouble, always speaking out of turn, but generous, gruffly kind, open-
hearted and now he was dead. She wept for him.
She wept for Rupert, for George, for Robert and for
Richard, for all the fine young men who had been
swept away into a world that was as alien and terrifying
as a far planet. She knew from Josie's letters and from
the delirium of the soldier in the end bed where he
hid, or was hidden, behind a screen, of waterlogged
trenches, for it had been a hard winter, of trench rats,
of crucifixion by barbed-wire, of fear and carnage. She
had helped to dress wounds and prepare gangrenous
limbs for amputation, going far beyond the duties
expected of her as a probationer VAD. She knew she
was a good nurse. She was not afraid of the soldiers
who were in her care as many of the girls were. They
took the tea round, did light cleaning, served the meals,

read to the patients, or wrote letters for those who
could not manage it themselves, tidied the wards for
Matron's rounds, but Grace was not satisfied with this
which was why, she supposed, Sister had asked her to
consider going to London, or even France, where *real*
nurses were needed. She had mopped up blood and not
been faint, she had dressed hideous wounds, soothed
the twisting bodies of men who waited for the relief the
drugs gave them from pain and had even once stood
in the operating theatre in readiness for an emergency
when Nurse Winter had been taken ill.

But in her heart she knew that what she had was
all she ever would have, for with three brothers in
the thick of the war she could not, in all conscience,
leave Pa to deal with Ma. And she could not leave
the responsibility to Nora of keeping an eye on John,
who would give them the slip and get to France by
any means he could, especially now that his brother
was dead.

And then there was Rupert who was never far from
her thoughts when she was alone. Rupert! What was
the meaning of that strange experience that had
occurred in Ma's bedroom? It frightened her, for in
that moment she had been as close to him as if she
had been with him wherever he was. Vivid, the feeling
of chaos, of disaster, of total disruption had been
something she would never forget. Something inside
her badly wanted to telephone Garlands and speak to
his mother but she could hardly ask baldly if Captain
Rupert Bradley was well, could she? Question whoever
answered the telephone on his state of health.

She fell asleep with tears still wet on her cheeks.

                    *   *   *

Ever since the beginning of January British shipping had been badly affected by the menace of German submarines. The SS *Western Coast*, out of Liverpool, had been sunk off Beachy Head. The SS *Bengrove* had suffered the same fate off Ilfracombe. The pleasure steamer *Victoria* was sunk almost in the mouth of the River Mersey, HM auxiliary cruiser *Bayano* off the coast of Wigtownshire with the loss of two hundred lives, seven British merchant ships in March and two more in April. During April another seven were torpedoed with over a hundred crew and passengers killed, but on 7 May, the day before she returned to the hospital, as Grace was in her parents' bedroom arguing for her right to fight for her country, the German submarine *U20*, lurking in the southern entrance to the Irish coast off the Old Head of Kinsale, saw the Cunard liner *Lusitania* on her final stretch of passage from New York to Liverpool. The submarine fired two torpedoes, hitting the liner and within twenty minutes the great ship keeled over and sank. Of the 2,000 passengers, 1,198 perished, including 291 women and 94 children. Among the dead were 128 American citizens, their bodies drifting on to the beaches of Kinsale.

The day she returned, Charlie had heard her coming before he saw her. He recognised the light tip-tap of her boots, restless and graceful and quick, and he turned his head on the pillow to watch her enter the ward, not wanting to miss a moment of her presence. He knew that her brother had been killed. He had been out of his mind when she didn't appear a week ago. He and the rest of the patients had begged Sister Randall for news of her; was she ill, on leave, and though he knew she would have told them if she had been planning to be absent, Sister was non-committal. It was none of their business where Nurse Tooley was, her manner said and nothing he could do would crack that austere demeanour with which she treated them. Kind, she was, and patient with them, but not like Grace who treated them all like *persons* and not just a body that needed mending, which Sister would do with the efficiency and patience of her calling. She was never found wanting but her maxim was that patient and nurse must be detached from one another if the nurse was to perform her duties properly. She was kind, but she was without the sweetness, the humour, the compassion that Grace could not hide no matter how many lectures Sister gave her.

That morning his mother and father had been allowed to visit him. His younger brother, just eighteen, had that morning entrained to the south coast with a brigade of the Lancashire Fusiliers, his own regiment, and Sister had softened her heart and given permission for them to visit him. Two sons at the front was hard to bear and as his mother said tearfully to him, she was glad she had only two sons and prayed that their Jenny would be sensible and not take it into her head to go gallivanting off nursing or ambulance driving like some.

"I imagine poor Mrs Tooley's wishing she had borne daughters instead of sons," his father remarked gloomily. "That poor family . . ."

"D'you mean Grace's . . . Nurse Tooley's family?" Though his neck was stiff from being immobile for so long, Charlie turned it on his pillow with such force he gasped with pain.

"No, darling, don't." His mother winced. "Lie still."

The sight of this boy of hers still flat on his back after all these months, though it meant he was out of those appalling trenches they were hearing so much about, was a great worry to her. They seemed to think his leg would heal now, thank God, and would not have to be amputated and he really seemed to have perked up no end recently.

"Yes, poor chap's lost another boy. Only eighteen as well."

"Like our poor Freddy."

"Now then, Mother. Freddy'll be as right as rain."

"Of course he will, Mother but tell me about Nurse Tooley's brother. She's been off all week and nobody knew why. Poor little girl. She must be heartbroken." Charlie's voice was infinitely tender and his eyes moved past his parents to the door which he watched constantly for her return. She had been pale this morning but her smile had been as sweet, and yet all the time she was carrying the pain of her loss about with her.

"Well, Mr Hynes, that's the chap who works for Tooley in the tobacconist's, says they have six sons; well, four now that this lad's perished. The oldest boy went down on the *Titanic*, you know, one is in the RFC, the youngest is still at home, of the rest, two are in France and the third is in the navy. Can you imagine the worry of that?"

His mother shuddered and took her son's hand in hers and at that moment Sister appeared in the doorway, her face as white as the enormous shovel cap she wore. Charlie could tell she was not her usual contained self, for her cap was slightly askew and her mouth kept opening and shutting like a fish that has suddenly found itself on dry land.

"Sister?" Major Crisp queried from his bed, holding the newspaper he was reading to one side, his face a picture of astonishment. "Sister, is there something wrong?"

Grace, returning from the sluice room with a bed-pan, appeared behind her and, with the respect due to a Sister, waited patiently for her to move out of the doorway, but Sister continued to waver about as though her legs had turned to jelly.

At last she found her voice. "The porter . . . in the newspaper . . . afternoon . . . yesterday. Dear God, are they to make war on children?" she groaned.

Major Crisp, a man of thirty, a regular in the army who had lost a leg and one of his hands at Ypres, was doing his best to get out of bed. He was a man of great compassion. He had seen three-quarters of the British Expeditionary Force slaughtered during the first months of the war and he could recognise shock when he saw it, for he had seen a lot of it among even soldiers of great experience.

"Major, please . . ." Grace hurried forwards and persuaded the soldier to lie back in his bed, and when she had done so turned to Sister Randall and took her arm, leading her to a chair beside the major's bed.

"Sister, what is it?" When Sister Randall seemed unable to speak she took it upon herself to stroke the Sister's cheek. "Sister dear, can you not tell us?" They all imagined that poor Sister, like everyone here in this hospital, had been struck down by some personal tragedy, but at last Sister Randall had pulled herself together enough to speak coherently, if violently.

"Those bastards . . ." They all gasped, shocked and speechless, for Sister was the soul of propriety and would take to task any man who used bad language on her ward.

"They've sunk the *Lusitania*."

For a moment none of them understood. Of course they had heard of the *Lusitania*, who had not. The *Lusi* as she was affectionately known by those who had built her and who had watched her sailing up and down the river. She belonged to Liverpool. She was one of the biggest Cunarders ever built and those bloody Huns had sunk her . . .

"Sister?" The major cleared his throat. "Survivors?"

"A handful. Women and children, their bodies floating up on the beach at . . ."

Mrs Davenport began to cry. She didn't think she could stand any more, really she couldn't. One son lying in a hospital bed and another on the way to the front and now this. All those poor souls, it just couldn't bear thinking about and she thought she'd like Norman to take her home now. They'd come on Sunday afternoon, she told Charlie, at the usual visiting time.

Charlie and Major Crisp exchanged glances over the heads of the other patients and the bobbing nurses who had been summoned to soothe those whose nerves were ragged enough without this disaster. Lieutenant Davenport and Major Crisp had been in this from the first and probably knew more about the state of the war than many of the soldiers and certainly the civilians. This was a horrific tragedy but at the same time, if Americans were involved, as later newspaper reports were to confirm, going down with the *Lusitania*, it might bring the greatest neutral power, the United States of America, towards the allied cause and help to shorten the war.

15

It was just after she had begun night duty that Robert was given leave. It was only right and proper, Ma said; after all, the boy had lost his brother and this leave proved that those who had control of such things in the army had compassion. When they heard he was to come home Ma emerged from her bedroom and began a frantic spring-clean of his room in Robby's honour, wondering out loud if she should buy new curtains, since the ones at the window had been there for years. How kind it was of his regiment, she kept saying to Nora and Grace, to allow her boy to come home to comfort his mother and what a joy it would be to see him after all this time. Grace, who had discussed Robert's leave with Charlie and the major, knew the army did not do such things otherwise half the serving soldiers would be at home instead of in the line.

"There are hundreds, thousand of families who have more than one son serving somewhere, Grace," Charlie said to her, holding her hand under the cover of the newspaper he had been reading. He had been allowed to sit up now, propped against a great pile of pillows which constantly needed adjusting, or so he told her. He lay still as a mouse when she leaned over him, breathing in the lovely fragrance of her which at such close quarters drowned the all-pervasive smell of lysol which did its best to hide the faint aroma of putrefaction of decaying flesh. Not on him, thank God, though it had been touch and go, apparently, but on the poor sod in the bed across the ward.

He watched her whenever she was on the ward, never taking his eyes off her and he swore, to himself only, that it was she who had put him on the road to recovery. At night he barely slept, for he could see her when it was her turn on duty at the table in the centre of the ward, one small light creating a halo round her head. She was like an angel, which he knew was romantic nonsense, an angel of mercy, for at his slightest movement she turned her head, then came to him, whispering his name, asking if he wanted a drink, or the bedpan to which he always replied vehemently in the negative. He might be dying for a pee but there was no way he would allow *her* to minister to him in that department. He loved her so much and his masculine need to tell her was so great it overwhelmed him at times but something held him back. Perhaps the knowledge that she had so much on her mind, so many responsibilities to her family, the grief of her dead brother, it seemed an impertinence to spring his own feelings on her at this time. Besides, he wanted to be on his feet when he declared his love. To be able to stand and put his arms about her, to kiss her as a man kisses the woman he loves. This was his dream and he longed to let the world see that she was *his*, meaning by the world the men she nursed and who all watched for her, loved her, needed her and took up so much of the time Charlie wanted spent on him.

"So many," he went on, gently caressing the heel of her thumb, "that it would be impossible to send

them home in such a case as yours. How long as he
been in? Since August, then Robert must be due leave,
wouldn't you say, Major? Your brother – George did
you say his name was? – who is somewhere on the
high seas has not been sent home, has he?"

Grace shook her head and hurriedly slipped her
hand from Charlie's grasp. It was not that she did not
like it, or him, she did, but it would not do for Sister
to see them like this. Sister had been most sympathetic
over Grace's loss but this did not mean Grace could
lower the standards Sister demanded on her ward.

But Ma knew nothing of the conversation Grace
had had with Charlie and the major. She was certain
that her boy had been sent home to recuperate from
the devastation of his brother's death. His impending
leave seemed to revive her and though she was far from
recovered she was talking of creating a small garden for
Tom next to Arthur's where she could plant flowers
until the day her hero son was sent home to her and
a proper funeral could be arranged. Though she was
about the house again, helping Edna with small jobs,
Grace dreaded the day Robby would have to go back
to France, for she thought that on that day Ma would
retreat once more into her misty world of memories,
leaving behind the *real* world with which her family,
particularly poor Pa, had to cope.

She went alone to Lime Street to meet her brother.
She had seen her share of soldiers come straight from
the trenches, for since the spring and the start of
new "offensives" the wounded in their vast numbers
were now being sent all over the country, London
hospitals being swamped. The Huntroyde Auxiliary
Military Hospital at Padiham, which was even further

up north near Burnley, had been opened recently to take the ever growing numbers of wounded, and Old Nook Hall had also opened its doors to the flood of casualties that flowed from the clearing stations in the south. These men came as they were from the front, spending days en route, still wearing their filthy, mud-clogged, blood-soaked uniforms, reeking of the dressings that had been hurriedly changed at the clearing hospital, so verminous the nurses donned special uniforms that could be boiled after the men had been deloused. The battles of Ypres and Neuve Chapelle had been disastrous to the British Army in as much as the Germans had, for the first time, used poison gas and the soldiers in the trenches who had taken a whiff and whose lungs had been damaged, came home convinced that the enemy might even get through to the English Channel.

It was a troop train that had brought him to Liverpool and all around him soldiers were being clutched at by weeping mothers and wives, but Robby just stood there waiting patiently for someone to tell him where to go, what to do, as sergeants and officers had been telling him for the past ten months. His uniform was stained with the mud – and blood – of the last battle he had fought in. It hung on his gaunt frame like a badly made sack and about him were attached various pieces of equipment, a helmet and some sort of knapsack fastened to his chest with straps and webbing and a rifle slung on one shoulder. He had several small khaki packs, slung here and there about his person, the contents of which she couldn't even guess at, and about the legs of his crumpled breeches were badly tied puttees. His boots were heavy with mud. His cap was raked at a jaunty angle but her brother looked far from jaunty. His face bore deep, unyouthful lines, etched by grief, fear and hard living, his boyish look gone for ever.

"Robby," she said gently, putting a light hand on his arm, for she had learned that soldiers just come from the trenches were inclined to be nervy of sudden movements or sound.

"Grace . . . Gracie, is it you?" He turned haunted eyes on her, the lovely glowing brown of them faded somehow, colourless and blank and as she watched he began to weep. All about them soldiers moved towards the exit, keeping their eyes sympathetically away from him, for they had been where he had but she could see that men and women, mothers and fathers, wives and sisters were shocked at the sight of a grown man in tears because it seemed unmanly somehow for a soldier to cry.

She got him into a cab, drawing him into the circle of her arms, his head on her shoulder and holding him tight in her clean, sweet-smelling embrace.

"Drive us to Newsham Park, please," she told the astonished cab driver who clucked to his horse and edged into the tremendous flow of traffic. She didn't speak to Robby, just rocked him and stroked his cheek, for she knew that he held something that was eating him from the inside and until it was got out she could not take him home to his mother.

The cab driver dropped them at the entrance to the park on Gardner Drive and she led her brother through the gardens to the shelter near the aviary. The beds were filled with the tall spires of lupins in colours from cream and white through to roselilac and butter yellow. Next to them were the vivid blue of delphiniums and at their feet the glory of petunia and the cheerful, daisy-like blooms of summer chrysanthemum. The aviary was filled with the music of songbirds and Robert leaned his rifle against the seat and lifted his head for the first time. He was dry-eyed by now but his dirty, ash-coloured face was still etched with a memory that was eating at him.

The sight of her brother standing like some lost child as if he had no idea which way to turn had wrenched her heart badly and while she shrank from what it might be she was aware that she must get him to speak, to empty his heart of all the horror that seemed to hide there and the only way, though it might be shocking, even cruel, was to do it now.

"Tell me about Tom," she said baldly. "He's not coming home, is he?"

"There's nothing of him to bring home, Gracie."

She flinched away from the picture his words had painted but this must be done, said, dealt with before his mother spoke of it. Ma was waiting for the official notification that would announce the return of her son's body. She was waiting for the dignity of the funeral she and Pa were planning, the decent laying to rest of her son which she had not been able to do with Arthur and if this was not to be, then some tale, some lie must be concocted now, before she and Robert went home.

"Tell me, darling," slipping her slim, chapped hand into his brown, hard and dirt-ingrained one, and as she glanced down at them for a moment they seemed to tell the story as words could not, of the changed circumstances of the Tooley family.

"We'd gone over the top, Tom and me and the others. We'd been told by the officer not to go together, to stand apart with other men between us so that if one of us was . . . got it then there would be a chance the other would survive. Brothers, you see, but we . . . there were whole families serving together but . . . they took no notice if they could get away with it. We ran together, almost shoulder to shoulder then the shell burst on top of Tom and he simply . . . disappeared then . . . then . . . bits of him began to fall on me . . . blood . . . his hand . . . the one with the ring on it Pa gave him. I was right next to him and didn't get a scratch but . . ." He fell silent as Grace began to moan.

"Oh, dear God in heaven . . . dear God . . . Tom . . . Tom . . ." She began to rock backwards and forwards, backwards and forwards and as though her reaction had broken some dreadful spell under which Robert had laboured since his brother's death, he put his arms about her, comforting her, shushing her, stroking her hair, and in comforting her, he comforted himself. They sat for a long time while she wept for handsome, cheerful, devil-may-care Tom Tooley who had exasperated her, teased her unmercifully, with whom she had fought and laughed and who no longer existed except in the heart of his family which, she supposed, was really all that mattered.

"We must tell Ma he was buried in the army cemetery in . . . wherever it is. You will know, Robby."

"Yes. And I have a letter from my officer telling her and Pa that he died cleanly and bravely without pain from a bullet wound to the heart. She will imagine him in a bed with . . . with people to care for him."

"You're a good boy, Robby," wiping her tears from her swollen face, the irony of calling this haggard man a boy escaping her entirely though he noticed it.

She had been on night duty for two months and was to change over to days when she got the telephone call from Josie. The bell was jangling as she ran down the stairs on her last night. It was August and just a year since the war started; though Ma still grieved savagely for her boy who had died so bravely but was honourably buried where she could not visit his grave, she had made her little garden for him and talked incessantly of when the war was over and she would be able to bring him home. She had survived again, going to the church bazaars, the sewing circles, the knitting bees, the bandage rolling with other mothers who had lost their sons as she had, and the sadness of it, the sharing of it, had given her strength and comfort.

"Hello," she shouted into the receiver, for the front door was open to a fine summer evening and in the garden John was playing a rowdy game with James next door in which Topsy, barking furiously, joined in. "Speak up, I can't hear you." She thought it might be Charlie who had gone home to convalesce with his family in Edge Lane and who had promised to take her to see *The Birth of a Nation* at the cinema in town. He was on crutches now and would be able, though he had not told his mother, in a month or two, to return to the front. A slight limp which would improve, the doctor had told him, with exercise, and he'd get plenty of that in France, though he had not said as much. Before he went, though he had not exactly said so to Grace, he meant to be engaged to her. Even married if he could persuade her to it. Since he had left hospital she had "escorted" him, his laughing words, since he could hardly be described as escorting her, to the cinema, to the music hall in town, and even to dine at the Adelphi on his birthday.

"I am speaking up, you fool," a familiar voice shouted. "The noise is at your end and it sounds like that obnoxious little brother of yours. What the devil's he doing, strangling the dog?"

"Josie, oh, how wonderful to hear from you. I wondered why I hadn't had a letter. What's up? Are you to—"

"Listen, Gracie, I've no time for a chat. There's a queue a mile long waiting for the one and only public telephone in the hospital so listen carefully and don't speak."

"Don't speak! Whatever's—"

"I said don't speak, just listen."

"I'm all ears."

"How d'you feel about being a bridesmaid?"

"A—"

"Don't say the word, for God's sake, somebody might overhear. Just listen and say yes or no in the appropriate places. Right?"

"Right."

"Can you get leave, first of all?"

"Probably. I haven't had any since I began."

"Good. Philip and I are to be married the day after tomorrow and for God's sake don't say anything now. Special licence and it's a secret."

"A—"

"Don't say anything, Grace, or I swear I'll strangle

you. We aren't allowed to be married without permission and if they knew they'd stop me nursing. I'm not telling Mother and . . . yes, yes, I won't be a minute, for heaven's sake," she said to a disembodied voice who could be heard complaining bitterly in the background, "but I must have someone I love with me. It must be you otherwise there would be such a stink. Will you do it?"

"Of course."

"You're a love . . . yes, here, take the bloody thing," again to someone who was clamouring, obviously, for their turn. "I'll meet you tomorrow on the ten thirty from Lime Street. If you're not on it I'll know you couldn't make it." The receiver was put down with a crash.

She wore a deep rose-pink face-cloth suit, a skirt and bolero with revers of velvet. The skirt was tubular, just touching her instep, and decorated with velvet round the hem. Daringly it was split at the side to just below her knee with vertical buttons covered in velvet along the opening. The bolero jacket had long sleeves, again with velvet round the wrist and a chiffon and lace fill-in collar. Her straw hat was wide-brimmed with a velvet ribbon to match that of her outfit and round the crown was a wreath of silk poppies. Her boots of cream kid matched her leather handbag which had a long gilt chain. Her gloves were of cream silk and she carried a long-stemmed cream silk umbrella. In her small fitted dressing-case, which dated back to the last century and belonged to Ma who had inherited it from her own mother, she had a change of underwear and a nightgown, plus sandwiches put up by Nora who was convinced she would die of starvation on that long train journey if not provided for. She had no idea where she was to sleep that night but the most trying aspect was the fact that she could tell no one of the real reason for her visit to London.

"I'm just going to have a day or two with Josie, Ma. A little break that I feel I deserve after two months of night nursing, don't you?"

"Oh, of course, dear but if I should feel . . . unwell I would like to know that I can get in touch with you."

"Ma, as soon as I get to London I promise you I will telephone."

"Dearest" – her mother was aghast – "you know I can't touch that thing."

"John will answer it, won't you, John?"

"I feel I should come with you, Gracie." John's voice broke just as he was doing his best to be manly. "A woman on her own in a city full of soldiers . . ."

Her mother's hand went to her mouth. "Oh dear, I hadn't thought of that."

"I shall be with Josie who has survived there all these months and is still in one piece, Ma, and John must go to school, you know that. Besides, Josie and I have a lot of catching up to do."

"And you don't want me along."

"Exactly. Would you want me trailing with you when you go off on these jaunts with your pals?"

Mrs Allen was quite tearful asking sadly why, if she had leave, didn't her daughter come home to visit her family, and when she telephoned him Charlie sounded horribly put out and very doubtful that she should go down south with the country in the state it was. She was to take care on the train, for it would be full of soldiers . . . he would miss her dreadfully . . . when was she to be home? Would she promise to telephone him? Those Zeppelin raids . . . he really thought it might be best if . . . bloody hell, he wished he could come with her . . . to travel alone . . . He was trying to be cheerful, she knew that, for she also knew his feelings for her by now and was sorry that the day was bound to come, and soon, when she would have to reveal her enduring love for another man, but she managed to reassure him that the moment she came home they would have a night out . . . a day out in his father's motor car which he had learned to drive before he went to France and at last, at last . . . *at last* she boarded the train to London.

She had never been further south than Buxton in Derbyshire where Pa had a cousin with whom they had stayed before the war. And she had never, ever been on a train by herself in her life.

"Now make sure you get in a compartment with other ladies in it, promise me," Ma beseeched her. "And keep the window closed at all times. Heaven knows what might fly in from those engines."

"I wish I was going," John muttered, kicking at the chair with his heels. "It's not fair, everyone's off somewhere except me."

"*John,*" Grace hissed, hoping Ma had not heard him and he had the grace to look ashamed.

"And don't venture into the corridor if there should be one, Grace dear," Ma went on, thinking probably of the men who hung about with chloroform pads rendering their victims unconscious the better to whisk them off into white slavery.

"I won't, Ma, but I'm sure, as Josie has already done the journey and survived I shall do the same."

Nevertheless it was a long and tedious journey with diversions here and there to allow troop trains to rattle past on their high-speed way carrying much needed soldiers to the trenches of France. There were soldiers standing in the corridors and lolling on their packs, dozing standing up, heading for training camps and God knows where and though she smiled and spoke to several, since soldiers held no terrors for her, the elderly ladies with whom she shared the compartment stared at her with horror, shaking their heads at her forwardness in addressing not only a common man, but a soldier!

Josie was waiting for her by the barrier where the ticket collector stood, smart as paint in a pale blue outfit which was evidently new, part of her "trousseau" she told Grace later laughingly. Standing next to her was Philip Booth in lieutenant's uniform, also smart as paint but his uniform had a somewhat worn look about it as though not only had the wearer been in the wars but so had his jacket and breeches. But his boots and Sam Browne belt were polished to a glass-like shine and his buttons and cap badge gleamed. He had Josie by the arm, smiling down into her face and for a moment they didn't see her. She felt her heart move achingly in her chest and in that moment envied her friend in a way that could almost be called jealousy. She supposed that was what she was. Jealous of Josie's love for this tall, thin soldier, and having that love returned. Josie had a glowing, rosy look about her, her skin as clear as a petal, her mouth rich with the ripeness of being frequently and recently kissed, and in that moment Grace knew that, if not in the eyes of the law, Josie was already Philip's wife.

Josie dragged her eyes away from Philip, turning to look along the platform and seeing Grace began to smile and move forward. Detaching herself from her lover she held out her arms and Grace ran into them. They hugged one another wordlessly, ready to laugh or weep, not sure which, with the emotion that had grown up between them since Arthur's death. Grace had not really been aware of how much she had missed her friend, for in the mad hurry of her life, divided between the hospital and the shop, not to mention Tom's death and her mother's illness, she had barely had time to dwell on anything but what the next day held and what she was to do in it.

"Gracie, you made it, you made it. Have you any idea what this means to me . . . to have you here. Oh, Grace . . . And will you look at me, ready to cry all over you when I'm the happiest woman in the world."

They began to laugh then, huge smiles of satisfaction until Philip coughed discreetly and the laughter grew as Grace renewed her acquaintance with the man who had once brought her and Josie home after that dreadful day outside the jeweller's. He was a quiet man, the exact opposite to the unquenchable vivacity of Josie but it seemed to Grace they were one coin with two sides, absolutely welded together though each side had a different pattern on it.

He put himself between them, offering an arm to each, quite happy to have them talk animatedly across him as he led them towards the entrance of the station.

"I'll see if I can find us a cab though with all these ambulances it might be tricky," he told them, standing them to one side of the concourse.

It was at that exact moment that the hospital train arrived on the next platform and at once there was a great clanging of opening doors and the eruption from them of nurses and orderlies and stretcher-bearers. Carefully and some not so carefully, since they were beyond being hurt again, they began to unload their cargo, hurrying them as fast as decency would allow through the totally silent and appalled crowds towards the waiting ambulances. Each stretcher had its bundle, a khaki-clad, unidentifiable bundle with rough dressings slapped to its wounds. They were all caked with the mud of France, with blood and other unidentifiable substances they had picked up on their journey from hell. Harassed nurses directed them, and though both Grace and Josie had seen it all, done it all, suffered it all before they could not help but hold their hands to their mouths as other passengers and travellers were doing. There was a sort of sighing, a sobbing, rippling through the station, come from a hundred mutilated bodies, and once a shrill scream as a stretcher-bearer lost hold of his end of the stretcher. Some men walked, their eyes bound, a line of stumbling soldiers in the same filthy state as those on the stretchers, a nurse leading, each man with his hand on the shoulder of the man in front.

For a moment there was a hitch and the line of stretcher-bearers halted, the stretcher immediately in front of Josie and Grace carrying what seemed to be an officer though he was just as filthy as any other soldier. He was caked with dried mud and blood and about his head and face was a stained bandage, completely covering it except for three holes, two for his eyes and another to allow him to breathe. He was conscious, breathing shallowly, deep in shock, the two nurses could see, and at once Grace dropped to her knees and put a hand to his which twitched on the rough blanket that covered him.

She didn't speak. Her hand held his, not gently, but with a firmness which told him someone was there, ready to comfort, to ease him, to help him endure. His fingers linked with hers, rigid with pain, then the stretcher-bearers moved on and his hand was pulled from her grasp.

"Where are you taking them?" she asked the orderly, her voice calm as though she had every right to question them. He muttered something and Josie drew her back, her own face pale, her vivacity gone, her rosiness drained.

"That's my hospital," she murmured, "perhaps I should . . ."

"You're getting married tomorrow. Philip is waiting." Grace's voice was harsh though she had not meant it to be.

The man on the stretcher was Rupert Bradley.

16

The wedding was one among the dozens of others that were taking place that day. Hurried, chaotic some of them, with dozens of excited guests throwing confetti and screaming good wishes, but for the few minutes it took Josie and Philip to become man and wife, with Grace a step behind next to the porter who had agreed to stand in as the second witness, they were wrapped around in a gentle circle of love and peace and quiet. The door had been closed on the previous couple and the next waited in the hall of the registry office. They made their vows, if their answers could be called that when not in a church, as if they were, and even the registrar seemed to be impressed by their stillness, their totally committed devotion which contrasted sharply with the near hysteria of many. Men were going in their thousands to the front and before they went they wanted to perform as men, males, to assert their virility, perhaps leave behind a part of themselves in an impregnated wife. But Grace's dear friend and the quiet man who was now her husband were dedicating their lives to one another knowing that those lives might be for ever or no more than a few days. After the ceremony she stepped into his arms as though she belonged there, which she did. Either of them might be killed next week or the week after and they understood this but they meant to condense weeks into moments, years into days if that was all they had. The absolute joy on their faces was almost unearthly. When Josie turned away from him she handed the small posy of forget-me-nots, the blue chosen to match her outfit, to Grace.

They were to go to Cornwall for three days and on the fourth Philip was to return to France and Josie to the hospital.

"They'd dismiss me if they knew I was married, Gracie, you know that."

"Well, I shan't tell them, but what about your mother? Do you think it fair to keep her in the dark?"

"I suppose not but she might do something, I don't know what, have me dragged back home. I . . . I've applied to go to France."

Grace turned to look at Philip who sat quietly, his eyes locked on his wife as though he were taking a picture of her, one that he meant to store in his mind to take out and look at when they were apart.

"Philip?" Grace questioned with amazement.

"I can't stop her, Grace, and I don't think I want to, if I could. She is a woman, a person, and if she makes no fuss about me going to war, why should I try to stop her?"

"But you're a soldier, Philip."

"And so am I, Grace," Josie interposed. "A soldier fighting for men's lives. Besides, we want to be as near to one another as we can. We will get leave together, even if it's only an hour here and there and if—"

"Shut up, my darling," Philip said, quietly. "You know what we agreed." He took her hand and turned the brand-new wedding ring on her finger. She would have to wear it on a ribbon round her neck as soon as he had gone but for now it rested between them, on her finger and under his.

The three of them were lunching at a small restaurant round the corner from the registry office, drinking champagne and eating the first of the grouse which was advertised as straight off the train from the north, the first of the season. She and Grace had spent the night at a private hotel off the Strand, with Philip in another room further up the hallway. Grace would have liked to tell them she would take the single room and they could have the double, since it was apparent to anyone with eyes in their head that not only did they long to be together but that they *had* already, probably the night before. Something had stopped her, though she would dearly have liked to have been on her own after the shock of seeing Rupert. It seemed to her that Josie, in this strange and unconventional wedding – Josie was not even of age – wished to have the traditional custom of seeing her groom for the first time at the altar, so to speak, and though everything inside her screamed to be alone to make some sense of what she had seen at the station and what she was to do about it, she managed to chat and gossip and laugh with Josie and Philip until the very moment Josie and her husband boarded the Cornish Riviera Express. She even waved as the train drew out of the station.

Without thinking, her mind telling her exactly where she must go, she found a cab and directed the driver to the London hospital where Josie was a nurse.

The hospital, which had been so overwhelmed yesterday with its avalanche of wounded come straight from the front lines of France, was calmer today, full to capacity, so that she was not even sure he would still be here. He might have been sent on to somewhere else but in her capacity as a nurse, or at least as a probationer nurse with six months' experience, she had felt that his head wound would not allow him to be moved again for a while.

The corridors were empty except for nurses and orderlies hurrying here and there on urgent business of their own with no time to spare for visitors. Though it was August it was a cool day with a small breeze coming from a window that opened on to a playing field. Boys were playing football and their voices, filled with the youth and vigour which had once been the right of those now occupying the beds in the wards off the corridor, floated on the air. There was the usual smell of lysol and the underlying pervasiveness of something which only those of the medical profession would recognise. Many of the men brought in yesterday had, even before they left France, the taint of gangrene on them.

There was a desk at which a nurse pored over a long list. She was only young, probably inexperienced in the ways of hospitals and their visitors, and when Grace enquired firmly the whereabouts of Captain Rupert Bradley, she consulted a list.

"I'm his sister, come from Liverpool," Grace added calmly, anticipating suspicion, but the nurse told her where she might find Captain Bradley though it was not really visiting time, she added.

"I'll wait," Grace told her, prepared to sit down on a chair by a table on which a bowl of roses stood. She wondered who had brought them in. She bent her head to smell a bud and the young nurse smiled sadly.

"Aren't they lovely," she said. "They were brought in for a boy who died. His mother . . ."

The clock ticked on the wall and the nurse was relieved by another and while they stood consulting over the list on the desk, Grace slipped quietly away and up the stairs to the ward in which she had been told Captain Bradley lay.

A nurse hovered in the doorway of the dreadfully quiet ward, bristling and officious, ready to do battle with any visitor who might have the temerity to approach a bed without her permission.

"Yes," she said. "Can I help you?" Her attitude saying Grace had no rights to be here at all.

"I am Captain Bradley's sister. I have come from Liverpool to—"

"It's about time someone turned up, poor soul," the nurse sniffed disapprovingly. "His wife was informed yesterday but . . . anyway, he's there, in the end bed. Please don't disturb him if he's asleep."

"Might I ask . . . the extent of his injuries, Sister?" Grace could feel her heart racing, thudding out of control in her breast and she could barely speak she was so frightened. Was he blind? But then they would hardly have cut eye holes in his bandage. Burned horribly perhaps or . . . Dear God, let her keep control of her senses, let her not faint, or scream; as if she would but the dreadful injuries she had herself seen had not been inflicted on a man she loved. She was fond of Charlie, of course, but . . . Her mind was wandering and as she approached the bed where Rupert lay, accompanied by the nurse, the woman's voice in her ear barely registered. She heard the word shell and cheekbone and eye and mouth and surgery then she was there beside him and his eyes, deep holes in which shock and horror and fear were reflected, looked into hers. He didn't recognise her.

"The doctor doesn't think he's lost his sight, at least not in both eyes," the nurse was saying with the appalling lack of tact that some displayed, just as though the man in the bed were not only blind but deaf and half-witted to boot. "The shell apparently exploded right in his face and—"

"Thank you, Sister." Grace cut her off sharply and sat down in the chair beside the bed, turning to give the woman a resolute glance which stated that they wished to be alone, and reluctantly the Sister returned to her desk.

There was a vase on the bedside table and, filling it with water from a jug that stood there, she put Josie's posy of forget-me-nots in it, then reached out a hand and took his between hers and he let her. His was still ingrained with dirt, the nails broken and blackened. Raising it to her lips she kissed it, rubbing her lips tenderly against his flesh, and her love, the love that had become part of her between one breath and the next years ago and which still flourished, flowed from her to him and she saw something move in his blank, stony eyes.

"Jess . . . ?" he quavered, slashing her heart to its core. His voice had a hopeful quality and yet it wavered weakly, controlled by the morphine that had been pumped into him.

"I'm here, darling," she answered tenderly and incredibly she saw the rigidity go out of his body and he relaxed. She placed the back of his hand against her cheek, then turned it over and placed her mouth in the palm and something beneath the bandage moved as though he had smiled a little. He sighed deeply and the eyes which stared somewhere into the high ceiling closed and he slept.

She would have stayed there for the rest of the day, the night, for as long as they let her, for she knew her presence was a comfort to him even if he did think it was his wife. He needed her . . . someone. Where were his parents, his sisters, his brother? Where, in fact, was his wife who had been informed yesterday that her husband had been wounded and was in this hospital? She was glad in her heart, though she knew it was not right, that no one was here, for it gave her this time with him that she might never share again. Soon, from wherever she was, his wife would come; perhaps she was away somewhere; but then . . . And she would have let his parents know, wouldn't she, this Jess that Rupert had waited for but until they came she would stay with him as long as they would let her. She had three more days' leave. She would ask at the hotel if they had a room and she would remain in London, hang about the bloody hospital. She wondered where Josie's room was; perhaps she could find out and sleep there if Josie had not shared it with anyone, but just at this moment all she wanted was to sit beside her love, hold his hand which still gripped hers even in sleep, and, as Major Crisp often said in his pleasant cultured voice, "Sod the lot of them."

She was so still, the nurses, who moved quietly in and out of the ward, leaning over motionless, silent men, over men who whispered in pain and one who woke up and cried for his mother, seemed to forget her until, with a rustle of quiet voices and the soft tap of quiet feet, a doctor arrived, his face set and tired, his eyes sunk in his gaunt face as though sleep was something he knew little of.

She stood up as he approached Rupert's bed.

"Sister?" he enquired of the nurse, not looking at all pleased, for like the Sister he was of the opinion that visiting time must be strictly adhered to otherwise there would be no order, order that was needed in the caring for wounded men.

"The patient's sister, Doctor. Come from Liverpool."

"Really, does she know that this is not visiting time and that" – he quickly consulted his notes – "that Captain Bradley is very far from well."

"He is sleeping, Doctor," Grace said quietly. "He wasn't when I came in. Surely that is good for him?"

"Miss Bradley . . ." He wasn't quite sure how to answer this question. He was stretched to the limit, worn to the bone, and next week he was to go with a medical unit to France, but this composed young woman was right.

"I would be glad to be told the truth about . . . about my brother, Doctor. I am a nurse."

"Are you indeed, then you will know the importance of regular visiting hours."

"I know they are of benefit to the staff though I'm not sure about the patients, but that is not the issue here. I have come a long way to see . . . my brother and before I return to my duties in Liverpool—"

"Whereabouts is that, Miss Bradley?"

"Liverpool?"

"No, of course not. Where do you nurse?"

She supposed there was no harm in telling him, since she was not breaking the law. She would probably never see Rupert again once his wife came to claim him, and his parents, but until then she needed badly to know how, or if, he was to recover.

"Old Nook Hall near Childwall. It has been turned into a hospital for wounded officers."

"Hmm, I can't say I have heard of it. How long have you been there?"

"Six months. I am a VAD."

"Ah . . ."

"But I am still able to understand if . . ."

The doctor relented, since he really did not have time to stand here talking to the very pretty young woman who was the patient's sister. He had heard that the man's wife had still not turned up!

"Very well. I had a good look at the patient's wounds this morning and they are pretty nasty."

"Gangrene?"

"No, which is a bit of luck. He will need extensive surgery: plastic surgery, you understand."

"His sight?"

He was pleasantly surprised by the young woman's calmness, her unflustered questions and the way she received his answers with no fuss or gasps of shock or gales of tears.

"We don't know. The blast, you see . . . It's early days, Miss Bradley."

"Yes, thank you, Doctor."

"And now I think you must go, my dear."

"May I return?"

He looked at his patient who appeared to be sleeping peacefully, a natural sleep which eluded many of the others who were twitching and sighing and murmuring in their pain.

"Yes, you seem to have . . . ask the Sister. She is in charge of the ward."

He turned away dismissively, bending over Rupert and though she longed to stay and hear what he had to say she knew she had been lucky to have had so much of his time and, more to the point, been given the opportunity to come again.

She was determined to see him again even for just a moment. She had wandered about London all afternoon, mingling with the crowds of soldiers and their girls who hung on their arms and promised all sorts of things with their eyes. They were going to have a bloody good time or die in the attempt, those who were on leave from the trenches were saying, to make the most of these few frenetic days that might be their last and Grace did not blame them. If she had Rupert here with her she would do the same, offer the same, share the same loving, if it could be called that, if it was all she was to have of him. Couples were pouring out of the Alhambra Theatre where they had watched a performance of *The Bing Boys* starring George Robey and Violet Lorraine and she was swept along with them. Many of the young soldiers, most of them barely more than boys, stared at her with admiring delight, asking her where she was off to and wouldn't she like to share it with them, but inevitably she found herself outside the hospital where, since it appeared to be visiting time, many motor cars were parked, for this, like Old Nook, was a hospital for officers, and officers' families travelled, for the most part, in style.

One even had a chauffeur standing to attention beside the gleaming bonnet.

She was not questioned as she walked past the nurse and porter who seemed to be manning the desk. There were other visitors, mothers and wives looking anxious, some ready to weep, others with the grim faces of those who knew their loved ones were in desperate straits, and she moved along with them, up the stairs and along the corridor towards the ward where Rupert lay. Though the hospital was crammed with casualties there were not as many visitors as might have been expected. Most of the men were from different parts of the country: Scotland, the north of England, even Ireland, and there would have been many difficulties for their families to travel this far. Large numbers of the men were to be moved on to other hospitals, for the London hospitals were in the front line, so to speak, clearing-stations almost, where men were assessed and then transferred to others. Some might even end up at Old Nook Hall or at the Huntroyde in Padiham. Still, the ward seemed crowded but not too crowded for her to make out the fuss that was taking place at the far end of the ward where Rupert lay.

"I demand to see the doctor at once," a voice was saying, "and I shall not move from this spot until he is brought here."

The voice belonged to a beautiful young woman, a fashionably dressed young woman who was just about to fit a cigarette in a cigarette holder and place herself on the chair next to Rupert's bed. Rupert's hands were shaking, plucking at each other on the turned-back sheet that crossed his chest and his head moved from side to side and Grace knew he was seriously disturbed.

"Mrs Bradley, the doctor who is in charge of your husband has just gone off duty and—"

"Then fetch another. I must have the full facts about my husband's injuries before I decide what to do with him."

It was as though she were talking of a piece of furniture that was littering up her drawing-room and must be disposed of. She produced a cigarette lighter from her dainty handbag and had not the Sister intervened, Grace, still hovering hesitantly in the doorway to the annoyance of those who wished to enter, would have marched down the ward and snatched it out of her hand.

The Sister was imperious in her annoyance. "You cannot smoke in here, Mrs Bradley."

"Oh, and who is to stop me?"

"I am, madam. There are men in here who have been gassed and whose lungs are . . ."

Jessica Bradley sighed dramatically and her eyes wandered with distaste about the ward but she returned her cigarette case and lighter to her handbag, before her eyes fell on the forget-me-nots in the vase.

"And who, may I ask, brought those flowers in to my husband?" There was a defensive note in her voice since it was noticeable she had brought him none.

"I believe it was his sister, Mrs Bradley."

"*His sister!* Which sister? One is in France driving an ambulance and the other two are not aware that my husband has been wounded." Her voice became suspicious and she glared about her as though suspecting some intrigue that she did not care for.

"I'm sure I don't know, madam." The Sister's voice was cold.

"Well, I might say I think it highly irregular that someone has been in here pretending to be a relative and bothering my husband when he least needs it."

"Indeed, Mrs Bradley, but whoever she was she seemed to calm your husband. I'll try to find out for you."

"I think you better had. Anyway," she challenged, "are you to fetch the doctor or must I speak to whoever is in charge? My husband needs to be moved to a hospital where he will receive" – she waved a careless hand – "the nursing he needs," as though to say it was plain he was not getting it here. "Somewhere in the country, perhaps. Anyway, please tell the doctor I am waiting."

Not once did she glance at the restless figure in the bed. It was as though she could not quite bring herself to turn to him, to speak to him, since he was, to all intents and purposes, a bandaged parcel whose wits would not enable it to answer her if she did. Her dainty high-heeled shoe, one made surely for dancing in, tapped restlessly against the leg of the bed and Grace saw Rupert wince each time it did so. Dear God, wife or no wife she could stand this no longer. She wished she wore her uniform which would give her the authority, not much, but some, to ask Rupert's wife to leave the ward, for she was disturbing her patient but she had underestimated the Sister in charge.

"Mrs Bradley, I'm afraid I must ask you to wait in my office where the doctor will be in to see you as soon as possible. Captain Bradley is . . . restless, you must see that and your presence is not helping. Please follow me."

Jessica Bradley turned for the first time and stared with what seemed to be perplexed curiosity at the wounded man in the bed. Her look seemed to say she was not awfully sure it *was* Rupert. How could she tell when he was swathed in bandages? And his hands were so dirty she hardly liked to touch them.

"Well, goodbye, darling," Grace heard her say. "I'll be in to see you presently." Then with a wave of her hand and a clipped tap of her high-heeled shoes she followed the Sister from the ward, pressing close to Grace, leaving a wave of expensive French perfume in her wake.

At once Grace sped up the ward and, careless of the watching visitors, since the men themselves showed no interest in anything, she knelt at Rupert's bedside. She took the twitching hands between hers and folded them gently in her loving grasp, lifting each one in turn to her lips. Again, as earlier in the day, she spilled out the endless current of her love, pulsing it through her hands into his and again she could feel the difference in him. His pathetic hands became still between hers. She didn't give a damn who watched her. She didn't really think they cared. They were too absorbed with their own agony to bother about hers. What the woman on her knees was doing, or who she even was, they neither knew nor cared. She dared not stay long, for his wife might return to argue over him with the doctor and when she did, if she did, then Grace wanted Rupert to be asleep, to be unaware that she stood there, debating over him with the doctor as to where he was to go that would, presumably, be convenient for *her*. She, Grace, couldn't come again, and so for those few moments she tried to instill into Rupert the peace, the calm, the steady assurance of the love she bore him.

He slowly, agonisingly turned his head and looked at her.

"Don't move, my darling," she whispered. "I'm here. I'll always be here. Wherever you go, I'll be there. Remember."

"Who . . ." the word was barely discernible, merely a breath on her cheek as she rested it for a moment on the pillow next to his.

"I love you, Rupert, remember that. I love you."

For a second his hands clung to hers, surprisingly strong, then as the familiar self-opinionated voice came floating up the corridor as his wife approached with the doctor, Grace kissed them, stood up and moved towards the door, passing Rupert's wife as she did so. The woman did not even notice her.

"Well, would you believe it, he seems to be sleeping," Grace heard her say to the doctor, as though her presence had brought it about, then she sped, her eyes clouded with tears, along the corridor and down the stairs.

17

"Yer could do a lot worse than marry that young chap, our Gracie. 'E thinks t'world o' yer, anyone can see tha' an' now 'e's off back ter't war, poor lad, it'd give 'im summat ter 'old on to, like. An' wi' that leg of 'is, an' all. It don't seem right ter send a chap off ter war wi' a bad leg. Nay, I know it's reckoned ter be mended but yer can't deny 'e's gorra limp."

Nora shook her head in disbelief and leaned even more heavily on the dough she was kneading. It was said, though how true it was nobody knew, that one out of every four British merchant ships that sailed the seas was sunk by German submarines and food shortages were beginning to pinch. It was generally acknowledged that the problem regarding goods was not the shortage of money but the shortage of ships in which to carry them from abroad and the inability of the shipyards to fill the shipping gaps left by the German submarine attacks. The likes of Nora and the housewives who had to make do with what was available were told to "Eat less bread and Victory is Secure" which made no sense, at least to Nora. They were told that women were doing nobly in the war but they must do still more, for the "kitchen is the key to victory and is in the fighting line alongside our undying heroes of the trenches and our brave men at sea". Nora raised her eyes to the ceiling when she was told that, letting them know what she thought of that daft statement, for how could her economies compare with what their Robert and George and Richard had to put up with! Anyroad, it seemed sacrifice was the watchword, with campaigns to save food and promote food economy. There was no rationing as yet but if it should come Nora would cope with it as she had coped with everything in her life from the death of her soldier sweetheart to the tragedies that had struck at these folk who were the only family she knew. The war was dragging civilians into its barbarous grasp whether they liked it or not. The attacks by Zeppelin which had killed and wounded over a thousand innocent men, women and children were absolutely criminal and it was no wonder, in Nora's opinion, that any person with a name that sounded the least bit German was treated to jeers and threats and sometimes worse. Even "sausage" dogs which were known to come from Germany were kicked in the street though Nora did not approve of that, for the poor animal had nowt to do with it, did it?

London and the south and east coasts were the worst hit by the Zeppelin air-raids but for protection lighting restrictions had been imposed throughout the country, causing great inconvenience and heightening popular hysteria. The disaster of the Gallipoli campaign, begun with a naval operation in February and ended with the ignominious withdrawal from Suvla Bay and Anzac Beach begun on 18th December and ended in January 1916 with the estimated number of Allied casualties at 252,000, was a severe blow and some, those who had survived it, believed the casualties to be considerably higher. One of them was Captain Rupert Bradley.

Grace was ironing her capacious white apron in readiness for duty the next day. Nora, though she had Edna to do the heavy cleaning, now did all the cooking. Ma, despite the fact that she was improving slowly after the death of Tom, could not settle properly, she told the others, until he was returned to her for a "decent" burial in the churchyard nearby. She knew, of course, that soldiers buried near the battlefield where they had died were committed to the ground with full military honours, rifles fired over their graves, bugles sounding and so on, but it would be a great comfort to her to be able to go whenever she wanted to put flowers on his grave. She brooded over it, spending many hours on her knees in the small gardens she had made for Arthur and Tom and when she was not there she joined the other mothers of dead and wounded sons at the church, working over any small item that might make the lives of those who were still in the trenches a bit more comfortable, among them her own son. They sent what were known as chocolate tins, which contained slabs of chocolate in a flat tin that just fitted in the breast pocket of a soldier's tunic. Princess Mary, daughter of their King, had started the custom and Rowntrees followed her with a special tin on which was painted a portrait of the King. Barker and Dobson, the toffee firm, had a special tin of Tipperary Toffee made up just for the lads in the trenches. The ladies of the Liverpool Presbyterian Church parcelled up Oxo cubes, khaki handkerchiefs, peppermint drops, Camp cocoa, and pipe tobacco and over Christmas had included plum puddings and turkeys, though how they were to cook them was a mystery. Ma was concerned with the welfare of the troops, knitting balaclavas, socks, scarves and mittens, for it was cold in Liverpool so what would it be like in those dratted trenches, she begged them to tell her. They sent parcels containing cakes and writing paper and something called Parasitox which helped with the bodily vermin, as Ma delicately called it, for Robert had complained of them. It gave her a great deal of comfort to know that she was doing her best to make the life of her soldier son that bit easier.

Richard had finished his training at the Flying School at Hendon and had been accepted into the Royal Flying Corps. He was now in France, one of the dashing young men who went out each day in their flimsy "flying machines" as those at home still called them, to observe the position of German troops and guns, indeed any movement of the enemy and to ascertain the position of their own troops. He wrote cheerful letters of landing in fields up and down the line, of French farmers staring in amazement as his machine set down in their fields before offering him hot coffee and bread and butter which he found most welcome. That cheered Ma up no end to think that her son was being shown hospitality by the people of the country he was defending! He would be glad of a silk vest and a cellular vest, he wrote, which he wore under his woollen vest and on top of that a silk shirt and his regular army shirt. The pullovers Ma had sent were ideal to go under his flying suit and the balaclava was a godsend and if she could knit one for "Chalky", Flying Officer

Charles White who was his pal, Chalky would be eternally grateful. Ma got out her knitting needles and began at once and the balaclava helmet was sent off within two days to keep warm the ears of the friend of her son's who, poor lad, apparently had no one to knit for him. Indeed she and Nora were never without a piece of knitting in their hands, making a balaclava for every flyer in Richard's squadron.

George was non-committal in his regular weekly letters except to say that he had been promoted, though he did not mention to what, and hoped to have leave soon.

"He never did have much to say for himself," Ma said placidly. George wasn't under fire like Robert, or so she believed, and her imagination had him almost on a cruise, sailing up and down the high seas, defending the shores of his country, and not for a moment, since she did not know of its strength, considered the might of the German Navy. Everyone knew that Britain ruled the seas!

When Grace was on night duty, after having slept for five or six hours in the morning, she would go down to town and look over the ledgers and accounts of the shop with Mr Hynes. Pa was there more often than not, since it was now considered possible to leave Ma with Nora, or with Mrs Allen who accompanied her to the church. With her daughter in France Mrs Allen believed herself to be the mother of a soldier, for what else was Josie when she was nursing those who were wounded in the line. She was accepted as such and knitted and sewed and rolled bandages with the rest of them.

Grace was surprised and delighted to find that in the past six months profits from sales in the tobacconist's had almost doubled but Mr Hynes was quick to explain.

"It's this advertisement, Miss Grace," he told her, though with a certain regret in his voice, producing a newspaper dated just before Christmas. The advertisement began:

Xmas is near. What shall I send him?
CIGARETTES DIRECT FROM FACTORY TO
SOLDIERS AT
THE FRONT BY POST.
A Christmas card will be enclosed with each parcel.

It then went on to list what could be ordered and despatched: "Wills' Wild Woodbine 3/3 for 280, Wills' Gold Flake 5/- for 280, Players Navy Cut 8/6 for 500," and so on, informing the public that orders may be handed to any tobacconist or posted direct to the factory.

"We're mekkin' a lorra money on this, Miss Grace, and though these items are needed by our lads," speaking in the slightly pedantic way he had, "it don't seem right ter be . . ."

"Profiteering, Mr Hynes."

"Aye, lass. That's warrit seems like."

Grace sighed. "I know, Mr Hynes, there are a lot of men making money out of this war but the soldiers smoke. It is a comfort to them. We *are* a tobacconist and we're selling the cigarettes at the proper prices."

"It's a dreadful thing, Miss Grace. A dreadful thing. A terrible time. Here's you what were brought up a lady, so to speak, nursin' men from't trenches an' seein' sights what no lady should see and then that there friend o' yours in France bein' shelled an' shot at an' . . . eeh, I'm right sorry, Miss Grace. I shouldn't o' said that but I don't know what the world's comin' to, really I don't. An' now Mr Davenport tells me only this mornin' 'is lad's bein' sent back ter't trenches as if 'e 'adn't done 'is bit already. I seen them young chaps in their twenties 'angin' about the town, smokin' an' enjoying theirselves instead o' doin' their bit like what Lieutenant Davenport done an' I'm glad conscription's bin' brought in, I am that. Single men wi'out responsibilities should be glad ter go an' I only wish I could."

"Mr Hynes, you musn't think like that. You have a family who depend on you and what Pa and I would do without you, I don't know. And if I'm not mistaken it won't be long before young Archie's off to enlist."

Now Grace lifted the flat iron from the stove where it had been kept hot and put the cooling one in its place. She often looked back on the Grace who had existed before the war, before Arthur died. That Grace hadn't known one end of a flat iron from another and ask her even to do the simplest thing like boil an egg and she would have been helpless. Ma was queen of the kitchen in those happier times, she did all the cooking and was glad to, for that was the job of a wife and mother. Then, Nora had done the shopping for the household and, with Ma, planned their meals. Nora did the laundry and the ironing while Edna tackled every dirty or heavy job that was needed. Between them they had kept the house running on oiled wheels with no need for Grace to bother with even making a bit of toast. The boys were not asked to iron their own shirts, were they, and so the seven children of the family had grown up like the children of the middle classes, not exactly pampered and spoiled but not expected to do a hand's turn in the day-to-day running of the house.

Now, thanks to her training as a nurse, and her mother's frailness which had forced Grace to fend for herself, she was capable of tackling many tasks about the house which her mother, once, would have been horrified to see her do. She could cook a simple meal, breakfast mainly, for when she was on night duty she resolved that she would not disturb Nora who needed her rest. And she had learned the art of ironing since she needed a clean apron every day. There was a laundry at the hall but that was concerned mainly with bedding and the patients' clothing.

She ran the iron smoothly up and down the apron front, leaning on it heavily, for it was an arduous task. Care had to be taken when using the flat iron because its intense heat could scorch the fabric and then woe betide her, for Matron was a tartar on appearances. She had tried to interest Nora in a box iron which was much cleaner than the old-fashioned flat iron since it was hollow and was heated by a red-hot metal "slug" from the fire which was inserted into the body of the iron. There was even an iron run on gas but Nora couldn't abide new-fangled things and what was wrong with what they had managed with for donkey's years, answer her that.

Nora gave the dough an extra thump. "Did yer 'ear what I said, lass?" she went on. She placed the bread to rise under its cloth, then, after pouring herself a cup of tea, sat down in the chair before the kitchen fire, scratching Wally behind the ear so that the sound of his purring filled the room. He had jumped gracefully on to her lap as she lowered herself into the chair and at her feet Topsy panted in the heat from the fire.

"Yes, I heard and I do know Charlie's feelings for me. He wants us to get married but I'm not ready for marriage."

In a strange way she knew she was lying. She perhaps wasn't quite ready to settle down yet but she was of an age when the thought of marriage to some decent, kind man – since Rupert was now far beyond her reach – was becoming increasingly desirable. She wanted the war over first, of course, then, with someone of whom she could be fond, even loving, she wanted a home of her own, a husband and, most of all, children. And didn't Charlie seem the most obvious choice? She was extremely fond of him. He made her laugh, he was kind, gentle, thoughtful and the thought of his embraces, some of which she had not managed to avoid, was not repugnant to her. He had a good future in the bank where his father was manager, not that that came into the equation, but it must be considered. As Nora said, she could do a lot worse than marry Charlie.

"An' besides, yer don't love 'im, do yer?" the quiet voice from the chair said.

Grace looked up, then lifted the iron hastily from the apron before it scorched the cotton. Her face was flushed, whether from her labour or from Nora's remark was not clear, then she went on with her job, her face suddenly saddened.

"No, I don't, though I'm very, very fond of him. I'm afraid for him, as I'm afraid for my brothers but—"

"Yer don't love him like . . ."

Grace turned in surprise but Nora was staring placidly into the heart of the fire, her face innocent of all expression.

"Like who?"

"Nay, it's not fer me ter say."

"To say what, for goodness sake?"

"I know wharr I know, an' I'm sayin' no more." Nora took a deep, satisfying sip of her tea. They were alone in the house. John was at school, Edna gone for the day, Pa at the shop and Ma had taken the tram with Mrs Allen to the church where a lady from the Royal Alexandra Nursing Corps was to give a talk – discreetly edited, for it did no good to frighten the wives and mothers of men at the front – on the efficacy of a nourishing diet for the invalid. Presumably those who were recovering at home from their wounds.

Grace spoke irritably. "I do wish you wouldn't make these cryptic and vastly annoying remarks, Nora. I have no idea what you're talking about. Now, I shall finish this bit of ironing and then I'm off to the shop for an hour."

"Rightio, lamb," Nora answered equably, having no idea what "cryptic" meant and barely before Grace left the kitchen Nora's spluttering snores wafted gently on the air.

At the last minute she decided that she didn't really feel like spending her precious and infrequent hours off hanging over a lengthy row of figures at the shop, besides which, with Pa slowly recovering his spirit and with Mr Hynes his usual efficient self, there was really no need for her to be there. When Arthur died there had been no one but herself to act as go-between for Pa and Mr Hynes. Then it had been necessary for her to take cheques for Pa to sign, to get to the bank to draw out cash for wages and the running of the household, to help Mr Hynes with the bookkeeping and a dozen other jobs that Pa had once done. Now there was no need and so, when the tram reached the corner of Lord Street and Whitechapel where she would normally alight for the shop, she jumped off as usual but continued on foot the length of Lord Street, past the splendid edifice of the Victoria Memorial, down James Street, passed the Dock Office, reaching the river and the glittering waters which heaved constantly with the passage of ships, turning south in the direction of Otterspool.

The soldier stood on Cressington Promenade which gave fine views over the River Mersey to the Wirral and North Wales. At the southernmost end of the promenade one came to the Garston Docks which were used for the importation of bananas, timber, chemicals and ores, and for the export of coal to Ireland. From here up to its northernmost point at the recently opened dock at Gladstone was a distance of sixteen miles and most of the docks from Gladstone to Garston were connected, giving miles of pleasant walking with the river to one side and the hundreds of warehouses and half-tide docks on the other, and along its entire length the bobbing heads and curtseying outlines of cranes. Even today, sixty or more years since the first steamships dirtied the sky with their smoke, square-rigged sailing vessels, tugs and flats and trawlers were still visible on the river and in the

docks against the skyline, gracefully silent but for the
snapping of their sails.

The soldier's eyes appeared to be fixed upon the
masts of the ships from which pennants of all colours
and countries flew. He leaned his elbows on the railing
that stood between him and the water, bending his
head to look down into the deep grey murk and
if anyone had cared to look they might have been
dismayed by the expression on his face. It was slack
with some remembered sadness and his eyes wore a
flatness that drained what might have been a rich
brown from them. He was tall and painfully thin
and the part of his face that was visible beneath the
peak of his officer's cap was not the colour of healthy
flesh. His shoulders moved beneath the fine khaki of
his jacket as if he shivered though the day was mild
and sunny. His belt and Sam Browne were polished to
a rich chestnut sheen, as were his boots. To denote that
he was a captain, there were three embroidered stars
on his tunic cuffs. He carried a short swagger-stick.

A ferryboat with the name *John Heron* painted on
her bow was fast approaching the landing stage further
up the river, the Princes Landing Stage, coming from
Seacombe and New Brighton, and the soldier watched
her, the ripples of her passage dragging a million stars
in her wake caused by the low March sunlight on
the water.

Seagulls wheeled overhead, screaming raucously,
their wings touched with gold, their beady black eyes
on the constant lookout for the scraps thrown over-
board from passing ships. The soldier glanced up at
them, shading his eyes from the sun which reached
under the peak of his cap. He breathed deeply, drawing

into his lungs the smells with which he had been familiar all his life. The fragrance of timber and the raw sting of the chemicals which were unloaded at Garston Dock and he thought he caught a pleasing whiff of bananas overlaid with the smell of oil from the nearby refineries. Tea, coffee, spices, exotic aromas come from exotic places and all converging here on this great port where, as a child, he had roamed with his brother Alan.

A dock "bobby" moved majestically along the promenade behind the soldier, doing his duty between St Nicholas Church and the Herculaneum Dock, making sure that there were no disturbances on his beat, his boots and buttons and helmet badge polished to perfection, the chain of his whistle gleaming in the afternoon sunshine. As he passed behind the officer he lifted his hand to his helmet in a salute.

"Mornin' sir," he said respectfully and was somewhat taken aback when the officer did not reply. He continued to lean against the railings and as the constable turned his head to glance at him he saw the soldier sigh and lean his forehead for a moment against his crossed arms.

The constable was uneasy. He knew that many soldiers came back from the front with strange, often incomprehensible mannerisms, incomprehensible that is to those at home, and he had heard that a friend of a neighbour of his had actually received a death certificate with her son's name on it, on which the cause of death had been "shot by sentence of FGGM for 'Desertion'" which had been an appalling shock for the lad's family. He didn't know whether to believe it himself, but if this chap leaning on the railings was thinking of throwing himself in the river, though God only knew why, he wasn't doing it on *his* beat.

He retraced his step. "You orlright, sir?" he asked politely.

The officer didn't turn his head as he answered. "Why shouldn't I be, Constable?"

"Well, I dunno . . ."

"Bugger off then, there's a good chap."

The constable was deeply offended. "There's no need ter talk like tha', sir, if yer please. I were only askin' . . ."

"Well, don't. Am I breaking the law?"

"No, sir, burrif yer don't mind—"

"I do mind so just sod off." The officer turned then and looked full into the constable's face and the constable gasped in horror; in fact he recoiled and the officer smiled.

"Will you go about your duties now, Constable, or have you not had a good enough look? I can come a little closer if you like."

The constable swallowed the bile which had risen in his throat and did his best to speak. It came out as a croak.

"Now look 'ere, sir, there's no call ter—"

"Be rude? Is that what you'd like to say?" He grinned and again the constable swallowed convulsively.

Grace saw the soldier and the constable in what appeared to be a sort of an altercation from some way off and though she had no idea what was happening or who was involved something made her quicken her step. The soldier had his arm raised and the constable, surprisingly enough, had the look of a man in mortal terror, backing away and yet at the same time doing his best to appear calm, as was his duty.

"Sir," she heard him say, "I don't want ter 'ave ter—"

"What, arrest me? Believe me, Constable, after what I have witnessed in the trenches a quiet cell sounds . . ."

Grace could feel the pounding of her heart beat like a drum in her chest, the vibrations pulsing through her body making her tremble, for though the soldier's back was to her as he appeared ready to knock the constable to the ground, she recognised his voice. The voice that had spoken to her in a thousand dreams, murmuring words that, out of those dreams, he would never speak, a voice that was as familiar to her as any member of her family. A voice she had loved for over five years, as she had loved the man.

Her voice, though she was shaking like a young sapling in a storm, was steady.

"Good morning, Rupert. I'm glad to see you up and about again. I heard you had been wounded but it seems you are recovered. Shall we walk along the promenade and let the constable get on with his job?" She managed to smile at the relieved constable who had not wanted to take the wounded officer into custody.

"Thanks, miss, I'll do tha'," he muttered, turning on his heel. For a moment he hesitated, for the officer seemed to be off his head, at least in his opinion and might not the young lady be in danger, but she smiled at him and with a gentle hand touched the soldier's arm.

"Rupert, won't you turn and shake my hand. After all, we're old friends."

The sun was suddenly obscured behind a thick stretch of white cloud in the shape of what might have been a stand of trees, and the promenade lost its brightness. It took the mildness from the day and Rupert shivered.

It seemed that he was reluctant to face her. She waited, her heart still lurching about in her breast so that she could feel her breath catching, then, slowly, he turned and when she looked into the wreck of his face, she knew the reason why.

18

It was as though some mischievous demon had drawn a line down the exact centre of Rupert's face, beginning somewhere under the peak of his cap, down his forehead, along the length of his straight nose, between his nostrils, bisecting his lips, and down to the cleft in his chin, dividing it into two parts. One half was as she had known it when last she saw him in the jeweller's with his wife, then about to become his fiancée. She did not count the occasion in the hospital since his head had been swathed in bandages. Pale and gaunt with illness, but beautiful as some men are beautiful, a strong, masculine beauty, with smoothly shaved cheek and chin, with a fiercely drawn eyebrow and eyelashes that were long and thick.

The other was like that of a gargoyle. A cruel freak of nature that was red and twisted, drawn into strange lumps and shallow valleys, pulled down beneath his lashless eye, up across where once had been an eyebrow, and into the shadow beneath his cap. It was raw, as a new scar is raw, shiny, hard-looking but healed. It finished at the strong, jutting curve of his chin leaving his neck above his military collar unblemished.

There was a pulse beating wildly in his throat and his clenched jaw quivered below his mouth which was clamped into a savage line as he waited, as he had so often waited, she supposed, to see the horrified expression widen her own eyes and crease her own face, first into lines of disgust, then of pity. But her gaze was centred, not on his dreadfully scarred face but on his eyes which were filled with hopeless anger, with pain and fear and the pitiable vulnerability of a man who has seen others flinch away from him. Who has watched *their* eyes look hurriedly over his shoulder, seen them glance at anything as long as it was not at him, whose mouths smiled and talked and uttered foolish remarks, for what can one say, face to face, to a hideous creature such as himself? All his life, from a handsome baby to a handsome man, he had been admired, sought after, not just for his amiability and wit and kindness but for his good looks. Now, not just women, but men turned away from him, not to be cruel, but for the simple reason they could not bear to look at him and therefore did not know how to address him.

But his eyes were still the same, a rich, chestnut brown, glowing, not with goodwill as once they had done, but with hatred and they glared at Grace as though she had offered him an insult, which he fully expected her to do, if not in words, then by an expression of repugnance on her face.

Her hand still rested on his arm but though she wanted, through sheer ignorance, a purely instinctive reaction that had nothing to do with her feelings, to drop it and take a step backwards, she did neither. Keeping her eyes on his, she smiled, a warm smile of welcome, then, another instinctive movement, one of natural simplicity, she stretched up and kissed him on his raw cheek.

He stood as still as a beast caught in a hostile clearing by the peril of the hunter but she felt the tremble run through him and she wanted to put her arms about him and draw his head down to her shoulder. To remove his cap and stroke his hair, to murmur of her love which had not faltered in five years and was not about to do so now. Instead she stepped back, still smiling, looking directly into his face, letting her eyes roam about it as she would have had he been the same Rupert she had known years ago.

"There," she said, "I think we have known one another long enough for a kiss, don't you?"

For the briefest moment she saw him relax and an expression of wonder, of relief, of thankfulness come into those eyes, then they hardened and his lip lifted in a sneer.

"Well, if it isn't the delicious Miss Tooley, and all grown up, I see. Very delectable." He allowed his eyes to run up and down her body in what was a most offensive way. He even took her hands in his, holding them out to the side as though to get a more thorough look at her and though it *did* offend her, or would have done had it been anyone but Rupert, she knew, for didn't she know every thought that was in this man's head, that it was no more than a defence, a pretence, a sham to hide the desolation that was in his soul. How did she know? She had met him perhaps half a dozen times over the past five years and then had barely been in his company long enough to be said to know him and yet she did. She could imagine as though it had happened to herself what he had suffered, not just the battle he had fought in the Dardanelles and which had caused the devastation to his face, but the surgery, the pain, the hope – hopeless as it turned out – the agonising changing and final removal of his bandages and the sight that met his eyes every day in the mirror.

She knew she must say something about his face. She could hardly ignore it, pretend it was nothing of consequence, act as though he were as she had last seen him and yet what to say that would not crucify him. Tear at what was the fragile link that allowed him to carry on with his life despite what he saw in other people's eyes when they looked at him.

"Shall we walk?" she said, and taking his arm turned him towards the long stretch of sand that was Jericho Shore. "And you can tell me all about it." And so surprised was he that he fell into step beside her, not speaking for the space of two or three minutes.

Abruptly he stopped and pulled away from her. His voice was bitter and cold and he slapped his leg fiercely with his swagger-stick. "Really, Miss Tooley, I can do without your condescension, or are we to call it pity, for I have had enough of that to last me a bloody lifetime." While he was speaking he looked straight ahead so that all she could see was the right side of his face. The beautiful side, and all the time the swagger-stick hit his leg like a lash.

"It is neither, Rupert. I suppose you might call it concerned interest. Or do you object to that? And might I be told why, after all these years, you have decided that I am Miss Tooley and not Grace? You used to call me that when—"

"When you were a child, Miss Tooley. Now that you are a woman grown, and a very lovely one, if you can take a compliment from a freak such as myself—"

"Dear Lord, are you always like this?"

"Like what, Miss Tooley?"

"Full of self-pity."

"Is that what it is? I had thought it was being realistic. I can hardly hope that those around me will not notice it."

"No, but surely a friend is allowed to ask how—"

"How I got this face, Miss Tooley? You want to hear every gruesome detail, do you, so that you can go home and tell your mother that you saw poor Rupert Bradley today with a face on him that would not only frighten the horses but would give little children nightmares. Tell her—"

Her voice was barely audible. "I would tell no one, least of all my mother who has lost two sons and is only now barely recovering. I have two more brothers at the front and another serving in the navy. Your injury can hardly be described as of vital interest to her, for believe me she would rather have both her dead sons back with her in your condition. Mothers are like that, you see. As are the many thousands of families who live in fear each day of that dreaded telegram. A face like yours would be welcome to the many soldiers I have nursed who have no arms, no legs, or sometimes no arms *or* legs."

He smiled sardonically as though none of this was of concern to him. "Well, well, Miss Tooley, I had no idea you were such a tigress in the defence—"

"And if you call me Miss Tooley once more I shall, as my brother Robert used to say, smash your teeth down your throat. Then how would you look? Not only with a face that, as you put it, would give children nightmares, but with a mouthful of broken teeth."

For the first time there was a gleam of genuine amusement in his eyes as he turned to look at her. He was watching her carefully, warily judging her reaction, just as though he would never believe that those who looked on his disfigurement would not be appalled by it, but her steady, direct gaze never wavered and her expression was tranquil.

"Tell me what happened to you, Rupert. I promise not to scream or faint. I heard your regiment had been sent to Gallipoli last year. I . . . I wanted to telephone your mother to ask after you and . . . I also heard that one of your sisters was driving an ambulance in France . . ."

"Where did you hear that?"

"I can't remember." Though of course she could. Out of the hard, red-lipped mouth of Rupert's wife on the day Grace had visited the hospital in London where he had lain wounded.

"But . . ."

"Does it matter? I wanted to. Anyway, I didn't. I didn't like to upset your mother. I remember she was so kind to me years ago, d'you remember when we all turned up on your doorstep, my brothers wrangling over who was to be first to inspect your motorcycle." She smiled up into his ruined face and saw his eyes change as the memory was reawakened. He returned her smile, this time, and though it was still a travesty of the one he had once had, it was natural, without bitterness. The unmarked side, though it was hollow-cheeked with the deep tracks framing his mouth that she had seen in Robert's young face, had a trace of humour in it and she rejoiced, for she thought for a wonderful moment that she had got through the hard carapace of his biting hatred, but it did not last.

"I'm afraid I can't recall," he said venomously, his intention to hurt. He swung away from her and began to stride along the firm sand avoiding the mud below the high-water mark and she was forced almost to run to keep up with him. He was deliberately doing his contemptuous best to leave her behind, to let her see that he really wanted nothing more to do with her or her happy memories of times before the war. She could have kicked herself for what she saw now as unfeeling on her part but it was not in her and never would be to give up, especially on this man, who, despite his dreadful disfigurement, she still loved.

"Rupert, for God's sake, can you not walk more slowly? Your legs are longer than mine and I want to—"

"I don't give a damn what you want, Grace Tooley, and if you would leave me alone I'd be mightily obliged. Can you not see I don't want your company? Jesus Christ, when will you women realise that I don't want your well-meaning sympathy. I don't need comforting, or cosseting, or any of the things women imagine a wounded man needs. I am recovered now. My wound is healed and yet I am fussed over as though I were a child with a fever. Leave me alone, damn you, and allow me to get on with my life, such as it is. I'm . . . sorry about your brothers but it's a bloody war after all."

His words floated back over his shoulder as he continued along the sands towards Jericho Cottage, his heels making deep impressions in the hard sand.

"All I want now is to get the doctors' report that they can do nothing else for me and then I can get back to where I belong."

"And where is that?" she shouted after him.

He whipped round then to face her, waiting until she caught up to him. "Where d'you bloody well think?" His voice was a snarl.

"Not . . ."

"Yes, back to the trenches with all the other poor sods where, with a bit of luck, I'll be finished off properly and my wife can . . ."

His face spasmed and in an almost boneless manner, like a young debutante making her curtsey to the Queen, he sank to the sand. He hugged his knees and bent his head until it rested on his arms, shuddering with some inner emotion, his shoulders heaving as he gasped for breath. Slowly, delicately, so as not to disturb his frail equilibrium, she sat down next to him. She picked up a pebble and turned it over in her hands, then, in the way her brothers had taught her, she threw it overarm towards the water where it landed with a faint plop, sinking out of sight. A seagull plunged to investigate what might have been something to eat, then swooped up into the pale grey air, squawking its displeasure.

Rupert, at the sound of the pebble hitting the water, lifted his head and seeing the widening ripples where it had landed, absently picked up another and chucked it, as she had done, like a cricketing fielder returning a ball to the bowler. Taking it in turns they continued for five minutes, then, standing up, searching about her, she found a flat stone and again, as her brothers had taught her, threw it so that it hit the water, jumped and skipped and eventually, after three strikes, sank from sight.

Without a word he did the same and when she sat down he crouched beside her, hugging his knees, his chin on his arms, his eyes on the far reaches of the river. They sat in silence for four or five minutes then, his voice soft, almost dreaming, as though he were back in a time of sad memories, he began.

"We landed on 25th April at Cape Helles and of the fifteen hundred troops put ashore on that first assault the Turkish machine-gunners on the cliffs mowed down twelve hundred of us. The Australians and the New Zealanders did the same at Gaba Tepe. We were supposed to link up on the high ground overlooking the Narrows but the Australian and New Zealand assault landed at the wrong place. Strong currents had carried them . . . well, they were trapped on the craggy headland of Ari Burnu."

He spoke these names as easily as he might have said Liverpool or Manchester since they were just as familiar to him; as though she herself must know them. She let him go on.

"It was all a bloody shambles. Weeks and weeks, months. I won't bore you with the details, for that was what we suffered more than anything, boredom. There were other things, of course: fifty thousand of us lost our lives, inefficiency, disorder, disease, fruitless assaults, inadequate maps, stores and ammunition lost. I had left by then – wounded – but hundreds of men simply froze to death . . . froze to bloody death."

"And you?"

"It was a flare that did for me. One of our own. The bloody thing simply went the wrong way. Oh, I don't blame the lad who . . . who let it get out of control. Half the time we didn't know what the hell we were doing." He paused and stared into the past. "Anyway, it caught me; you can see the results. I was put on a hospital ship but instead of being taken to Egypt which was a damn sight nearer I was sent – another mistake in a long line – back to Blighty. It didn't do me any good, the delay, but there was no gangrene."

"I know, the doctor—" Suddenly aware that she had said too much she bit her lip and pretended an interest in a bit of seaweed at her feet.

His head snapped round and she felt his eyes on her.

"You know . . . how do you know?"

"I was told."

"Told, by whom?"

"I am a nurse, you know, and . . . and my friend Josie Allen nursed at the hospital."

He seemed to lose interest and she searched about in her mind for something to say that would persuade him to continue with his story. She knew, for had she not nursed them, that soldiers who allowed their suffering, their appalling experiences to fester inside them were susceptible to terrible nightmares from which they woke screaming into the high ceilings of the wards. If they could speak of them, just a murmur into the ear of a nurse, a doctor, a professional someone as distinct from a family member, it acted as a catharsis, like lancing a boil. It drained away the badness which was followed by healing. She had a feeling this was the first time Rupert had spoken of his ordeal. She would not have expected him to unburden himself to his wife but surely, the comfort of female arms about him, the intimacy of husband and wife should have healed him, even in a small way. And yet he was filled with fire and fury, with a biting hatred, a resentment which, it seemed to her, was eating him alive. She could feel it throbbing inside him, a small volcano waiting to erupt and she longed with all her loving, loyal heart, which had never once turned aside from its passionate devotion towards him, simply to draw him into her arms and spread her love about him.

For want of something to say that would not upset him she asked after the woman who had been making such a fuss in the ward when he had first been brought in wounded.

"Your wife is at home with you?" For was it not the most natural thing to assume that a wife would be with her husband in his adversity?

With a violence that astounded her, even in his present state, he stood up and flung himself this way and that as though he were doing his best to escape some terror that pursued him.

Then he stopped and smiled, not a nice smile. A smile in which so much emotion was mixed it was difficult to decipher.

"My wife? *My wife!* What wife is that, Miss Tooley? Certainly not the woman I married just before the war, or is she? That is the paradox. I thought her then to be the most enchanting creature I had ever known but it seems I was wrong. I cannot count the number of lovers she has had since our marriage; more than a few I was reliably though reluctantly told by a friend. I somehow – I don't know why – had suspicions. I had to drag it out of him. The whole regiment knew, apparently, but like the blind fool I was I did not believe it until . . . until this happened. She was always ready to climb into bed with me whenever I got leave and apparently with half the officers in every regiment. She had two abortions, I was told, though whether the child, children were mine . . . I couldn't say and neither could she, I suppose. Do you know she actually screamed when she first saw me without bandages and ran from the ward. That was a day, I can tell you. Visitors gaping at her, and then at me, with her voice echoing down the corridor telling the world that if 'that monster expected to be seen about London with her on its arm it was sadly mistaken'. That monster was, of course, myself."

"Rupert, don't." She had sprung to her feet when he did and now she attempted to put her hand on his arm but he shook it off as though it were a cobra about to sink its fangs into his flesh.

"She . . . she destroyed me, and yet . . . when I was bandaged . . . in the first days, she was there, holding my hand; she called me darling and told me she loved me, would always love me . . . be with me. It got me through, I believe, so I suppose I have that to thank her for. Of course, I was bandaged then and she could not see my face."

He was shaking now and without thought of a rebuff, not caring if he should throw her off, she put her arms about him. He shuddered, his arms down by his side, his fists clenched. His teeth chattered and he moaned deep in his throat, so badly damaged, not, she thought, by his dreadful wound, but by the one his wife had inflicted. She held him fiercely, protectively, her cheek against his, not knowing or caring which one it was, for this was Rupert, the whole of him was

Rupert and if one part was broken she would mend it and if it could not be mended she would accept what was left.

"Darling, my dearest love . . . my only love . . . don't . . . don't despair. Hush now . . . hush now, you're safe. Rupert, you're safe . . ."

She could feel the tension slipping out of him, little by little, then he stiffened again, pushing her away so that she almost fell, catching her heel on the shifting pebbles, and when she had recovered her balance he was striding away from her.

"Go and nurse some other poor sod, Grace Tooley," he shrieked over his shoulder, "and leave me alone. I don't want your bloody sympathy. You women won't let a chap alone, will you, forever interfering, doing your damnedest to . . . to . . ."

"Rupert, wait . . ." But she knew she had lost him. He was in the grip of a nightmare so appalling it would take more than a few kind words and an embrace to fetch him out of it. His mother and sisters must care about him, must do their best to comfort him. Especially his mother who would love him no matter how he looked. As she had told him, mothers were like that. She knew that his brother had married a pleasant girl from Old Swan and a child had been born so perhaps new life, a baby in the family, might soften the rigid heart that had formed inside his chest and which would allow no human emotion to touch it.

But it was not what he needed and the worst of it was she couldn't give it to him. A woman who loved him, which was her but she could hardly declare her love to him, could she? "Oh, by the way, Rupert, did you know I love you, have done ever since I was thirteen and that if you wanted me I would do anything, anything in this world a woman can do for a man if it would give you peace. If it would heal you. I would show you that all women are not like that bitch of a wife of yours, if you would let me." But it was pretty evident that it would be a long time, if ever, before Rupert Bradley trusted a woman or even believed that a woman could love him as he now was. Jessica had crippled him, castrated him, she supposed was the way to describe it, taken away that part of himself that a man cherishes, for it was what made him the man he was. And until Rupert could fight his way out of the ties she had put on him, the cruelty she had inflicted, he would never recover.

Sadly she began to follow his striding figure along the sands, watching as he became smaller and smaller along the promenade by Garston Docks. She wondered where he was going, longing to shout after him, to force him to wait for her, to listen to her, but her heart's instinct told her it would do no good. He was bent on destruction, his own destruction which his wife had started and which he himself would finish. He was fit enough to fight again, she as a nurse who had seen many men returned to France and the trenches knew that. His men might shudder away from the sight of his face but the rest of him was capable of being their officer again, the man who would lead them over the top and into the enemy fire. He didn't care whether he lived or died but she did. By God, she did!

She began to hurry then. She knew it would need great fortitude, a strength she hoped she would find and hold on to but she would not, *would not* let him go off to kill himself. That was what he intended. Since the end of the Gallipoli evacuation which had taken place in January the war seemed to have come to a full stop. A lull, so to speak, but the soldiers whom she nursed at the hall knew this would not last. Another big push was talked of at a place called Verdun to get the Hun back to where he belonged, but even though the recruiting of young, able-bodied men went on, even more were needed which was why the Military Service Act had been passed. Unmarried men were being conscripted but Rupert would move heaven and earth to get back in it again and the doctors would not stop him. Nor his mother, who would be bound to think he had done enough. No one, in fact, could deter him from his path of self-destruction but by all she held most dear she, Grace Tooley, meant to try. In one way or another! And if she didn't, then she'd give him something to take back with him that would, in whatever the future might hold for him, prove to him that all women were not the monster his wife had turned out to be.

19

As Grace entered the front room Charlie rose awkwardly from the sofa in front of the blazing fire, throwing the cigarette he was smoking into the flames, before turning back to her. His leg would always be stiff, the doctor had told him, but it was perfectly usable and certainly capable of carrying him back to the trenches and over the top in those screaming charges at the enemy. Like all those who had fought in France for the last eighteen months, those who had been wounded and even those who hadn't, he dreaded the thought, but if he had the love of this beautiful girl to take back with him it would sustain him, give him the promise of a future to carry with him as a bright, protective shield against the horrors he had already witnessed and would undoubtedly witness again. A French soldier who had lain next to him at the clearing-station behind the lines and had lost an arm had told him of a gigantic gun disgorging a German shell that had exploded in Verdun. Tree branches, whole trunks, were blasted into the air, then fell to the ground, only to be interred or repeatedly thrown upward by further explosions, along with mangled machinery and dismembered human bodies and those of horses until the landscape was one of lunar bleakness. Severed human limbs, heads and trunks lay scattered over a wide area and many French soldiers, himself one of them, still manning their guns, were bespattered with the blood, brains and bowels of their stricken comrades. With pictures like these in their minds and behind their eyelids every time they closed their eyes, what soldier would be blamed for being reluctant to return to them.

But Charlie was going. He smiled that particularly sweet and endearing smile of his with the considerable charm which he was not aware of, pushed his hand through his thick, fair hair and took a step towards her. Though he loved her quite desperately he knew he must not be too precipitate, which was not easy, since he knew she did not have the feelings for him that he had for her.

"Charlie." She smiled affectionately at the sight of him and he was not to know that it was because she was glad to see a good-humoured, uncomplicated face after the devastation and bitterness of Rupert Bradley. Charlie seemed so *young*, so *untouched* despite what he had been through, the pain and the memories he carried within him but which had not warped him as they might have done. But then he had not known the mental torture to which Rupert had been exposed.

"I came to see if you could do with a night out, Grace, but Nora tells me you are on night duty. Anyway" – he grinned infectiously – "I hung about just the same. John here has been entertaining me with the football match his team have just won."

John lounged, hands in the pockets of his flannels, his legs stretched out, his stockinged feet to the blaze, on the low sewing chair which stood to the side of the fireplace. Topsy lay at his feet, her tongue hanging from the side of her mouth, her eyes rolling in Grace's direction in greeting.

"Really, jolly good, John."

"Three goals to one, Gracie, and I scored two of them." John preened proudly, waiting for some more praise but Grace was not really listening to either of them, for her mind was still wholly focused on the scene played out on Jericho Sands between her and Rupert. She felt battered, bruised, as though she had been engaged in fisticuffs. Her body ached strangely and so did her head and she would have given anything to be allowed to slip quietly to her room and live the scene again in her own mind. To go over it carefully to see if she had missed anything, some small hopeful thing that would lead her to what she must do next.

John was still talking, words that made no sense to her even if she had been a football devotee, which she wasn't, about "off-side" and "penalties" and "referees" and she wanted to tell him to shut up for God's sake. But it was Charlie, with that instinct that comes to those who are in love, a keen perception of the beloved's feelings, who stopped him since Grace was just standing in the middle of the room, her eyes wide with some distress, her face pale, her body stiff, her voice flat as she did her best to show an interest in her brother's prowess on the football field.

"John, old chap," Charlie said, cutting through a detailed description, which he had already heard, of how John had got the last goal in the net, "how about asking Nora for a pot of tea and some of those delicious biscuits she makes." For this was not the first time Charlie had been a visitor at number ten, Sheil Road and partaken of the confections baked by Nora. Ever since he had been discharged from the hall and put in the care of his mother, convalescing until such time as the doctors pronounced him fit to return to the front, he had been a welcome guest at the Tooley house. Ma and Pa liked him enormously. Who could not, for he was a most engaging young man and so obviously taken with their Grace, who seemed to like him. He had good prospects when this awful war was over and the two families, the Tooleys and the Davenports, had high hopes of a match.

John looked surprised, for he had been enjoying re-living his success but he hauled himself to his feet, disturbing Topsy who looked up at him reproachfully. It was a while until their evening meal and after his strenuous afternoon he could do with some nourishment which was what Charlie had counted on.

Charlie was dressed in a pair of grey flannels, a tweed jacket in a mixture of oatmeal and brown with an oatmeal-coloured polo-necked jumper underneath it. Time enough for his uniform when he went back, he had told Grace, besides which it would only upset his mother if he wore it when there was no need. His light woollen overcoat, cut somewhat on the lines of his army greatcoat, was thrown over the back of a chair. He wore no hat and though he was pale and lean after his long illness he looked most attractive. Though he was not handsome as Rupert Bradley had once been handsome, his impish grin, his narrow-eyed intelligence, the humour in his long mouth, the keen expression which, as a soldier who must be on his guard, he had acquired early, gave him a masculine charm which drew admiring glances from young women and had he wanted he could have started a romance with a number of the nurses at the hall.

But he loved this woman, not with the boyish infatuation of young men but with the strength and depth of maturity. He was twenty-two years old but he had experienced in the eighteen months since the start of the war more than many men experience in a lifetime. A youth becomes a man, a man matures rapidly in the trenches, or goes under, and Charlie Davenport had not gone under. He had so far survived and he meant to continue to do so since this woman he loved, he hoped and prayed, would be waiting for him when he returned. Tomorrow he would know.

"What is it?" he asked her softly, longing to put his arms about her, as she had longed to put her arms about Rupert. To comfort, to protect, to take her burden from her, if she had one, and it seemed to him that something was troubling her though he could not guess what it might be.

Grace attempted to throw off the numbness which the events of the afternoon had placed on her like a heavy cloak. She could not get rid of the feeling that she must do something, say something, make Rupert understand that . . . that what? That the world had not come to a harsh end because one woman did not love him. That he had been cruelly humiliated but . . . Oh, dear God, what was she to do? She couldn't even put into words inside her own head what she felt . . . *knew* she must do but her anguish told her that Rupert was teetering on the very edge of madness and needed a hand, a strong hand, to draw him back. She did not even know if he still loved his wife but if he did she knew she must . . . *must* . . .

She felt the arms go round her and so far was she in her nightmare that she allowed it, not really aware now whose arms they might be. Comforting arms holding her lightly so that if she wanted to she could draw away with nothing to stop her. Arms that said "we are here to comfort if comfort is needed" but nothing more and she sank against Charlie's chest with a sigh of relief. He smelled good, some sort of cologne, or perhaps the lavender in which his mother had lain away his jacket while he was at the front. Charlie was tall and as she placed her head beneath his chin his cheek came to rest on her hair. She had gone out in her nurse's uniform with a red woollen scarf wound about her neck. She had left off the stiff collar and cuffs, meaning to put them on, with her cap and apron, on her return. Over her uniform was her nurse's warm, woollen navy blue cape. Her arms crept out from beneath the cape and clung round Charlie's waist and she heard him sigh in what seemed complete content and at once she stepped back, horror-stricken in case she had given him the hope, the belief that there was more to the embrace than she had meant. It had been no more than an involuntary response to his encouraging arms.

"Heavens, Charlie, what must you think of me?" Her voice was deliberately light. She put her hands to her hair which, as usual, was drifting about her cheeks but he took hold of them and smiling down at her brought them to his lips.

"What must I think of you? You know what I think of you, my darling, or if you don't you are not as bright as I think you are and tomorrow—"

"Charlie, dear, I really must get a bite to eat before I go on duty," she interrupted him. She tried to free her hands but Charlie, now that he had known the lovely feel of her in his arms, and in the mistaken belief that his courtship was progressing as he hoped, grinned down infectiously and would have kissed her, not on her fingers but on her lips had she not, quite violently, dragged her hands from his.

"Charlie, I must go, for if I'm late Matron will have my hide. You know how she is. I haven't a moment to . . ."

Charlie sighed but his good nature, his happy optimism did not desert him. "Sweetheart, there is nobody who knows better than me and the other poor chaps in the ward how Matron is. How many times has she reduced me to a blubbering infant with her complaints about the untidiness of my bed or my locker or my pyjamas. Go then, but I warn you, I shall be back tomorrow. Father has promised me the loan of the car seeing that I am to be . . . well, I will tell you tomorrow when . . ."

His voice slowed to a stop and the smile slipped from his face, for she was shaking her head and her mouth had opened on a silent denial.

"What?" His own voice sounded strangely harsh as he had suddenly become aware that there was something odd about the woman he loved and had it not been for the few moments she had rested in his arms, he might have noticed it sooner.

"I can't manage tomorrow, Charlie, I'm sorry. I have to . . ." *I have to go to the house of the man I love and make him understand, how I can't imagine, that he is not the freak he thinks he is. That all women are not like the one he married. That there is a future for him, if the war allows, with another woman. I must* force him, if necessary, to face me, to see . . . Sweet heaven, am I deluding myself that of all the people he knows, friends who are fond of him, his family, his parents, that he will listen to me? What am I to say — something, surely — that will give him hope?

"What have you to do, Grace? What is it that has put that desperate look in your eyes, which, it seems to me, are avoiding mine? I wasn't going to tell you this until . . . tomorrow but I am to return to France at the beginning of next week."

"Oh, Charlie, no . . ." Her face spasmed and he took hope from the stricken look in her eyes.

"So won't you please come with me tomorrow? If it's a nice day we can take a picnic."

The door was pushed open and, blundering awkwardly with his burden, John came into the room carrying a tray loaded with the tea things and a plate piled up with Nora's biscuits. Topsy followed him prancing eagerly on her back legs, her tail wagging furiously.

"Nora says she hasn't time to be waiting on us hand and foot when she's a meal to get ready. Her words, Grace, not mine, honest. Ma will be home soon, she says, and we must help ourselves. Grace, will you look lively and pull that damn table out. You look as though you've seen a ghost."

Charlie turned away and reaching into his pocket took out his cigarettes and matches. Selecting a Gold Flake from the packet he put it between his lips, struck a match, lit the cigarette and blew smoke at his own haggard reflection in the mirror above the fireplace. Something was wrong and he didn't know what the devil it was. There was something wrong with Grace, something she was keeping to herself. Why couldn't she come with him tomorrow, for God's sake, or was he finding trouble where none existed? Was he imagining the desolation in her eyes, the tension that wouldn't allow her to look him straight in the eye and tell him simply that she had a dentist appointment; she had promised her mother; that they were busy at the shop and she was needed. She had been . . . odd, distracted ever since she had come into the room, and the surprising way in which she had walked into his arms – at first delightful – was something he was not sure about. Not that he hadn't liked it but it had not, now he thought it over, been the act of a woman putting her arms about the man she loved. Desired. Comfort had been asked for, and freely given but on what grounds? Oh, Jesus, he was being paranoid, wasn't he, or was it simply that he was sensitive to every nuance, every small degree and hue of the woman he idolised?

"Come on, you two," John said resentfully. "You sent me for the damn tea and now the pair of you are standing about like 'one o' Lewis's'." A favourite expression of John's meaning one of the dummies in Lewis's shop window. "Give us a hand, Gracie, will you?"

Grace dragged herself from the turmoil Charlie's disclosure had thrown her into, the turmoil she had already been struggling with before she even came into the house. She kept hearing Rupert's voice railing against his wife and the words "she has destroyed me" banged like a child's drum inside her head. At the same time, making a muddle of it all, she could not escape from Charlie's revelation that he was to go back to the trenches next week and that tomorrow he would declare himself. To her! He probably had a ring already picked out for her approval. Poor, poor Charlie. She felt numb with the pain of it. She had allowed Charlie to believe that she felt more for him than she did. She had been introduced to his mother – she already knew his father – and he had been to Sheil Road and been made welcome by her parents. They had gone about together, to the cinema and the music hall and she had told herself that she was merely helping in the recovery of a young soldier who happened to live in the same city as herself. But she had seen what was in his eyes, in the expression that lit his face when she walked into a room, heard it in his voice and, she supposed, it had soothed some part of her that had yearned hopelessly – for so many years – to see it in Rupert Bradley when he looked at Grace Tooley. Who had the greater need for her? Dear God in heaven, who?

John was staring in bewilderment at the two backs that were turned to him and, had her mother not come in, taking the pins from her hat and, unmindful of the tension, smiling at the three of them, who knows what he might have said. Something tactless, no doubt, Grace was to think later.

"Charlie, dear, there you are, and it seems I'm just in time for tea. Put the tray down, John, and run and ask Nora for another cup, will you? Now then, Charlie, won't you sit down, and Grace, are you coming in or going out? I see, well take off your cape, dear, or you won't feel the benefit when you do go out. Are you to cycle? I must say it worries me somewhat knowing it is almost dusk and you're going out among the traffic."

"There is little traffic when you leave Prescot Road, Ma."

"And with nothing inside you but a biscuit. Surely you have time to eat something hot?"

"I get a hot meal at the hall, Ma."

"And what about you, Charlie? Will you stay and eat with us? Mr Tooley will be home soon." Without waiting for an answer she continued in the same vein, pronouncing on the happenings at the church hall that afternoon and poor Mrs Jenkins's son who had been wounded . . . no, not seriously, but she felt so sorry . . .

John ate his way through the plate of biscuits and accepted a second, then a third cup of tea, listening to his mother but hearing not a word she said, wondering how soon he could escape to his room, his *own* room since his brothers had gone to war. He was sixteen and though the almost hysterical patriotism which had been promoted at the beginning of the war had died down, he was still keen, with two of his pals from school who were the same age, to try and enlist as soon as possible. He was tall for his age, athletic, broad-shouldered, though he wasn't so sure "Ratty" Ratcliff, his special pal who was a bit on the short side, would manage it.

"Mother would like you to come to tea on Sunday," Charlie blurted out, stopping Mrs Tooley in mid sentence. "Freddy's on leave and it's his birthday. His nineteenth." The significance of the remark – that Freddy had survived a year in the trenches – was lost on Mrs Tooley though both Grace and John grasped it immediately. Grace had the sense to keep her mouth shut but she might have known John would open his.

"Did he see action then?" he asked eagerly. Freddy was Charlie's brother.

"Yes." Charlie's answer was abrupt.

"Action?" Ma asked, bewildered, for as far as she knew Freddy was articled to a solicitor in town. He had only left school the year before and had a bright future ahead of him.

"In France, Ma. Where else?" John leaned forward and helped himself to the last biscuit, ignoring Topsy's unwinking gaze as she waited for a tit-bit. "Will he tell us all about it?" Unlike all the other servicemen he had met, he was ready to ask.

"John, don't be a bigger fool than you already are," Grace muttered as she rose to put an arm about Ma's trembling shoulders. It was a strict rule in the house that no one mentioned anything remotely connected with the war, with France, with the trenches unless it was to ask what Ma had done at the church that day. When a letter came from one of the boys it was read out to the family by Pa who had made it clear to his sons that absolutely nothing of a frightening nature was to be included in them. They wrote of the weather, the poppies that bloomed in the fields, the wonderful scenery that was spread out beneath Richard's wings, the wonderful sunsets witnessed from George's ship and were fulsome in their thanks for Ma's parcels. The war, as far as it was possible, was not to touch the fragile susceptibilities of their mother.

"Oh dear . . . oh dear, your mother will be upset, Charlie. Are you sure she wants us to come on such . . ." The last thing Mary Tooley wanted was to be present at a party for another young man who had seen action.

"Well, perhaps . . ."

"Let's wait and see, Ma, shall we?" Grace said soothingly. "If you don't feel up to it, John and I will go, won't we, John?"

"You bet." And Grace was left with the feeling that the last thing Mrs Davenport would want was the enthusiastic antics of her brother who would be bound to question Freddy on every aspect of his life at the front, again quitting his mother's protection, though John would not put it like that, and going forth with her other son who had already been wounded, into the unknown. A big adventure it would be to John and Mrs Davenport's feelings would not even be considered. He was not old enough, despite the example of his own mother's frailness, to take cognisance of the young warrior's mother, or her fear for her sons.

They sat and drank tea and when it was time for Charlie to go Grace accompanied him to the front door, telling him in her mother's hearing that they would telephone Mrs Davenport about Sunday tea.

They stood face to face in the growing dusk, the silence between them filled with the tension of Charlie, who longed to take her by the forearms and shake out of her what she might be doing the next day that would not allow her to come on a picnic with him, and with the tension of Grace, who prayed that he would do no such thing.

"Well, you'd best be off, Charlie, and so had I or I shall be late for work," she said nervously, wondering why she should feel nervous.

"Yes, Matron an' all."

She laughed. "Yes, she'll give me the rounds of the kitchen if—"

Abruptly he interrupted. "What is it, Grace? What's happened? Why can't you see me tomorrow? What is so important?"

"Don't, Charlie. You have no right to question me. No right at all." She put on a show of anger, hoping that would steer him away from this awkwardness that had sprung up between them but though he might be a mild-mannered, good-humoured chap, Charlie Davenport was not daft, nor was he easily put off. He had a stubborn streak in him that his mother could have warned Grace about.

"Come with me." His young face was set in a mould of determination.

"I can't."

"Why?"

"There is . . . someone I must see. Now please, leave it at that, Charlie."

"You're afraid I might not approve?"

"It makes no difference whether you do or not. I must go."

Charlie turned away from her and pushed his hand through his hair and she longed to put her arms about him, rest her cheek on his back, murmur words of comfort but she didn't know where that might lead. Why did she have this frightening feeling that she must go to Garlands and demand to speak to Rupert? Why did she have this feeling of premonition – how silly, her logical mind said scornfully – and that she must go at once? If she had not been on duty tonight she believed she might have ridden her bicycle up there this very moment. But she didn't want to hurt Charlie by telling him the truth. Dear God, she said to herself, are you deliberately not revealing the truth because if you do Charlie will go away and you want to keep him in reserve in case . . . *in case of what?* She was so fond of him and when she had believed that Rupert was happily married she had considered Charlie as a husband and as a father for her children. Was she so shallow?

She sighed, putting a hand on Charlie's arm then hastily withdrawing it in case he should think she was relenting.

"I'm sorry, Charlie," she said tiredly. "I can't explain but I must go and visit . . . a friend of mine. Perhaps you and I could arrange—"

"It's a man, isn't it?"

"Yes."

"I see." His voice became brisk. "Well, I'd best be off. Goodbye, Grace." And at a brisk pace he strode down the garden path, closing the gate quietly behind him.

20

It was not the sort of day to go out on a bicycle. Nora told her so vigorously. What on this earth was so important that not only was she missing her sleep – she had just come off night duty – but she must get on that dratted machine and go off on a madcap jaunt just as though the sun were cracking the flags, which it wasn't. Would she not just wait until the rain had stopped – which it showed no sign of doing – or if she must go out use that infernal machine in the hall to call a cab from the rank on the corner of Prescot Street?

In the numbed state into which the meeting with Rupert had flung her, Grace barely heard Nora's exhortations, nor was she conscious of Edna's sly, inquisitive looks from her stool at the end of the big kitchen table where she was drinking her mid-morning cup of tea.

"I have to go out, Nora."

"Aye, queen, I gathered tha' burr all I'm sayin' is can't yer wait until it lets up a bit? An' wharr I wanner know is where yer goin'? What'll I tell yer ma when she asks?"

"Tell her I won't be long," Grace answered absently.

"That's all very well but she'll not like it an' neither do I."

There were a lot of things that Nora didn't like

in this world since that damn war had started. Here was their Grace, a well-brought-up lass, dashing off all over the blasted place, as free as a chap, which wasn't right. Gone were the days when good-class young girls were kept at home, protected by their menfolk and who, when they did go about, went in the company of their mothers. Now, it was off whenever they wanted, wherever they wanted – look at that lass next door, in *France* if you please – with whoever they wanted and not a word of complaint from anyone, or so it appeared. Mind you, since the tragic drowning of young Arthur followed by the death of that imp Tom, Mr and Mrs Tooley had not been as they should and could you wonder? Even young John was missing, often for hours on end, his answers on where he had been vague and unsatisfactory. It was a sad world, it really was, Nora thought, shaking her head as she began to knock up a few scones for tea.

Though the rain continued to slant across her path, driven by a sharp wind, as Grace was passing Fir Grove Farm on Black Horse Lane she could hear the soft warbling song of the swallows which were mating and nesting in the farm outbuildings as they did every year. The sound broke through the shadowed mist that had wrapped itself about her yesterday and for a moment she felt a stirring of what might have been hope cut through her strange foreboding. It was as though the spring melody presaging the annual recurrence of nature's way of life had momentarily reassured her, telling her that everything would eventually be as it should in these challenging times.

The wrought-iron gates to the entrance of Garlands stood wide open and on the top bar, impervious to the weather, it seemed, a robin sat, a fat little robin with its feathers ruffled by the wind, singing his rich and musical aria, a somewhat wistful noise but again it cheered Grace's fearful heart. It flew off as she approached.

Leaving her bicycle resting on the stone urn at the bottom of the steps she ran up them to the front door and rang the bell before she had time to lose her nerve. She was a bedraggled sight though she was not aware of it, for she had left her hat at home and neglected to put up the hood of her cape. Her wet hair had sprung into a mass of curls about her forehead and over her ears, the rain dripping from them on to her eyelashes which she blinked to clear her vision.

The elderly maid who answered the door surveyed her in astonishment, her eyes going over Grace's shoulder to the bicycle then back to the rain-soaked figure on her step.

"Yes?" she said coldly, ready to order her round to the back door. But Grace had dealt with doctors and nurses who had tried to intimidate her by their superior knowledge and was well used to dealing with those who imagined they could put the wind up anyone beneath them in the order of things. But in her eagerness to get to Garlands and confront Rupert in some way or other she had not thought out a plan of action. She didn't know what she was going to do or say and in consequence she didn't know who to ask for. Rupert or Mrs Bradley.

She hesitated and the maid was irritated. She was overworked and underpaid, at least by the standard of the day when all the young women servants had gone off to work in munitions factories where they earned twice as much as she did. Only the elderly servants remained, in the house and in the garden and this . . . this apparition on her doorstep had interrupted her from her scullery where she was attempting to scrub the floor which was not her work but that of a skivvy.

"Did you want something?" she asked truculently, not quite daring to order the caller off the doorstep which she dearly would like to do.

Grace made up her mind. "I would like to see Mrs Bradley."

"I'm not sure madam is at home," the maid answered, for she came from the era where "at home" or "not at home" was a serious business and not one to be ignored in the Bradleys' social circle.

"Perhaps you could find out. I'll wait." Moving up another step Grace settled herself in a corner of the vestibule, dripping, the maid noticed, all over the vari-coloured flags which she had scrubbed only yesterday.

"Madam is not usually . . ." the maid began but Grace merely looked at her, unsmiling. "I'll see," she muttered ungraciously. "Who shall I say it is?"

"Grace Tooley," wondering if Mrs Bradley would recall the name.

"Wait here," the maid said and moved towards the closed door which Grace remembered from the last time she was here. It led into the crowded drawing-room and through to the conservatory. She gazed up the wide staircase and memories from four years ago came flooding back. She could see Rupert racing up them, taking the stairs two at a time to change from his oil-streaked clothes. He had been an arresting figure, not quite aggressive but sure of himself with a vigorous physique which had bemused her young girl's senses. His strong body and handsome, merry face had filled her with a yearning, a fire which ran through her veins and left her trembling with something she did not recognise, and she recalled quite clearly the strange frisson that had passed between them at that moment when he had looked at her at the gate. Even at such a young age she had recognised the admiration in his eyes and felt the strange sensation of being in a silent world in which only he and she existed. She had let it slip away in the pain of the last years, his marriage to another woman and her own determination to forget him and get on with the life she had instead of the one she had wanted. That silent exchange between them had been real and yet it had come to nothing. She had been a child and he had realised it, she supposed, not knowing of the loving, faithful heart that beat inside her breast.

Mrs Bradley peeped cautiously round the door frame as though, before she let anyone into her home, she needed to know who they were and what they wanted. They had few visitors these days and though she was elderly, forgetful, vague sometimes in a pleas-antly gentle way, she was aware that it was to do with her son. People were not deliberately unkind but Rupert was . . . difficult, convinced that friends came merely to stare, and his manner towards them was bitter, rude even, and if this was to be the case today she must make certain that whoever it was should be thoroughly vetted.

"Yes . . ." she said uncertainly, wavering in the doorway like some lost ghost. She had aged dreadfully in the four years since Grace had last seen her, her hair more white than grey, her face sad and lined, just like her own ma, and Grace wondered how many women up and down the country had this look about them.

"Mrs Bradley." Grace moved forward slowly, her sweet grave eyes looking deep into the older woman's, her tender mouth curving in a smile, her wide tranquil brow giving her an expression which calmed Mrs Bradley and made her attempt a small smile of her own. "It's Grace, Mrs Bradley. Grace Tooley. My brothers were friends of Rupert's. Arthur particularly. We were here . . . oh, four years ago just before Arthur went . . . went away. You were so kind. You and I had tea in your conservatory and you told me about all the plants there. I will never forget it . . . it was so lovely."

Mrs Bradley's face broke into a smile of recognition and without hesitation she put her arms about Grace – to the amazement of the maid who still hovered there – and held her close for a moment. She stood back and looked at Grace, holding her by her forearms with hands that were stained with soil.

"I remember, I do. The boys were so excited about Rupert's motorcycle and left you and I to take tea, which is what we'll do now, I think, Elsie, or perhaps coffee, if you would prefer, Miss Tooley."

"Grace, please, and tea or coffee, I don't mind. Whichever is easier for Elsie." Elsie at once relaxed, for it seemed this young woman was sensitive to Elsie's workload which many weren't.

"Come through, Grace. I was just potting some geraniums," looking down ruefully at her hands. "Come through, dear. This is a lovely surprise. Alan and Victoria – his wife, you know – have just gone off with the baby. They have a son, Harry, and Caroline, now that the horses have gone, has decided to fill her time with . . . well, I don't know what young girls get up to these days. Some sort of war work at the nursing home in Old Swan. Louise is still at school, of course and Eve is driving an ambulance in France. I live in fear and dread; but then, you don't want to hear my worries, I'm sure. As I recall you had brothers of your own who must be . . . well . . . We seem to have nothing but sad news to tell each other, don't we?"

Her voice rambled on as she led Grace through the remembered clutter of small tables, gilt-legged chairs, rosewood sofas and the elephant's foot which had so fascinated John and into the conservatory. No wonder she spends her time in here, Grace thought, for it was a haven of peace, rest, tranquillity and beauty. The birds sang and the water from the tiny fountain Grace did not remember from the last time played a musical accompaniment. The rain lashed at the windows and the curtain it made hid the garden but it didn't matter, for the garden was in this room, all around them.

"You're wet through, dear." Mrs Bradley frowned. "Do take off your cape and let Elsie put it to dry before the kitchen fire." She started in surprise when she saw that Grace wore the uniform of a nurse beneath the cape. "I didn't realise," she began but then Elsie came in with a tray of coffee and a plate heaped up with hot, buttered crumpets, putting the tray down on the small, round table next to the chair in which Mrs Bradley sat.

"Cook thought you might like these," she said to Grace, to whom she seemed to have taken a liking.

"Thank you, I'm starving. I've only just come off night duty."

"Poor lass; well, tuck in." She took the cape Mrs Bradley handed her and trotted off with every appearance of amiability.

Mrs Bradley seemed starved of someone to whom she could talk, not of anything urgent or important like her children and her fear for them but of inconsequential things, as she used to do before the war. Gossip, Grace supposed it would be called, and she let her, watching Rupert's mother relax a little, become less strained, knowing quite well what had caused that strain. They drank coffee and Grace ate the crumpets, for she found she really was hungry, then, knowing she must do it, she began to speak of why she was here.

"Mrs Bradley, I think it only fair to tell you, and I would be grateful if you would let it go no further, that I love your son. Rupert, I mean, naturally. I have done for years." It was said in a matter-of-fact voice as though she were telling Rupert's mother of some inconsequential event in her life that she thought might interest her.

Mrs Bradley, her face as pale as the plate on which the crumpets had been piled, watched her, her eyes no longer vague and smiling, but pierced with an intensity that told Grace exactly what the older woman was suffering on her son's behalf.

"I saw him yesterday on Jericho Beach and it seemed to me that I must see him again. I cannot leave him, loving him as I do, in the state of mind that . . . please forgive me for being so frank but I could hardly come here and ask to speak to him letting you believe that it was nothing but an idle visit. I love him, you see."

Her direct eyes, as soft and golden as amber, looked without excuse into Mrs Bradley's and she put out a hand, not touching her but letting it be known she would be glad to have it taken. Mrs Bradley took it.

"Grace . . ." Mrs Bradley's voice broke and she bent her head in great pain. "He is . . . she does not love him, his wife . . . and to hear you say that you do, looking as he does now . . . you can have no idea what it means to me. Oh, my dear, my poor son who was so handsome, so admired, so loved and yet she has . . . I will say no more but I believe you will find him in the summerhouse near the lake. He sits there for hours on end, whatever the weather. Go to him. Tell him what you have told me. Let him see that he is not the monster he believes he is. Thank God . . . oh, thank you, dear God for sending this woman to us."

She had flung her still damp cape about her shoulders, thanking Elsie who was not at all pleased to see her put it on before it was dry and, following Mrs Bradley's instruction, walked through the garden at the back of the house, her head still uncovered in the driving rain, and down the sloping lawn to the wooden building with its back to the house which looked out over the lake. Ducks swam busily near the edge, hoping for crusts, and two swans glided gracefully across its rain-dimpled surface. The grass was springy and wet and her feet made no sound in it but her heart was thumping so loudly she was sure he would hear it.

Though Mrs Bradley had called it a summerhouse it was more like a small pavilion. It was octagonal in shape with a wide double doorway which stood open to the lake, and round the inside, set below curtained windows, were seats on which padded cushions of maroon-coloured plush were scattered. There were deckchairs, cricket bats, tennis racquets, a clutter of croquet hoops and balls, even ice skates as though at some time the lake froze and the Bradley children had swooped and swirled and screamed with laughter on it.

Rupert lounged in a folding canvas chair, his left hand in his trouser pocket, his legs stretched out before him, his ankles crossed. He wore his uniform and as she studied him in that moment before he saw her she became aware that it was only when he was dressed as a soldier that he felt he had some identity in the world in which he was lost. It was immaculately pressed by some careful hand, Grace suspected Elsie's, his knee boots polished as were his badges and Sam Browne. His chin was on his chest as he stared unseeingly across the lake, his face brooding, his mouth twisted into the same bitter line she had seen on Jericho Beach. In his right hand he held a revolver.

She cried out then, and leaping forward grabbed it from his hand, startling him to such an extent he froze, giving her enough time to step back from him, holding the gun behind her as though under no circumstances would she allow him to take it from her. Her face had drained of all its colour and her eyes were wide with shock, for she believed that in his total despair he was about to shoot himself.

Recovering from his shock he sprang from the chair and made a lunge for her, his face, the good side, losing all its natural colour.

"You bloody fool," he snarled, "what the hell d'you

think you're doing? The thing could go off at any minute."

"That's what I thought and if you imagine I'm going to let you take the coward's way out and—"

"I mean the safety's off, you bloody idiot. For God's sake don't touch the trigger or you'll kill—"

"Myself? Or you? I thought that was what you wanted." And still she backed away from him, keeping the revolver behind her while he crouched, ready to fling himself on her and wrestle the dangerous weapon away.

"Don't be daft, woman. You don't know what the devil you're talking about, nor do you realise how dangerous that revolver is."

"Why did you have the safety catch off then?"

"I . . . don't know."

"Tell me how to make it safe and I'll give it back to you."

"Oh, don't be so bloody dramatic, woman. Give it to—"

"No, I'll shoot myself in the foot, believe me, if I have to. Just tell me how to do it. No, stand back," as he began to edge towards her.

He instantly took a cautious step away and held up his hands palms facing her. "All right, all right, I give in." He watched her as she brought the revolver round until she held it in front of her, then, carefully, watching her every move, he told her what to do. When she had done it, he strode forward and wrenched it from her hands.

Shoving it in the holster he wore on his belt, he turned on her savagely and for a moment she thought he was going to strike her. His face was almost the same colour on both sides, he was so livid with anger, but she stood her ground, lifting her chin, almost offering her face for his blow. For a moment it was touch and go then he swung round, turning his back on her as though he couldn't bear the sight of her.

"What the devil are you doing here? I thought – hoped – I'd seen the last of you the other day. Are you in the habit of forcing yourself on people who want nothing to do with you? And how did you know where I was?"

"Your mother . . ."

"My mother has no right to tell intruders where I am. I shall have something to say to her."

"Will you? It seems to be a knack of yours to threaten those weaker than yourself. Your mother is a lovely woman who loves you."

"Oh, don't talk such blether, woman. I'm sick of it. She's my mother so I suppose she does but I don't need you to tell me. I'm tired . . ."

"I suppose you are. This war has plunged us all into a weariness."

"Platitudes."

"You really are the rudest man I have ever known and the most foolish, for if you can't see that . . ."

He turned to face her then, his eyes savage with hatred, for her, for the war, for the world that had chosen to lacerate him, to break him cruelly on a wheel that he had not the power to be free of and as he faced her she took a step up to him and without thought for the consequences placed her mouth on his. It was not really a kiss for she had never kissed a man before and was not sure of the procedure. She needed her arms about him to hold herself and him steady, but she had intended merely to stop his mouth, to stem the flow of bitter words that poured from it. She was taken by surprise when his arms came round her in a vice-like grip and his lips took hers, not in a kiss but what might almost be a bite. A leeching of one creature on another. She thought her lips would break open his were so ferocious, and strangely, since she had her eyes open, she thought he was smiling.

He dragged his lips from hers. "So this is what you're after, is it, madam? A fancy to be kissed by a freak of nature. Which side is the best, d'you think, the still pleasant features of one side or the monstrosity of the other? Shall we try again, my dear, or have you had enough?"

"Rupert . . ." Her voice was a whisper, a pleading for something and her heart was in great pain, for it was evident that his was breaking. She lifted a hand and placed it on the ugly side of his face, caressing the wrinkled flesh but he wrenched away, laughing, dangerously close to hurting her.

"Oh no, my dear. Not allowed to touch, you see, or at least you're not." And with a gesture that was a cruel parody of love his hand gripped her breast and squeezed, his fingers taking her nipple, crushing it until she cried out.

"Ah, you've had enough, have you? Well I'm not sure I have, so let's have a look at what is being offered to me with such generosity. Remember, my pet, you started this, not me." Laughing, ugly with menace, out of his mind, she knew, also knowing she was in grave danger from this damaged man who wore his uniform even now, months after the battle in which he had been so grievously wounded, she stood as still as a doe cornered by an attacker while he tore at her apron, the buttons on her nurse's dress, her camisole until her breasts were exposed, high, proud, white, her rosy nipples ready for his hands, his teeth or any other insult he cared to offer.

"Well, you really are up for it, aren't you?" he sneered. "And who am I to refuse such an offer?" His hands reached out and he began to stroke her breasts, watching himself doing it, twisting her nipples between cruel fingers, and when he had done that to his own satisfaction he pushed her cape and her dress back off her shoulders and down her arms, drawing them down until she was naked to her waist. He stood back for a moment, never taking his eyes from her, running them speculatively over her nakedness, waiting, she supposed, for her to make some resistance, but as she continued to stand quietly, he fumbled with his jacket, his tie, his Sam Browne and his shirt, throwing them to the seat behind him, then pulled her forward, pressing himself against her, his breast to hers. His hands smoothed her back, moving to the nape of her neck beneath her hair and as he did so she began to feel the change in him. His hands became gentler and in the pit of her stomach something warm stirred and her breathing quickened. His hands rose to cup her face and his lips came down on hers. This touch, after the hard cruelty of the first, was a pleasurable shock to her, warm, moist, his tongue exploring her lips, the delicious feeling spreading through her body like the ripples on the lake the swans had caused. He raised his head and his eyes, normally so rich a brown, were dark, almost black, as they stared into hers. He frowned and it was as if he were analysing the expression on her face, her reaction to his caresses and when she smiled his lips took hers again. Slowly he drew her clothing down the length of her body, kneeling to spread his kisses across her flat stomach, the tight triangle of dark curls at its base, the inside of her thighs. She held his head to her, her fingers clutching at the dense thickness of his hair. She threw her own head back, her eyes closed, offering herself to him, offering her lovely, untouched body to him, loving him, telling him so in the abandonment of her pose. Straightening up, he quickly stripped himself, took her in his arms and laid her down on the cushions he had dragged from the seats.

"I love you, Rupert," she said, taking his head between her hands and drawing it to her breast. His frown deepened as though what they were doing had nothing to do with love, and perhaps, to him, it didn't, but he was too far gone in his masculine need to stop and question it. She was a magnificent female body in his arms, something he had not experienced for a long time and without a thought for her he entered her, deeply, swiftly, painfully and when she cried out he cried out with her though not for the same reason.

Afterwards she lay dreaming, her eyes narrowed, ready to purr like a cat, for she had just been loved by Rupert, but even as she clasped him in her arms, her hands smoothing his tousled hair, he dragged himself from them, sprang up and reached for his clothes. Assiduously he avoided her eyes, not even glancing at her beauty, at her hair spread out like a fan behind her head, at her breasts which were rich as cream tipped with rose, at the long length of her spread so trustingly for his gaze.

"Rupert . . . ?" Even then she did not cover herself.

"Oh, for God's sake, woman, what now?" His voice was irritable.

"Rupert . . . I love you, Rupert. I wouldn't—"

"Have done it had you not loved me." His voice was top-heavy with sarcasm. "I swear to God you women are all the same. You always want to make it into something it's not. Romance! Romance has nothing to do with what we've just done. It was a good—" Here he used a word she had never heard before though she could not help but understand it. "Confound it, will you get dressed and then we'd better get back to my mother or she'll think I've thrown myself in the bloody lake."

He turned his back on her as she blindly, numbly, fumbled her way into her clothes then walked stiffly beside her as she stumbled, stunned and trembling, up the sloping lawn.

Not another word was spoken between them. In her eyes was desolation, in his, which might have been filled with satisfied male triumph, was an expression that was unreadable.

21

She thought that had it not been for Charlie she might have broken down in total despair. He was waiting for her at the gates as she pushed her cycle down the drive from the hall the next morning after being on the night shift.

"I can't let it . . . be like this, Grace," he said without preamble. "It's no good pretending. You know how I feel about you but if there's another chap . . . then I'd rather you told me. I'm to be off on Monday" – making it sound as though he were to start a new job in another town, no more than that – "and if there's no chance for me then I'd rather know." His boyish face was twisted into an expression of wretchedness, his carefree male virility which had always appealed to her was drained from him. His tall, lanky frame was hunched as though it hurt him to straighten up. She knew exactly how he felt and for a moment she had an almost hysterical desire to laugh. What a bloody farce life was, she thought, using language which if she had spoken it out loud and Nora had heard her would have precipitated having her mouth washed out with soap. But it was. A bloody farce. Here she was, yearning after a man who had treated her like a common tart, not that she knew much about tarts, only that they got paid for their services and all she had got was a slap in the face.

And here was Charlie, dear Charlie whom she loved as she did her brothers, offering her the kind of love she did not want, at least from him.

She was totally drained, exhausted to the point where she wondered if she would have the strength to cycle home. She had not slept for what seemed days . . . she couldn't remember when and last night on the ward had been harrowing.

She had gone home after leaving Garlands. Without saying goodbye to Mrs Bradley she had climbed painfully on to her bicycle, aware that there must be blood in her drawers, and without turning to Rupert who, probably, had gone into the house anyway, she had ridden down the drive, taking a circuitous route home, not knowing where she was, banking on her own instincts to get her to safety. They had done and flinging her cycle against the wall she had let herself into the house and run up the stairs to the bathroom.

"Grace, is tha' you?" Nora shouted up the stairs, obviously surprised that she had not come into the kitchen.

"Yes, I'm going to have a bath. I'll be down in a few minutes," she had managed to answer before banging the bathroom door behind her, locking it, then sinking down on her haunches, her back to the door, her arms about her knees, her head bowed in black sorrow. She supposed she should feel shame, since it was an accepted fact that "nice" girls did not share any kind of physical love with a man until he was her husband. But it was not this that was devastating her, far from it. She had wanted it as much as he seemed to do, gloried in it, responded to his hands and his mouth and even to the hurt he did her, for in her foolish heart she had imagined that this must be the turning point. In her naïvety she had thought that the fact that a woman did not find him repulsive, indeed was exultant in his arms, would heal that great scar that festered inside him but it was not so. He had looked on it in the way a man looks on some casual encounter that means nothing to him. He had degraded her, humiliated her, told her not to talk such bloody nonsense when she had revealed her feelings. He had *dirtied* her and if she didn't get in the bath and do her best to wash it away, she would fall apart and run screaming down the stairs for Nora.

She had stripped off her torn clothing, run herself a bath and when she was in it, scrubbed herself almost raw, even that place between her legs which still ran pink with her blood. She had even washed her hair. Her underwear was bundled into a parcel which she meant to burn at the hospital. She put on a clean set of clothing, her nurse's dress, apron, cap, collar and cuffs and, slapping a false smile on her face, ran down the stairs and into the kitchen.

"Well," said Nora, her hands on her hips. "What's up wi' you?"

"What d'you mean? I was wet through so I had a bath."

"Yer'd best gi' me yer uniform then an' I'll get it washed an' ironed." Nora was not best pleased, for she was part of this family and did not care to have secrets kept from her, which Grace was evidently doing.

Her apron, from which the buttons had been torn, her dress the same, were stuffed at the back of her wardrobe, for how to explain to Nora how they had come to be in such a state. She couldn't burn those for she had only the two uniforms but when she was alone she would mend them, sew on new buttons and wash them. Perhaps on Sunday when she knew Nora was to accompany her mother to a sale of work in aid of the war effort.

"No, I can . . . well . . . I'll do it, it needs a stitch."

"Fetch it 'ere then," Nora said, suspicious though she didn't know why.

"Leave it, Nora, I said I'll do it. Now I must be off." For by now dusk was falling.

Nora was aghast. "But yer've 'ad no sleep. I dunno, on night duty nursin' them poor souls then out all day wi'out a bite to eat an' 'ow yer gonner get through tonight's shift wi'out a rest? See, sit yerself down an' I'll mekk yer a sandwich. Put yer feet up on that there tuffet and rest yerself fer ten minutes." And so she had done what Nora demanded, knowing it was the easiest way.

Somehow she had got through the night without coming to the notice of Sister Randall. A young soldier had been brought in with the last batch of wounded, just a boy who had evidently gone straight from the playing fields of school to the battlefields of France. He had been gassed, his whole company had been gassed, choking, blinded, the men vomiting and unable to stand let alone fight. Though he had received treatment at a dressing-station behind the lines and again in a London hospital, treatment that was worse than the actual gassing, he had not recovered. His skin where it had been exposed was burned and was a mass of infected matter. He was slowly drowning in the muck that filled his lungs and his bubbling, sighing agony had racked her with pity. He had called constantly for his mother in a high, treble voice as though, in his pain and terror, he had regressed to childhood and Grace, overwhelmed with compassion, had stayed for most of the night by his bedside, holding his hand, smoothing back the curly tangle of his hair, doing what his mother would do had she been there and it appeared to soothe him. She was not glad, of course, that he was there, but his suffering took every shred of her concentration as she tried to ease it, keeping her mind off what had happened to her. The doctor had come in the early hours and given the boy a shot and he had eased into a troubled sleep.

Now, here was Charlie wanting something from her that she was not able to give him, but as she stared at him, almost senseless with misery, for the boy had died just before dawn, her eyes deep in dark caverns of pain and weariness, she realised that it was not so. Charlie was not here to take but to give.

"Grace, darling, what is it? What's happened? Jesus, you look ghastly."

She chanced a small smile which did not reach her eyes. "Oh, a bad night, Charlie. A boy who was gassed . . ."

"Poor sod, and here am I babbling on; let me take you home. See, I've got Father's car." And there just beyond the gates stood Mr Davenport's Ford Model T, or Tin Lizzie as it was affectionately called. It was not as glorious as the Vauxhall that Mr Allen owned, that dazzling silver monster that had taken them to see the opening of the Gladstone Dock at Bootle in 1913, but it was reliable. The Ford wasn't used much these days except when Charlie borrowed it to take her out, but now and again it could be seen drawn up outside

Tooley's Tobacconists when Mr Davenport popped in for his cigars.

"He said I might borrow it today, Grace, so I thought . . . seeing that we didn't have an excursion yesterday we might have a spin out to . . . but you're exhausted, I can see that, so I'll run you home and we can go another day."

"What about my cycle?" She tried to smile, to show some enthusiasm for the loving man whose usually carefree boy's face had constricted into lines of strain, caused, she knew, by her.

"It'll fit in the back, see . . ." And it did. He jumped into the driver's seat, making sure she was well tucked up with rugs and her scarf tied warmly about her chin, since it was a cool day and there was very little protection from the weather beneath the hood of the motor car.

"Charlie, this is so good of you . . . to meet me . . ."

"My pleasure . . ."

"And after all I think I would like it if you would take me somewhere. I'll telephone home and tell them."

"There's nothing I'd like more, my dearest love," abandoning all pretence that what he felt for her was no more than friendly affection. "But what about the dreaded machine? You know you're the only one who dares to answer it." He turned to her, his sweet, wide smile filled with humour and with his love for her.

"It's Saturday so John will be there."

"But you look so tired. Not that I'm complaining but after working night duty . . ."

"Please, Charlie. Take me somewhere . . . any-where."

"Put on your goggles then."

"Goggles!" She thought she would never laugh again but when Charlie handed her a pair and helped her to put them on she found herself to be quite convulsed. Charlie had a pair as well, and a leather cap which he pulled down over his forehead, for when the motor car started and began to pick up speed the wind whipped under the hood and through the open sides. She felt her hair come loose from its pins, flying out like a dark curtain behind her and she began to laugh. The speed at which they went took her breath away, for though this wasn't the first time she had been in a motor car it was the first time she had been with Charlie who, he told her, liked a bit of speed. With Mr Allen they had scarcely crawled along for Ma and Mrs Allen were not at all sure they cared for the experience and when she had driven with . . . with Rupert, he had moved at what he considered to be an appropriate speed for she had just lost dear Arthur.

Now Charlie roared along at what must have been twenty or more miles an hour and through the eyepiece of her goggles she felt her eyes widen with excitement. Charlie watched her, narrowly missing a horse and cart plodding along the road that led to Rainhill. Charlie began to sing.

It's a long way to Tipperary,
It's a long way to go,
It's a long way to Tipperary,
And the sweetest girl I know
Goodbye, Picadilly, Goodbye, Leicester Square
It's a long, long way to Tipperary but my heart
   lies there.

They thundered along open country roads with

high banks in which grew crocus, marsh marigolds and anemones. They were stopped once by a herd of cows, the farmer shouting furiously at them since he evidently considered this to be an accepted route for farm animals from field to farmyard and not for the infernal machines which littered up his lane.

They sat for fifteen minutes on a dry-stone wall with the pale March sun on their backs. Charlie held her hand and she let him, comforted somehow by the smooth, hard firmness of his palm, the tenderness of his fingers entwined with hers. He didn't speak as though he knew it would be a mistake to press his love at this moment. The country air was sweet with the aroma of newly growing grass, the good smell of manure from a farmyard further up the lane, hawthorn blossom coming into bloom and threading the hedge dividing the field, of dogwood and the white field pansies which came earlier than their purple-blue cousins. There was no sound but the bark of a dog, rooks cawing in the denuded trees and the low bleat of sheep in a field.

They clattered through quiet villages and hamlets, Old Heath, Great Sankey, turning heads, for the vehicle seemed to have many parts that shook and rattled, along the outskirts of Warrington, through more sleepy villages and then they were in Cheshire. They drove into the Delamere Forest at noon and the tall conifers closed in about them. The sunshine shone through their high branches, touching light and shadow to the quiet clearings and when Charlie stopped and turned off the motor the peace, the perfect solitude wrapped itself around them and entered her heart. He turned to smile at her and she wanted to take his hand, perhaps kiss him but she knew it would be a mistake. He had brought her here in the goodness of his heart because he loved her and, she thought, perhaps with the hope that he might persuade her to love him, but instead he had done the opposite.

He had made her see that her love for Rupert was not an emotion she could turn off simply because he had hurt her. She had, in the small hours while she had held the hand of the young soldier who had cried and babbled in delirium, convinced herself that she could no longer give her life to Rupert but here, in the almost cathedral-like mysticism of the forest, she knew she had been wrong. Rupert, the *real* Rupert, was still there deep inside the man who had hurt her so badly yesterday. Not physically, though there had been that as well, but in the offence he had offered her. Surprisingly she had not been offended, insulted, affronted, in whatever way you wanted to put it, by his lovemaking. His body had been beautiful, lean, dark, powerful, long, graceful bones, flat muscles that ran from the curve of his chest to his concave belly and thighs. No, *he* had been glorious but his words had mortified her, cut her to the bone, slashed at her loving heart and brought her almost to her knees. She had thought he *had* brought her to her knees but it was not so. And it was Charlie who had brought her round to this reasoning. Charlie would always be dear to her and how she was to let him go, say goodbye, wish him well and see him go, knowing how he felt about her was something she could barely contemplate but it must be done.

They walked for a while and Charlie took her hand. He brought it to his lips and kissed each finger before tucking it with his into his pocket but he did not speak and she thought that he knew. He had not asked about the "other man" as she was certain he had meant to and when he dropped her off at the gate of number ten he merely saluted, as a soldier salutes a superior officer, smiled and drove away.

When she telephoned his home the next day to accept Mrs Davenport's invitation to tea the maid who answered told her the family was not at home. She was surprised that the boy who had been sent with a note had not yet delivered it to Mr and Mrs Tooley. Oh, yes, Lieutenant Davenport had gone with them. Where? She believed it was to London where Mr and Mrs Davenport were to see their sons off to war. Was there any message for her mistress when she returned? No, then she would tell Mrs Davenport that Miss Tooley had called and would telephone . . .

She slept for the best part of three days, the three days she was allowed between moving from night duty to being on days, only waking to eat the food, good nourishing food Nora prepared for her, to have a bath and then to climb back into bed and slip into the almost unconscious state the events of the past few days had induced in her. She had vague recollections of her mother coming to stand by her bed, to kiss her and smooth back her hair and then it was her last day off.

"I'm going out for an hour or two," she called up the hall to Nora.

"Yer've only just gorrout yer bed," Nora complained. "Yer can't go wi' nowt inside yer. Anyroad, where ya off to now? See, I'm not 'avin' this. Either yer come inter't kitchen an' get summat inside yer or

I'm callin' yer pa." She appeared in the doorway, her hands and apron covered in flour and on her face was the expression they all knew and dreaded.

Grace sighed. She was dressed today in her cycling skirt of navy blue wool, sturdy black ankle boots, a warm woollen shirt in a small check of blue and red and over her arm was her bright red cape. Her hair was brushed to a high gloss and plaited, the thickly curling end of the plait tied with a ribbon to match her cape. She looked rested, the bloom back on her cheek, her eyes bright with something that Nora wasn't sure she cared for.

"Now then, where ya off to? Sit yer down an' I'll mekk yer a decent breakfast. No, no arguments, my girl. It's bacon an' egg an' 'appen a few sausages. Pass me that fryin' pan an' will yer get this dratted dog from under me feet. Pour yerself a cuppa tea, it's just medd. I'm not listenin'; yer either get summat inside yer and tell me where yer off or I'm telephonin' yer pa."

"You! On the telephone!"

"Don't you think I can't, my lass. 'Tis not ter me likin' but if I 'ave to I'll master the thing. Now, where ya off."

"I'm going to see Mrs Bradley." Grace poured herself a cup of the black liquid Nora called tea and, after putting in several teaspoons of sugar and plenty of milk, sat down at the table to drink it. Topsy sidled up and leaned on her knee, her face looking up imploringly, for she did love a bit of sausage.

"Mrs Bradley? Name sounds familiar. Weren't 'e a friend of our Arthur's?" Nora put a plate in front of Grace, all neatly arranged with two rashers of crisp bacon, two sausages, well done, a fried egg the white of which was firm the yolk soft and runny, two strips of crisp fried bread and three mushrooms. Not overcrowded as the lads liked it, but dainty with no trace of fat on the piping-hot plate. She watched with great satisfaction as Grace ate the lot, though she did share the sausage with the dog.

"That there beast be spoiled," grumbled Nora, but her lass had eaten a good breakfast and that was all she cared about.

"Yes, Mrs Bradley's . . . sons were with Arthur at university."

"Both at front, I suppose," Nora said sadly.

"One is, I believe, but Mrs Bradley was very kind to me when Arthur died and so I thought . . ."

"But why now, my lamb?"

"Just a ride out, Nora," Grace answered airily and grabbing her bright red woollen beret that matched her cape she flung them both on and fled the kitchen before Nora could ask any more awkward questions.

He was in exactly the same spot where she had last found him though this time he had his swagger-stick in his gloved hand. He might have been just about to stride off for the parade ground he was so immaculate, breeches brushed, boots, belt and badges polished, even his cap set at a dashing angle on his carefully brushed hair. And in that moment she knew she had been right. Only in his uniform, his insignia of rank displayed, the symbol of dress that told the world, even if the world wasn't here to see it, who and what Rupert Bradley was, could he manage to maintain his feeling of self. The war had taken his looks, turning him, or so he thought, into a hideous monster from which his fellow human beings shuddered away, and his wife had done the rest.

He was, as he had been the last time, gazing, his eyes clouded, across the lake to the small stand of trees on the far side. Presumably because the sun was shining he had placed the canvas chair on the grass just in front of the summerhouse door. The ducks gathered in hope of bread and the same two swans dipped and bowed in one another's wake. There was a liver-coloured spaniel leaning on his leg, his head on Rupert's lap and Rupert's hand smoothed his silky fur.

The dog sensed her presence first and immediately straightened up, ready to lift his lip in a growl as he turned towards her. Rupert swivelled his head indifferently, perhaps expecting a maid, or his mother, and certainly not her, though the dog's growl should have warned him it was a stranger, at least to the dog. For just the fraction of a second it seemed he was going to smile; instead his eyebrow lifted sardonically and his wide, strong mouth twisted in a sneer.

"Dear God in heaven, it's you again." His voice was lazy. "Do you never give up or were my embraces so intoxicating you have come back for more? Well, I'm always ready to oblige, my pet, so if you'd care to lie down . . ."

"You're a bastard, Rupert Bradley. You think because you have been wounded and your wife has been in the bed of every officer in your regiment it gives you the right not only to feel immensely sorry for yourself but to insult everyone who holds out a friendly hand to you. I can certainly understand why you are sitting here, all alone except for your dog. People get tired of offering sympathy."

At once she knew she had said the wrong thing. He had smiled with what seemed genuine amusement when she first turned on him but as soon as the word *sympathy* was uttered, his expression changed to one of white-lipped anger, a fierce, knife-edged anger which told her she was in mortal danger. He sprang to his feet and the dog, alarmed at the tension, began to bark in fright. He backed away, then ran into the summerhouse where he hid behind the open door.

"You bitch, you stupid bitch. How dare you come here mouthing your meaningless irrelevancies, telling me how to run my life, expounding on things that don't concern you and which you know nothing about. Believe me, sympathy does not interest me, nor the no doubt well-meaning interference of so-called friends. All I want is to be left alone. I don't need anything from you though I must admit our . . . activities the other day were very enjoyable. Now, if you care to repeat them then I am quite amenable, if not, then bugger off to wherever it is you came from. I neither want—"

"You remind me of my younger brother when he is sulking over something he wanted but has been refused," she interrupted him. She was appalled by the terrible blankness in his eyes, put there by the physical and mental torment he lived in but she could not stop now. She wasn't at all sure what she was going to do, or say, or what she hoped to achieve, she only knew she must do *something*, link him to something, even if it was only hatred of herself; even if it was to drive him to retaliation and anger so cold, or so violent, she would be the one to suffer. "He shouts a lot, too, like the schoolboy he is, but then one can excuse him on the grounds of youth."

"Really, I don't know why the hell you have decided to come here and make me the target of your philanthropy. I don't want you, except perhaps to have another good—" – again he used the word he had used before – "if you're willing which I must say you were last time, and very nice it was too, but apart from that I wish you'd go to the devil and take your . . . well, whatever it is you think you're doing for me, with you. Now, get out of my sight and leave me in peace."

"Peace, is that what you want? You call this peace? Hiding away like a criminal waiting for . . . what are you waiting for, Rupert? For your face to become as it was? Or perhaps for your wife to decide she doesn't find it quite so monstrous as she first thought and that she doesn't mind returning to your bed instead of the—"

"You filthy bitch." His rage was lethal now and he shook with the force of it and somehow, though she couldn't for the life of her think why, she felt she had reached some festering sore in him that needed lancing. But she wasn't ready for what came next.

Holding her with one hand, he hit her twice across the face, viciously and accurately so that her neck muscles wrenched in agony and her head, reeling backwards, struck hard against the wooden wall of the summerhouse.

He stepped back, breathing hard, and as though the rage that had blinded him, taken his senses and turned him into a wild beast, had drained him of the matter that came from the lanced wound, he passed a trembling hand across his face, then covered his eyes with it.

"Jesus Christ . . . I'm sorry, I'm sorry. Really, that was unpardonable. Forgive me . . . I don't . . ."

Her lip was bleeding and she had bitten her tongue, but she mumbled what she thought was something on the lines of "No . . . no . . . it's all right," but he turned, and stumbling with the dog at his heels, he fled along the lake, round its top end and disappeared into the wood. She picked up his cap which had fallen from his head and placed it carefully on the chair, then turned and moved slowly up the lawn to the side of the house where she had left her bicycle.

22

The letter from Charlie came a week later.

Dearest girl,

I call you that because that is what you are to me. I cannot pretend it to be otherwise. I couldn't bring myself to say goodbye to you which I knew was cowardly but there it is. I shall treasure the day we spent together and I wanted it to be the precious memory I would carry back with me. As you can see I'm already back on the Western Front and Freddy's with me, for which Mother is truly thankful since she imagines I can keep my eye on him. It would be a priceless gift to me if you would write, darling Grace, perhaps to tell me you miss me. I know the chaps yearn for letters from home. I shall wait and hope for one from you.

My heart is yours,
Charlie

It made her cry. She felt she had let him down by not seeing him off, as a girl sees her sweetheart off, but she knew that Charlie would have seen through any pretence on her part and would have resented it. He had chosen to slip away without troubling her, troubling her guilty heart which was centred on only one man, given to one man, and at once she sat down

to answer his letter. She would fill it with ordinary
things, events as they took place in her own world,
the periwinkles that suddenly rampaged, blue as his
eyes, in a corner of the garden, the starlings that took
flight and swirled about the fields as she cycled to the
hall, the swallows that were nesting in the rafters of the
den, the scene between Matron and the new doctor, a
Scot called MacDonald, who was far too *sympathetic*,
Matron's word, towards the patients. She didn't care
if Doctor MacDonald *had* served at the front, this was
her hospital and he would bide by her rules. Knowing
Matron he could imagine the scene, she was sure!
She would keep him up to date on that one, Grace
told Charlie. She had taken a walk on Princes Parade
and watched the famous Cunarder RMS *Mauretania*,
the *Mauri* as she was known in Liverpool, entering
Sandon Dock at the end of a voyage. The *Mauri*
had won the coveted Blue Riband, taking it from
the illfated *Lusitania*, having crossed the Atlantic in
four days, seventeen hours and twenty minutes, the
fastest crossing between Bishop Rock in the Scilly
Isles and Ambrose Light, off New York. Did Charlie
remember the liner, which she was sure he would being
a Liverpool man? What a wonderful sight it had been,
then and now. Small things she described to him.
John's success on the football field, a day in the shop
when she had chatted to his father who looked well, her
mother's continued improvement and involvement in
the Church, Topsy's naughtiness in digging up Ma's
newly planted phlox and a score of run-of-the-mill
happenings which might paint a peaceful picture of
her life to him.

She did not tell him about Captain Rupert Bradley

nor the telephone call she had received from his mother. It happened about a month after Charlie had left. The end of April. The battle for Verdun raged on with appalling losses on both sides with the French and Germans losing the best of their young manhood. This, naturally, was not mentioned in the Tooley household.

"There's a telephone call for you, Gracie," John, who almost always answered the machine, shrieked up the stairs before crashing the receiver down on the hall table and flinging himself along the hall towards the kitchen where Nora was threatening to "spiflicate" him if he didn't get to the table at once. His bacon and eggs were going cold and if he didn't look sharp she'd give the lot to the dratted dog.

"Who is it?" Grace had called, since she was just about to lower herself into a bath. There was no answer from John so, sighing, Grace wrapped a towel about herself and made her way down the stairs.

"Grace Tooley speaking," she said into the mouthpiece, for if it was Matron on the line, she liked to be precise with no time wasted in chitter-chatter.

"Grace, dear, is that you?" an anxious voice asked.

"Yes, who is this?" For Grace had become as efficient as Matron in her no-nonsense approach. Time was something that might mean life or death in their business.

"Oh, Grace dear, how lovely to hear your voice. I'm hopeless with this machine and I wasn't sure whether I had got it right," the tinny voice continued somewhat breathlessly. "I usually ask one of the others to do it but I wanted to speak to you privately. Are you there, dear? Is that you?"

Grace distinctly felt her heart lurch sickeningly in her chest as she recognised the quavering voice of Rupert Bradley's mother. So far she had said nothing, merely listened since she could hardly cut across Mrs Bradley's nervous verbiage. She longed to scream down the telephone, "What is it, what's happened, what's wrong? Is Rupert ill, what . . . what . . . what?" But still Mrs Bradley babbled on about the difficulties of using this dreadful machine until at last Grace could stand it no longer.

"Mrs Bradley . . . it *is* Mrs Bradley, isn't it?"

"Yes, of course, dear." Mrs Bradley sounded surprised as though the very act of speaking into the telephone disclosed who she was as clearly as if the person at the other end could see her.

"What is it, Mrs Bradley? Is there something . . . ?"

"Grace . . . oh, I do wish I could see your face. I'm not very good at addressing someone who isn't there."

"I'm here, Mrs Bradley, but would you like me to come round?" Grace asked her urgently, visions before her eyes of Rupert lying on his death bed – that damned revolver – but then Mrs Bradley would hardly call for her, would she, if . . . if . . .

"Oh, no, dear, there isn't time."

"Time? Time for what, Mrs Bradley? Please . . ."

"I sensed, you see, that you were . . . sympathetic to my poor boy and so I thought . . . I'm at my wit's end, Grace. I'm sure he intends to throw himself into the enemy fire and . . . I don't know what to do. If you could speak to him. Make him see that there is something worth living for despite what has happened to him. He mentioned you . . ."

"Mentioned me?" Images of the scene that had taken place in the summerhouse, images of herself in Rupert's arms, their bodies . . . naked bodies pressed . . . surely he had not . . . no . . . *to his mother* . . .

"Yes, last night; he and I were alone for a moment. He began to speak of the day, d'you remember, when you and your brothers came to Garlands."

"Yes, oh yes."

"And when he spoke your name there was a . . . a softness in his eyes; a mother recognises such things in her children."

"He asked for me?"

"Oh, no, dear, not at all."

"Then?"

"He is going back, Grace. To the war. He is to take the eleven thirty train from Lime Street. He will allow no one to see him off and I cannot bear the thought of him all alone. You . . . you have a feeling for him, don't you? Forgive me . . ."

"Yes." Grace's voice was steady though inside there was a vast quivering terror, a dread, for she knew Mrs Bradley was right in her instincts. Rupert believed he had nothing to live for. He believed he was a freak, the sort others shuddered away from. That his face offended people and that no one, no *woman* certainly, could ever love him. His own wife had shrieked in horror when she saw him. Besides, he had had his hopeful young manhood destroyed by her promiscuity, by her affairs with men who were his brother officers, and his belief in himself, the part that is in all of us, the small fortress where our inner being is protected, had been torn away.

He had not believed her, Grace, when she told him of her feelings. He thought she was a generous-hearted nurse who had seen many sights that other women had not been privy to. That she was accustomed to such things and her pity, her compassion had given her the strength to allow him to make love to her. God knows why, for women of her class and upbringing did not throw themselves into men's arm on a whim, not for any amount of compassion. His mind, altered as his face had been altered by his battle scars, could not believe that Grace Tooley loved him, no matter what she said, and to allow him to go back to France believing these dangerous thoughts would surely be the end of him.

"I'll go, Mrs Bradley," was all she said before replacing the receiver.

The station was acrid with smoke and the sudden hiss of steam. There was a great crush as there was at every station in the country as soldiers returned from or went back to the war. There was fighting in many parts of the world, on land, at sea and in the air and the movement of troops was constant. Men, or rather *boys*, or so they seemed in rough khaki, tunics with brightly polished buttons, pantaloons neatly wrapped from ankle to knee with puttees, webbing belts and ammunition pouches, enormously heavy black boots, to withstand the mud of the trenches, she supposed, hitched their rifles across their shoulders. Service caps at a jaunty angle, all a-glitter and gleam, tin hat, haversack and water bottle and ready to be off to the great adventure, embarrassed by their mothers' fussing. But these were the ones who were *going*!

Those returning were a different sight altogether. Their upright young figures were dragged down, not by the paraphernalia of war but by what they had seen and suffered in eighteen months of trench warfare. They still bore traces of mud about their uniforms and their faces were old and strained. They were *glad* of the comforting arms of their tearful mothers about them.

Carriage doors banged, engines screeched and whistled, porters shouted and in the midst of the turbulence Rupert stood alone with his back to the wall. He was smoking a cigarette. Travellers waiting for the same train which was coming down from Preston and stations north glanced at his tall, immaculate figure. He was an officer and so did not carry the clutter of the private soldier and, until he turned to face them, they, especially the women, cast appreciative looks in his direction. It was when they saw his face that they looked hastily away, afraid to meet his eyes, appalled by his disfigurement. Surely he could not be returning to the front with a face like that, they speculated, you could see it in their expressions, but Rupert met their gaze impassively as he had taught himself to do.

She had not consciously made the decision to wear her most attractive outfit but she was aware, from the admiring glances that were cast in her direction, that she looked her best. She wore a pale grey broadcloth skirt and a short military jacket to match – very fashionable at the moment – with rows of black braiding. A black straw boater with a broad white ribbon was pinned to her piled-up hair. To complete the elegant picture was a white cambric shirt with a high frilled collar that framed the line of her jaw, and well-polished black boots.

He had his head turned away from her, studying a young couple who shyly held hands, longing to fling themselves into one another's arms, a soldier and his girl saying goodbye, perhaps for ever. She touched his arm and when he swung round she smiled.

"Good God," he said, so taken by surprise he was ready to smile back in welcome. Then he remembered who he was, who she was and what was between them.

He drew himself up in evident indignation. "Good God in heaven, do you never give up?" he said icily. "Am I never to get a bit of peace from your attentions? Haven't you realised that I am not interested in the . . . the romance you seem determined to heap on me. That whatever it is you wish me to—"

"Stop it, Rupert." Her voice was so gentle he barely heard it above the tumultuous bustle which heralded the arrival of his train. But he did hear it and his face spasmed in what might have been pain.

"Goddammit, woman, can't you leave me alone? Let me go to the devil in my own way. Stop this crusade you seem bent on, though God knows why you should think it necessary."

"I have told you why though you seem determined not to believe me. I love you. I have loved you for years and nothing will ever change it."

"Stop it, stop it. Stop making such a bloody fool of yourself. How many times have I to tell you I'm not interested in your pitiful advances. God, you women, you don't know when to back off, do you? Now leave me alone."

His voice was harsh and he stooped to lift the small leather portmanteau that was at his feet, gripping it in his gloved hand, turning from her with the evident intention of striding across the platform to where the train would come to rest.

"I'll never stop it. I'll never leave you alone. Do what you like, say what you like but I cannot allow you to return to the front without—"

"Without what?" he snarled. "The loving farewell of a good woman to speed me on my way? Is that it? *I don't want it.* Can you not get that into that obtuse head of yours? Love! Jesus Christ, what do you know of love? I thought I had it but I was wrong and by God, I'm not going to be taken in again, so go home to your mother, little girl, and then look out for some young knight in shining armour to make your romantic dreams come true. I have nothing for you and I want nothing from you. Is that understood?"

"Your mother—"

"So that's how you came to be here? My mother had no right—"

"She loves you."

"Sweet Jesus, all this talk of love is making me feel quite nauseous and horribly bored so if you'll excuse me I'll get aboard and leave you to . . . to whatever it is you do."

The train had pulled into the station and there was a concerted surge towards it from all those who were to travel. Passengers were disgorged and in the general mêlée they became parted as those who had alighted mixed with those who were to climb aboard. She stood still and through her ran the wretchedness, the sheer misery, not just of his going but of the way he went. She had demeaned herself so often for this man, and would do again if she had the chance, she knew that, wondering idly at the sheer bloody strength of feeling which would not leave her be. She *could not* let him go believing he was unloved, unlovable. She had no idea what she had hoped for; perhaps in her naïvety that at the last moment he would relent, allow her to put her arms about him, let him see what his return to the trenches meant to her, what his return to *her* would mean to her, but he had spurned her advances, the love she had offered him, for the third time. There was a great emptiness inside her, a sadness, a numbness, for no man should go to war without the knowledge that he would be missed by some woman. That he was treasured, even if it was only by his mother and he had refused even that. Something inside her was shaking so violently it was as though her heart had come loose.

For some reason, perhaps to tell her more forcibly to leave him alone, now and for ever, he had put down the window of the first-class carriage and stuck his head out and without conscious thought she plunged forward, elbowing aside those who were making their own farewells. She flung her arms about his neck and fastened her mouth on his. She moved her lips, caressing, loving, soft, then hard and passionate as they had been taught by his in the summerhouse, and with a singing gladness inside her she felt his response.

"Rupert, I do love you," she whispered, her mouth still on his, then, as the train began to move off with a great whistle of impatience, she was dragged for a moment along the platform.

People were staring in great consternation but then there was a war on, their expressions said and soldiers and their sweethearts were sadly parted. They watched as the eyes of the officer, the one with the dreadfully shattered face, searched the lovely face of the woman who was left behind on the platform and were saddened themselves by the haunted look in them.

It had begun to rain as she moved slowly down the wide, graceful steps outside the station and the weather matched her mood of total desolation. She was pushed and jostled as people shoved passed her, struggling to grab one of the cabs that waited at the foot of the steps but she scarcely noticed, for it seemed she had done no good in coming here. For a moment she had felt hope when his lips had responded to hers but then, that was probably the natural response of male to female and nothing to do with emotion, of any sort.

There was a motor ambulance parked at the foot of the steps and from behind her a voice was pleading with those about her to "Make way, please, make way." Moving to one side, she turned indifferently, doing her best to make a path for the stretcher which two stalwart porters were heaving down the steps. A still figure lay on it, a man with a thin, pale face and a certain tension in his prone figure that spoke of pain. His lean hands were clenched on the blanket that covered him and they twitched and moved as though searching for something to cling to in the jostling he was suffering. From the shape beneath the blanket it was obvious that both his legs were missing from below his knees. At his side was a woman, a nurse. She was doing her best to help with the carrying of the stretcher and from her lips came soft, soothing murmurs.

Grace watched, aware of the sigh of sympathy that rustled about the crowd, for it must be one of their brave soldiers returned from the war. Though she did not recognise the man on the stretcher the woman beside him was Josie Allen.

"Josie?" Her voice was no more than a whisper but the sound of it in her own ears galvanised her to action. Moving forward and down the last few steps she put her hand on Josie's arm.

"Gerraway, if yer please, miss," the porter told her importantly. "Can yer not see't poor chap wants a birra peace?"

"Josie . . . it's me, Josie. God in heaven, Josie, it's me."

At last the nurse turned distractedly, caring only that her patient should be got as painlessly as possible into the ambulance. She was drawn, her face fallen into hollows, deep circles of purple beneath her eyes, her nose a beak in her gaunt face. She was ready to spit and fight with anyone who disturbed her patient but when, finally, she recognised Grace, she looked ready to fall apart with relief.

"Grace . . . oh, Gracie, thank God."

"Josie, darling . . . what . . ."

"It's Philip."

"Philip? Where?" Grace asked, bewildered, ready to look round to find the familiar face of Josie's husband.

"Here, you fool, on the bloody stretcher," Josie snarled. "Get into the ambulance, Grace. For God's sake, can't you see we need some room," turning on the crowd and the porters who were struggling to get the wounded man into the vehicle. The driver had climbed down from the front and was doing his best to help but the confusion, without the trained medical men needed in cases like this, was doing neither Josie nor Philip any good.

It was clear that Josie was almost at the end of her strength, for who knew how far she had travelled with Philip, but with Grace's own training in handling wounded men, the stretchers that brought them to the hospital, the men who carried them and the way in which she herself received them, quietly, efficiently, with no care for her beautiful outfit, Grace had Philip comfortably settled, Josie beside him, and herself next to her.

She turned and took her friend's hand. "Where are we going, darling?"

"Home."

"To Sheil Road?"

"No, to Philip's home. Derwent Road. Will you tell the driver, Gracie. I'm about done in."

Though the ambulance driver did his best it was plain that the journey from Lime Street to Derwent Road in Old Swan was a torment to the man on the stretcher. He did not complain but now and again a groan, sometimes a whimper, was wrung from him. Josie hung over him, not touching him except for a tender, gentle stroke of her fingertips on his hand, her voice a strand of sound on his ears telling him of her presence, of her love, of her devotion.

"Soon be there, my darling, soon be there. Not much longer. I know, I know . . . but when we get home I'll give you something. Not far, my love, not very far now. See, we're just on Green Lane. Grace is here to help and we'll soon have you comfortable. There, my darling, I'm here . . . I'm here, always."

Spring Cottage in Derwent Road was small, detached, whitewashed and with a roof of thatch, the garden pretty with spring flowers thrusting through the grass which had not been cut for a long time. The gate stood open and there was smoke coming from the single chimney. The cottage stood alone in a large garden and at its back was an orchard white with blossom. A dog barked from inside the cottage and as the ambulance drew up at the gate the front door was flung open and a stout, florid-faced woman stood anxiously on the doorstep, a black and white dog beside her.

With the dog, which was going mad with joy, firmly shut in the scullery, it took the four of them to get the stretcher up the narrow stairs to the bedroom, the driver, the stout woman, herself and Josie and the whole time Philip Booth moaned helplessly. It was not until she and Josie, expertly as they had been trained, had Philip comfortably in the vast, clean, double bed, his pain taken away with the morphine Josie administered – against all the rules, she murmured to Grace – that the two friends were able to sit down with the cup of tea the stout lady made them, and Josie was able to tell their tale. Hers and Philip's.

They had met as often as they could, knowing the joy of eating in cafés behind the lines, of sharing an occasional narrow bed in cheap French inns, of strolling along empty sands and through woods denuded of anything that might be called foliage. They wrote to one another knowing the relief that at the time of writing the loved one was alive but aware, both of them, even with the delivered letter in their hand that the other might be dead. She ate with it, slept with it, had gone mad with it, and so had he, and when word was got to her that he had been wounded by a shell which had exploded when he trod on it she had gone to him. She had deserted the other men in her care and gone to him and she would do it again, she told Grace fiercely. That had been in January and since then she had followed him from dressing-station to hospital after hospital, staying as close as she was able and when they had cut off his remaining leg, the first having been blown off by the shell, she made up her mind she would bring him home. No, not to a hospital, but home. She was a nurse. The doctor was to come later and besides, she was four months pregnant and Philip's child would be born under the same roof as his father.

She wept when Grace took her in her arms. Not once had she broken down in her need and care for her husband but now, she was home, her dearest friend was here and she gave herself up to the relief of letting go. It was the first and would be the last time!

23

The stout, florid-faced woman went by the name of
Bessie Marsden. Her husband owned Spring Farm
which stood at the end of the lane leading from
Derwent Road where Spring Cottage was situated and
though, being the wife of a busy and successful farmer,
she had more than enough to do about the farm she
could no more turn her back on them at Spring Cottage than she could fly to the moon. She remembered
the lad, young Philip, as a fresh-faced, bright-eyed,
engaging youngster who had helped about the farm
when he was not at school, for ever begging her sweet
almond macaroons and lemon biscuits. He was always
in the thick of it at harvest time and had proclaimed
stoutly that he meant to be a farmer when he grew up
but, of course, he hadn't. He'd been a well-educated
lad and had gone into some profession in the city, she
couldn't remember which, when he left school and
then, when war was declared, had rushed, like the
rest, like her own elder two sons, into the army. His
parents, who had been older than most when he – their
only child – was born, had died a year or two before the
war and within a few months of one another. She had
promised to keep an eye on his cottage while he was
away and had sent their Clarry, her eldest daughter
who had never married, to give the place a bit of a

clean each week. He had sent them a lovely letter when he married a nurse in London and when, a couple of months ago, his wife had written to say that Philip had been wounded and they would be returning as soon as possible, she and Clarry had scoured the place from top to bottom, stocked it with good farm food, made up the bed with freshly laundered linen, lit fires to air the place out, but nothing had prepared her for the sight of the ambulance, the poor chap on the stretcher and the gaunt creature who was his wife.

"Won't you sit down with us, Mrs Marsden," the gaunt creature had asked politely once they had got Philip to bed and given him something to alleviate his pain. You could see she herself needed a decent night's sleep, poor lass, but it seemed the other young woman, the one who had been so efficient in getting Philip comfortably in to his bed, was also a nurse and within half an hour she had everything sorted out.

"I am Philip's wife, Josie, as you have probably gathered, and this is my dearest friend, Grace Tooley. I happened to meet her at the station, thank God. Oh, Grace" – turning with a lovely gesture to her friend, a gesture that took her straight to Bessie's heart as nothing else could – "what guardian angel put you there just when I most needed you?"

"Never mind that, Josie. I want you to go straight to bed. Is there a second bedroom, Mrs Marsden?" Miss Tooley asked, turning to Bessie. "I want Josie to get to bed at once."

"Oh, no, Gracie, I can't. Philip might—"

"I shall be here, Josie, so let's hear no more. You're exhausted and need a rest before you can begin to look after Philip." When she entered the cottage she had removed her black straw boater and thrown it carelessly on to the dresser. Now she swung round again to Bessie, her dark, glossy hair, which had come unpinned in her endeavours with the wounded man, flowing about her head in a heavy mass, curling slightly at its ends. Bessie, who had just lowered herself into the rocking-chair to the side of the old-fashioned, blackleaded range, thought how lovely she was, all flushed at her cheekbones yet at the same time not at all flustered. "Is there a telephone at the farm, Mrs Marsden?"

Bessie almost laughed and would have done if the situation had not been so serious. These modern young women lived in another world to her and Monty. A telephone, indeed! The nearest was probably across the fields at Garlands where the Bradleys lived and the lass could hardly tramp across there in the get-up she was wearing. Them smart boots would be inches deep in mud, for they'd had a lot of rain recently.

"Nay, burr our lad could tekk a message on his bicycle."

"Could he bring back something more suitable for me to wear?"

"Aye, if yer was ter tell 'ooever's at t'other end what ter give 'im. 'E's a basket on't front fer't butter an' that. We deliver, yer see."

"That would be wonderful. I shall stay here until Josie has had a good rest, then, with you to keep an eye on things, Mrs Marsden, she and Philip will be in good hands. I shall come—"

"Gracie . . . Gracie, slow down. You have a job to go to."

"I'll send a note to the hall asking for a few days off. Just to give you time to rest. Have you looked at yourself in a mirror lately, Josie Allen . . . sorry, Booth?" Though she did not say so she was appalled by the state of Josie's lank hair which had once been springing with silvery fair curls, her thin, pinched face and tired eyes which, on her wedding day, had been a sparkling merry blue. "Where have those peaches and cream gone?" she added lightly. "D'you remember? I was bronze, rose and honey and you were peaches and cream. What a pair of idiots we were, children, and now look at us. You married and with—"

"A husband who may never walk again and—"

"Don't, darling. He loves you and you love him and surely, that's all that counts."

Bessie drank her tea and watched the two women impassively. She knew nowt about either of them but she considered herself to be a good judge of character, animals and humans, and she knew that these two were not only good friends to each other but would be to others in need. They had chosen to nurse men who were wounded in this life-taking war and she admired them for that. They were what she would call "ladies", brought up to be the wives of men of the middle classes; nevertheless they had rolled up their sleeves and thrown themselves, like the soldiers who fought in the war, into the thick of it, seeing and dealing with horrific wounds and, in the case of young Philip's wife, doing it in dangerous conditions. She wasn't one for fuss or demonstrations of affection, even when she felt it, but she thought she might "take" to these two. She listened to their conversation and though much of it meant nothing to her she could tell there was something being said that was causing upset to Miss Tooley.

"Rupert . . . ?" Josie queried, knowing exactly what was in Grace's mind.

"Gone."

"To France?"

"Yes."

Josie's face brightened suddenly and she took Grace's hand. "You were seeing him off."

Grace shook her head sadly. "Against his will." Then she lifted her head and smiled artificially. "But enough of that. Mrs Marsden must need to get home and if . . . er . . ."

"Andy," Bessie said, supplying this straightforward young woman with her youngest son's name.

"If Andy would . . ."

Bessie made as though to heave herself to her feet but Josie put out a hand to stop her.

"Stay for a few minutes and drink your tea, Mrs Marsden. I want to thank you—"

"Nay, I want no thanks, lass. I've known young Philip since he were born an' ter see 'im . . . well . . ." She shook her head fiercely, for Bessie Marsden was also not one for tears. Her own two, Owen and Davey, twins of twenty-one, were somewhere in the trenches and she prayed whenever she was on her own that God would keep them safe, though why he should single her boys out when there were thousands of mothers doing the same, she did her best not to dwell on. But she had not wept when they marched jubilantly away with the Liverpool Regiment and she didn't mean to start now. Young Philip was the first wounded man she had seen and the sight of that shortened body which had ended at what looked like his knees, had badly distressed her. And if she wasn't mistaken Philip's wife was in the family way and would need all the help she could get. Happen it was a good thing, for there was nothing like a baby for cheering folk up.

"I'll be off then and send up our Andy, an' if there's owt yer need just run up ter't farm. It's burra hop, skip an' a jump. We'll soon 'ave the two've yer on yer feet . . ." Then could have bitten her tongue, for Philip Booth had left his in France.

Nora was startled when the rosy-cheeked lad who looked as though he lived on the fat of the land, which he did, and who stood on her doorstep, speechlessly handed her a note.

"Wharris it?" she asked him suspiciously. For a heart-stopping moment she had mistaken him for the dreaded telegram boy but it was not a yellow envelope he handed her but a scrap of lined paper.

"Me mam sent me," he said, then waited.

"Oh, an' 'oo's yer mam?"

He sighed dramatically, for the daft things old people said was most irritating to his twelve-year-old mind.

"It's in't note. I've ter wait burr I've another note ter deliver." So look sharp, his manner told her.

She read the note before she let him in and for five minutes wrung her hands and addressed Edna with such heat the whole thing might have been Edna's fault.

"I can't just 'and over Gracie's stuff to a perfect stranger," she declared, "an' where's this . . . this" –

she peered at the note – "this Spring Cottage when it's at 'ome? I never 'eard of it."

"It's Mr Booth's place," Andy began, eager to be away, for he'd a football match that afternoon and he was the goalie.

"I don't know no Mr Booth," Nora wailed. Both Mr and Mrs Tooley were out and it wasn't up to her to make decisions about their Gracie's things.

"Look, missus, I've ter gerrover ter't th'ospital wi' another note from . . . from" – he racked his brain for the name of the pretty lady at Spring Cottage – "from Miss Grace Tooley, that's right, an' then ride" – he nearly said "hell for leather" but remembered in time the lessons his mam had taught him about language – "as quick as I can back ter't cottage."

Nora still looked bewildered but their Gracie's note, in their Gracie's handwriting and her inability to master the intricacies of the telephone to get in touch with Mr Tooley meant she had no choice but to do what the note told her.

"I'm going to France, Josie." Grace's voice was soft but steady, her face composed, and Josie, who had been half dozing by the bright fire in the range, lifted her head sharply to stare at her. She looked better. It was three days since she and Philip had returned and when Grace put her to bed in the second bedroom, without even the bath she craved, she had slept for twenty-four hours. Though it was not spoken of Josie had known that her husband was in good hands and even when the doctor she had arranged to call examined Philip and supplied the morphine that was needed and which she and Grace were not officially qualified to administer, she had not woken.

"I'll call again tomorrow," the elderly doctor, too old for the front, told Grace, "and I'll speak to his wife then. In the meanwhile, let her sleep. She's going to need her strength."

"She's four months pregnant," Grace told him bluntly.

"Good God alive." The doctor was clearly dumbfounded by the folly of the young.

"But Mrs Marsden up at the farm will keep her eye on them when I've gone."

"And where are you to go, young lady?" he asked disapprovingly. "Couldn't you arrange to stay with Captain and Mrs Booth until Mrs Booth is quite recovered and able to nurse her husband?"

"I'm afraid not. I'm to go to France."

The old doctor shook his head but there was an admiring gleam in his eye. "They'll need help."

"They'll manage, Doctor," Grace told him firmly as she walked to the gate with him.

The next day when the doctor called Josie had bathed and washed her hair and though she was far from the attractive young woman who Grace had last seen in August, she was considerably improved. Philip was eating a little, sleeping a lot and had actually had a bed bath given him by his wife and her friend. His eyes followed Josie about the room and whenever they thought themselves to be alone, they kissed one another with great tenderness. They would get through this, Grace knew it and, though it was a tragedy for so young a man to be without legs, and for his wife to share the loss with him, she envied them.

Now, she continued her conversation with Josie. "Matron asked me if I wanted to go several months ago. I lied, you see, about my age, and she knew I was lying. She asked me just the same but I said no, I couldn't abandon my parents but they are better now and I can safely leave them. Your mother is wonderful with Ma and when Ma is all right, then Pa is too. Nora is devoted to them."

"You're following Rupert, aren't you?"

"Yes, I suppose I am. He is . . . very frail, Josie. Oh, not physically but what his wife did to him and then the scars to his face. I told you all about it in my letter. He believes he is repulsive, that people shrink away from him and perhaps they do, but I don't. I love him as I have loved him for five years and if he won't allow it I shall force myself on him. I already have!"

Josie sat up and unfolded her legs which were curled beneath her. "You mean . . . ?"

"Yes, I mean . . . exactly what you're thinking."

"You have no idea what you're taking on, Gracie."

"You did it."

"I was with Philip. I loved him and he—"

"He loved you. That's what you're going to say, aren't you? And that Rupert doesn't love me, but he will, Josie, he will. I'll make him love me."

"Oh, darling Gracie." Josie's face was compassionate and she put out a hand to Gracie. The old dog, who had been bought as a puppy for Philip when he was a boy and who had lived up at the farm while his master was away, padded gingerly down the narrow staircase and stood at the door waiting patiently to be let out. Despite the doctor's misgivings he slept beside Philip's bed and would not be shut out and when Philip dropped his hand out of the bed the dog licked it lovingly. Philip stroked his silky head, the action soothing both man and beast. He was called Gyp.

Grace rose from the chair and opened the door. Gyp slipped out and disappeared for a moment, then came back, glanced up at her politely as though to thank her, then trotted up the stairs to his post.

"When do you mean to go?"

"As soon as I can. There are things to be arranged, so Matron told me. You'll have been through it when you went but when I get back to Old Nook Hall I'll speak to Matron. But before I go I want to make sure you and Philip are all right."

Josie smiled. "Come off it, Gracie. Mrs Marsden will make sure of that. She's dying to get her hands on Philip, fatten him up and all that, get him out into the fresh air and fill his lungs with the smell of manure. And when the baby comes I dare say I'll have a hard job getting my hands on it. Though two of her daughters are married she has no grandchildren. She'll be over here every second God sends, which will give me time to get Philip on his feet. Oh, yes, I mean it when I say feet." She paused. "D'you know what she told me?"

"Go on."

"That when Philip was a boy he wanted to be a farmer."

"Did he really?"

"And I mean to make him into one."

"Josie!"

"The old doctor says there is no earthly reason why Philip shouldn't eventually be fitted with artificial legs and when he is there's a job here for him on the farm."

"And shall you like being a farmer's wife, Josie?" Grace asked gravely.

"As long as the farmer's Philip."

She stayed a week and when she left she knew that Josie and Philip would not only survive but would succeed.

"Well, where've you bin?" Nora asked in an accusatory tone, just as though Grace had been off on a holiday to Blackpool instead of a mission of mercy. "Wharra ter-do there's bin wi' Mrs Allen not knowin' till this mornin' that their Josie's back from France wi' a wounded 'usband, an' stoppin' at *Spring Cottage*. Yer've just missed 'er. 'Er an' Mr Allen's just gone off ter see 'em."

"I told you in my note, Nora, where I was."

"'Ere, don't you go blamin' me, miss. I were told ter send yer clean underclothes an' such wi' that cheeky lad. There was nowt else innit."

"Nora, I'm sorry, but Josie was in a terrible state. Her . . . her husband has . . . has lost both his legs and . . ."

Nora sat down abruptly and her rosy face turned the colour of the dough she was kneading. "Eeh, never. Eeh, that poor lad, an' there's me shoutin' me 'ead off an' that poor lass wi' such trouble. Wharra shock fer her mam an' dad."

"I didn't know she had written them a letter. I suppose Andy posted it for her." She lifted Nora to an upright position and put her arms about her. "Don't cry, Nora, if there's a couple who can stand what they will have to stand, it's Josie and Philip. They love one another, you see, and really they are in the best place. The farmer's wife, Mrs Marsden, thinks the world of Philip and they'll be well looked after until Philip's up and about."

"Up an' about. What, an' 'im wi' no legs!"

"You wait and see, Nora. They can do wonders these days. Now, I'd better get off to the hall and face Matron. Where are Ma and Pa?"

"Yer pa's at shop as usual an' yer ma's gone to a lecture somewhere or other on't best way ter grow vegetables."

Grace had been just about to go and change when she turned back. Topsy, who could smell Gyp on her, sniffed cautiously at her skirt then went to lie down by the fire, hitching herself up close to Wally who made no objection.

"Nora."

"Yes, lamb?" Nora wiped her eyes sadly and resumed her kneading of the dough.

"Will you sit down for a minute?"

Nora looked up in surprise and her hands became still. "Sit down? I only just stood up."

"I know, but I have something to tell you and you'd be better sitting down." Nora began to look alarmed but she sat obediently.

"You see . . . well . . . ." Grace looked at Nora and then away again.

"Go on, my lass."

"I wanted to tell you . . . ."

"Out wi' it, our Gracie."

"I'm applying to go to France, Nora. Now I know it will put an enormous responsibility on you . . ."

Nora's face went even paler if that was possible and though her mouth trembled she straightened her shoulders courageously. She'd stood a lot in the care of this family she loved and could stand more, her attitude said.

"Nay, lass, don't think o' me. I don't matter an'—"

"Of course you matter. Quite simply we could not function without you, Nora, but you know how Ma will be," Grace cried, and for no reason at all tears began to run down her face.

"Give over, yer great soft 'apporth. Yer mam's survived a lot these last years an' it's my belief it's medd her stronger. She'll survive this an' all. We'll all stick together and if yer can 'elp just one o' them brave lads at front then yer go wi' my blessin'. Don't worry about yer ma. I'll see to 'er. I reckon if she can 'elp Mrs Allen through what's come to 'er Josie, it'll mekk 'er feel right important. Now, off yer go an' let me gerron wi' me bread or there'll be nowt fer us tea."

"Nora."

"Yes, queen."

"Josie's going to have a baby."

"Eeh, there yer are, yer see. Close one door an' another opens." They were both smiling as Grace ran lightly up the stairs.

She was dressed in the depressing uniform of a VAD nurse when she said goodbye to them all. An unflattering hat pulled down over her hair to her eyebrows, swallowing her wide, tranquil brow, overshadowing her sweet, grave eyes, a dark blue coat and skirt, white shirt and black tie and a wide Red Cross band circling her arm to denote she was on active service.

At the last minute, though she had been so brave in the interim, Ma clung to her and cried, for, apart from her schoolboy son, this was the last of her family to go. Six of them and if the war lasted long enough John wouldn't be far behind. Pa patted her shoulder, his eyes blind with tears, and Nora held her in a vice-like grip, her arms stiff with fear but her face grimly doing its best to smile. John was gruff and awkward, Edna sniffled into her apron while Mrs Allen, who had come to the gate to wave her off, with Mr Allen and the others behind her, smiled through her tears, her mind no doubt on her own daughter who had set off last year just as Grace was doing and look what had happened to her. A husband they'd known nothing about who'd lost his legs and a baby on the way. Her drawn face told its own story.

She crossed the Channel a week later with ten others in the group, all dressed alike and all looking as apprehensive as she felt. The Channel steamer was filled with soldiers, some young, fresh, excited, longing to get to grips with the Hun, others, just as young but quiet, withdrawn, obviously returning from leave and knowing exactly what was waiting for them.

She leaned on the rail and hitched the knapsack with which she had been issued more comfortably on her shoulder, watching as the coast of France appeared through the slight mist that lay on the water. The harbour of Boulogne came steadily closer and as she watched the picture disappeared and another image took its place. She saw Rupert's face, not as it was now but as it had been years ago when she first met him at the field where Mr Melly took his fragile monoplane skywards. His tanned face had been smiling then, smiling with the joy of being young, of being alive at such an exciting time, nothing on his mind but enjoying himself. Handsome, so handsome, tall, graceful, glowing with health and ready to be kind to the young sister of one of his friends. She had known then that this was the only man to whom she could give her heart, her love, her constancy and so it had proved. Where was he? How would she find him? She hadn't the first idea where to look, besides which she could hardly wander about in this country torn by war enquiring after Captain Rupert Bradley. But she *could* ask where the 2nd Battalion, King's Liverpool Regiment might be stationed. Let her get settled wherever she was posted and when she had a day, or an afternoon off, she would begin. And there was Charlie, dear Charlie who loved her, so he said in the last letter she had received from him. She must find him and Robbie and Richard . . . her brothers whom she had not seen for months. All the men she loved who were here.

She squared her shoulders as the steamer nudged its way into the harbour. Her tender mouth lifted a little at each corner in a smile of resolve.

24

Grace and a quiet girl called Amy Duncan were posted to the Number Two British Red Cross Hospital west of Amiens on the edge of a vast forest, where men who had been hurriedly treated at the dressing-stations behind the lines came by ambulance. Ambulances driven by women who had answered the Red Cross advertisement for those with driving experience. The Western Front was blasted each day with thousands of shells and was disgorging wounded at the same rate and these women ferried them about with what seemed the fearless ease they might have shown on a country road in England. Not only could they drive but they had learned the mysteries of motor maintenance, for there was no handy garage to drop into for help should they break down. From the advance dressing-posts and casualty clearing-stations to the field hospitals and on to the hospital trains which took the wounded back to Blighty, they drove through the muck, the muddle, the trackless wastes of the battlefields, sometimes becoming wounded, or even killed themselves, and Grace and Amy, who shared a tiny hut with two other VADs, grew to have great admiration for them.

Amy was older than Grace by a year or two, a softly spoken young woman from Leeds whose fiancé was serving with a Yorkshire regiment somewhere in this hell on earth called the Western Front. There was Matron, grey-haired and with a face on her that would frighten the horses, Grace heard an orderly say. She was firm and eagle-eyed as she gave them a lecture on exactly how they were expected to behave, remembering that they were on active service and as such must obey the rules, making it quite clear that should they deviate from them they would be sent home immediately. They were introduced to Sister Ryan and the other VADs, nurses and orderlies, and then taken round the big ward where Grace was soon occupied, much as she had been at the hall, with the emptying of bedpans and bottles in what was described as the sluice room, with taking temperatures, with changing dressings, giving blanket baths, writing letters for the "Tommies" unable to do so, cleaning wounds and scrubbing floors. And the worst job of all, writing to the parents, the wives of soldiers who had died, perhaps screaming and writhing in agony, of how peacefully they had left this world with the names of their loved ones on their lips and not the obscenities they often shrieked. They were young and did not want to die and they told God so in the language of the trenches.

The Tommies called her and Amy "Sister" which embarrassed them at first but the real Sisters didn't seem to mind, for the need for nurses was so great, indeed was overwhelmed by the number of casualties, the Sisters could not have coped without them. Many of the soldiers who had been wounded in the battle for Verdun, over which the French and Germans fought so bitterly, still remained in the hospital, asking one another each day as the ward round began, whether today would be a "Blighty one", that magical phrase which meant they would be going home. To get a "Blighty one" was the dream of every wounded soldier and when they were procured the soldier fiercely protected the label tied to his pyjama button. BL meant "boat lying", for the serious cases, or BS "boat sitting", for the fitter men who would nevertheless require long convalescence. Even a red label for the cases that would need careful watching was coveted.

She had imagined that she had seen the worst of what man could inflict on his fellow man at Old Nook Hall but she was mistaken. The casualty who had reached Liverpool had been cleaned up, patched up, and treated at the receiving hospitals in the south and had been several weeks into his wounded state, but these men for whom she now cared were in such a pitiable state, suffering unimaginable wounds, straight from the battlefield, that she found that she had to creep away to some corner now and again to hide her weeping. If Matron had found her she would have been hauled over the coals, for every nurse and every VAD was expected to acquire a clinical detachment for her patients. It was no use whingeing and whining, as one tender-hearted VAD was told, since it did the men no good. Men struggling for breath and blue in the face with the acute bronchitis caused by the inhalation of gas could do without hysterics, Matron told them icily. Amputations that resulted from sepsis and gas gangrene, the limbs and wounds treated with hypochlorous acid solution, the smell of which, added to the smell of the wound itself, Grace could not get out of her nose. The agony of the men so treated, for it had to be done every three hours, was such that the wounded man shrank from the sight of her coming towards him. Irrigation, it was called, the cleaning of a suppurating wound. She and Amy found it very hard at first, since they were not trained nurses, but so great were the number of wounded still coming in the nurses couldn't cope and it was left to VADs to do the best they could with wounds, some so horrendous they were both ready to faint. But they didn't!

She and Amy sometimes managed to get an hour off together and walked from the hospital in their heavy shoes through fields still grassy and filled with wild flowers and on into the forest, though the far-off vibrations of the big guns in the distance still attacked their ears. There was to be a big offensive soon, a big push, and there was a spirit of optimism and excitement among the men, for they felt, and had been led to believe that this was the offensive, carefully planned and prepared for, that was going to smash the German Army and bring an early end to the war. The front stretched from Gommecourt in the north to near Chilly in the south and it was rumoured that soon, no one was quite sure when, the attack would begin. The Somme began where the harsh industrial north country of France left off, a land of rolling downs, of meadows and woodland, of gentle hills, quiet streams, peaceful villages and hamlets that reminded the British soldiers of home. A quiet sector of the line which was soon to change.

May was nearing its end: she had been in France no more than a month when she heard her name called as she trudged from the draughty hut she shared with Amy to the main ward. It had rained heavily during the night and though duckboards had been placed from hut to hut it was difficult on the slippery wooden surface to avoid sliding into the mud that the ambulances had churned up.

During the month she had been at Amiens she had picked her way through all the wards, with Sister Ryan's permission, naturally, who sympathised with her anxiety over her brother, asking every patient if they knew the whereabouts of the 2nd Battalion, the King's Liverpool Regiment, or the Lancashire Fusiliers.

"I hearrrd the Liverrrrpool lot were up norrrth with Allenby and the Third Army near Gommecourt." The speaker was a pipe-smoking Scots sergeant-major who'd lost one eye and was wounded in his arm and leg. The orderly had to lift him up to have his dressing done and the doctor and Sister had just done the dressing together. It was a terrible torment to him and the man had clamped his teeth about his pipe in order not to scream. He was as white as the snowy bandages that festooned him but he managed to speak round the chewed stem of his pipe.

There was a pot-bellied stove in the middle of the ward, the chimney from it going up through the roof. A badly burned airman lay in an angled bed on a high frame, his feet higher than his drawn, youthful face. Morphine had just been administered and his eyes were cloudy but at peace. There were men in cane chairs, some without legs, others without arms and some thoughtful person, probably a young nurse who had been given time off to walk in the surrounding fields, had placed a vase of wild flowers on a table under the window.

"The Liverrrpool 'Pals' Rrregiments," the sergeant-major continued in his broad Scottish accent. "'Pals' Rrregiment!" It was obvious that had he been outside he would have spat with disgust. "Fight together an' effin' die together, whole streets of 'em." Suddenly aware that he was swearing in the presence of a nurse, which was strictly frowned upon, he closed his mouth like a trap. He was also aware that this pretty nurse was asking after the regiment for a reason and the reason must be that whoever she was concerned about was in it. "Not that it happens all the time, ye ken," he went on hurriedly, "and anyway, what wi' this big push they'rrre talking aboot it'll bring an earrrly end to it all. You wait an' see, Sister."

"Thank you, Sergeant." She did her best to smile but his words were like shards of glass in her heart for it was not the first time she had heard this said about the "Pals" Regiment. Got together in the first months of the war, it had been supposed by those who had raised them that the "boys", sometimes a dozen from one street, would settle down with their own and make a better fighting machine. Lord Derby had been one and she herself had seen them, the Liverpool "Pals", route-marching through the streets of Liverpool. Every town and city in the country had sent their own regiments to the front and they had been slaughtered, lying in their own blood and the blood of the pal who had lived next door to them.

Another patient, also a sergeant, a regular from the old British Expeditionary Force, thought the Liverpool 2nd Battalion, which was the one the nurse was enquiring about, might be with the Fourth Army under Rawlinson just south of Albert, so he had heard, and gradually word got round the hospital that Nurse Tooley, who was not only a "looker" but a kind and patient nurse with time for every man on every ward, was searching not only for the Liverpool regiment but the Lancashire Fusiliers where, it was rumoured with many a nod and a wink, she had a sweetheart.

She turned round quickly when she heard her name called, almost sliding into the mud. For several moments she could not make out who it was among the hurrying medical staff, the ambulance drivers, the stretcher-bearers trying to keep to the duckboards who had called her name. The men in khaki all looked the same, tired, strained, muddy, some of them borne down by the heavy equipment they were forced to carry into battle. Along the road that lay beside the hospital compound they marched, some stepping out from their rest behind the lines on their way back to the trenches, others dragging their weary loads in the opposite direction.

He was standing at the entrance to the compound in which the hospital was situated on the very edge of the broad duckboard that ran past the row of tents where the orderlies slept. He was an officer so he did not carry the mass of equipment the men did, sometimes half their own weight, but he still looked dragged down, infinitely weary and plastered with mud which came from the trenches when it rained.

"Grace." He said her name as though it were a prayer, then began to limp towards her along the duckboard. It was a limp that was very familiar to her though as yet it was difficult to recognise Charlie beneath the mud, the unshaven face, the tin helmet.

"Charlie . . . Charlie? Is it really you? Oh, my

dear . . ." And unconscious of the grins of the watching soldiers, the wrath of Matron should she be seen, she ran along the duckboard, light as a drifting feather and straight into Charlie's opened arms. They closed round her and clung, tight as a vice, and Grace was aware that Charlie was hanging on to a slender tether which was keeping him from simply spiralling away into a state of madness. Already what was called "shell-shock" when applied to the men, and "neurasthenia" to an officer, was beginning to be seen among the troops and Charlie had already been wounded, had already nearly lost a leg and had already been in the line for over eighteen months.

"Darling . . . oh, my darling . . ." His mouth was pressed into her neck beneath her chin and the stubble on his jaw grazed her flesh. Aware that they were on show for all to see, she pulled herself from his arms, took his hand and drew him off the duckboard and behind a tent, tucking him between the guy ropes, then leaning again into his arms.

They stood for several trembling minutes in one another's arms and she was surprised by her own intense feelings. She loved another man, a man who had suffered just as much, if not more than Charlie, a man who was fighting as hard a war as Charlie, and yet her depth of feeling for the soldier who shuddered in her arms overwhelmed her. Charlie needed her now and could she refuse him the warmth and haven of her arms, the softness, the gentleness that was the other side of the coin to life in the trenches.

At last she moved a fraction away from him so that she could look into his eyes. They were wet with tears.

"Oh, Charlie," she said sadly, "where have you been?" Which was the silliest question a woman has ever asked a man straight from the trenches, she knew that, but it wasn't what she meant. She was asking him in which hell had he dwelt since last she saw him, for it was evident from his old-young face that he had seen it.

"Away from you, my lovely girl, that is all it takes to put me in purgatory. You are my peace and rest." He removed his helmet and gently placed his mouth on hers. His breath was stale. She supposed a soldier in the thick of battle hardly had time to clean his teeth but it didn't matter, this was Charlie, and she loved him.

"How did you know where I was?"

"You'd told me you were coming to France in your last letter, and when it got round – a stretcher-bearer, I believe – that a nurse from the hospital here was asking for the Lancashire Fusiliers I knew, hoped, I suppose, that it might be you. I've got twenty-four hours, that's all."

"Where are you going? Tell me and I'll see if Sister will give me a few hours off."

"Into Amiens. The officers have a billet there which I'm told is quite spectacular but I want to take you somewhere quiet and make love to you."

It was said simply and she replied with the same simplicity. "I would like that." Not for herself, she knew that, but for him. She wanted to heal him, to "make him better" as her mother used to say when she was a child, to take away the hurt and make him forget for a few hours the horrors of his war. It was the only thing she *could* do.

* * *

The patron of the small hotel looked at them knowingly as he handed over the key. They climbed the stairs to the first floor but Charlie was beginning to shake uncontrollably as she shut the door. She sat him on the edge of the bed, then knelt and removed his mud-caked boots. One by one she gently stripped him of the clutter an officer carries about on his person: holster, Sam Browne belt and cross-belt, pack, cap which had replaced the helmet, jacket and breeches, as though he were a small child. She placed his revolver carefully on the chest of drawers, then when he was totally naked eased Charlie between the sheets of the bed. With the same care and refusal to be hurried she took off her own clothes, letting him watch, wanting him to watch, and he wept as she did so. Then, when she was naked, when he had studied her, drawn into his soul the cleanness, the wholeness of her body, she lay down beside him.

She had made love to only one man, a man who had taken her with passion, with a rough sort of tenderness, since he was not a brute, with great skill, bringing her to an explosive orgasm – she believed that was the word though she had never spoken it – that had left her sighing and stretching and yawning like a cat just awakened from sleep. Charlie made love to her reverently, enraptured more by her naked beauty, her smiling acceptance of his, than with desire. He wanted her, naturally, and at the last fell on her with a trembling moan, burying his head on her breast, taking her nipple into his mouth, holding her like some rare porcelain that might break while she wrapped him about with her loving arms.

He slept then, holding her in arms of such strength it was as though he clung to the only thing that made sense in a world that had gone mad. She could not move and gradually her arms and neck became numb but when he awoke and began again she responded with warmth and love, the feelings he roused in her far from those Rupert had awakened but still worth while. His delight had the wondrous, almost innocent quality of a child discovering the beauties of the world, a slow second wandering – the first had been hurried – through enchantment as his hands took her breasts, moved slowly across her flat stomach, along her thighs and down the long slenderness of legs to her ankles. He sighed as he touched her forehead and cheek, her mouth and throat, and she stretched her arms above her head, turning slowly so that his body might enjoy hers. The bed was hard and lumpy and there were a great many street noises from beyond the window but it did not concern Charlie as he enjoyed for the second time the forthright explosion of male joy which enriched her own body though she did not achieve it. His long, lightly boned body moved her to exquisite tenderness and she let him see it, since she knew it strengthened him and he would need that strength in the months to come. She had no idea, and neither had he, when they would see one another again but she was here, near the front, near where he was.

Her heart ached, though it was overflowing with tenderness for Charlie, for the man who was lost to her, longed for him, strove to push away the thought of him, and the memory of his rejection of her filled her with savage pain. For a moment, as she smoothed Charlie's tumbled hair, she remembered the sweetness and humour she had first seen about Rupert's lips, the quiet amusement behind his alert gaze, the luminous joy she had felt in his arms and she was consumed with a deep and terrible grief for which there were no words. With her loving of Charlie she had lost irrevocably what might have been with Rupert.

It began to grow dark and she knew she must go. Amy had promised to cover for her if she should be missed and though Sister had given her permission to spend a couple of hours with her "brother", raising a sardonic eyebrow as she spoke, she knew that those couple of hours were long gone.

"When we get out of this bloody mess, will you marry me, Grace?" Charlie asked her quietly from the bed, as she dressed herself. He looked peaceful, hopeful, rested and she knew he would be all right now. The haggard, shambling wreck had been healed, healed by what she had given him. She didn't want a song of praise for herself. She wanted nothing said in her favour. She was a woman, a nurse, and she had done what women and nurses did for a man. She loved him. It was enough.

"I ask because you don't seem to be . . . connected to anyone. You told me once that—"

"It's over, Charlie, and yes, I will marry you."

The smile began in his eyes, crinkling them up at the corners, spreading to his lips then breaking in an irradiation over his whole face. It shone from him like a beam of sunlight and she felt its warmth, the love he held her in and she moved to the bed. Kneeling down she put her arms about him and kissed him.

"I love you, Charlie," she told him and though she knew it was an entirely different love to what was in her heart for Rupert, he didn't, and it was enough.

*   *   *

It was several days later when Matron sent for her and her heart sank. Someone must have seen her with Charlie. They had been open in their movements from the hospital to Amiens, climbing aboard a passing truck whose driver, a grinning soldier, told them to "hop up". There had been hundreds of men and women in the town, any of whom might have known her by sight from the hospital and this was the result. She would be sent back to England in disgrace, for one of the strict rules Matron had insisted upon was that there was to be no fraternising with the opposite sex!

"Sit down, Tooley," Matron said and Grace noticed for the first time that though Matron did indeed have a stern, even forbidding face, her eyes were kind. Grace's heart was pounding, for the last thing she wanted was to be sent home in disgrace. It would mean she would be away from Charlie, whom she had promised to marry, and, though she had done her best to erase it from her sorrowful heart, there would be no chance of catching sight of Rupert, or her brothers, Robert somewhere in the trenches, Richard somewhere with his flying unit, though where that might be she had no idea. She was ashamed of herself for the thought. Putting her brothers second was shameful and if what she had shared with Charlie was to continue and be meaningful, which she was intent on, why should she consider, even yet, the possibility of finding Rupert? But Matron was speaking and it was not of her visit to Amiens with Charlie.

"Nurse Tooley," she said, her gaze very direct. "I don't know whether news has reached you of a battle at sea which took place last week. Jutland which is in the North Sea. The German Fleet . . . well, several of our ships were sunk. One of them was the *Indefatigable*. It was hit and was . . . there were no survivors. I believe your brother . . . I'm afraid, my dear, he is lost. I am so sorry. You will, of course, be sent home on compassionate leave. I know you have only been here a few weeks and your work has been well thought of. You have a brother in the lines, so I was told, and he is to be given compassionate leave too, as is your other brother in the Royal Flying Corps. Your family has given much to this war and your mother needs you at home for a while. When she is—"

Grace stood up abruptly but Matron took no offence. She was accustomed to giving orders and having her orders obeyed instantly. None of them sat or stood unless she said so. A stickler for discipline was Matron, but she was kindness itself as she summoned Sister Ryan and explained what had happened and what was to be done with Nurse Tooley. Nurse Tooley was in a state of shock, she told Sister Ryan and until her brother, who was with the Liverpool Regiment, was brought to her to take her home, she was to rest in her hut. Perhaps Nurse Duncan who shared her hut could stay with her for a while.

Somehow, she didn't know how it was arranged, Robert was there and had they not told her who he was she would not have known him. Gone was the cheeky lad who had teased her so maddeningly, the light-hearted, engaging boy who had marched off to war in search of the big adventure, and in his place was a worn-out man, expressionless, showing none of the terror he had known, the horrors he had seen. Only in his eyes was desolation as he put his arms about her.

"Gracie . . ." It was all he could say.

Richard was waiting for them at Boulogne and the three of them clung together for a moment then broke apart, saying nothing. The men lit cigarettes and watched the chaotic jumble which was the disembarking of soldiers for the front and the embarking of men going home on leave. There were wounded on stretchers carried by orderlies, some of them moaning, one screaming in agony as his stretcher was jolted. There were walking wounded, nurses, doctors accompanying them and the three quiet figures watched with what looked like indifference. Robert was twenty years old and Richard and Grace just nineteen and in their short lives they had seen more than anyone ought to see, and still be sane.

"Jesus Christ!" Richard muttered, then stubbed out his cigarette against the wall before taking Grace's hand in his and leading her towards the Channel steamer that was to take them home.

25

The three of them stood before the seated figure of their mother and waited for her to recognise them but such was the depth of Mary Tooley's devastation, the extent of the damage done her, they might have been strangers. Strangers who were standing in her house come for some reason she could not even guess at, if she was capable of thought, that is. She simply wasn't there. The mother of Arthur, of Tom, of George had gone away where nothing could hurt her. And the mother of John, the last of her babies who had vanished when the telegram about George had been delivered and had broken her heart beyond repairing. The arrival of Grace, Robert and Richard had stirred up the crippling grief again, dug its claws into the open wound and so great was the distress, so extraordinary the catastrophe, Nora had deserted her kitchen and occupied the chair opposite her mistress, weeping quietly into a large tea towel, her head bowed, her shoulders heaving. At the window, staring blindly out into the lovely summer day, the lovely summer garden which had helped to save his wife's sanity, was their pa. Someone was in the kitchen, for Grace could hear the quiet clatter of crockery. She guessed it must be Edna, or perhaps Mrs Allen who, in the awfulness of the situation, might have torn herself away from her pregnant daughter and her pregnant daughter's legless husband to give what she could to her neighbours in their hour of need, which was how she would see it. Dear God in heaven, what was this war doing to the families of this country, tearing them apart and throwing the pieces hither and yon like some careless child? Grace thought. Her own family was slowly being decimated, its sons dragged into the war machine, the last of them her baby brother who was just seventeen and had been swearing for many months he would go despite the fact that he was under age. Conscription had begun in January of this year, applying to single men of nineteen to thirty years of age but John, it seemed, could not wait.

Richard, the first time they had seen him in his uniform, looked extremely dashing in the uniform of a pilot officer. It was similar to the uniform worn by an army officer, a khaki service dress of well-made jacket and breeches with knee-high boots. His cap, which he had removed, had been worn at a jaunty angle to the side of his well-brushed hair and above his breast pocket was the badge of the Royal Flying Corps. In contrast poor Robert, who was a private soldier and, what's more, come straight from the trenches – the mud still clung to his boots, puttees and trousers – was slung about with the usual pouches, webbing belt, rifle, bayonet holder, backpack and tin helmet, and Grace had time to wonder tiredly why the army felt it necessary for a soldier to carry all his equipment when he was going home to his family. She herself wore her nurse's uniform, the long, belted coat, the hideous hat, and in the two days it had taken them to get from Boulogne to Liverpool had scarce had the time or the opportunity to have a wash. She knew that Richard fretted over his inability to shave but Robert, who was eerily quiet, didn't seem to care about anything, let alone shaving.

She knelt down at her mother's knee and took her flaccid hands in her own.

"Ma, we're home. See, Richard is here and Robby. Won't you give them a hug?" Her voice was almost a whisper as though she didn't want to startle the worn, sagging woman in the chair but when Ma slowly lifted her head Grace looked into eyes that were empty, the woman behind them gone out somewhere, unfocused, blank and flat as a lake on a windless day. Not a ripple of life, not a gleam of light, nothing, and as Grace rose slowly to her feet and turned to look at her brothers she supposed that really it was for the best. Ma was not hurting.

"Pa." Walking wearily across the room she lifted her hands and took hold of her father's upper arms, resting her cheek against his back. "Pa, we've come home," she murmured. "They let us come home."

Her pa turned stiffly, looking down into her upturned face and though he was not as comatose as Ma there was little expression in his face.

"Grace . . . Gracie, is that you, child?"

"Yes, Pa, and Richard and Robby. We've come home."

"George is dead, did you know?"

"Yes, darling." And by the fire Nora continued to weep noiselessly, rocking in anguish back and forth, back and forth.

"Drowned, they said, like Arthur. And John, our little John has gone . . . all gone . . . none left . . ."

A moan tried to escape from Grace's throat and Robert made some sound that could not be identified.

"Your ma is . . . is . . . upset."

"Yes, but I'm here now, Pa, and Richard and Robby. See . . ."

"Richard . . . Robby . . ." He turned his gaze on them and with a movement which almost had him over his two strong boys surged forward and put their arms about him. He was frail, even frailer than when Grace had left and she knew, sadly, that she could not leave them again. As much as her brothers and all the others involved in this war, her mother and father were the victims of the carnage.

While her brothers held their father, awkward, embarrassed but staunch in their own grieving compassion, Grace went to Nora. She lifted her from her chair and took her in her arms, patting her back, saying nothing, just holding her, letting her know that she was no longer alone in this terrible time.

"Grace." A gentle voice from the doorway between the family room and the kitchen made her turn her head and there was Josie and behind her Mrs Allen. Josie was in her sixth month of pregnancy now. That awful expression of acute weariness, of strain and sorrow had disappeared and, though her face showed her sadness for her friend and her family, she looked bonny, serene, her hair cut short and brushed into a shining halo of bright curls, her face rosy, her eyes as blue as once they had been. Peaches and cream.

"Oh, Josie, darling, what are you doing here? You should be at home with your husband, not . . ." But even as the tears started, the first she had shed, Josie was across the room and dragging Grace into her arms. Mrs Allen watched with compassionate eyes.

"Oh, shut up, Grace Tooley. Father brought me over in the motor. If I can't come to help my . . . well, you know what I mean. And Philip is in good hands. Mrs Marsden can't wait for me to go out so that she can get her hands on him. Mother and I . . . we . . . well, here we are and tea is made so take off your coats. Robby . . . Richard, give me a kiss, then sit down and tell me . . . No, Nora, stay where you are," as Nora rose automatically to go to her post in the kitchen. "Mother will bring in the tea and some scones she made."

"I should be out there doin' summat," Nora argued but Grace pushed her back into her seat, then squatted on the floor by her mother. The men leaned against the windowsill, one on either side of their father as though protecting him, and as Grace sipped her tea she was thankful that neither Josie nor Mrs Allen offered sympathy or the condolences thought necessary at a time like this. Richard and Grace talked of the difficulty of travelling, Josie brought them up to date on Philip's progress, which was slow but good, Grace gave them an edited description of her work at the hospital near Amiens and the first hour was got through. No mention was made of the future. The boys would go back to their units at the end of the week, their compassionate leave of short duration. Grace suspected they had been given it because George was the second son to have laid down his life in the defence of his country, but she herself had been allowed fourteen days, that presumably being enough time for a daughter to settle her bereaved parents into an acceptable pattern of life after the loss of their son.

But that would have to wait. She knew she was needed to nurse the growing number of casualties that the war spewed up but there were hundreds of girls, most of them privately educated and groomed to be a "lady", longing to get out there, to be on active service and be as much a part of the war as "Tommy Atkins". She was honest enough to admit to herself that her application to go to France was mainly due to her need to be near Rupert, perhaps to nurse him should he be wounded. And if not, to look for him, to convince him one way or another that she truly loved him. To give him something that perhaps might prevent him from throwing himself in front of a German machine-gun as she felt he intended to do. Instead she had met Charlie. She had made love with Charlie. She had promised to marry Charlie, which, naturally, one day, she must do. Charlie had taken that promise up the line with him, a shield to protect him from the dangers, the terrors, the horror that he would meet. It had given him a purpose and whether that purpose would protect him was in the hands of something stronger than she was. Oh, she still loved Rupert; she had pondered on the sad fact all the way back from Boulogne, the distance growing between them and hurting her as if something of her was fastened to something of him and was being pulled in two. She should have been dwelling on George but her thoughts had been of Rupert. But Rupert was married to Jessica. And Rupert did not love Grace, not as Charlie did. She needed love and Charlie was ready to give it to her, had already given it to her in his enduring devotion.

So, if it was possible, with Ma in the state she was in, she might get back to Old Nook Hall or one of the other hospitals in Liverpool. She had a talent for nursing; she had been trained to it by her time at the hall and the few weeks she had spent in France. Though she had been told firmly to remain detached from the emotional needs of the wounded, dying men, she had not been able to cultivate that detachment and the men had sensed it in her and she had given, she hoped, an added something, a piece of herself, she supposed, to those who needed it. She could withstand the swollen ankles, the reddened hands, the aching feet which were the lot of a nurse, and if she could arrange for someone to care for Ma until she recovered, or at least was able to bear her grief, she meant to approach the hospital authorities to transfer her back to Liverpool.

Her brothers had gone back. Nora had recovered enough to resume her duties in the kitchen and the general management of the house, and Ma was not a scrap of trouble, sitting in her rocking-chair, oblivious it seemed to what went on about her, her face serene, her eyes empty. Pa was persuaded to return to the shop and it did him good to get out of the house and have some purpose other than anxiously watching for his wife to return to him. Mrs Allen, with the other ladies of the church, took it in turns to sit with Ma, to talk to her of what was happening in their circle, to drink the tea Nora brought in and eat her delicious biscuits, the recipe for which they begged from her. Ma was got up each morning by either Grace or Nora, dressed, washed and led to her chair until bedtime when the process was reversed, and so when Grace cycled up to the hall two weeks later it was with the peace of mind of knowing that life at Sheil Road, as it was to be at the present, was slowly falling back into place. She had written to Charlie, telling him what had happened and was waiting for a reply.

"I won't say we wouldn't be glad to see you back, Nurse Tooley," Matron told her after commiserating with her on the death of her brother, "but do you think you will be able to perform your duties bearing in mind the condition of your mother?"

"My mother is well looked after, Matron and if I stay in Liverpool I'm not far away should a crisis arise. I want to go on nursing but I'm afraid I can't return to France, much as I'd like to. My younger brother, though he is only seventeen, has disappeared and though it has been reported to the authorities since he is too young to enlist, I'm afraid he will find some way of doing it. He's a big lad, tall and strong and could pass for nineteen so by now he's probably already in the army."

"Probably, my dear. There are so many youngsters who have no conception of what is waiting for them over there who are lying about their age and getting away with it. Also, at the beginning of the war the standard of fitness required was very high but now, with men . . . I'm sorry, my dear, but you will know what I mean. They need men so desperately they are willing to overlook many things and age is one of them."

"Yes, I know that, Matron, but until we hear from him there's nothing to be done and by then it will probably be too late."

"My poor child, your family has been singularly unfortunate." Matron sighed sadly over the Tooleys' misfortune then she became brisk. "But I'll admit you would be most welcome back here. The casualty list grows longer by the day. I hardly dare glance at the newspapers but there, it's no good crying over spilled milk . . ." Which was her way of saying there was a job to be done and they'd best get on with it. "When can you start?"

"I'd like to give my mother another few days but perhaps next Monday. It's the end of June now. I have been home three weeks and she seems to be . . . well, I was going to say settled but she is really not that. Sometimes I wonder whether one of the doctors who deal in this illness of the mind could help her, or perhaps she is best left where she is."

"Doctors qualified in psychiatry are few and far between. The tension of trench warfare . . . well, you have seen it for yourself. Hysterics, as the men in the ranks are being called, are becoming more and more frequent. There's a hospital for shell-shocked officers in Edinburgh which deals with nothing else, but your mother . . . my dear, give her time. With you at home she will be herself again soon."

"Thank you, Matron." Grace stood up. "I'll see you on Monday morning then."

She was at Spring Cottage when the news of the rumoured offensive on the Somme began to trickle through. It had begun on the first of July, a beautiful summer's day with the sun shining down from a cloudless blue sky, so Grace was to later hear in a stained and crumpled letter from Charlie. He and thousands of others had attacked shoulder to shoulder, line after line, wave upon wave, straight into the sights of the German machine-guns. Far from being pulverised by the bombardment of the British guns which had gone on for days, the enemy was waiting for them. Before they left the trenches the young soldiers, many of them in their first battle, many of them standing shoulder to shoulder with their "Pals", smoked their cigarettes and winked at each other in high old excitement, giving the thumbs-up sign, full of confidence. Within an hour half of them lay dead and wounded, among them Private Robert Tooley and Lieutenant Charlie Davenport. Thirteen British divisions went "over the top", that day, nineteen thousand of them were killed, fifty-seven thousand wounded, the greatest loss in a single day suffered by any army in the war.

Philip sat out beneath the heavy foliage of a massive oak tree on the special cane armchair stretcher with wheels which Josie had obtained for him. The sun was turning his pale, wasted look to one of tanned health and but for the amputation of his legs, hidden under his rug, he looked as normal as any man who lived in the good country air of Old Swan. He was adored by his wife, who had confessed privately to Grace, without even a blush, that they had resumed their lovemaking, with a great deal of clumsy manoeuvring, she admitted, on both their parts, since she was pregnant and he was wounded! Grace had been inclined to blush but then was ashamed of her silly modesty and was tempted for a moment to tell Josie about her and Charlie, but Josie forestalled her by asking diffidently about Rupert.

"I know you went to France to be near him, as I

did Philip. Were you . . . successful in finding him?"
Her face was filled with affection and a longing to
help her friend but she needed her to know that she
wasn't prying. It was concern that made her speak.
Grace was dreadfully thin, grieving for her brother
and the sadness in her home but there was something
about her that spoke of . . . well, Josie didn't know.
Some strange tranquillity that was at odds with her
sadness.

"No, I wasn't there long enough. Just a few weeks
but I did see Charlie."

"The soldier you nursed at the hall?"

"Mmm." Grace stared down at the flowers she had
picked in Josie's garden and which she was arranging
in a vase. Her hair was tied back carelessly with a bright
ribbon but a swathe had come loose and hung over her
forehead, hiding her eyes.

Josie peered at her, trying to analyse her expression.
"And . . ."

"We went into Amiens."

"Really. Was he well?" Meaning not wounded.

"Oh, yes."

"And he still loved you?"

Grace lifted her head abruptly. "I didn't tell you that
he loved me. I spoke of it to no one."

"But he does."

"Yes."

"And you?"

"I shall love Rupert I think until I die, Josie. No
matter how I try I can't get him out of my mind. No
matter what I tell myself . . . about his wife and . . . all
that, he is my love. I still love him so much, so much
I cannot imagine that it will ever end. You will know

that from loving Philip. But Charlie means . . . means a lot to me."

"Yes." Josie was not satisfied, for she was certain her friend was keeping something from her, but she merely took the flowers from Grace's hand.

"Well, whatever it was you learned at the hospital it didn't include arranging flowers. Go and talk to Philip."

Philip was reading *The Times*, the front page of which was filled with a report of the great offensive on the Somme, its headlines announcing FORWARD ON THE WESTERN FRONT. START OF A GREAT ATTACK. FIERCE BATTLES ON THE SOMME. Having been involved in a fierce battle himself, however, Philip privately was not at all certain he could feel the elation that seemed to be shared by the rest of the population, the rejoicing over the glowing newspaper headlines. Bessie had been over that morning to bring him the newspaper.

"Eeh, lad, it'll be over before long, just you wait an' see," she told him, giving his breakfast tray a good look to make sure that his wife was feeding him to the standard Bessie demanded. Mind, that Josie, as she had begged Mrs Marsden to call her, was right sensible. Well, she would be being a nurse, but she took Bessie's advice and gave the lad plenty of milk, eggs, cheese, and was getting halfway to being a decent cook under Bessie's guidance. Good broth with plenty of vegetables in it, grown on the farm, of course, home-baked bread, egg custards, as much nourishing food as his small appetite would allow, Bessie's own apple pie lathered with fresh cream and then, of course, there was the coming bairn which was

enough to put the life back into any man. A chap had
been out to talk about false legs and the difference in
the wounded lad did your heart good. They'd have
him out in the fields by harvest time, or so he told
them and dear Lord, she hoped it was true.

"What d'you think, Philip?" Grace asked as she lay
down on the rug Josie had spread on the ground next
to Philip's chair. Josie had promised them some iced
tea – the ice come from the small ice-house Philip's
parents had had put in years ago – for the weather
continued hot, not just in France where the battle
raged, but here in this peaceful corner of England.
James, Josie's younger brother, had enlisted as soon
as he was eighteen and was somewhere in France.
Mrs Allen, like all mothers, had been devastated by
her young son's departure for the front, for not only
had she the casualty lists in the newspapers to frighten
the life out of her but the symbol of the ghastliness of
war living next door to her. With Josie in the kitchen
Grace felt she could ask for the truth from Philip.

"Oh, they will soon break through, Grace," Philip
said cheerfully, conscious of the fact that Grace not
only had two brothers in the fighting, one in the
trenches and one in the air, but Josie had told him
that Grace was involved, in what way he did not
know and neither did Josie, not fully, with a captain in the 2nd Battalion, the King's Liverpool Regiment.

"I want the truth, Philip," Grace said quietly, sitting
up and shading her eyes from the sun. She had
recovered her lovely colour, the bronze, honey and
rose she and Josie had once laughed over, and was to
start work again the next day.

"They're being butchered, Grace. I'm sorry to say that to you who have—"

"No, I know. Mr Hynes – he works for Pa – his nephew came in on a hospital train a day or so back, into London. Mr Hynes's sister, the boy's mother, has gone . . . She telephoned Mr Hynes at the shop; she says the hospitals are overrun and simply cannot cope. They, the wounded, are being sent, or so Mr Hynes has been reliably informed, to hospitals all over the country. Ah, here's our maid with the tea," turning to smile at Josie. "And a plump little maid she is too. And getting plumper." They all laughed as Grace sprang up and took the tray from Josie, then brought another cane chair for her to sit on.

Mrs Marsden came over with a batch of scones she'd just taken from the oven, far too many for her, her Monty and Andy to eat, so Philip was to get them inside him with plenty of butter. She sat for a moment, telling them of a letter she had received from Owen and Davy, who seemed to share the letter-writing between them. She was so obviously relieved to have heard from them, which meant they were still alive and well, that even in this terrible time and in the midst of this terrible battle it had not occurred to her that even with their letter in her apron pocket, her sons might well be dead.

Grace was at the hospital at seven thirty and was at once swept into the routine that she knew so well. The irrigation of wounds was not done so much in England, for by the time the wounded reached the hospitals it was too late for the procedure, but everything else was the same. Changing dressings,

cleaning wounds, taking temperatures, emptying bedpans, writing letters, scrubbing the sluice and locker
tops, taking round drinks, holding the hands of the
dying, and there were more of those than there had
been, comforting them, washing them, feeding those
unable to do so themselves and at the end of the day
cycling wearily home to fall into bed and sleep like
the dead.

Her ma continued in the senseless state that merciful
nature had put her in and with Nora to keep watch and
the good ladies of the church, those who had as yet
suffered no loss themselves, she was in good hands
and Grace was able to concentrate on her work at the
hospital.

Grace, as a nurse, could have run the hospital herself. There was little she did not know about wounded
and sick soldiers but her knowledge of the female condition was sadly lacking, and when she suffered a bout
of sickness she did not attribute it to anything more
than something she had eaten which had disagreed
with her. It was not until certain other things happened
to her, or more precisely *didn't* happen to her that she
began to realise that perhaps this was not the case.

She was at the shop, taking Mr Hynes's place on
his day off which coincided with hers, when she
finally admitted to herself as she clutched faintly at
the counter, her stomach threatening to empty its
contents on to a box of fine Havanas that she was
pregnant. On the same day and at the same time
the wounded from the Somme reached Lime Street
Station.

26

They dragged themselves from Lime Street Station, a long procession of walking wounded, those who were the most likely to survive the endless journey from the battle that was taking place on the Somme, going to any hospital with a bed to take them. The sun beat down into the chasm of the streets, cliffs of tall buildings on either side, affording the exhausted men some shade from the heat, but where it struck the windows of the shops it flashed off the polished surfaces directly into their sunken eyes. Above them a serene arch of blue sky stretched down to the river, the smoke belching from factory chimneys not yet obscuring its endless beauty.

The stream of traffic, as usual on a weekday, was continuous. The constant scream and clangour of the maroon and yellow tramcars was strident on the ear. They were colourful with advertisements for Hudson's soap, Horniman's tea and Fry's chocolate on their swaying sides. They were crammed with shoppers, surging down Whitechapel towards the Pier Head, their occupants leaping off at every stop to the annoyance of cyclists and motorists who were forced to swerve round them. Waggons lumbered by pulled by patient Clydesdales with huge splayed feet, the brass of their fittings glinting in the bright sunshine.

The young soldiers, some of them hardly more than boys straight from school, did not concern themselves with it. They were too absorbed with putting one unsteady foot in front of the other, disorientated some of them, flinching from the sound of the traffic, the neighing of horses unsettled by the confusion, the great thud of hooves on the road, the screech of brakes from bicycles and motor cars which were still swirling round them until the constables hurriedly summoned to take control had made a way for them.

The scene was being repeated all over the country, from Scotland to London, from Liverpool in the west to Hull in the east, and those who watched, stunned – though they were becoming aware that the number of casualties was not as light as the newspapers reported – were appalled. They had heard that some of the wounded were being sent to Liverpool and other cities in the north but not in the numbers that were stagger- ing out of the station and being directed towards the hospitals. The ones coming along Elliott Street and into Church Street were to go to the Old Bluecoats Hospital in Hanover Street, so a constable who was holding up the traffic said. Others were to go to the City Hospital, to the Highfield Infirmary which was a fair walk; and not only to hospitals but to wherever they could be herded in for treatment. Some, the less seriously wounded, were to be boarded out in these first chaotic days, so it was rumoured, and already harassed Red Cross workers were on the telephone ringing local vicars, schoolmasters, even friends and private householders to beg a few nights' shelter for these shocked casualties from the trenches.

Grace and her pa edged slowly out of the shop

and stood in the silent crowd that had gathered along the pavements, watching in frozen horror as the dirty, unshaven, bloodstained, shambling figures with their pathetic bits of filthy bandages slapped on their wounds, probably two days ago, did their best to step out bravely, though God alone knew what they had to be brave about. Hadn't they suffered enough in the place they had come from and shouldn't they be entitled to a clean bed, and an ambulance to get them to it? Instead they must walk, or limp, or stagger painfully and still they managed to smile at the sympathetic crowds who stood, many of the women in tears, to watch them go by. The authorities had rounded up as many private cars and motor lorries as they could for the worst cases, and amid the chaos Grace caught a glimpse of Mr Allen's magnificent Vauxhall Prince Henry, the vehicle stuffed with filthy soldiers, the worst cases, but the rest were making their tortuous way on foot to the hospital to which they were directed. They were doing their best to be cheerful, one helping another and some of the least wounded pushing their comrades in bathchairs which had been rushed down to the station.

The Red Cross helpers were everywhere and from the crowds men and women began to move hesitantly forward to give a hand to a soldier who leaned on another, to push a bathchair, and from the shops along the way shopkeepers emerged to pass out drinks of water, lemonade, anything they had, biscuits, chocolate. Grace missed Pa for a moment and when she looked round he was emerging from the shop with boxes containing packets of cigarettes. He ran into the road and passed them out, patting a soldier on the shoulder, encouraging another who stumbled, marching along with them until they reached Waterloo Place and the beginning of Hanover Street. As Grace watched him she saw him speak to a Red Cross worker, then stride back towards her with an expression on his face and a lift to his head she had not seen for years.

"I've told them we can put up six, Grace, and with you being a nurse they were very grateful. After all we've six empty beds at home. I'm closing the shop to give a hand so I'll get home and . . . . I want to help, Grace."

She put her arms about him and hugged him, tears in her eyes for this brave man who had in the last four years lost three sons, two to the war, with three more fighting in the battle from which these poor boys had come.

She rang up the hospital from the shop listening to the sound of Sister Randall's frantic, almost *snarling* voice, just as though she were furious at what had been done to the boys pouring into her wards and the call was something she could well do without on this chaotic day. She who was usually so calm, but it was enough to tell Grace that things were just as bad at the hall as it seemed they were in every part of the country. She was, for the first time in years, leaving Pa to make his own decisions, to find his own way home. Archie, of course, had enlisted and Mr Hynes, taken by surprise as they all were, was on his day off. Pa would be fine, he told her, a new look in his eye which seemed to say he was determined to clamber his way out of his own suffering, at last, and give a hand in the ending of this appalling war. His first step was to close the shop by himself and then he would be off, to see to the soldiers he meant to put in his sons' beds for as long as they needed them. Grace had telephoned Nora, letting the machine ring and ring until Nora had finally answered, sounding so frightened Grace knew she was sure she was to get bad news. It was terrifying enough to answer the thing, let alone have words coming out of it that might finish her family off altogether.

The news that they were to have six wounded soldiers staying with them, that there must be plenty of hot water, six clean beds and plenty of her nourishing broth on the stove had put new life in her. Yes, Edna was here and would lend a hand and Mr Tooley and Grace weren't to bother about a thing.

"Grace, dear Grace, get over here as soon as you can," Sister said and put the telephone down.

As she stepped from the shop, cramming her straw hat on to her head, a motor car she thought she recognised eased its way past the weary soldiers and seated in the back of it next to two more men in khaki was Rupert Bradley. She stopped so abruptly her pa, who had come to the door with her to reiterate that he would be perfectly all right on his own and perfectly capable of catching the tram back to Sheil Road, almost bumped into the back of her.

"What is it, child?" he asked her, looking uneasily at her pale face, but she turned a quick smile on him, kissed his cheek and hurried to the tram stop, leaving him to close up. Her thoughts, though she had sprung quickly into action in this emergency, seemed to be deadened, nothing much making sense and she had no time to dwell on the possibility that Rupert might be among the wounded.

A tram ride, a quick scramble into her uniform, a word to Nora who was in her element preparing for the heroes who were coming from France, a frantic bicycle ride to Old Nook Hall, and at once she was thrown into a confusion she, and the other nurses, had never before known. The state of the hospital was unbelievable. Every room was occupied by sprawling soldiers, many of them in the death-like sleep of the exhausted. In the recreation room there were men lying across the billiard table, and in the wards beds had been pushed together into pairs to accommodate three wounded men. There were four times as many men as the hospital could nurse and Matron told her, when she stopped for a brief moment to drink a cup of tea, their hospital was only one of the hundreds up and down the country that were frantically trying to arrange nursing for the casualties. The most critical cases, those unable to travel, were being taken to hospitals as close as possible to the ports of their arrival.

Grace spent several hours along with Nurse Knowles picking tiny pieces of shrapnel out of a young soldier whose eyes were burning pits of pain but who never made a sound, and when she had finished, she couldn't help it and bugger Matron's sermons on detachment, she bent over him and kissed his cheek, telling him he was a brave lad.

"You'll cop it if Matron sees you," Nurse Knowles said, but the smile on the boy's face was well worth the risk. Their wounds were mostly of the straightforward kind, shrapnel, gunshots, in the arm or neck or shoulder, men who could no longer hold or shoot a rifle but must be restored to health and sent back to the lines as soon as possible. She and the others worked for twelve hours without a break except for the welcome cups of tea that they drank on the move, and when the last straggle of men came in and were attended to, most of them in ambulances by this time since the rush seemed to have slackened, she flopped down into a chair in Sister's office and promptly fell asleep.

She was awakened some time later by Sister's hand on her shoulder. "Go home, Tooley," she said, "but be back in six hours. That's how we're to work, six hours on, six hours off until we can get some nurses and orderlies from the smaller auxiliary hospitals. I don't know how since they are all simply swamped but we are taking a delivery of extra beds. God knows where we shall put them. Go home, my dear, you look absolutely terrible. Get some sleep and a bath and report back in the morning."

She wasn't awfully sure how she did get home, cycling like an automaton up past her old school and along Prescot Road. It was dark, almost dawn. From the hedgerows and trees on their far side came the first sleepy twitter of birds and the delightful aroma – or so it seemed after the stench of vomit, excrement and suppurating wounds that remained in her nostrils – of sun-drenched grass and wild flowers.

She was surprised, since yesterday seemed so far away, to find a soldier sitting at the table in the kitchen, his drawn face deep in a cup of Nora's strong tea. He tried to stand when she slipped into the room but Nora told him stoutly to "Sit yer down, lad an' drink yer tea," and he did as he was told. His young face was grim but he was trying to smile and Nora put a hand on his shoulder, patting it awkwardly. He looked as though he might cry.

"This 'ere's Billy, our Gracie. 'E's 'ad a birrof a sleep but . . . well . . ." Her expression seemed to indicate that could you blame the poor young fellow if what he'd been through kept waking him up. "So 'e came down fer a cuppa an' a birrof a chat, didn't yer, lad?" The lad nodded and drank deep of his tea and Nora patted him again. Topsy crept up to him, confused by the strangers in the house but as though she knew suffering when she saw it she put her head on the soldier's knee and his hand dropped to it, stroking, soothing, not the dog, but himself.

Despite her own depthless weariness Grace looked him over with a professional eye. Apparently a team of medical people were checking on the wounded boarded out and a doctor and nurse had seen to his wound. Billy had a clean bandage on his upper arm but his drawn face was flushed as though with a fever. She put a cool hand to his forehead, then smiled down at him. He blinked and did his best to focus on her but she could tell it was an effort for him.

"You'll do, Billy, but I think you should get to bed." She turned to Nora. "Did the doctor leave . . . anything?"

"Aye, 'e did that. I told 'im we'd a nurse in th'ouse and 'e said you was ter give . . ." She looked with great compassion at Billy as she handed Grace a bottle of pills.

"Here, Billy, take a couple of these," Grace told him, taking his hand and putting two of the pills into it, and when he had done so, drinking the last dregs of his tea, he turned to smile gratefully at her.

"Thanks, Nurse," he said and allowed her to lead him up the stairs and into what had been her brothers' bedroom. One of the beds was occupied by a soldier who twitched and moaned in his sleep but Billy did as he was told, climbing into bed in his unwashed undergarments. Grace knew that Nora and Edna would have them off him and washed before he left the house. She held his hand until he fell asleep then went downstairs again to check on Ma. Ma was sitting by the fire in the family room but not, as she had been for weeks now, staring at nothing in particular. She had a bit of knitting in her hand, a sock on four needles and she turned as Grace entered the room.

"I'm making Billy a pair of socks," she said, and Grace breathed a silent thank-you to Billy who, though so sorely tried himself, had unwittingly brought Ma back to them.

"Wake me in five hours, Nora," she said, then fell fully dressed on to her own bed.

The Battle of the Somme continued, but with less ferocity until the twentieth of July, when a new offensive on a greater scale was launched, and by the end of the month it was reported that an advance of two and a half miles had been made.

The soldiers who had slept in her brothers' beds were all now accommodated at the hall or in other hospitals in Lancashire, and for the first time in almost a month Grace was given a couple of days off. Without the constant call on her nursing skills, and the desperate need to fall into an unconscious state whenever possible, Grace had time to consider her own predicament. For weeks it had lurked at the edge of her mind. It had not seemed important when measured against the magnitude of the suffering she had seen and heard of in the last few weeks; besides, she had not had the time, nor the inclination to dwell on it but now, now she must.

She had not heard from Charlie and neither had his parents when she telephoned them, but as they had not had one of the dreaded telegrams which told them either of their sons was "missing believed killed", which was the one most received, they drew comfort from it. It happened all the time. In the chaos of battle men simply disappeared, blown into many pieces, their remains rotting down with thousands of others into the earth of France.

During those weeks it was as though her condition was of no consequence. Now she had time to consider it she supposed it was because she had been in a state of shock, of stunned weariness, as though it was happening to someone else, and the strange thing was she could not imagine how it had happened without her noticing. Not the actual moment of conception, of course, since that day with Charlie, his simple joy and wonder, his loving acceptance of her body which she had given without stint, would never be forgotten, but when had she had her last "monthlies"? The simple fact was she couldn't remember. And she must not forget that Charlie was not the first man to make love to her. Her mind flinched from it, from the scene in the summerhouse at Garlands but it must be considered. How she had loved him, Rupert Bradley, and in her innocence she had told him so and in answer he had humiliated her. But not before he had made love to her so thoroughly she knew she would never love another man in that way again. That had been at the end of March. It was now the end of July. *Four months!* Could she be four months pregnant? She had spent the day with Charlie at the end of May. *Two months*, which meant she would probably have missed her monthly bleeding once? The bald truth was that she didn't know. She couldn't remember. Her life had been so chaotic over the last few months that unless it had to do with the war, with her nursing, with worry over her mother and her own grieving for George, it had not concerned her! She knew very little about the facts, the progress of pregnancy. The only child born at Sheil Road after her had been John and at the time she had herself been two years old. She had never nursed women, never been trained in midwifery. It was not needed where she had been! So was this child she carried inside her the child of Rupert, or of Charlie? It seemed ludicrous to ask herself this question and what's more to have been so *unconcerned* about it. She was to have a child and surely she should be beating her breast, or in a state of terror, for nothing could be worse to an unmarried woman than a child, and what made it a more tangled predicament in her case was not to know who the father of that child might be. Was she out of her mind, or had the last weeks been such that her mind had simply switched itself off the better to deal with her duties? There was only one person with whom she could discuss it.

Josie was kneading the dough for bread when Grace leaned her bicycle against the wall under the kitchen window and knocked on the pane of glass. Josie looked up and her face split into a joyous grin, for they had not seen one another for weeks. She was seven months pregnant, almost eight with perhaps six weeks to go – she herself was not sure – and had developed that waddle that women assume when, top-heavy, they are almost within sight of the end. She opened the door, smiling with delight, and drew Grace into her kitchen.

"Come in, come in and sit down and let me get you a cup of tea. Philip has gone off . . . yes, can you believe it? He is being pushed in a special wheelchair by young Andy . . . oh, he won't allow me to take him since he is convinced I shall give birth in a row of potatoes or in the cow shed but . . . Oh, Gracie, it's lovely to see you but how tired you look. This bloody war . . . Have you been run off your feet? What a stupid question, of course you have. Now sit down."

Grace held Josie's hands, steadying herself for the words she must speak, then without preamble blurted them out. "Josie, I'm pregnant."

Josie's face whitened and she reeled back against the table and Grace could have kicked herself for her lack of care. Just to come right out with it like that, which was not the way she meant to do it was unforgivable. Josie might have gone into labour in her shock but then Josie was made of sterner stuff than that, as Grace well knew.

"Sweet Jesus, you certainly know how to catch a girl's attention, Grace Tooley. Dear God . . . who? I don't know what to say . . . When? No, not when did it happen but when is it to be?"

As she talked she fumbled her way to the chair by the range which was lit to receive the bread and sank down into it. "Tell me . . ." Grace sat down opposite her and her voice was strained. She could feel her heartbeat quicken in dread, for though Josie was her friend, promiscuity – if what she had done could be called that – was not something a decently brought-up girl likes to admit to.

"I don't know."

"You don't know what?"

"I don't know who, or when."

Josie was appalled. "Grace . . . Gracie dear, what have you been up to? You don't know *who* the father is? Surely, it's . . . it's . . . What in heaven's name do you mean?"

Grace ignored the question. "If you had a look at me, as a nurse and a woman – a pregnant woman – could you tell how far . . . how far along I was?"

Josie looked even more dumbfounded, staring at Grace in what seemed to be horror. "Grace, I don't know what—"

"Never mind how you feel or what you need to say on the subject. Just have a look at me"

"But don't you know? Your monthlies . . . when . . ."

"That's just it. I can't remember, so much has happened . . ."

"I can see that."

"Please, Josie, don't judge me."

"I'm not, I just can't understand what—"

"*Josie*. Help me with this, for God's sake. I don't know what to do. I have to know whose child this is."

"Oh, Grace." Josie's voice was sad but she drew in a deep breath. "Stand up."

Grace stood up and Josie studied her. Josie, like Grace, had never nursed women and until she herself became pregnant had never really seen a pregnant woman. She had only her own condition to go on.

"Turn round. Lift your jumper and let me see. You're so thin but you have a small bump. Lord, I can't believe you haven't noticed it. Are you totally blind, my lass?"

"I've been so busy, Josie, so distracted what with George and . . . Ma and now this battle in which Rupert and Charlie are both fighting. At least, I'm not so sure about Rupert. I thought I saw him brought in with the wounded at Lime Street but . . . well, I just haven't had time to—"

"Well, you'd best make time because it's my belief you are three or four months but then I'm not qualified."

"You're pregnant, aren't you. You told me you were four months when you came home. Do I look like that?"

Josie grimaced and let her gaze run over Grace's still slender figure, focusing on her slightly swelling belly.

"Well . . . I'd say yes, but then I believe all women are different. Mrs Marsden would know, I suppose, or . . . Dear God, Grace, tell me when you . . . when you think you might have conceived and then . . ."

"Either the end of March or sometime in May." Grace's voice was flat, expressionless but in her eyes was dawning the comprehension of what this would mean, not only to her as an unmarried mother, as a nurse who would have to give up her vocation, but to her family whose reputation would be in tatters.

"With?"

"Rupert in March. Charlie Davenport in May."

"Oh, Gracie, you fool . . ."

Grace turned on her like a tigress defending her young but it was not the child inside her that she thought of.

"They were wounded . . . needed something . . ."

"And you, like the bloody, generous fool you are, gave it to them and now you don't know who made you pregnant."

Grace dropped down into the chair opposite Josie and bent her head. Her hands twisted in her lap and leaning forward Josie took them, quietening them, and her friend. They sat for several minutes like this until a sound from the garden lifted Josie laboriously to her feet. She lumbered to the door, standing in the doorway so that Andy could not enter.

"There you are, the pair of you. We have a visitor, darling. No, it's all right, Andy, my friend and I can manage the chair, but later, if your mother could come across . . . thank you, thank you . . . yes, see you later."

They manoeuvred the chair between them into the kitchen with Philip giving Josie the length of his tongue, ordering Grace to fetch Andy back to help but Josie told him abruptly to give it a rest.

"Grace is upset," she told him shortly and at once he was full of concern, and again Grace envied Josie for the good man she had married. Despite his own very obvious upset he was only too willing to listen to whatever was troubling his wife's friend and when the tale was told, by his wife, while Grace sat like a pale ghost at his fireside, all he said was "She must stay here with us, if it's needed, my darling." What he meant was that it was not unknown for a woman's family to turn her out in such a case as this.

But Philip Booth, of all men, knew what comfort a woman's body, a woman with love in her, could give to a man about to go into battle, to a man who had been deeply wounded, and Grace Tooley was just such a woman.

27

Had the world gone mad? Why was it so beautiful, so filled with the lilting song of birds, the scent of growing things, the warmth of the golden sun on her back when a few hundred miles away men were being slaughtered by the thousands and in a carnage so obscene it was hard for those who had not seen it to visualise its horror. Men who were gassed, blinded, emasculated, shelled, made limbless, mutilated beyond description and yet there were cowslips in the grass verge at the side of the lane. As she passed farm gates a pair of whitethroats chased each other above her head, darting into the achingly blue arch of the sky, and far out of sight a lark poured out its heart in liquid song. She stopped for a moment and tipped her head back to stare upwards. As she watched the bird dropped like a stone from the sky then rose again just before it touched the rippling corn in the field. She resumed her journey, shaking her head in honest bewilderment. Had God decided to turn his back on the millions of men and women who were suffering, not just on the Western Front but in the homes of the families they had left behind? Her thoughts were sad as she pedalled along the lane which was deep in its hedges of hawthorn and tangled honeysuckle. Its rutted surface jolted her bicycle and it entered her mind idly that the juddering might cause her to miscarry. It didn't, of course.

As she whirled along, cycling furiously lest she lose her nerve, the afternoon sunshine put a glow on the fields on either side of her, fields ready to be harvested, and when she sped through the open gates she could smell the rich fragrance of Mrs Bradley's rose garden and of the newly cut grass. She did her best to make her mind blank, to keep from it the slippery thoughts that slid in and out of it as she braked, putting her foot down to the gravel drive, propping her machine against the post at the bottom of the steps.

She straightened her boater, smoothed down her skirt with her gloved hands, making sure she was perfectly presentable for an afternoon call, mounted the steps and rang the bell. The elderly maid who answered knew her, for had she not been a visitor a time or two, so politely she asked Grace her business.

"Yes, miss?"

"I'd like a word with Mrs Bradley, please," Grace told her.

"I'm not sure the mistress is at home," the maid answered, still living in the past when such things as visiting, calling, leaving cards was normal. In fact she would herself not have answered the door. Before the war, not so long ago when men servants were in abundance, the butler, gone now to the front since he had not been as old as herself, would have been standing on this step giving this young woman his careful scrutiny.

"Will you ask?" Grace suggested.

"Well . . ."

"I'm sorry, but I have to see Mrs Bradley and as I have

only an hour before I return to my duties at the hospital it is somewhat urgent."

The maid relaxed visibly, her face softening, for anyone who nursed their poor boys was acceptable in her eyes. She stepped back and ushered Grace over the doorstep. "Who shall I say is calling?"

"Grace Tooley, if you please."

"Wait here, Miss Tooley," she told her in a more kindly tone, then hurried away into what Grace remembered was the cluttered drawing-room leading into the conservatory.

Taking a deep breath, she stood for a moment looking at a watercolour of what seemed to be the summerhouse and the lake at the back of the house, the one she remembered so vividly, so vividly it brought a flush to her cheek and she did not hear the unsteady step, the gentle tap and bump as somebody came down the stairs and it was not until his voice spoke from behind her that she was aware of his presence.

"I do believe it's the charming and . . . obliging Miss Tooley," the voice remarked sardonically and when she whirled about there he was on the bottom stair, leaning on a stick, his face arranged in that same arrogantly amused expression she had come to know so well. The words were spoken with cutting disdain, making her aware that her attentions were as welcome to him now as they had been earlier in the year. She had infuriated him, taunted him as a coward and he had hit her, then, appalled by his own behaviour he had apologised, for he had been brought up to be a gentleman, and taken to his heels round the curve of the lake. Even then she had not given up but had made her way to the station to see him off when he returned to the line. She had kissed him goodbye – against his will – and told him *again* that she loved him and again he had told her to leave him alone.

And it appeared nothing had changed. He was as bitter and full of loathing now as he had been then, not of her, she had begun to understand, but of the circumstances that had overtaken him. He had gone back to the trenches to get himself killed and instead had suffered another wound, as the stick seemed to imply.

Her heart was pounding in her ears with shock, for she had not expected to see him though why she had thought that she could not imagine. She'd seen him in his brother's motor, presumably coming here so was she fooling herself? Probably. Her whole body yearned, as it always had done, towards him, wanting nothing more than to be drawn into his arms, her face pressed to his chest, just below his chin against the warm, once brown flesh of his strong throat. She felt hollow, dragged out and down by an unutterable sadness, for it seemed it would never be any different between them.

He saw her eyes go to the stick and he grinned. "Oh, don't worry about me. It's only a flesh wound and is healed already. I'm off again at the end of the week so perhaps I'll have better luck next time. I can't wait to get back actually," he lied. "I'm bored stiff hanging about here. I can't even get on a bloody horse since the army took them except for an old nag who was no use to them, and walking far is a bit of a problem. But then a soldier doesn't have to walk far to get himself killed or wounded. Sometimes no more than over the top of the trench so you see . . . But here am I babbling on, forgetting my manners when I'm sure you must have some good reason for being here. I just hope to God you're not going to declare your undying love for me again, Miss Tooley, since the repetition of it is becoming somewhat tedious." He paused, beginning to grin. "So, have you nothing at all to say to me, or are you to hang like a fish on the end of a line with its mouth open?"

The fury rose in her in a rising tide, drowning her solicitude and sadness like a great roaring breaker. It crashed in her incensed brain as the sea will crash on the shore and she took a step forward, lifting her hand to strike him full in the face. Her own was as red as the crimson roses in a copper bowl on a table against the wall and her eyes were a brilliant gold, flashing their maddened fury at this man who did nothing but insult her. He staggered back, caught unawares by her ferociousness and for a fleeting moment there was an expression in his eyes which, if she had not known him better, might have been called remorse, a sad regret, then it was gone and he laughed.

"Bravo, Miss Tooley. How much more admirable than your everlasting protestations of love."

She took a deep breath. "Believe me, Captain Bradley, you have heard the last of that. I think I might have finally realised that you are not worth loving, by any woman. I came to see your mother, to ask after you since I saw you a few weeks back being brought from the station. But it seems you are quite recovered so it only remains for me to say give my regards to Mrs Bradley and to tell you to go to hell where I hope you will roast for all eternity."

His laughter followed her down the steps.

* * *

She wept all the way to Josie's, blinded by tears, swerving wildly whenever she met another vehicle, all of them horse-drawn, for petrol was becoming scarce as the war rationed the civilian quota. A man on horseback shouted after her to look where she was damn well going since she nearly had him and his animal in the ditch, and on the rutted track between Black Horse Lane and Derby Lane she actually fell off as her front wheel caught in the furrowed surface. Her boater tipped over her eyes and so maddened was she, she flung it over a hedge, badly alarming a few peacefully grazing cows. Her knee was bleeding where it had hit a stone, she could feel the blood trickling down her leg and her hair was all over the bloody place but she didn't care if she met their majesties taking a stroll in the summer sunshine. She didn't care about anything, she told herself, fiercely, least of all that bastard who had, for – what was it? – the fourth or fifth time insulted her, humiliated her, shamed her and she would never, never seek him out again. She no longer loved him, for surely this thing . . . this . . . could she call it love? No, it was nothing more than girlish infatuation. It still might turn her heart in her breast but it was not love, was it? Obsession, that was what it was, something that had flowered in her years ago and had become a habit, that was all there was to it, she said out loud this time as the tears poured down her cheeks while she pedalled furiously up the lane that led to Spring Cottage. She had been caught in some vast and emotional vortex and now it was over. He had killed it at last. It was shattered for ever by his contempt, his sneering, despising insults, his rejection, and he could go back to the bloody trenches and she hoped he got himself blown to kingdom come . . . she did, she did; he was no use to anyone, least of all himself and certainly not to her who was to be the mother of his child.

As this last thought filtered into her demented brain she came to a juddering halt at Josie's gate, appalled, horrified, frightened, for the sound of her own voice which had ranted and raved for the past ten minutes was suddenly loud in her own ears and she knew she didn't mean a word of it.

"Sweet God in heaven, don't listen to me," she said out loud. "Take care of him, don't let him be killed or wounded or even grazed. He doesn't want me but that is not to say that somewhere there is not a woman who will make him happy, who will . . . I can't stand the thought. I lost him once to another woman and now here I am offering him—"

"Gracie?" Josie's voice, soft and wondering, came at her from the other side of the gate. "Who are you talking to?"

She shook her head and laughed, a harsh laugh that had no humour in it. "God knows; I don't, Josie. To myself, I thought, or perhaps it's to some God who is supposed to love us and yet is destroying the men I love. I've just come from Rupert's . . ."

"Ah," in vast understanding.

"What does that mean?"

"Just . . . that explains it. You're crying, do you know?"

"Am I? And I seem to have lost my hat."

"Come in, sweetheart and I'll put the kettle on."

She leaned her bicycle against the gatepost and shut the gate behind her, trailing after Josie's lumbering figure. The dog ran out and she absently patted his head as he nudged against her skirt. Someone called to her and she turned to wave at Mrs Marsden who was collecting eggs and she knew that within five minutes the farmer's wife would be over with a dozen to take home for Ma. At least that would be her excuse, but in reality it would be to see how Grace was. Besides Josie and Philip Mrs Marsden was the only one to know of her condition.

She slumped down in the chair beside the range which was not lit, for the bread had been made yesterday. Her hair fell about her and she stared off somewhere into the corner, her eyes blind and unfocused as she considered, no matter what she had told herself on her ride over, the strength of her love for Rupert. She had told herself, and him, that she hated him but it wasn't true, of course. She loved him, no matter what might happen in the future, the future which, she admitted to herself, would never contain Rupert. If he didn't kill himself in the madness of the war, he would never recover from it, from what had been done to him. His mind had been turned and if he would let no one near him, meaning herself, how was it ever to be mended. Her love was strong, steady, the love of a mature woman, patient and honest. The romantic love, the dazzling emotions that she had known as a girl had been replaced by the enduring, indestructible – no matter what Rupert said or did – love that filled her heart and mind and she might as well face it, for it would never change.

"Well?" Josie said quietly. "What happened?"

"What always happens. He sent me off with a flea in my ear. Told me never to darken his doorstep again and if I did he would set his gamekeepers on me."

"He didn't!"

"No, he didn't, but he has no time for me, Josie and my . . . attentions, as he called them, are not welcome. He's returning to the front. I think he said at the weekend and so that's that. I can't keep going over there to . . . to throw myself at him."

"The child?"

"Well, we'll see, won't we. When it arrives, nine months presumably from the date it was conceived, then I shall know who is the father."

"Oh, love . . ."

"Don't pity me, Josie. I can't bear it."

"What can I do?"

"Josie, I couldn't have gone on without you and Philip. You two and Mrs Marsden know about the baby but I can't keep it from Ma and Pa for much longer. I've got to tell them and decide what . . . what my future is to be. I'd like to go on nursing for as long as I can but . . . well, we'll have to wait and see. In the meanwhile you can use your skills as a nurse and do something about my damned knee. I fell off my cycle and . . . oh, Josie . . . Josie." Broken-heartedly she began to weep again.

As she entered the house she could hear quiet voices in the family room and from the doorway of the kitchen Nora's face beamed. She pointed excitedly in the direction from where the voices came then vanished as a tall figure in the uniform of an army officer moved slowly, woodenly into the hall, standing rigidly as though at attention. He was clean, shaved, his hair brushed, his uniform quite immaculate, someone having put him together when he returned from France, she supposed, but there was something about him that spoke of horror, of nightmares, of sights he could not speak of and she knew he had come straight from the battlefield. He looked at her with eyes that were dulled, still in his private nightmare, and she began to move slowly up the hallway to meet him. The expression on his face was despairing, for it seemed he was still sharing the experiences with the damaged men he had left behind up the line, the ones he knew so well and who could barely cope with what they did. With those who would never come back, for there were many ways for a soldier to die at the front and he had seen them all. She made no effort to touch him but stood at arm's length, afraid even to put out a hand to this stranger. Afraid not of him but for him.

"Grace," he said, his eyes like a child who is lost and has, perhaps, found his protector.

"Charlie . . ." Her voice was thick with tears.

"Grace . . . oh, Grace . . ." And his own broke on her name. His arms rose and frantically, desperately he held her to him, holding her so close the buttons on his tunic cut painfully into her breast. He bent his head and crossed his arms fiercely behind her back, burying his face in her neck and she felt him tremble violently.

"Charlie . . . darling, Charlie . . ." She held him to her, her hands in his hair, smoothing the back of his neck, her lips warm and loving against his cheek and eyes and for several minutes, disturbed by no one, though they were all there, Ma and Pa, Nora and Edna, she began the process of healing him with her love.

He had brought Freddy home, he told her simply later, when Mr and Mrs Tooley had gone to bed, since he had no wish to upset them with a bald statement of his brother's death. He had been given a week's leave to bring back the nineteen-year-old body of his

brother. It was not the custom of the army to be so
compassionate, for a soldier is there to fight and if
he is capable of standing on his feet fight he must,
whatever the circumstances. The Tooley boys had
been the exception, since two of their brothers had
given their young lives, but Charlie had been ill with
dysentery, a subject he was reluctant to talk about, even
to Grace who was a nurse. Weakened, they had sent
him home and he had brought his brother with him.
For once it had been true that a soldier, a dead soldier,
had been shot cleanly through the heart by a sniper's
bullet and so Freddy had come home to his mother in
a condition that could be seen by her. He would have
the funeral a dead hero should have, decently washed
and dressed appropriately in his uniform. Flowers and
black horses with black plumes in the old way and his
mother and father would be comforted by the decent
mourning, the respect due him as a young warrior, a
boy taken so tragically and so young from his family.

He held her hand as he spoke, his voice low with
what seemed to be hopelessness, his face despairing,
and when she told him, for what else would give Charlie
back his life, that she was to have his child – since it
might be his child and if it wasn't Rupert certainly
didn't want it – it was as though she had taken a jug,
a large jug labelled *life, love, hope, the future* and poured
it into him. She watched as the strain emptied out of
him, emptied from him in a weary torrent and when
he was emptied, was replaced with the sweetness of
her love. The haggard, slightly crumpled look about
him, the sagging of his young body, the bowing of his
head as though he were just too exhausted to hold it up
as he once had done, vanished as though it had never

been and he lifted his face to the shadowed ceiling and smiled joyfully, began to grin, then turned to her and took her hands.

"My dearest love, I can't tell you . . . a child, our child. This is what I need. I can get through it now, with you and the child to come back to. I *will* come back, Gracie."

"I know, Charlie, and I will be here," sorrowfully burying the ghost of Rupert Bradley in the deepest recesses of her heart where he would lie for ever.

"We must be married." He was grave now. "Before I go back. I will speak to your father. What? Why are you smiling?"

"Oh, Charlie, my dearest, darling Charlie. You are to be a father. A child is to be born to us so the idea that you must ask my father for my hand in marriage . . . I'm sorry, I shouldn't laugh." No, she shouldn't laugh and to tell the truth she had never felt less like laughing in her life, for she had just, finally and irrevocably, given up all hope that one day – one day, some day when he came home for good, when his bloody war was over – she and Rupert Bradley might . . . she might still be given the chance to heal him, to give him back the joy he had once known.

Her thoughts were swept away on the magnitude of Charlie's rapture, his laughter which brought Nora suspiciously to the door, her hands still holding the saucer she was drying.

"We're to be married, Nora," he cried, lifting Grace to her feet and waltzing her round the table, his young face as it had been before he was dragged off into the clutches of the war. He stopped suddenly, contritely, placing Grace carefully on the sofa from where he had dragged her.

"Darling, I'm sorry, I suppose . . ."

"Charlie . . ." she warned, for it was her place to tell her parents they were to be grandparents as it was his place to inform Mr and Mrs Davenport.

"*Married!*" Nora shrieked, then threw her apron over her head and began to cry. A wedding! The first in the family and who knew that it might be the only one with them lads in the thick of battle, and when Ma and Pa crept timidly down the stairs to find out what all the fuss was about, fearing the worst, for that was what all families in these days of horror feared, they were swept into the wonder of it by Charlie Davenport's rejoicing.

They were married a week later, the following Saturday, two days after the funeral of Charlie's brother; and Mrs Davenport, though she liked Grace and was glad to have her for a daughter-in-law, was not sure it was proper to have a wedding so soon after a funeral.

"The boy's to go back, my dear, and who knows when he will get leave again," Mr Davenport told his wife, or even if he will ever come home again, though he did not voice this last to the grieving mother of Freddy. Young couples who could not be guaranteed a future were grabbing at the chance of a bit of happiness before the husband marched off to the front, perhaps never to return, and the number of marriages, many of them rushed jobs, squeezed into a seventy-two-hour pass or a few days' leave, were on the increase.

"I know but with Freddy . . ."

"Sweetheart, times are not as they were."

"I know, Norman, but Freddy—"

"This is Charlie we're talking about, my dear, and we must give him this. You know he has loved Grace for a long time and we are fond of her. Perhaps there will be a child . . . a grandchild . . . should Charlie . . ."

"Don't you dare say another word, Norman Davenport, but you're right. We must be brave."

It was a bright August day and almost two years since the start of the war. In France the conflict continued, the struggle, so it was reported, becoming more equal in the churned-up, bloodstained mud, the shell-holes which made the scene one of pitted lunar desolation, with rotting corpses and mangled abandoned weapons littering the ground. Poppies grew and the legend began which said that Genghis Khan, the Mongol warlord, brought the seed of the white poppy with him on his advance into Europe during the thirteenth century. The legend had it that the flowers turned red when they sprang up after a battle and on the Western Front the scarlet poppy proliferated on devastated battlefields, starting with the Somme.

They were married by special licence. They were all there, those who could: Nora, Edna, both in their sensible, old-fashioned floor-length dresses of navy blue serge, their only concession to the festivities a silk flower on their wide-brimmed hats; Mr and Mrs Davenport in mourning as was proper; Ma and Pa quietly dressed not in black but dark shades of grey. Mr Hynes and his Martha were invited, Mr Hynes given permission to shut the shop, hanging out a sign to inform customers that it was closed for a wedding! Josie and Philip, Philip pushed in his wheelchair by a rapturous Mrs Marsden and Josie, such a size now, smiling that it should be her in the wheelchair and not her husband, bringing unsure smiles to the faces of the guests.

Grace was not in white as her mother would have

liked her to be, giving no reason to any of them why she had chosen a rich shade of golden yellow. She was not a virgin, as her new husband was aware, though as yet she had not told her family, nor had Charlie. Time for that later when Charlie had gone, since she did not want him upset in these happy days, and nights, that were left to him.

They spent them at a small hotel near Formby overlooking Formby Point and the sandhills, the sparkling waters of the estuary, not speaking much, walking hand in hand along the firm sand, drowsing in the sandhills, the sun on their strained young faces. At night, after her smiling reassurance that it would be all right, Charlie made love to her in every way his male body could devise, turning her in the lamplight, exploring with loving attention every inch of her body in the lavender-scented comfort of the deep bed.

"I love you, Grace Davenport," he murmured, his mouth against the bounteous beauty of her rose-tipped breast, moving down to the small swell of her belly where his child grew, then on to the mound of dark, springing hair at the base of it until his fingers parted the smooth, secret warmth of her. Again and again he plunged himself into her, making her pregnant again and again, he laughed, then slept in the deathlike sleep she gave him.

When he left her he was straight-backed, quiet, but within him was the love with which his wife had restored him and it was enough. Charlie Davenport now had the strength to go back to the bloody hell which had killed his brother along with hundreds and thousands of others; the bloody "cock-up" which those who fought in it knew it to be.

28

"I see that nice young woman got married the other day." Eleanor Bradley nodded round the breakfast table at the members of her family who were present, smiling in that slightly vague, sweet-natured and, in her daughter-in-law's opinion, dotty way she had. They all looked up politely, smiling too, for they were well used to her small eccentricities which came from her placid way of life, her husband's inclination to protect her from the dangers of the world and her memory, which was not as sharp as once it had been. Her husband was the same now that he had retired and to see them together dithering, as her daughter-in-law described it, round the garden, often hand in hand, was a familiar sight. Mrs Bradley, Eleanor, or Elly, as her husband Hugh called her, was fond of gardening and now Hugh had taken it up. He was too old for riding, he said, and a bit of exercise round the garden and into the woods at the far side of the lake did his arthritis good.

"Oh, and what young woman is that, Mother?" Louise Bradley, the youngest of them at seventeen, buttered a piece of toast and bit into it with her strong white teeth, not unduly interested but trained by Nanny in the nursery to be respectful of adults. She was late and she really had no time for the idle chit-chat which her mother loved. As soon as she

had breakfasted she would cycle over to the small
auxiliary hospital for convalescent officers which had
been converted recently from the home of their dear
friends the Greenways. She did no nursing, of course,
no *real* nursing that is, since she was only seventeen,
the gently reared daughter of a gentleman, and her
family would not allow it. Besides, the soldiers were
well on their way to recovery, or waiting to be invalided
out of the army. She read to them, or wrote their letters
for them, served them tea or cocoa, straightened their
beds, pushed them round the extensive grounds in
their wheelchairs and generally felt she was doing her
bit for the war effort and surely no more could be
asked of her.

They were an army family, a son from each generation serving his country as far back as Waterloo.
Hugh Bradley's elder brother, once an officer in a
Lancashire regiment, dead now, had been the one of
his generation to go. Alan Bradley was the elder son of
Hugh and Eleanor Bradley. He had a weak chest and
so was considered unfit to be a soldier, his younger
brother going in his place. He had risen to his feet,
since he must be in the city very soon where he had
taken his father's place in the family business when
Hugh Bradley retired, so he kissed his wife on the
cheek, said he really must dash and was away before
his mother could answer.

Hugh lifted his head for a moment and peered
amiably over the top of *The Times* at his wife, and
his second son, Rupert, who was to be off on Monday
back to the war, gazed out of the window at the
rolling slopes of the lawn beyond. He should have
returned a week ago but the doctor, after examining

the healing wound in his upper arm, had considered another week at home would be beneficial. Absently he lit a cigarette and his mother, who considered such things "common" and fit only for the working classes, frowned a little, but then the boy needed something, she supposed, to calm his wounded spirit and though it was not polite to smoke in the breakfast room she said nothing.

"I can't remember her name but Rupert will know, won't you, darling?"

Rupert Bradley turned to stare at her. He was dressed casually in a pair of grey flannels and an open-necked shirt, the sleeves of which were rolled up to just below his elbow, revealing the tapering end of the wound in his arm.

"*I* should know? What *are* you talking about, Mother?" He would have liked to show his irritability, his impatience, his sheer bloody inability to cope for much longer with his mother, with every person he spoke to, who wanted to know what it was like "over there". He knew they found him difficult. They were bright and cheerful, courteous and attentive and he did his best to respond, to say all the correct things and listen to whatever it was they wished to say to him. Like all the men who were engaged in it he loathed the war that was being fought in France and what it was doing to a generation of young men. It was dirty and dangerous and it had shrivelled something inside him when he was forced to be the man sending the young soldiers into attacks, going with them and having them fall on either side of him. But he could not tell these people, his family. His world and theirs was too far apart and could not be bridged. Despite this he couldn't wait to get back to it for that was the *real* world to him. There was a hard and bitter stone in his chest where once his heart had beaten and he thought he would never get over it.

"Darling, you must know who I mean," his mother said. "Really, my memory is not as it was. She was so sweet and thoughtful and it must have been so sad for her family to lose those boys. I can't even remember how many except that one went down with the *Titanic*. Such handsome young men and she was quite beautiful . . ."

He turned from the window and looked blindly at his mother and she was startled by the look on his face. The side of it that was unharmed lost its colour, the healthy tan he had acquired over the last few weeks of wandering about the garden, the woodland, round the lake and lounging in the wickerwork chair on the terrace, turning to an unhealthy shade of putty. His eyes narrowed and his lips clamped themselves together as though to keep in some dreadful thing he might inadvertently say to her and they all gazed at him in some consternation. They were well used to his moods, his silences, his erratic behaviour, but surely this was . . . well, what was it? His mother had merely mentioned the marriage of someone she, and he, presumably, had known and he looked as though for two pins he could cheerfully strangle her.

"Rupert?" she said anxiously.

"Are you speaking of . . . of Grace Tooley, Mother?" His voice was quite normal, if a bit staccato, and his father, reassured that all was well, returned to his newspaper. Louise, doing her best not to look at her brother's face, which, in the shaft of sunlight that fell on it, looked quite fiendish, rose from the table and after kissing her mother's cheek ran from the room, babbling of the lateness of the hour. Victoria, Alan's wife, also rose, saying she must go and look at the child in the nursery, and still Rupert and his mother studied one another. Eleanor Bradley might not be the brightest of women but she had a kind heart and where her children were concerned an intuition which was given to most mothers. Her son had been dreadfully wounded by the carnage in France, twice physically, and also spiritually by the carnal indecency of his promiscuous wife, and now, or so it seemed, something else had come to hurt him and she could not imagine what it was. There had been nothing between him and the Tooley girl, at least that she knew of, so why was he looking as though someone had stuck a knife between his shoulder blades, and was twisting it cruelly?

Rupert Bradley himself didn't know. He had hardly given the girl a thought these last few years except when she intruded – was that the word? – into his life and interrupted his bitter thoughts with her blithering insistence on declaring that she loved him. Good God, as if he gave a damn about that, but she seemed to think it important and had told him so every time they met. She had been a child to him, a very pretty child, true, when they first met at the field where Melly took off in his monoplane that day – when was it? Jesus, five years ago – and he remembered, though why he should, that he had been strangely drawn to her. Her brothers had been there but had left her to her own devices and he had taken her under his wing. Sweet

Jesus, how was it he remembered it in such detail? He had been so sorry for her when – what was his name? – Arthur, that was it, had disappeared with the *Titanic* and had – yes, he remembered – he had taken her to lunch. Why did he remember it so well? his darting mind asked him. And then he had met Jessica, who had inflamed him, burned him in a fire so scorching he had been drawn into her magnetic bewitchment, dazzled, blinded and had seen no one but her.

And yet that . . . that child had kept coming back, bravely, he realised it now, offering him her heart and then . . . her body and, bloody hell, since he was a man after all, he had taken it. Even then he had flung back in her face all her sweetness, her declarations of peace and love and hope for the future. He had rejected her, hurt her, sneered at what she offered and so . . . she had offered it to another man.

But so soon! She was married. Only a few days after he had thrown her love back in her face she had gone away, she had married someone else and why the hell did he feel as though the very ground he walked on had fallen in at his feet? So much for love, his embittered heart said. So much for the loyalty of these bloody women who declared undying passion for a man and then did the dirty on him with someone else. *Did the dirty on him!* What the hell did he mean by that? he asked himself. She was not committed to him in any way, as Jessica had been, nor he to her so what the hell was wrong with him?

"Rupert." His mother's hand was on his arm and he looked down into her anxious face and did his best to smile, to let her see that there was nothing wrong but there was. Of course there was, but the question was *what*?

"Who did she marry?" he managed to ask in a normal enough sounding voice, then wondered why he asked, for did it matter. She was married . . . married. Gone for ever. Dear God in heaven, *did it matter*? he asked himself. He was to be off the day after tomorrow and it was doubtful he would come back. Indeed he would continue to do his best *not* to come back.

He bent his head and gently kissed his mother's cheek, patting the hand that rested on his arm. He smiled and it was the smile he had once possessed as a young man. He was only twenty-four now but he was no longer a young man.

"I'm off for a walk, Mother." He snapped his fingers at the spaniel which dozed in a square of sunlight, bringing him to his feet, then opened the French windows that led to the terrace. He and the dog moved down the steps, the dog leaping ecstatically and himself sauntering across the lawn towards the lake. His mother watched him go then sighed deeply, sadly.

The baby perambulator was standing in the shade of a magnificent horse chestnut, said by Monty Marsden to be a hundred feet tall. The flowering spikes, or candles, blossomed in May with the large leaves which among all the trees were the first to appear in spring. Now the leaves were turning to yellow and deep gold and were beginning to drop, floating like butterflies caught in a gentle breeze and the "conkers", which her brothers used to collect every year at this time, would be next. The canopy was still dense, almost reaching the ground and the perambulator had its hood up to protect the child sleeping in the warm autumn sunshine, but as Grace walked towards it several more leaves spiralled down, falling softly on the hood. She peeped under it, sighing deeply, studying the infant's face which was round, rosy under the swansdown edge of its bonnet, knitted by Bessie Marsden. The baby lips pouted and began to suck on an imagined nipple and Grace smiled with delight.

A male voice hailed her and from the gate and the lane that led up to Spring Farm, Philip Booth trundled his wheelchair towards her.

"Isn't she the most beautiful female you ever saw, apart from her mother, of course? I'm supposed not to disturb her but I'm afraid I just hang about waiting for her to wake up. I can lift her out, did you know that, and when she's settled on my lap and fastened with these straps Monty devised I can take her about with me. I know she's only three weeks old but I can't imagine what we did without her, and—"

"Philip, darling, do leave poor Grace alone. We know you are quite besotted with your daughter . . ."

"And you are not?" Philip tilted a sardonic eyebrow in the direction of his wife who had appeared at the door of the cottage and was walking towards them.

"Well . . ." Josie laughed and putting her hands on Philip's shoulders bent over to kiss him lovingly on his mouth.

"Now then, you two. If Bessie Marsden sees you she'll be over here to make sure you're not overtiring yourselves."

Grace and Josie exchanged a smile and a hug and Grace bent to kiss Philip's cheek, her heart strangely sad, for the magic of the happiness these two had found together, despite what they had been through, never failed to move her. With the birth of their daughter – and they meant to have more, Josie told her, leaving Grace with no mistake about the meaning of the words – their joy in one another, in their child and the small cottage that housed the three of them was like a shining bubble protecting them, a bubble that would never burst. Philip's dog strolled over from the sun-warmed step, wagging his plumy tail and sniffing at the strange, sometimes noisy newcomer that had appeared on what was his territory. He apparently seemed happy with them all, sinking down next to Philip's wheelchair. Grace considered them, this lovely family. She loved Charlie and no doubt when he came home she and he would settle down, with the child, to a content that would fulfil her, *fill* her days as Josie's were filled, but she knew that with Charlie she would never have what Josie and Philip had. Her love, her true love was battened down in the depths of her wounded heart, unreturned, she knew that at last.

Philip tore himself away, trundling off in the direction of the farm where it seemed he had a number of jobs waiting for him, and Grace and Josie settled down by the open window of the cottage where Josie could keep her eye on her daughter who was to be called Elizabeth. They chatted in the amiable, relaxed way of long-standing friends, drinking tea and eating the biscuits Mrs Marsden had shown Josie how to make.

"So, have you told them yet?" Josie asked her at last, setting her cup carefully in her saucer and offering Grace another biscuit.

"No." Grace took a bite and turned to look out at

the pretty garden which was just beginning to fade from summer to autumn.

"Why not? They've got to know some time, and sooner rather than later, I would have thought," eyeing Grace's thickening waist. Not that anybody who didn't know could have realised her condition, since she had always been slim and was one of those women, apparently, who "carry well". Her build, her stature, her erect carriage concealed her condition. It was September and Grace was either *four* or *six* months pregnant but it was hard to tell which. There was *one* way to tell, of course, but perhaps Grace, with her lack of knowledge of childbearing, would not have noticed it and if she had, had not thought it important enough to tell her.

"I . . . don't know. I suppose I don't want a fuss. And if I don't say anything it will be more . . . more difficult for them to work out when . . ."

"When it was conceived?"

"Mmm."

"It's not like you, Gracie, to be underhand."

"I've got to be, for Charlie's sake, and for the baby. It might even *be* Charlie's, and if it happens not to be then I . . . well, if it's not wanted elsewhere, which it isn't, and neither am I, I might as well make somebody happy. Anyway, I'm having enough trouble with Mrs Davenport, or *Mother* as she says I've to call her. She says I should live in my husband's home and as my husband has not as yet got one it should be with his parents. Dear God, Josie, can you imagine it? Once she knows I shall be cossetted like a kitten in a basket and I want to work for as long as possible. The wounded from the Somme . . . when will it end, Josie? They

pour in on every hospital train, poor bloody sods . . .
I'm sorry, my language. I must pick it up from the
men I nurse, for when I change their dressings they
don't care what they say. They are sorry afterwards,
of course, and apologise profusely." She watched a
late bumble bee lurch from flower to flower beyond
the window. "Besides, I'm not happy about leaving
Ma, which is my excuse at the moment. When Charlie
comes home we'll look for a small house somewhere;
a cottage like yours would be nice."

"Oh, Gracie, darling, it seems another world, another
you and me since those days, d'you remember, when
we flounced round town thinking we were so grown
up. Peaches and cream, bronze, honey and rose.
We thought even that was smart, clever, and now
look at us."

"You're all right, Josie."

"I know, and so will you be one day soon. When
that baby comes you'll wonder what you ever did
before."

It was six weeks later, the first week of November, and
a dreary sort of a day which didn't know whether to
rain or not, so it settled for a drifting drizzle. Grace's
cape was wet through when she tramped dismally
into the nurses' room, making for the fire. It seemed
there was a bit of a lull and Sister Randall was taking
advantage of it, removing her shoes and sitting with
her toes to the fire. Nursing was hard on the legs and
feet, and in any free time, which wasn't much, God
knows, they sank thankfully into a chair and put their
feet up. She watched as Grace slung her cape over the
back of a chair and propped it in front of the fire to

dry. Had Grace cared to study her, which she didn't because she was already running late, she might have noticed the sudden perplexed frown on Sister's face and the narrowing of her eyes. She sat up slowly.

"Davenport." Her voice was hesitant. Grace turned and smiled in her direction.

"Yes, Sister?"

"I hardly know what to say but . . ."

Grace looked surprised, for if there was one thing Sister could not be accused of that was not knowing what to say! She was firm, fair and wonderful with the "boys" but just let one of the nurses or VADs put a foot wrong or do something of which she didn't approve and she had no hesitation in carpeting you. If it needed a higher authority she would even report you to Matron, and that, as one young nurse had said, weeping loudly, was a "hanging offence".

"Sister?"

Sister cleared her throat and Grace had the strangest and silliest feeling that Sister was actually embarrassed.

"There is no way to say this except straight out so: Davenport . . . Grace, are you to have a child? You have put weight on, I can see that. I saw it just now when you lifted your arms to throw your cape over the chair but . . . I'm sorry, Grace but really, if you are I shall have to tell Matron, you know that."

Grace sank down into the chair over which she had hung her cape. She studied her fingers which squirmed in her lap, and sighed deeply. It had come. She wondered how she had got away with it so long, for when she looked at herself naked in the mirror she had a belly on her . . . well, no one could mistake what her condition was. And contrary to Josie's silent thought she had not been unaware of the movement of the child inside her. When the strange fluttering had first been felt she had taken the tram down to town and slipped into the free library in William Brown Street. Asking for the medical section, she had found a book on pregnancy. It had told her the incontrovertible truth that she was, at that time, five months into her pregnancy. She had what was called "quickened" and if that was so – and how could she deny medical facts, she who was a nurse? – she was carrying Rupert's child. It had been the end of March when she had found him at the summerhouse with the gun in his hand. She even knew the exact date, for like most young girls of her class and education she had kept a diary. She had not, naturally, written down the incident – *the incident*, what a way to describe the rapture of that hour she had spent in Rupert's arms – in so many words but the mark she had put against the date reminded her. She and Charlie had made love in May so if the child was his she would have quickened in October or thereabouts! The facts, the plain, unequivocal medical facts, which, even if her heart had not told her, knew that this was Rupert Bradley's child she carried under her heart.

"Well?" Sister Randall was not criticising her, since Grace was a married woman and married women – and sometimes *unmarried* women – got themselves pregnant, nor did she even question Nurse Davenport's wish to keep her pregnancy hidden for as long as possible. Davenport was a nurse totally committed to her work, to her patients. She had brothers, and now a husband, serving at the front and her dearest wish was to heal those who had been wounded there, but this wouldn't do, of course. There was heavy lifting involved and, besides, once her condition became more obvious it was not proper for her to be among the young men. The full skirt of her cotton dress, the enveloping folds of her long apron had concealed her condition all these months but now, unfortunately, for she was well liked and respected, she would have to go, and as soon as possible. Now that Sister Randall had had a good look at her she was of the opinion that she and her husband had anticipated their married state – they had been married in August – by several months. Still, that was nothing to do with her. Young men who were off to risk their lives, their healthy bodies, their manhood in the dreadful carnage of France did not want to do the *proper* thing and wait, neither did the women who loved them and longed to comfort their fear.

Grace lifted her head and looked directly at her, her gaze steady and honest. "I believe I became pregnant in March, Sister, so that makes me seven months."

"Good God!" Sister was visibly startled. "I would never have guessed. You've kept it well concealed."

"I know. I didn't want to leave nursing. I don't even now. Is there *anything* I could do that would allow me—"

"No, child, there isn't." Sister took her hands and helped her to her feet. "You must go home now and take it easy. This is no place for you. Your husband—"

"Sister . . ." Grace interrupted the nurse's fervent words, bringing them to a sudden halt. "Sister, may I ask that you say nothing, except perhaps to Matron who, of course, will have to know the reason I am leaving. You see . . ." She hung her head and in that moment Sister Randall realised that her first suspicions had been correct. The child Grace Davenport was to bear had been conceived before her marriage.

She patted Grace's hand sympathetically. She herself had never married; in fact she was as virgin as the day she was born and had had no desire, ever, to change that condition. But she was an exception, she knew that, so who was she to judge the rampant feelings of these men, and women, who lived in a time when the next day, the next hour, might find them dead, or, even worse, so badly wounded they might never recover.

"Come along, my dear, we'll go and see Matron together. You are an exceptional nurse, d'you know that, and who knows, if there is someone who can look after your child when it is born, she might be persuaded to let you come back. Good nurses are not easy to find."

29

Nora crossed herself reverently, threw her apron over her head and wept, this time with joy. Grace could see she wanted to caper about with delight since it was time this tragic family had a bit of good news, something joyous, and what was more joyous than a baby to help to replace all the young men who had been taken from this house.

"God love yer, child, an' thank the Blessed Holy Mother," she shrilled, unusually, even though she had been raised in the Catholic faith. It was a long time since Nora had attended mass, or even confession, but, as her mother would also have said, had she been alive, once a Catholic always a Catholic and the words and actions came easily.

"Dearest, oh Gracie, how wonderful, how absolutely wonderful," Ma beamed, standing up and moving to embrace her daughter, her thoughts more or less like Nora's, for this had been a sad house for many years and a baby would bring back something that had been lost.

"Grace, my dear, how splendid. A grandchild . . . imagine, a grandchild," said Pa, passing a trembling hand over his eyes.

"When, lass, when's it ter be?" Nora asked tremulously, not knowing whether to laugh or cry. She turned to nod at Edna who hovered, made up with it, as they said in the north, at the back of her. "Wet the tea, Edna, there's a good lass, or will it be somethin' stronger?" looking at Mr Tooley, for surely the first grandchild warranted a sup of something special.

The rain which had drizzled all the way to the hospital and back again was coming down in buckets now and Grace stood and dripped on the carpet and suddenly they all became aware of it, of this precious vessel which carried the hope and joy of them all and at once, as she usually did, Nora bustled forward and took control.

"Wharr in heaven's name are we thinkin' on. Lamb's soaked ter't skin an' needs ter gerrin a hot bath an' get changed. See, Edna, I said put't kettle on while I get this lass sorted out an' then we'll celebrate. Eeh, Gracie, I'm that delighted an' wait until yer tell that lad o' yours."

Nora did her best to lead Grace from the room but her lamb was resisting, for there was a question that had been asked and must be answered before she lost her nerve and though Grace allowed her dripping cape to be removed she was doing her best to stand out against Nora's persuasions. She must tell her family, and Charlie's family, that though they were married in August the baby was likely to arrive a lot sooner than the nine months they envisaged and she was well aware that they would be shocked.

"Come on, chuck," Nora was saying, "let's get yer outer these wet clothes before yer catch yer death. That babby needs a strong mam who'll be healthy."

"I have something to say, Nora, if you don't mind." But she allowed Nora to take her wet cape and hand it to Edna who had put the kettle on the hob but had hurried back to the doorway lest she miss something.

"Can it not wait, me lamb. Let's—"

"No, Nora, please. I must . . . I've . . . well" – she took a deep breath – "the baby will be born in . . . in . . ."

Abruptly she stopped speaking as a voice from the past came at her. A young Tom, lost now in the carnage of France, used to tease her when, daring her to perform some deed which he, as a boy, considered to be nothing at all. "Lost your nerve, Gracie dear?" he used to say and that was just what she had done. *She* knew it was to be December but dare she tell these people, *her* people when it was to be? If Charlie was to be . . . to be – God forgive her – *deceived*, made to think this was his child it must be made to look like a premature birth. Oh, yes, she had read all about it in the medical section in the Free Library. So, she must be vague about the date, muddy the waters, so to speak. Oh, Charlie, I am so sorry but . . . it was the only way to protect him, her child, and indeed her family who trusted her.

"I'm not sure."

"Not sure?" Nora echoed.

"No, you see, things have been so muddled and when I told them at the hospital . . . well, I was . . . Sister Randall noticed and she . . . she insisted that one of the doctors had a look at me and confirmed. I can't work any more, not until the baby is born so . . . The doctor thought January or . . ."

Her words tapered off and her head drooped a little as it had once done as a girl when she had done something of which her parents had disapproved.

Her hands twisted together and the glow from the fire caught and shone on the wedding ring Charlie had put on her finger. She played with it as though drawing – unintentionally – their attention to it, for it was a symbol of the respectability into which her and Charlie's child would be born. She simply stood there while both Nora and Edna, diverted for a moment, ran a critical eye over her. Nora had never borne a child herself but she had been present during the pregnancy and birth of all seven of the Tooley babies, and Edna was the mother of a great brood so she should know. They were both struck with the same thought and that was, how the dickens had they missed the thickening of young Grace Tooley's . . . no, Grace Davenport's slim figure, for now, even in her enveloping apron you could distinctly see the bulge beneath the wide belt.

"January?"

"Or thereabouts."

"Thereabouts?" Mary Tooley quavered and Pa put his trembling hand on her shoulder. "But, darling, you were only married in August." She looked so perplexed Grace wanted to smile but this was not the time for amusement. Nora had folded her arms across her ample bosom and a look of stern disapproval hardened her face which moments before had been soft with gladness. Edna, though she was happy here and though the Tooleys were grand to work for, was not so judgemental, for sure hadn't she been three months up the spout when she and Joe were wed.

Grace didn't know what to say next so Nora said it for her.

"So, Grace Tooley, you and that lad of yours were 'at it' before you were married." She couldn't think

of another way to put it and it was noticed that Mary
Tooley winced and shrank back a little in her chair.
These days it did not take much to upset her.

Grace lifted her head, for it seemed they were going
to put the interpretation on the situation that she had
hoped for. God forgive her and she prayed Charlie
would too though she hoped with all her heart that
Charlie would never know. Not because of what he
might do to her but what it might – *would* – do to
him. He was vulnerable, as all the men who fought in
the war were vulnerable. How many of them had been
– what was the word? – *cuckolded* by the women they
left behind? How many men had been told that their
wives had been unfaithful to them, by neighbours, or
by the wives themselves and who longed to get home
and sort out the "fancy man" who had wrecked their
marriage. She had not been unfaithful to Charlie, for
what had taken place between her and Rupert had
been before her marriage, even before the afternoon
she had spent with Charlie, so could that be considered
as being unfaithful? No, her brutally honest mind told
her, but passing off another man's child on him was,
surely. She told herself that it was for Charlie's sake,
for the child's sake, for they were both blameless and
perhaps she meant it with one part of her mind but it
was still not right.

"Grace . . . oh, Grace, I can't believe that you and
Charlie . . ."

"I'm sorry, Ma, but . . ."

"I know you love one another, and, thankfully, you
are married but why did you not marry sooner? You
must have known you were to . . . to have a baby long
before August and yet . . ."

"I don't know, Ma . . . please, forgive me but Charlie and I . . ."

"Darling . . ." She turned to her husband and put a trembling hand in his. "I think I will go upstairs now, Edwin. This has been a great . . . shock. I am pleased to be having a grandchild and I know it will bring great joy to us all but I cannot forgive Grace for forgetting her upbringing. Oh, I know I will . . . eventually but for now . . ."

The old couple, clutching at one another, moved slowly towards the door that led out into the hall and Grace watched them, wondering why she had called them the old couple, since she knew that neither of them were yet fifty. She supposed, with the part of her mind not involved with the scene that had just taken place, that the last four years, ever since Arthur had died, had aged them, taken what Nora would have called "the stuffing" out of them. And then again they were Victorians, born in the old Queen's era and had not caught up with this dashing modern age in which women had found freedom and the choice to leave their parents' protection and go out into the world, as she had, to a certain extent, and do things that once had been solely the prerogative of the male.

"Come on, chuck," Nora said gently, putting an arm about her shoulders. "'Tis not the end of world. What you and that young 'usband o' yours did 'as bin 'appenin' since the world began."

"Oh, aye," said Edna feelingly from the doorway.

"'Tis human nature, lass, an' there's no 'arm done. Yer a married woman an' though I were shocked at first an' it'll be whispered round't church 'all fer a bit, 'appen upsettin' yer ma, but it'll be a nine days' wonder, you'll see. Yer ma an' pa will be made up wi' it when they've 'ad a chance ter get used to it. Yer ma'll be sortin' out her knittin' needles an' baby patterns, off down ter town ter choose baby wool before week's out. Just think, a babby! Eeh, yer ma'll be that thrilled when . . . anyroad, let's get these wet clothes off yer an' then we'll sit down an' 'ave a nice cup o' tea."

It was the same at the Davenports when she and Ma and Pa went over to Edge Lane the following day, for they must be told, Ma said sternly, though she was inclined to smile a little and was heard to be humming, *humming* as she put on her hat in front of her dressing-table mirror. She was most solicitous with her daughter on the walk over there, begging her to tell them if she felt tired because if she did they would call a cab, wouldn't they, Edwin, turning to the prospective grandfather. Grace was not to over-exert herself in any way. She could remember when she was having her first baby, dear Arthur, looking sad for a moment, how excited she and Pa had been and no doubt Charlie must be the same.

They were as shocked as Ma and Pa, especially Mrs Davenport, though Grace thought Mr Davenport had that look about him that men seemed to acquire when another man has been "a bit of a lad". Males were like that, rather admiring in another male what was totally frowned on in a woman. His son had proved himself to be a man and what was wrong with that in these terrible times? He patted his wife's arm when she wept a little but in Jean Davenport's mind was already the rather pleasing thought that now her lovely daughter-in-law would have no choice but to come and live in her husband's home, *her* home until Charlie came back and settled his wife and child in one of his own.

She said so and at once Ma put her cup and saucer on the small table next to her and rose to her feet. She straightened her back, tugged at her hat and spoke firmly for the first time in years.

"Oh, no, Mrs Davenport, I'm afraid not. I quite agree that when her husband returns from the war he and Grace will have their own little home but until then my daughter must remain with her family."

"No, Ma—"

"Mrs Tooley, the mother of my son's child surely must—"

"Mary, dear, let us discuss this—"

"Now then, Jean, there is time for—"

Mrs Davenport turned on them all, a lioness spitting and clawing in defence of her grandchild, her son's child, a Davenport who must be born in the home of the Davenports. She was not normally an aggressive woman but had she not just lost one of her sons and surely should be allowed to find consolation in this new child who was to come into the family, under her close guardianship! She liked Grace, in fact she was fond of her and had not been averse to Charlie marrying her, though they were both very young, but this determination on her mother's part must be dealt with at once.

"No, Norman, I'm afraid there is no time." She turned a forbidding glance in her daughter-in-law's direction. "That is what we don't have. Grace . . . Grace chose to leave it until almost the day of the birth before telling us of the coming child and arrangements must be made. She and Charlie . . . well, the less said

about that the better but I think it would be best if you
got out the motor and took her over to Sheil Road to
get her things, then we—"

"I beg your pardon, Mrs Davenport, my daughter
will do no such thing. She is to remain with us
until—"

"Oh, for God's sake, stop it the lot of you,"
Grace shouted, alarming them all considerably, but
then she was in what was known as an interesting
condition and women were known to be off balance
at such times. She stood up and strode across the
comfortable living-room, almost knocking over a
table on which Mrs Davenport's cherished knick-
knacks were carefully arranged. A glass ball teetered
on the edge and the snowstorm inside whirled prettily in the light from the flickering flames of the
fire. She twisted about and the four people, her
parents and Charlie's, were left in no doubt as to
the true condition of Charlie's wife as the pleated
skirt, held together with a safety pin at the waist
under her full blouse and cardigan, clung to her
rounded figure.

"Grace, darling, really you should not stride about
so much. The baby . . ."

"Ma, only the day before yesterday I was on my feet
for ten hours nursing, *lifting* wounded men, changing
dressings, emptying . . . well, I'm not suddenly going
to become fragile."

"Please, Grace, your mother is only—"

"I know, Pa, and I'm sorry but this must be said
and said quickly. I am not going to live with Mrs
Davenport. I'm sorry" – as Charlie's mother fell back
in her chair and her own mother smiled in triumph –

"and I'm not going to live at home." This time it was her mother's turn to fall back in her chair.

"There is a cottage to rent near Spring Farm. Only a stone's throw from Josie's. Josie Booth. It's been empty for months now. It was lived in by Mr Marsden's cow man – Mr Marsden is the farmer at Spring Farm – but he was killed on the Somme and his wife, who's not a country girl, has gone back to her family in Manchester. There is some furniture in it and with a bit of work which Andy Marsden is willing to do when he's not at school and with Bessie's help . . . Bessie? She's the farmer's wife, and of course, with Josie close by . . . Now, Ma, it's no use crying. You . . . and you, of course, Mrs Davenport, can get on a tram along Edge Lane to Old Swan and be there – Rose Cottage, doesn't it sound lovely – in ten minutes. I want to . . . to make a home for me and the baby . . . and Charlie when he comes home. Josie and I had a look at it the other day and Mr Marsden said I could have it. Bessie is getting a woman to scrub it out for me and a chap to slap a bit of whitewash here and there, so . . . so there it is. I'm sorry . . . all of you, but I must make a life, a separate life for us. I have Charlie's allowance as his wife and some money saved so until I . . ."

She had almost said until I get back to work, to the job I love, to the hospital and the soldiers I nurse, I shall manage, but she stopped herself in time. She and Josie had made an arrangement but she knew it would not be one to suit the grandparents of her child.

They wept, her mother and mother-in-law but it did no good and at the end of the week, with Andy's help and the farm waggon, pulled by the biggest horse Nora said she had ever seen, she moved into Rose

Cottage. Her mother and mother-in-law begged to come with her, get her settled in to their satisfaction, but she gently refused, the only one she would accept being Nora. Nora might not approve of her lamb moving out of her home and going to live on her own, and said so, but she was a willing workhorse, steady, strong, capable. One thing she did insist on and that was bringing Edna with her, for no matter what their Gracie said Nora was unwilling to trust the scrubbing, the deep scouring and polishing she considered imperative to anyone but Edna. She didn't know this Bessie, nor the woman Bessie had employed and, until she looked the place over and found it to her satisfaction, Edna was held in readiness to do what was necessary. Grace was of the opinion that Nora was a mite disappointed to find the cottage was like a new pin. And, better still, she found Bessie, a sensible woman, to her liking. After all, as Grace said, it was only ten minutes on the tram to Old Swan and with no one else to interfere with, her boys – bar one – all gone, her two youngest lasses gone, Bessie'd plenty of time on her hands to keep her eye on Grace and the new babby when it arrived.

For the next few weeks, spending some of her savings and in the company of Josie who was thrilled to have her best friend for a neighbour again, she made the cottage into a cosy home. There was already a pine dresser in the kitchen and Bessie, who said she'd never used the thing since she and Monty were given it as a wedding present over twenty years ago, had arranged a complete dinner and tea service of blue willow-pattern crockery on the shelves in true cottage style. There were brass candlesticks with white candles in them, for there was no electricity. There was, fortunately, water piped to an old stone sink in the tiny scullery. On shelves were copper pans of all sizes and terracotta jars filled with wild flowers from Mr Marsden's fields that Josie had dried in the late summer. There was a scrubbed deal table in the centre of the kitchen on which Grace had placed a copper bowl filled with winter hyacinths. Around the table were four rush-seated, ladder-back chairs she had picked up at the market in Old Swan. A basket of applewood logs for the fire which Andy brought over each day and before the hearth two kittens rolled in play, come from the litter which arrived punctually in the barn up at the farmhouse.

In her front parlour was an occasional table or two, old ones, purloined from the attic at Sheil Road, an old chintz-covered sofa and a couple of deep armchairs to match that Ma said were of no use to them. There were two bedrooms, one of which was to be a nursery, the other, hers and Charlie's, low, slope-ceilinged with an enormous brass bed, over which she had thrown a colourful patchwork quilt, a pine dresser and wardrobe and a few worn rugs on the polished wooden floor.

Not to be outdone, Mrs Davenport provided the bed linen of pure white cotton, enough for a dozen beds, never mind one, with enormous white towels so thick and fluffy they were a delight to use when she stepped from the zinc bathtub which was placed before the kitchen fire and filled painstakingly with kettles of hot water heated on the old range. And if they caught her trying to empty it herself they'd skin her alive, Monty and his son Andy told her. He and Betty were made up with the newcomers who had arrived to fill the somewhat empty place his own childless daughters had left in their lives and they watched over Elizabeth as if she were their own. And would do the same for Grace's when it arrived, their manner said.

For as long as she could remember she had kept a diary, writing about the sweet, girlish, totally innocent, probably boring details of her life as a schoolgirl, as a female on the threshold of a woman's life, her days at Old Nook Hall, in France with Charlie and of her love for one man. His name was never mentioned in the diary, just the initial R; and when she had entered her day's doings the diary was locked with a tiny gold key.

When her labour began it was exactly nine months to the day since the entry that had spoken of the incident with the gun. The last day in December and though the first pain took her by surprise for a moment as she drowsed in the rocker before her kitchen fire, the kittens purring in her lap, she knew her "time" had come. She was alone, as she had been alone for the past two months, in the semi-dreaming state of the breeding female, in this place of peace and comfort where she had settled placidly, as pregnant women do, to wait. Charlie's letters were ecstatic at the prospect of being a father and at the prospect of them, all three of them, living in their own home when he returned. Oh yes, he conceded, he had understood her desire to continue with her nursing, since he certainly would have insisted that she give up at once, but still, she was taking it easy now and as soon as he could get leave he would come home. Perhaps when his child was born, wouldn't that be lovely. He loved her so much. He loved the coming child. He loved everything in his happiness, except the bloody war which separated them, he wrote, but his part in it he kept from her as all the men beside whom he fought kept it from those at home. She was to take care of herself and make sure she had some way to let Josie know the minute she felt the first pang.

Which she did, *and* Bessie who sent for the midwife, and six hours later with very little trouble, either to her or to the three women who watched over her, Tamsin Georgina Davenport was born.

"Isn't she the most beautiful thing you ever saw?" she asked Bessie, sighing as she looked down into the furiously scowling face of Rupert Bradley's daughter. There was no doubt of it. The dark, curling fluff on her head, the shape and dark chocolate colour of her eyes. The slightly sardonic lift of one fine, silken eyebrow in an exact imitation of her father as though, when she had stopped shouting her displeasure at being dragged into it, she might find the world somewhat amusing. Even the chin, a baby chin as yet, and female, but which would be as determined as his. When she was washed her rosy pouting mouth had reached greedily for the nipple, as was her right, her starfish hand resting in a companionable way on her mother's full white breast.

"Can I hold her?" Josie begged but Grace couldn't bear to part with her.

"No, you can't, at least not yet."

"She's *his*, isn't she?" Josie's voice was gentle with a wealth of understanding in it. Grace understood.

"Yes." And not another word was spoken on the parentage of Tamsin Davenport.

Charlie was fair, blue-eyed but their child had
Grace's colouring, which was something of a bone
of contention between her two grandmothers when
they hurried over the next day to examine her, both
swearing that the baby was a replica of *her* child at
the same age. They were not at all sure of *Tamsin*,
they told one another but when Grace explained that
she had named her daughter for her own two dead
brothers, Ma was overwhelmed with the rightness of
it. Tamsin Georgina. Mrs Davenport felt that it would
have been rather nice – with a disapproving sniff – to
have had a *Davenport* name in there somewhere, but
when Grace promised to give the next child, winking
at Josie who hovered in the background with Elizabeth
in her arms, a name that her mother-in-law fancied,
she was mollified. The firm certainty in Grace's
declaration that she and Charlie would have another
child comforted her, giving her hope for the future
which would not have her younger son in it. Grace
seemed to say that Charlie *would* come back to them
and Jean Davenport, holding Tamsin Georgina in her
arms, looked forward to that day.

30

"Oh, Jesus, make it stop . . ."

Charlie Davenport, Lieutenant Charles Davenport, placed a compassionate arm about the shoulder of the young soldier who crouched beside him. The soldier had his face pressed so desperately into the rotting matter of the mud wall of the trench his helmet tipped up at the front. They were standing with the rest of his platoon along the slipping, sliding trench, in mud up to their knees and what Charlie wanted to know was how the bloody hell they were expected to drag their booted feet out of it when the signal was given to go over the top. The men were loaded down with all the paraphernalia that was thought necessary for a fighting soldier to carry, almost half the weight of his own body and, not for the first time, or even the hundredth, Charlie wondered what went on in the minds of the men who were directing this war.

"Oh, gentle Jesus, make it stop," the soldier wept, bending his head in despair and Charlie patted his shoulder, then, reaching into his pocket, withdrew his wallet. Though they could barely hear each other speak, he took out a photograph and pressed it in front of the soldier's face. It was of a baby, smiling, plump-cheeked, two front teeth displayed proudly as she sat on the knee of a pretty woman.

"My wife and daughter," Charlie told him, yelling into his very ear and the soldier looked at it and the look of terror slipped for a moment from his face. "They are my peace and rest. I'll lend them to you until we get back. Fix them in your mind, soldier." Again he patted the boy's shoulder then reverently returned the photograph to his wallet.

The noise was like a great, crushing solid weight mercilessly bearing down on the waiting men, grinding their nerves and their bodies to bits and it had been going on without a moment's relief for the past two weeks. Some clever prick, probably Private Hardcastle who always seemed to know everything that went on, though where he got his information from was a mystery, said that 3,100 guns had fired four and a half million shells during that time, so was it any wonder that the nerve of the young soldier who huddled against him had gone.

> . . . Bonsoir, old thing,
> Cheerio, chin-chin,
> Napoo, toodle-oo, Goodbye-eee

Some seasoned Tommy sang defiantly down the line, the song heard only by his immediate neighbours, hardened by three years of trench warfare, as Charlie was, as all those who had survived it were.

Abruptly the preliminary bombardment stopped and the silence it left was so eerie the soldiers lifted their heads, not above the parapet, of course, since they didn't want their sodding brains blown out before they even stepped out of the trench, and looked about them, the expressions on their faces saying that they knew what the silence heralded and perhaps the bloody noise might be the better of two evils. Now that it was quiet they could hear the soft cooing of the pigeons which were vital for communications and which would be sent back with messages to those behind the lines, and their faces brightened as the ordinary sound from their past lives came back to them, for many were country lads.

The dawn was lightening the sky as the whistles blew, one of them Charlie's, and one hundred thousand troops went over the top. Charlie was in the second wave. The young soldier had gone with him bravely and just as bravely fell down again, silently, without a word of protest at having his eighteen-year-old life ripped from him, huddling this time, not against Charlie but among the hundreds and hundreds who had gone with the first wave. Some were dead, some not, a great rippling, moving, sighing sea of men, and though he did his best not to step on them Charlie found it very difficult to find a bit of muddy ground that did not have a soldier on it. The sound of the enemy machine-guns – where the hell were his men? – exploded in his ears, then there was a kick in his left shoulder and before he knew where he was or who had kicked him he found himself in a shell-hole. Smoke and noise continued to fill the air and the dead and the dying littered the ground behind him and in front of him, and in the hole with him was a young soldier who covered his head and moaned for his mother, and a dead German who, from the state of his rotting body, had been there for some time. In fact the rats had already been at him and Charlie turned his head away in horror before he passed out.

It was 31 July 1917 and at four o'clock in the

afternoon it began to rain heavily. Charlie and the young soldier, with the dead German for company, had been in the shell-hole for ten hours by then.

Captain Rupert Bradley was shouting something or other, he was not awfully sure himself what it was but it served to get his badly mauled men over the top. They were in the second wave, the 2nd and 3rd Battalions of the Liverpool Regiment, along with the Lancashire Fusiliers, cramming into the trenches along the Ypres salient. Rupert was tired, physically and spiritually. He had not been on leave since autumn of last year and what he had seen and done since then had sickened him. For three years they had fought over the same bit of ground, breathing in death and destruction along with the stink, the smoke and the disillusionment, and at the end of that first day of the Third Battle of Ypres he was not a bit surprised to be told that they had advanced no more than half a mile. He and what remained of his company squatted in what had become a quagmire in the last few hours, what his sergeant called a bloody porridge of mud, and prepared to pitch their bell-tents. It was raining cats and dogs but his men worked in a dogged silence, as though the frail shelter that they were preparing to hide in during the night was the most important task of their war. Almost thigh-deep in mud they were by now and every time they put a spade in the ground it caved in. They did it at last, then crawled into their tents and lay down, exhausted, wet to the shivering skin of them, coated in clinging, liquid mud, but they tried to sleep. What else was there to do until it was light but it really was no use and he knew it. The tents were sinking. His

men were sinking. Their weapons were sinking, so in
the end he gave the order for them to make a dash to
a nearby crater.

As they crept from the tent and prepared to run
across the bit of open ground to the shell-hole, a
burst of fire from a machine-gun caught them and
though he was not hit, ten of his men were, falling
into the shell-hole on top of those already there. Those
who were unhurt, only himself and a corporal who
spoke with a Liverpool accent, threw themselves in
among them.

Fifteen men, one of them dead, and at the bottom, in
the company of the sleek rats and the rainwater which
crept steadily up the sides of the crater, was Charlie
Davenport. He was conscious but for some reason he
couldn't move, neither could he make a sound to tell
them that he was being slowly buried alive. Or perhaps
drowned. He didn't know which, and as the night drew
on and a rat poked an inquisitive bewhiskered face into
his, he began to go mad.

Dawn revealed the full extent of yesterday's casualties. They were strewn over no-man's-land like debris
tossed up by the tide. Because they had not been dead
long and, indeed, some of them were not yet dead,
there was movement, sounds, a writhing and moaning
which Rupert, when he gingerly poked his head over
the edge of the shell-hole, told himself must be a scene
from hell. In the dark he and the corporal had moved
about among his men, reaching for the small first-aid
packs they all carried, asking them where they were hit,
doing his best to slap a dressing in the general direction
they indicated. He gave them a sip of water and told
them it wouldn't be long, lads, sitting for a moment

with one who died holding his hand, doing his best to comfort, though it was bloody hard when you couldn't see the face of the man who whimpered, or moaned for help. One chap, not one of his, he thought, for he was not wounded, cried bitterly for his mother, begging her to come for him and in the end, seeing that it was upsetting the others, he struck him deliberately across his face which shut him up.

Night fell again. He was filthy and exhausted and covered in blood, his own or the others' he didn't know, but since no one, no stretcher-bearers had come for them during the previous night he thought he might as well, with his corporal, have a shot at getting some of them out. The battle had continued to rage about them all day, bringing fresh casualties into the fragile protection of the shell-hole and as he whispered to the grim-faced but chirpy Liverpudlian, it wouldn't hold much more.

He and the corporal, between them, carried ten men back to their own trenches and when he went back for the two remaining he found they had died in the fifteen minutes he had been gone. There was just one man left who still breathed though his body was as stiff as a plank.

"Come on, soldier," he said hoarsely. He was so tired every single bit of him hurt, his skin, his teeth, even the roots of his hair but he carried Charlie Davenport on his back, dropping him into the trench from which Charlie, fifty hours ago, had climbed.

From the back of her cottage, across the two fields and the wood that separated them, Grace could see the chimneys of Garlands. On the day that Captain

Rupert Bradley and Corporal Edward Bracken were earning the medals the King at Buckingham Palace would, if they survived, pin on their chests, she and Josie with seven-month-old Tamsin and ten-month-old Elizabeth walked in the fields which were golden with buttercups, patched with the red of sorrel and the blue of cornflowers. The hedges they climbed by way of a wooden stile were bright with wild rose, elderberry and honeysuckle and on the rise at the top of the slope a cutting machine was at work, the buzz of it like a bumble bee on the warm summer air. There were cows, Monty Marsden's cows, standing up to their knees in wild clover, their heads down as they grazed but lifting to watch the progress of the two women who carried their babies on their hips, tied in a shawl as peasant women did. Two young cats and a dog followed them, the cats skittish and ready to dab at everything that moved with their paws, the dog resigned but prepared to put up with them. His master was trying out his new legs up the field which would soon be ready for harvesting and the dog, protective and anxious, was inclined to get in his way.

The perfume of wild flowers was heavy and sweet and the two women breathed it in deeply before flopping down on to the warm grass. Tamsin was placed on a rug where she sat, or rolled on to her front then back again, clutching at anything that would give her a hold to sit up once more. Elizabeth was crawling now and was off the minute her mother put her on the rug, like a small, scuttling animal, to investigate the hundred delights of the field, among them a blade of grass, a daisy, which went in her mouth, a couple of ants which were foolish enough to crawl on to her baby hand, and a cowpat which intrigued her greatly. Tamsin watched enviously before setting up a great howl, and it took fifteen minutes for the mothers to quieten their children into a peaceful sleep. The dog decided he had had enough of these noisy humans who had come to destroy his peace and sloped off towards home, but the cats continued to play their feline games in the tall grasses.

"So what's new from Charlie? Is there any likelihood of him coming home to see his new daughter, does he say? Well, not so new now at seven months." Josie put out a hand and gently touched the cheek of Grace's beautiful sleeping child. Her face was unutterably sad. "Dear God, what is the matter with this world when a man has a seven-month-old child whom he's never seen. Philip and I were . . . well, you can imagine how we felt when he lost his legs but sometimes I think we were the lucky ones. He sees his child every day, plays with her, watches her sleep at night and there are thousands, more probably, who will die without seeing their own children. Oh, dear Lord, I didn't mean . . . Jesus, me and my big mouth, of course Charlie will."

"Josie, there's no need to be so apologetic. I'm well aware, as, I suppose, are woman all over the country, the damn world, if it comes to that, what the chances are; women who live with the knowledge that . . . well, you know what I mean. Children who will never know their fathers. Charlie loves his daughter as though she were his—" She stopped speaking abruptly and the hand that had been stroking Tamsin's rounded cheek lifted and moved to place itself lightly on Grace's arm.

"She is, Gracie, if that's what you were going to say."

"Yes, I suppose I was but I also meant that though he's never seen her except for photographs he loves her as much as I do. I believe it's what keeps the spirit in him. Dear God in heaven, I wish he could get leave, then we could make a baby who is truly his."

"You will, darling, soon."

"I don't know." Grace sighed and stared sightlessly off towards the chimneys of Garlands. Her heart dragged heavily in her breast and the feeling grew in her, she couldn't even explain it, but it was absolutely imperative that soon she must walk over there and seek out Mrs Bradley. It was almost a year since she had last been there. Almost a year since she had seen him and she felt that her own spirit was slowly being chipped away and it was growing worse with every month. She had told herself that she would put him out of her mind, out of her heart, or at least bury him so deep in it she would not be aware of his presence there. She was married to another man, to her dear Charlie whom she loved as she had loved her brothers, a strong bond which she would honour, but it was all very well to say you were to do something, and then *do* it. She could not help herself. She scanned the lists of casualties in *The Times*, which daily grew longer and longer. The smiling faces of young men who were "missing" and whose families begged for news of them from other soldiers who might have seen them or knew of their fate. So many who had just disappeared off the face of the earth and where, in the midst of them all, was Rupert Bradley? Was he dead or alive? She had sat beside the bed of a badly wounded soldier on the night before Sister had told her she must give up her nursing, listening to his ramblings of unburied corpses which rotted and burst on the fields of battle, the stench that stopped him from breathing, the shell-holes and dugouts and gun pits, the fear of death, the fear of life, the loss of a pal, the waves of shell explosions which simply drove them mad so that even the rats screamed in terror. They wept like children, cold, wet and needing their mothers so desperately they *were* children again. Where, in this hell on earth, were Rupert and Charlie?

"I should get back," she said abruptly.

Josie started to rise and Grace put out a hand. "No, Josie, not home, but back to the hospital. I've let Tamsin keep me from it since I've just not been able to tear myself away from her. I'd seen you with Elizabeth and been told about how much I would love my child when it was born but I didn't believe it; but now, of course, I've found out it is so. She is . . . so exactly him. I know she's female but in every detail she is his replica. To look at . . . her eyes and hair and even that way he had of lifting one eyebrow when he smiled. I'm afraid someone is going to say something, though fortunately Ma and Pa don't remember him. Anyway it wouldn't occur to them; but if Mrs Bradley were to see her. She's got his sweetness, the way he was before the war, and yet she's stubborn . . . lively." Her head drooped and her hair, which she had never cut, and which was pulled back into a thick plait, had unravelled slightly and drifts fell over her face and hid her expression. "I love him still, Josie." Her voice was muffled with tears. "And yet I don't know if he is still alive . . . wounded perhaps and only Mrs Bradley can tell me."

"Wouldn't it be in the local papers?"

"Yes, I suppose so." She sniffed and wiped her nose on the back of her hand like a child, then lifted her head. "Anyway, if you'll take Tamsin, now she is weaned, like you said, d'you remember? I'm going to go and talk to Matron and see if they still want me."

They were glad to have her, Matron told her fervently and when could she start? The sooner the better.

The wrench at leaving Tamsin was almost more than she could bear and Mrs Davenport was highly indignant that Charlie's daughter was to be left in the care of a stranger when she should be with her mother, for was that not what mothers were for? To look after their own offspring.

"Josie is not a stranger, Mrs Davenport." She had still not been able to bring herself to call her "Mother". "Tamsin sees her every day and when I go shopping I usually leave her at Spring Cottage. And I look after Elizabeth. The babies know one another and play together. She won't suffer from my absence and I shall ask Matron if she would keep me off night duty. Believe me . . ."

"I don't like it, Grace," Mrs Davenport sniffed, "and I don't think Charlie will when I write to him."

No, she supposed he wouldn't but then perhaps he would understand her thinking, which was that every man or woman who could possibly help, in any way, to end this foul war, and thereby bring *him* home sooner, must be allowed to do it.

They were at full stretch at once. The new offensive of the Third Battle of Ypres, commonly known as Passchendaele, provided Old Nook Hall, and other hospitals up and down the country, with more casualties than they could cope with, or so it seemed. They received men who had been shot, wounded by shrapnel, gas bacillus cases, amputees and men who had received a "whiff" of chlorine and could barely breathe. The rain that had begun on the day of the first battle turned the trenches and dugouts, the shell-holes and gun pits on the Western Front into a quagmire, four feet of mud through which the soldiers did their best to march in good order, which was a sheer bloody impossibility, the weary men swore. They stood in the stuff for days on end and if the mud didn't drag them physically into its depths, which often happened and had it not been for the efforts of their mates frequently would, their poor old feet swelled to three times their normal size and were as numb as if they had been frozen. Stick a bloody bayonet in it and you wouldn't feel it, one soldier told Grace. That mud was a killer, another said, and worse than the enemy who, he had heard, had been seen giving a helping hand to a French soldier who was up to his waist in it.

She had been back a week when Sister Randall tapped her on the shoulder and told her she was wanted in Matron's office. She was tending to the wound of a brave lad who, despite the shrapnel wound in his own back, had volunteered to give blood to a young officer, no more than a boy, who had lost a leg through gangrene. It was a new procedure done in the operating theatre, the two soldiers head to head, and one that most soldiers would have considered daunting. Strangely, the experience had given the lad something to focus on even though the giving of the blood had been painful. He had seen the colour literally come back into the young officer's face, he told Grace, when *his* blood, and himself only a private, a miner's son from St Helens, had been pumped into the vein of the soldier on the other bed. He had had five stitches in the cut where the tube had been put into his vein and that small wound was more to him than the quite horrendous one in his back.

"I won't be a minute, Sister," Grace said, for she liked to stay with a patient for a minute or two after attending to his wounds.

"Right away, Nurse, if you please." And both the soldier and Grace turned to look at Sister in surprise, her voice was so sharp.

"What have I done, d'you think?" she whispered to Sister as she was hurried from the ward and into Matron's private office.

Matron was sitting stiffly at her desk and as Grace entered the room she was surprised to be told, gently, that she was to sit down.

Matron stared at her own hands for a long moment and it was then that Grace became aware that she was about to be told something that she could not bear. Rupert . . . no, don't be daft, girl, Matron knows nothing about Rupert. So . . . so what? She could see that Matron was at a loss for words which was unusual in itself, so what could that mean, she asked herself while her heart banged frantically in her breast and her mouth dried up. She held her own hands tightly clasped against her apron that, she noticed, had a small stain of something on it, for which, if she saw it, Matron would haul her over the coals. She could feel her mind desperately shying away from pictures; had she not seen them again and again as the men poured into this very hospital, the men she loved: Charlie, Robert, young John . . . and which one was it that Matron was going to tell her about?

"I have something . . . I am so sorry, Nurse, but you must forgive me if . . ."

Oh, bloody well get on with it, her mind shrieked while her expression remained impassive. This might be hurting you, as you seem to be telling me, but I'm certain it's going to hurt me more and the quicker it's over the better. The sooner I know the worst, then the quicker I can get away and . . . and . . .

"I'm afraid it's your husband, Nurse . . ."

"Dead?"

"Oh, no, my dear." Matron leaned forward compassionately as though she would drag Grace from her chair and put her arms about her but then that wouldn't do, would it, so she leaned back, her face inordinately sad.

"What . . . are his wounds? Is he . . . has he . . . ?"

"He is not wounded, my dear. There wasn't a mark on him when . . ."

Grace leaped to her feet and Matron did the same, prepared to get a hold of her nurse before she ran amok, which it seemed she might, so intense was the expression on her face.

"Grace, sit down, dear,"

"Are you going to tell me what is wrong with my husband or are you to dither about until I—"

"Grace, do sit down and at once if you please." Obediently Grace sat down and waited.

Matron returned to her seat, her face composed.

"Your husband was in the battle, the one they are calling Passchendaele. He was . . . he was buried in a shell-hole for . . . for a long time, Grace, and when he was brought out he had suffered . . ."

"How long?"

"Now there is no need for you to know."

"I am a nurse. How long?"

"Fifty hours."

"Oh, Jesus. He is . . . where?"

"He has been taken to a hospital in Scotland . . ." Where they put the men who are so badly shell-shocked they can no longer function. Matron did not say those words but Grace knew what she was telling her.

Grace stood up so violently Matron's desk shook. "I must go to him." She whirled about and made for the door but Matron, despite her bulk, was up out of her seat and had hold of her arms in hands of iron.

"No, Grace, no . . ."

"Yes, yes, let go of me, *let go of me.* He needs me and I must be there when . . . when he recovers."

"No, Grace. You must not go. It will be a long time" – "if ever" Matron wanted to say – "before you can visit him, so . . . go home, my dear, be with your family and if . . . when you feel up to it . . . come back to us."

Grace sagged against the door and surprisingly she found Matron's arms about her.

"Are you telling me that my husband has . . . lost his mind?"

"Yes, Grace, that is what I am telling you. Now go home to your baby." For though Matron was not a mother she knew the healing properties of a child.

31

The autumn sunshine shone through the leaves in
shafts of misted gauze, turning them from the lime,
the sea green, the emerald of their summer foliage
to the soft and mellow colours of yellow and gold,
of amber and copper and russet and the blush of
crimson. Some of the leaves had already begun to fall,
spiralling gracefully to the mossy ground where they
formed a crisp carpet. They rested among browning
bracken and drifted over fallen logs and the cut stumps
of trees and in them small creatures hid from the
quiet mare as she passed. The sun was low, slanting
through the leaves that remained on the high branches
of oak, hornbeam, sycamore and beech, and the mare's
legs brushed against the ferns that clustered against
each tree trunk. Rabbits and hedgehogs and birds
crept close to their hiding places and among the
undergrowth pheasants and woodcock, those that had
multiplied during the man's absence from home, hid
in their nests.

The man on the mare's back saw none of these
things as he rode slowly along the overgrown track.
He had one foot out of the stirrup, his leg bent
across the pommel of his saddle, for the mare was
old and not likely to be skittish. Indeed his hands
had relinquished the reins, letting them trail on the

mare's neck, allowing her to find her own slow way along the woodland path. He stared ahead of him in brooding silence and in his eyes was a kind of death-like blindness as though he saw not the loveliness of the autumn wood but something else that was haunting his thoughts.

He had once been the handsomest young man among his school fellows and in the battalion in which he served. He had reached full manhood now at the age of twenty-five with a tall, muscular frame, arresting, a vigorous physique, a strong body faultlessly proportioned, which set off the officer's uniform he usually wore to perfection. Nothing remained of the young man he had once been. His eyes, fringed by thick, black lashes, were the rich brown of the treacle toffee his mother's cook had made him and his brother and sisters in their childhood and his hair, uncut for a while by the look of it, was an unruly tangle of brown curls in which the sunlight had placed the gloss of chestnut. His face was strong, determined, unsmiling for the most part. Once he had laughed a lot, finding the world, especially the women, vastly diverting; now he was grave, an air of vulnerability about him, a sadness that weighed him down so that his shoulders slumped. One side of his face was badly mutilated, the flesh puckered and raw, the eye dragged down, the mouth dragged up. A spaniel trailed at his heels, darting off now and then to trace the source of a smell that caught his attention, then ambling back to his place at the mare's heels.

"Dear God, George," the man said sadly, "in this peaceful bit of woodland who would guess that a few hundred miles away the world's in bloody chaos. It's hard to believe . . ." His voice faded away and George, the dog whose name it was, cocked his head and looked up at him enquiringly. When nothing further was forthcoming he put his nose to the ground and sniffed, following the scent of the fox that had moved silently through the undergrowth the previous night.

The trees began to thin out as the man on the horse neared the edge of the wood and sunlight fell on a smooth green clearing. There was a wild guelder rose growing in profusion, the seeds of it brought by birds long ago, and the crimson berries on it glowed against the leaves. Sprawling along what had once been a hedge were bramble bushes, the branches of which were thick with luscious purple fruit.

"Season of mists and mellow fruitfulness . . ." the horseman said out loud. He supposed it was appropriate. It was September and there was still warmth in the sun. It touched his back in gentle benison, the goodness of it felt through the shirt and beige corduroy waistcoat he wore. The sleeves of the shirt were rolled up to his elbow to reveal arms that were golden brown with a scattering of dark hairs on the forearms and the backs of his hands which were scarred here and there as though he had been in a fight.

Leaving the woodland he urged the mare, who really did not need any urging, through a gap in a dry-stone wall and into a smooth and undulating field in which were scattered a number of rocks and small, stunted bushes and trees. A meadowlark sang and cows lifted their heads to watch him go by, one of them lowing mournfully. Giving the mare her head, scarcely caring where she went, he plodded through knee-high grass thick with clover, through another gap and across another field which, like the first, had a dozen well-fed cows in it. Ahead was a low hawthorn hedge. Above it the thatched roof of a cottage could be seen and it was then that he suddenly became aware that George was no longer with him.

He turned in the saddle and gazed about the field through which he had just ridden, expecting to see the animal leaping up among the tall grass; he scanned the fields and the scatter of buildings, a farm and several barns, to his left.

"Bugger the animal," he muttered, then putting his fingers to his lips gave out a piercing whistle. The mare pricked her ears, swivelling them on her well-shaped head, continuing to pick her dainty way towards the hedge.

"George," the man called. "Where the bloody hell are you, you damned idiot? If you're stuck down some rabbit hole I swear I'll leave you there."

There was a flurry of brown and white, of lolloping ears and bright eyes, a wet nose, a quivering tail and George appeared through the hedge ahead of him, but instead of racing towards him, the spaniel turned and dived back through the hedge.

"Bloody fool," he roared, then seeing it was no use expecting the animal to come of his own accord since he was a young dog and still not properly trained, he jumped down from the mare's back and strode to the hedge. Parting the top branches he peered through and was taken aback to see a woman, pegs in her mouth like a line of long teeth, pegging out what looked like towelling squares on a washing line that stretched across the wide, lawned garden. She was staring at him in frozen incredulity. There was what looked like a laundry basket on the ground and in it was the most beautiful infant he had ever seen and he was not a man who looked too closely at children, even those of his own brother. It was standing up, clutching the sides of the basket, rocking back and forth and squealing in delight at the sight of George and another dog, wrestling playfully on the grass.

He could not stop staring at the child. It was dark, with a riot of loose curls, a round-cheeked face the colour of amber and rose and deep, deep brown eyes. A little smudge of a nose, lips the colour of a poppy, wide with laughter, in which several little white teeth glistened. Suddenly its own exertions caused disaster and the basket tipped on its side, the child spilled out of it on to the grass and the woman with the pegs in her mouth instantly turned, spat them out and ran towards it.

"Darling, oh darling, what happened?" she crooned tenderly, picking the child up and holding it close to her shoulder but it seemed the child wasn't hurt, for it struggled to escape her arms, longing, it seemed, to be among the larking dogs.

He watched the woman and child with the fascination of a man looking at a species he had never seen before. The mare was peacefully cropping at the grass and George was engrossed in his game with the woman's dog, and across the hedge, across the months, across the anger, the acrimony, the heartbreak which both had known, Rupert Bradley and Grace Davenport looked at each other as if for the very first time.

The baby was beginning to shriek its displeasure and, coming slowly from her trance of amazement, the thunderbolt his sudden appearance at her back garden hedge had caused, she placed it on the grass where it headed at once towards the dogs.

His own dog was not used to babies despite those in the nursery at Garlands, for it would not occur to the nanny Victoria employed to allow her charges to lark about with an animal. You never knew where it had been, was her private thinking. But George and the other dog parted at once as the child scuttled towards them and to his own consternation both dogs allowed themselves to be pulled and pushed and climbed over with the greatest of goodwill.

"I wasn't sure . . ." he began. "My dog isn't . . . he's a good dog, good-natured, I mean, but I wouldn't have believed he would . . . the baby . . ."

"Oh, Gyp is used to . . . to children. He's not mine but he comes through; the people next door own him."

"Oh, good," he answered foolishly, wondering why he felt so bloody tongue-tied. "The child is . . . what name did you . . ."

"She is called Tamsin; after my brother."

"Of course. I remember Tom. I was sorry . . ."

"Thank you."

They stood then, both of them watching the lively baby and the patient dogs. Two young cats sauntered gracefully, one behind the other, round the corner of the cottage and the baby, spying them, began to crow and point her fat finger at them, grinning at her mother. The cats came to a sinuous stop when they spied George, ready to turn tail and run but George was busy licking the baby's hand and when he did notice them treated them with indifference. After all he had seen cats in the stable yard at Garlands and considered them to be nothing out of the ordinary.

"How old is . . . Tamsin?" Rupert asked diffidently, still looking at the child and Grace felt her heart, which was already banging away like the drum that boomed on the bandstand in Newsham Park every Sunday, quicken its beat. At the sight of him it had felt as though it were being squeezed by a vice-like fist, then, when it was released, began to hammer at three times its normal pace. Should she tell this man that the child, *his* child, was just over eight months old and if she did was it likely he would count back the months to that day when he and she had . . . sweet Lord, when they had made love in his mother's summerhouse? Or, man-like, would he just accept what she told him with the unconcern of a stranger? For that was what he was. A stranger. She had seen his photograph in the Liverpool *Echo* stating that Captain Rupert Bradley was to be awarded a medal for his bravery at Passchendaele when he and his corporal had carried a dozen severely wounded men from a shell-hole in no-man's-land. They had gone back again and again under enemy fire, risking their own lives and Philip had told her that they were to go to London to receive their medals from the King himself.

She turned to look at the child who was sitting up now and clapping her hands. A joyful child, a happy, beloved child, Charlie's child she had begun to think of her as, and yet she had only to look at Rupert and see his daughter in him. The same colouring, the same turn of the head, the same smile, the same impish good humour which, though now sadly lacking in her father, his daughter had inherited.

Now that she had turned her deep and velvety eyes away from him to look at her child, Rupert studied the woman in the garden. She was as lovely as he remembered. Perhaps a trifle fuller in the breast but that was not to her detriment. She wore a plain cotton dress in a shade of lavender blue, the hem just touching her ankle bone. The sleeves came to her elbow and the neck was high but she had undone the top buttons to reveal the deep, shadowed cleft between her breasts and her nipples strained against the fine material. Her hair was tied carelessly to the top of her head with a knot of lavender-blue ribbons, the curly tangled ends hanging down her back between her shoulder blades

"And your husband?" he managed to get out, speaking as though he had a blanket in his mouth. She turned to him then and on her face was an expression of unutterable sadness.

"Charlie was . . . he was in the battle . . . Passchendaele. He is still in hospital . . ." Her voice faltered.

"I'm sorry. Where was he wounded?" Meaning legs, chest, stomach, any of which could be death-dealing.

"No, he was not physically wounded. He is in a hospital on the outskirts of Edinburgh for . . . shell-shocked officers." She hung her head as though she might give way to something she barely had under control and immediately he knew what sort of a state her husband would be in.

"Poor bugger," he said, his voice soft and compassionate, for wasn't that one of the worst things that could happen to a soldier. Shell-shock, the inner migration to madness. In the ranks it had been diagnosed as "hysterics" which often took the form of paralysis and he had seen it a dozen times when the men in the front lines, unable to bear the tension, had simply gone mad with it.

"They won't let me see him. He's totally paralysed, even his . . . his mind. So you see, he's not able to recognise . . . but perhaps later when he has been treated I may be able to . . ." She was beginning to shake and the baby, sensing something out of the ordinary about her mother, stopped clapping her plump little hands and her bottom lip began to tremble.

Rupert didn't know how he got through the hedge. Through it, over it, under it, he only knew he was on the other side and his arms reached out and folded Grace Davenport in their warm and comforting strength. She had seen so much, he knew that, for she was a nurse. He had seen so much, suffered so much and in those first few moments they merely clung to one another in the companionship only damaged soldiers can share. For some reason his mind drifted hazily back to the beginning of the Battle of Passchendaele when he and Corporal Bracken had brought out the chaps from the shell-hole. He hadn't thought much about it at the time. He was alive and unwounded, they were in need. Besides which he didn't give a damn whether he lived or died so he had just got on with it. But there had been one, the last one at the bottom of the hole who had been rigid with paralysis, whose eyes, when he saw him later in the field hospital where they had taken the wounded, stared unblinkingly into the maws of hell. By then they had cleared his mouth of the mud, the mud that had pressed on his eyelids, filled his ears and forced its way up his nostrils. They had wiped it away from his face and his hair but he could see that the man, a young officer of the Lancashire

Fusiliers, still imagined himself to be at the bottom of
that pit where, they told him, he had been buried for
fifty hours.

The baby began to scream and at once the woman
in his arms tore herself loose and ran to pick her up.
"There, sweetheart, Mother's here. Don't cry, there's
nothing to cry about." Though her own face was wet
with tears.

For several moments she stood with her face buried
in the child's neck then she turned to face him.

"It was you, wasn't it? The newspaper said you
had saved a dozen men from a shell-hole and Charlie
was . . ."

He shook his head, doing his best to smile. "Grace,
there are a hundred shell-holes in France and your
husband could have been—"

"No, Rupert, it was you. The report of how you
carried—"

"Don't, Grace. I tell you what, let me tie my mare to
the hedge and then you can offer me a cup of tea." He
grinned disarmingly in the way he once had done, then
turned to look about the garden so that she could not
see the expression on his face. It was a country garden
with tall hollyhocks in shades of crimson, pink and
white, Livingstone daisies against the wall in the sun,
rose-campion, the "flower of love", he had heard it
called though by whom he could not remember, sweet
william and marigolds and up the wall of the cottage,
climbing to the thatch, a fragrant, vibrant pink rose.

"I had no idea you were living here," he told her,
following her across the garden towards the open
back door of the cottage. He had to bend his head
to enter the kitchen and something taut within him

was instantly eased by the homely comfort, the bright bowls of flowers, the sparkling rows of blue and white crockery on the pine dresser.

"I've been here since . . . ever since Tamsin was born. I wanted a place of my own for when my husband came home."

"Of course," he answered politely. He watched her as she put the baby in a basket which was padded with a blue checked material then turned to the enormous range on which a kettle steamed. The baby, quiet now, her mouth firmly plugged with her thumb, regarded him gravely, then, to his delight, grinned at him without removing her thumb from her mouth. As he watched, her eyes began to close and, falling back, she was instantly asleep.

"How wonderful," he marvelled.

"What?"

"To be able to fall asleep like that."

"You don't sleep well, Rupert? Dear God, will you listen to me? I'm sorry, are there any men who have returned from the front who know what it is to get a good night's sleep?"

"I . . . don't suppose so."

Grace could feel his eyes on her as she put the tea in the big brown pot Bessie had passed on to her, then poured on the boiling water. She might have sat down, as he had done, at the table, while the tea "mashed", one of Nora's sayings, but for some reason, confusion, disorientation, *enchantment* and a vast disbelief that this was actually happening, held her rigid and she continued to stand with her back to him, staring at the pot. He was – what was he? – different, of course, the sharpness, the bitterness scoured out of him, it seemed, leaving something that was not as once he had been years ago but that was softer and more easily handled. There was embarrassment, for could either of them forget that hour in the summerhouse? Could either of them forget her fervent declarations of love for him? Could either of them forget that she was now married to Charlie and – in her mind at least – had borne him a child?

"Do you take sugar?" she asked him politely, then looked up at him sharply when he did not answer.

"I'm sorry." His voice was so soft she could barely hear it.

"I asked you if you—"

"For the way I have treated you in the past. I was a bastard. You were young . . . and I didn't take you seriously and if I hurt you, which I suppose I did, I can only say I'll never forgive myself."

Her face was pale as she stared at him but in her eyes was an expression he found hard to decipher. She had married another man which surely told him that she was – well, he hardly liked to put it into words – that she was no longer *in love* with him, as she had once protested. But there was a shining, a glow in the depth of her golden-brown eyes that was perplexing. She was very lovely, he had always thought so, a delicate loveliness, even as a young girl, fresh, innocent, an inexperienced child who had looked at him as though he were the sun and moon all rolled into one and he had been amused in a kindly way, naturally, for that had been his nature then. Kindly, tolerant to the sister of his friend who had looked at him with such awe. But later, much later, after Jessica, after the dreadful disfigurement to his face, he had not been kind. He had taken her quite brutally, taken what she had offered and she had responded with an ardour that had taken him by surprise. He could see her now, naked and sighing in his arms, her eyes unfocused, her body arched to meet his, her head flung back as he impaled her. She had been a virgin, the physical proof of it on her thighs, but she had wrapped her arms about him, taken his head to her breast and enveloped him in a love he had failed to notice, or if he did it did not concern him.

Neither of them knew what to say, how to continue, but both of them were aware that something had changed between them. They sipped their tea, elbows on the table, the homely kitchen, the smell of roses which drifted in through the kitchen door, the deep breathing of the baby settling about them like a soft blanket. The two cats, twined together on the rug, purred with deep satisfaction. George poked his nose enquiringly over the doorstep, then, seeing his master, padded across the flags and put his muzzle on Rupert's knee. He looked down at the dog and placed a hand on his smooth head. A deep contentment washed over him and putting down his sturdy beaker of tea he looked up at Grace. He sighed deeply.

"May I come again, Grace?"

"Yes, of course." No hesitation.

"I've a bit of leave before I go up to . . . well, I don't mean to be pretentious but before I go to Buckingham Palace. It sounds as if I'm to take tea with Their Majesties but I'm afraid—"

"You don't want it, do you?"

"No. There are hundreds and thousands who deserve it more than me. Your husband for one."

"Charlie is brave, I grant you. He has been wounded twice and now this. Do you know he has never seen his daughter."

A long silence then. "*His* daughter, Grace." There was a wealth of sadness in his voice. At once her face turned a fiery red before every vestige of colour slipped away.

"I don't know what you mean, Rupert. What are you implying? Charlie and I—"

"Grace, you are not the sort of woman who makes love to two men at the same time. A year last March . . . I'm sorry to bring it up again but it's not something a man forgets when a woman as lovely, as sweet as you . . . offers herself. I'm sorry, I don't know how else to put it. The child is as lovely as her mother but she is . . . so like the babies in the nursery at Garlands, a true Bradley. I *can* count, Grace, and I believe that your daughter is also *my* daughter. Oh, please, Grace, don't get upset . . ." as Grace stood up and flung herself about the kitchen. He tried to follow her, to take her arm since she seemed in danger of hurting herself on one of the sharp corners she encountered but she threw him off, her face like fire, her eyes burning brands of rage.

"How dare you . . . how dare you try to say that Charlie's child is yours. Yes, you are a bastard, for what man will try to take another man's child."

"I'm not trying to take her, Grace. Jesus wept, what kind of a man do you think I am?"

"I've just told you and haven't you proved it time and time again in the past. A bastard and Charlie is worth two of you. I love him and I will never—"

"Never what, Grace? Never what? I'm asking nothing

of you, nothing, d'you hear me. By sheer coincidence I've turned up on your doorstep."

"Damn you . . . damn you."

"Oh, I'm damned all right. But I mean it when I say I make no claim on the child."

"You *have* no claim on the child. Now, I must ask you to go and never come back. Charlie will be home soon . . . one day . . . and . . . and . . ."

She began to weep with the broken-hearted despair of a child, putting her hands to her face in a spasm of sorrow that drove spikes into him. The dog whimpered and the two cats raised their haughty heads to stare at her.

"Oh, darling . . . darling," he whispered, drawing her into the circle of his arms. "Don't . . . don't. I can't bear it. Don't cry, my lovely girl . . . don't."

They were both bewildered by what was happening and when she lifted her wet face to look into his he tucked her head beneath his chin, rested his cheek on the knot of blue ribbon in her hair and wished to God he had ridden in any direction but this when he left the stable yard at Garlands.

32

Too late, far too late, it had begun. What she had dreamed of, longed for ever since the day when, as a young girl, she had watched Mr Melly take to the skies with Rupert beside her. Now he was beside her again, sitting at her kitchen table, his eyes wandering from her to Tamsin as though he were in a daze of disbelieving wonderment, unable to grasp what had happened, what was happening. His face was dark and forbidding, seemingly without humour as though the few minutes they had spent in one another's arms had never happened and if they had it was of no consequence, since he had been merely comforting her distress over her wounded husband. Just the same she could not help noticing a strange quiver in his hands for which there seemed to be no reason. But when he smiled at the baby who was clapping her hands for him she was bowled over by the warmth and beauty of his expression. Her heart missed a beat, several beats, and she could feel the colour flood her face whenever he looked at her, and though she longed for him to stay, at the same time she longed for him to go, for surely, the way her pulses were racing, it could only cause mayhem with her life, hers and Charlie's.

She was not to know that Rupert's heart was doing the foolish things he himself had heard that hearts did in romantic novels and his throat was so dry he could hardly speak. The glow in his heart when he looked at her was simply there. One moment it had not been, now it was. Beyond reasoning so why try to explain it. Irrational, he knew, just as he knew that what he felt for her was madness, since he was married to another woman and she was married to another man. He had known her for years. *Known* her in the biblical sense and yet he didn't know her at all really except that she was showing, had always shown the most remarkable courage. She had lost three brothers. He had heard, he didn't know from whom, probably his mother who got it from friends, that her parents had gone to pieces and she had held them together. Her husband, the one he himself had brought from the water-filled, mud-filled crater, was paralysed by the horror he had suffered and she was left to pick up the pieces of the wrecked man who would come home to her. Or *never* come home to her as the case might be. She was as much a survivor of the battles as any man who had fought in the trenches but she had not gone under.

She was fiddling about at the table, buttering some scones she told him she had made, making another pot of tea, rinsing the cups they had used under the tap at the stone sink in the scullery while he watched her with an unreadable expression on his face.

Suddenly he got to his feet, knocking his hip against the table making the milk jug and sugar bowl rattle. His face was forbidding and the brown of his eyes was like the mud flats on the Mersey when the tide went out.

"I must be off." His voice was ragged and she stared at him in alarm. Had she said something, offended him in some way or was it that he . . . he . . . what? Perhaps the baby . . . or was it the thought that he was sitting in the home, or what *would* be the home of Charlie Davenport when he was recovered? Perhaps he was remembering that he himself had been cuckolded by the many men who had slept with his wife and the thought that he might do to Charlie what had been done to him was more than he could stand.

"Rupert, will you not have another cup of tea?" What a stupid, banal question in the midst of the tamped-down emotion which was likely to blaze round the homely room if not extinguished.

"No, really, I have things to do . . ."

"Of course."

She walked slowly through from the scullery into the kitchen, the tea towel still in her hands. The pale honey of her face was flushed with rose at the cheek and her eyes were the glowing colour of the conkers her brothers used to collect at this time of the year, and the silence was thick with some tension that stood between them. He took a step towards her, perhaps to say something polite such as thank you for the tea but instead he took the tea towel from her hands and dropped it to the floor. She began to shake and her lips formed a word that might have been "no" but both of them knew that it was not meant.

He sighed deeply and as though it were something he had no power to resist he drew her towards him, holding her by the shoulders. Gently he put his mouth against hers and the bolt of lightning struck them both, going from one to the other, and when he took his mouth from hers she almost fell. He kissed her again, more vigorously this time.

"I must be off my head . . . if I'd known I wouldn't

have . . ." he was murmuring against her lips, recognising that whatever had lain between this woman and himself for all these years had awakened at last.

"I know," she answered, though she had not the faintest inkling what he was talking about. Her own practical good sense, her loyalty, her love for the man in the hospital in Scotland were lost, scattered to the four winds, and she found she didn't care. To do her justice she was in no state to care, for her senses were reeling away from her, emptying her mind of everything but her love and need of this man. *This* man and no other. Even the baby prattling to herself in the basket was no longer considered. Rupert's tongue began to flick and probe the soft inside of her mouth and the desperate, hungry need in her and in him erupted between them.

"Rupert . . ." she murmured huskily, her mouth against his brow as his lips slid to her throat and lower, dipping into the open neck of her bodice and an electric bolt of passion fused them together as though their separate bodies had become one.

"Darling . . . darling . . . I didn't know . . . I didn't realise . . . all these bloody years . . ."

He was mesmerised, bewitched, so that all decency, all thoughts of the rights and wrongs of what they were about vanished like smoke in a wind. He didn't know, nor care and neither did she, and if at that moment the child had not decided to stand up and repeat the performance with the basket as she had done earlier he thought he might have laid this lovely, *willing* woman on her own kitchen floor and taken her right there.

The basket tipped, the baby howled, George barked

and leaped about thinking it was all a game for his entertainment and the cats fled for the back door.

They sprang apart guiltily just as though Bessie Marsden and Josie Booth had bustled in and caught them, both of them flushed and breathing heavily, she pulling at her bodice, doing her best to draw the neckline higher, he adjusting something at the front of his dreadfully tight breeches.

"I'm sorry . . . I should not have . . . taken advantage, but . . ."

"No, please . . ."

"I don't know what happened to me." His voice was stiff.

"Don't you?"

"It was inexcusable; your husband is . . . I'd best get home."

"Yes."

Then, in a voice harsh and explosive, turning violently towards her so that she flinched away from him, he told her, "No, I'm *not* bloody sorry, Grace. I should be, I know that, whatever you may think of me. Jesus God, the times I was a bastard to you and now you will think that this is the same, but it isn't; but to try it on – not that that's what I was doing, it just happened – but to *approach* the wife of a man who is wounded . . . it is unforgivable."

"Yes, Charlie is a good man." Her voice rasped in her dry throat. "But you were not forcing me, Rupert, whatever *you* may think. You know . . . you knew how I've felt about you for years and years. You married and were lost to me so . . . I wanted a home, a family of my own, children, so I married Charlie. I love him, you see."

"Because of the child; no, don't try to tell me the child is his."

"I'm telling you *I love Charlie*. Charlie wouldn't . . . survive without me. When he comes home I shall—"

"I know. Christ in heaven, d'you think I don't know? Now I really must go. I'm sorry. Please forgive me . . . this, and everything."

She had the baby in her arms as she watched him run from the house the dog at his heels, and across the garden. At the hedge he stopped for a moment to stare back at her and the child, then pushed his way through it. She heard him speak to the mare, then there was the thundering of hooves as he raced the animal across the field. He even leaped the low dry-stone wall, risking himself and the elderly mare's legs, for she hadn't done a jump like that for years.

His photograph was in the Liverpool *Echo* two days later: LOCAL HERO RECEIVES MILITARY CROSS. CONSPICUOUS BRAVERY UNDER FIRE. The headline was followed by a report of how *Major* Rupert Bradley had saved the lives of a dozen men and had this day received not only a promotion, but his medal from His Majesty the King at Buckingham Palace. There was a forbidding photograph of Rupert in his officer's uniform scowling defiantly, and Grace could imagine the photographer hopefully asking him if he would mind presenting his "good" side to the camera and being snarlingly refused. His mother and father stood one on either side of him, his mother proud and tearful, his father stern as though having a hero for a son was a lofty burden to bear.

He was knocking at her back door the following day,

having come the same way as previously. His mare was tethered to the hedge at the bottom of the garden and when she opened the door he pushed his way in and took her in his arms with a trembling violence which told of his wretchedness.

"I can't see beyond you." His voice was savage with his own fury, at himself for feeling or at her for making him feel it, she wasn't sure. "I swore to myself I wouldn't come again," he mumbled into her hair, "but I couldn't bloody stay away. I know I shouldn't have come but I just found myself heading straight here. Poor bugger, that poor bugger up in Scotland. D'you realise that if I hadn't brought him out he would have died and perhaps, who knows, he would rather be dead. Sweet Christ, what have I done? Condemned him to a life of . . . indescribable misery. Will he recover, Grace, d'you think, and if he does what is to happen? And if he doesn't will I ever forgive myself?"

"Rupert." She knew he expected no answer. She held him in her strong young arms, not sure whether he was grieving for himself, what had happened to him, or for Charlie, who, because of him was probably to live the rest of his life in a frozen casing of shock brought on by his experience in the shell-hole. Was Rupert saying he was sorry he brought him out for Charlie's sake, or because he wanted Charlie's wife – *after all these wasted years!*

"Grace, what is to happen?"

"To Charlie?"

"No, to me . . . and you. You must realise that I want you."

"I can't say I do, Rupert," she answered carefully,

afraid to upset even more what seemed to her to be his terrible fragility. He was on the brink, as so many were, of falling off this world into another and without someone – *her* – to hold on to him would he slip? It appeared there was no one else!

"I'm to go back at the end of the week, Grace." He let go of her then and, running his hand through his hair which she noticed had been cut, probably for the ceremony at the palace, he looked round him in what seemed to be puzzlement. Sighing, he thrust his hands deep in the pockets of his breeches and moved slowly to the window, looking out on the garden. The baby carriage stood under the protection of an oak tree and in it Tamsin Georgina Davenport slept. There was a line of baby clothes drying in the mild autumn sunshine, the scene peaceful, homely, something, his expression seemed to say, to take back with him.

"Have you a photograph, Grace? Of . . . of the baby. It would give me something . . . clean to look at when . . ."

"Of course. I had some taken for Charlie. Of Tamsin by herself but he wanted me on it so . . . but I think—"

"Just of Tamsin."

"You won't show it to your mother?" Then could have bitten her tongue when his head bowed as though in defeat.

"You really do think I'm a bastard, don't you?"

"I'm sorry, but in the past you—"

"I understand."

She was suddenly frightened and she moved to take his arm. "Rupert." Her voice was soft. "Rupert, promise me you'll be—"

"Careful?" He laughed harshly.

"Your wife might—"

"My wife has a fancy to be the wife of some earl of other, I forget of where, and has asked me to divorce her. Or rather to provide her with the means to divorce me since she believes I am a gentleman and . . . anyway I told her to go to hell. I imagine she will do so one day; in the meanwhile she will do what she has to in order to be a countess."

"Rupert . . . oh, my love . . ."

"Am I, Grace, am I your love?" He turned fiercely and glared into her face, his own spasming with some dreadful emotion. "You used to say I was once but I trampled on you so I can hardly expect you to—"

"Hello, anyone at home?" a familiar voice called. "I've left Elizabeth next to Tamsin . . ."

It was doubtful who was the more confounded, Rupert and Grace, or Josie as she pushed open the door and stepped over the threshold. The door opened inwards so that Rupert and Grace were behind it and when she peered round it and saw them there, their faces almost touching, she looked ready to laugh in disbelief.

"Ooh, I'm sorry. I didn't know you were . . ." It was clear she had been about to say "entertaining". "I'll push off and let you . . ."

Rupert straightened his tall frame which had been just about to collapse around Grace, his arms ready to lift her to him and she had been ready to acquiese. Already their passion was mounting, their eyes becoming unfocused in anticipation of the sensuality of loving. His glance had begun to wander towards the steep, narrow stairs and the deep, soft, lavender-scented bed he was sure she would have, but Josie's appearance brought him to the erect stance of the officer he was, his smile polite, correct.

"Josie . . . no, please, don't go. I don't think you have met my friend" – she laughed somewhat shrilly – "and next-door neighbour, Josie Booth. This is Major Rupert Bradley, Josie."

They exchanged polite greetings.

"I was just about to put the kettle on for tea, wasn't I, Rupert?"

"Indeed you were, Grace, but I'm afraid I must be off. My mother . . ."

"Of course, and thank you for . . ."

"Don't mention it."

With a courteous nod in Josie's direction he strode from the house and down the garden. He hesitated at the baby carriage that held his daughter and for a fraction of a second glanced inside, then pushed his way through the fence and was gone.

Josie sighed sorrowfully. "He knows then?" as Grace continued to stare at the hedge where he had disappeared.

"What?"

"About Tamsin?"

"Yes, he recognised her."

"How long has he been home? I saw the report in the *Echo*."

"I don't know. He came a day or two back."

"Did you tell him about Charlie?"

"Oh, yes. Actually it was Rupert who brought Charlie out."

"Oh, God, Grace! What a bloody muddle. From

the way the two of you were ... almost in each other's arms I take it he has decided he ... he has really loved you all the time? And it also seems you believe him."

"Don't be daft, Josie."

"I don't think so, Gracie. Now then, did I hear you say you were to make a cup of tea? I have left Philip struggling with some paperwork Monty asked him to look over and Bessie's 'turning out' the attic bedroom since her eagle eye has spotted that there is to be an addition to the family and we'll need another room for it."

Grace was dragged out of her blind and senseless state as the impact of Josie's words were made clear to her. She began to smile, a smile that grew into a grin, then with a cry of joy, for it seemed Philip Booth was still man enough to father a child despite his infirmity, she threw her arms about her friend and began to waltz her round the kitchen.

"Hey, carefully does it. Don't forget I'm in what is known as an interesting condition and if Bessie was to see us she'd give the pair of us a smack bottom."

"Oh, Josie, I'm so pleased for you, and for Philip. He must be beside himself."

"I told you we were not to stop at one, didn't I?"

"You certainly did. When is it to be?"

"Oh, ages yet and how Bessie could spot it, I don't know. I'd hardly noticed it myself." Josie drew in a deep breath, lowering herself into Grace's rocking-chair and accepting the cup of tea Grace put in her hands. She sipped it, gazing into the small but bright fire which glowed behind the bars of the blackleaded range. Grace squatted on the battered velvet pouffe on the other side of the fire and the two cats twined about one another at their feet. The Chime clock which stood above the fire on a shelf chimed the quarter hour and both women glanced at it automatically though time did not mean much to either of them. Josie's life revolved round her husband and his needs, her baby and her needs. When it was light they rose from their bed and when it was dark they lit the lamps. When they were tired they went to bed. They ate when they were hungry, their only concession to the passing of time in the seasonal demands of the countryside which moved from planting in spring, haymaking in autumn, the mating and birth of the animals on the farm. Grace found that, with no one but herself and Tamsin to consider, she did the same. Ma and Pa came a couple of times a week, taking enormous joy from their granddaughter, and most weekends Mr Davenport drove over with Mrs Davenport to do the same. She found she drifted rather pleasantly through her days and had it not been for the constant worry about Charlie she would have asked for nothing more. Her intention to take up nursing again had been curtailed after only a few days when the news of Charlie's illness had been given to her and though she still tried desperately to persuade the army medical authorities that she must see him for herself they were adamant that it would do no good, to her or to Charlie, at least for the time being.

"What are you to do then?" Josie's voice was casual, just as though she were asking when Grace intended to put on her coat and go into town.

"About what?" Though of course Grace knew exactly what she meant.

"Come on, Grace, this is me! You know what I'm talking about. Your face was like a beacon and just as illuminating when I came in. You love this man. I know you always have, you told me so but it seems that he returns your feelings now. No, don't argue. I could see it in his eyes when he looked at you. Oh, he was being the perfect gentleman bidding us both farewell but it was there when he turned to you. And the way he stopped to look at the baby . . . *his* baby."

"Don't, Josie, for God's sake don't take Charlie's daughter away from him. She is all he has."

"He has you?"

There was a long silence then Grace raised a sad face to her friend. "Yes, he has me."

"That is the answer to my question then. You are not going to run off with—"

"Don't joke about it, Josie, please, I can't bear—"

"I'm sorry, darling, but I don't think Major Rupert Bradley is going to stand idly by and watch you, and his daughter, play happy families with Charlie. I know I sound flippant. I always do when I'm being totally serious but . . . well, you know what I mean. Now, I must go before Bessie begins to give Philip a good 'bottoming' with that bucket of soapy water I saw her heaving up the stairs."

Tamsin had been bathed in the oval galvanised-iron bath which Bessie had unearthed from the back of the barn and, after a good scouring, had passed on to her. It was ideal for Tamsin though a bit on the small side for herself. Nevertheless, after Tamsin was tucked up and asleep in her cot, she decided to add some more hot water to it and bathe in front of the fire. The curtains were drawn, the door bolted and when the tap came she knew at once who it was.

She began to tremble and the water she crouched in made small ripples up the side of the bath as though it were a pond in which a stone had been thrown. The flesh on her body rippled with it and she could feel it prickle with goose bumps and some sound made itself heard in the back of her throat. A small moan, whether of pain, or joy, or terror, she did not know. The lamps flickered, one on the table, the other on the windowsill and the tapping became more insistent.

Slowly she stood up, the soapy water running down her naked body and though with some gesture towards decency she reached for the towel and wrapped it about herself she wondered, with the part of her brain not darting ahead to the rapture to come, why she bothered, for there was no doubt that the minute he came through the door he would have it off her.

He did. He nailed himself to her wet body, his arms crossing over at her back and hers went round his neck, her hands clinging in his hair quite viciously.

Strangely he leaned back from her, his eyes a deep, warm, gleaming brown in the lamplight. He put up one hand to cup her cheek. His thumb caressed her smooth skin, feeling the bloom on it, the warmth of it as she came slowly towards her own real blooming as a woman at last. His face was stern and uncompromising but she did not see it as she pressed closer into his arms.

"Rupert . . ." Her eyes were closed, her voice husky.

"Yes, my darling. You are safe with me."

He laid her down on the rug before the fire, booting aside the indignant cats and in the light from the lamps and the flames of the fire, studied every sweet curve and hollow of her, his hands gentle on her breasts which were rich as cream tipped in rose. His mouth was warm on her belly, drifting to every part of her arching body, taking her nipples between his lips and teasing them with his tongue. She was scarcely aware of it when he removed his own clothes and with delicacy, with the tenderness he had not shown her before led her in the true ways of loving. His penis stood proudly from the mat of dark hair at the base of his belly, a lordly lift and thrust of his loins before he entered her. He threw his head back at that last moment, crying out her name.

"I love you . . . I love you," he cried, carrying her on his own incoming tide of passion, taking her with him until she wept.

They made love again later and in between they slept in one another's arms. It was the same on the following night and the one after that. They made no plans. How could they? And when he left her that last time just as day was breaking, so did her heart, for, despite Josie's words two days ago, she knew she would not see him again.

33

The train drew up alongside the platform and those in the carriage with her, mostly soldiers going home on leave, stood up, those who had not already done so, as though they hadn't a moment to spare, which she supposed they hadn't, and must be off to that dear haven they had dreamed of in the trenches. The door was flung open and even before the train came to a full stop the carriage emptied, leaving her sitting alone in a frozen attitude of – she didn't know what to call it – dread, trepidation, even terror. She had no idea what she was to find at the end of her journey but it must be made no matter what anyone said to the contrary.

Slowly she rose from her seat and reached down the small suitcase some polite but stony-faced young officer had placed in the rack for her. They had all been the same, the men with whom she had travelled from Liverpool, through Preston and Carlisle to Edinburgh and the dozens of stations in between. She was an attractive woman, she was sensible enough to admit that and was not unused to men eyeing her admiringly, even to engaging her in conversation, but these were not of that sort. They barely glanced at her in her smart, dove-grey outfit, her pretty peach flowered, wide-brimmed hat, their whole being, each one of them, appearing to be holding itself together until they reached the safety of someone's arms. They would have to go back, they knew that, but at the moment they were heading towards something that they prayed would give them the strength to go on and Grace's lovely womanhood was of no concern to them.

She stepped down from the carriage and at once there was the usual mind-numbing tumult of a busy railway station, hissing steam, acrid smoke, shrieking voices and piercing whistles, of clatter and clamour and movement as porters raced here and there with their overflowing trolleys. There was a war on and all manner of folk were moving from one end of the country to the other. On the opposite platform, away from the pitying stares of passengers, was an ambulance train and from it were gently led the "walking wounded", those who were able to travel the long distances from the south to the north. Stretcher-bearers did their best not to jostle those they carried but still they whimpered and moaned and longed for the peace that had been out of their reach for such a long, long time.

Grace turned away and moved steadfastly towards her own objective beneath the vast arches, the fancy columns, the winging roof and delicate tracery of Edinburgh Station.

At its wide, imposing entrance she stood for a moment, drawing a deep breath of clear air into lungs that had been filled with the smoke from the cigarettes the soldiers had incessantly puffed on for the whole train journey. The sweet spring air still had a chill in it so far north, but in the gardens along Princes Street were the brave, defiant trumpets of daffodils, nodding their golden heads in the breeze, tulips of red and white and yellow, and along the edges of the neatly mown grass were low blue cushions of periwinkle and the snow white of primula.

There were motor taxi-cabs drawn up at the bottom of the steps and though she had been born and bred in a big city she was hesitant as she approached the first in line. The driver sprang out and took her suitcase, saying something to her in what she supposed was the English language but which she couldn't decipher.

"Pardon?" she asked him politely, but he grinned cheerfully and repeated whatever he had said before.

She gave up. "I want to go to Craiglockhart," she told him diffidently and at once the grin slipped from his face and he took her arm solicitously, compassionately, for did they not all know who went there, and why.

"Aye, lassie," he said, putting her in his cab as though she were as precious and fragile as a snow-flake.

Josie and Philip's son had been born on a wild and stormy night in March 1918, shouting his fury at being dragged from his warm nest into a world that seemed to have gone mad. The wind was shrieking through the thatch on the roof, and leaves that had fallen during the previous autumn whirled up about the windows, pattering against them as though they wanted to come in out of the storm.

"Well, he's got a good pair o' lungs on 'im, bless the lad," Bessie shouted over the hullabaloo, gloating over him as though he were her own flesh and blood.

"Can I have a hold?" Grace begged her.

"No, you can't, not until he's been cleaned up decent. Poor wee chap . . ."

"Well, perhaps I, as his mother and the one who's done all the hard work might have a peep at him," Josie said from her bed, "and someone should fetch Philip."

"Lass, lass, 'ave a birrof a rest first," Bessie begged, but Philip Booth, on his new legs which managed to take him wherever he had a fancy to go, clambered up the stairs and snatched his boy from Bessie's protesting arms.

They drank champagne that night, even Josie being allowed a sip, though Bessie said she didn't know what people saw in it, she'd rather have sup of ale any day of the week. She had the boy in her arms and eighteen-month-old Elizabeth scrabbling for space on her capacious lap, and, being Bessie, room was found for her, and Josie said she might as well go and stay with her mother since she was not needed here. A happy, happy time for the family whose tragedy had turned to such bounding joy and through it all Grace did her best not to let her own grief mar Josie's gladness.

Daniel Booth was three weeks old when she told his mother she was going to Edinburgh.

"Charlie's been there nine months now, Josie, and all they do is put me off and put me off. How have I allowed myself to be so spineless? He's my husband and he is suffering. I love him and I must go and see for myself. They won't even tell me what hope he has of recovering, or even if he is to recover. The times I have been up to see Doctor Prentiss at the hall but all he will say is to give it time. *Time!* How much time do

they need to decide when he can come home? I really
don't think they even know themselves. He says that
there are so many soldiers with the same . . . the same
illness. They don't call it by that name any more. That
the use of the term 'shell-shock' has been abandoned
and that on medical records the Field Medical Officer
is to enter 'NYDN' which means 'not yet diagnosed,
nervous'."

"Gracie, Gracie, slow down, darling. Do try to
remain calm."

"Calm? Would you remain calm if it was Philip?"

"No, I wouldn't, but do you think it wise to disre-
gard what Doctor Prentiss is telling you and just go
barging up—"

"I'm not barging up there, as you so quaintly put
it. I have thought of nothing else ever . . . ever . . ."

"Ever since Rupert went back?"

There was a deathly silence broken only by the
sound of the child at Josie's breast suckling heartily
and, from the garden, the shrieks of Tamsin, who was
walking now, and Elizabeth, being chased round the
bare garden by Andy Marsden and Gyp and a couple
of excited puppies the bitch up at the farm had given
birth to before Christmas. One belonged to Elizabeth,
the other to Tamsin, given them as presents by the
fond and indulgent farmer and his wife.

Grace bent her head in great distress, doing her best
to gain control of her emotions which were inclined
to slip badly at times. Josie, somewhat pinned down
by the demands of her son, put out a hand to her
and sighed. Ever since the day last September when
he had returned to the trenches Grace had had no
word from Rupert Bradley. It was as though he had

vanished over the edge of the world and what must have been the rare and exquisite days he had spent with her were no more than mist before a breeze, as easily dispersed and as easily forgotten. Grace had told her nothing but she had known that something special had taken place as Grace, for several weeks, had glowed all about the place, a look of sleek fulfilment, of polished completeness shining from her which Josie recognised. For a while she had worried in case her friend might have heaped further trouble on herself by becoming pregnant but when it became apparent that she had not she breathed a sigh of vast relief. But gradually that look of wonder Grace had carried about with her, that starry-eyed bewitchment, had disappeared to be replaced by such a dragged-down look of wretchedness Bessie had hesitantly asked Josie if that lad up there, meaning Charlie, had passed on.

"When he left I told myself it meant nothing," Grace told Josie at last. "I told myself I'd never see him – Rupert – again but I didn't really believe it, Josie. He was . . . different. I truly believed he loved me . . . at last. He didn't say he would write but I thought . . ."

"That he would. Perhaps it's because of Charlie, and your marriage, and his."

"Perhaps. I don't know but I can't go on like this, hanging around waiting for something to happen. For Rupert to . . . I need to know what is to happen to me and Charlie so *I must go and see him*. They say the war will end this year. It can't go on like this much longer, Josie. Not with the Americans in France. If it is to end I must know what . . . have some plan. God, I don't know. What I am to do with my life, with Charlie? Or if he is not to come home . . ."

"Go then, Gracie. We will look after Tamsin, you know that, unless you would rather your mother . . ."

"No, with you, please. She loves you and Philip, and will hardly miss me."

But she missed Tamsin. The journey had been endless, with constant unexplained halts and diversions, moving into sidings to let the urgent ambulance trains race by, stopping for what seemed hours in small stations as soldiers were put down or picked up, stations swarming with weeping women who knew quite categorically that they would never again see the man who was clutched despairingly in their arms.

"This is it," the cab driver said, or that was what she guessed he said. He helped her from the cab and when she asked him how much the fare was, he shook his head, took her hand and told her to put her purse away before he drove off.

She rang the bell twice and when no one came put her hand hesitantly to the gleaming brass doorknob and turned it, expecting it to be locked, but the door opened and she found herself in a wide hall, the wooden floors scrupulously polished. There was the familiar smell of carbolic but not of the underlying odour of wounded men, for the soldiers who were incarcerated here were not physically damaged. There was a wide staircase disappearing into the gloom of the first floor, woodlined walls on which several dismal paintings hung and a square table in the middle of the hallway on which a great blazing bowl of daffodils stood.

A nurse came running down the stairs, stopping in surprise when she caught sight of Grace hovering in the open doorway, then hurried forward as though she expected the visitor to go dashing off into some part of the hospital and do untold damage to her routine.

"Excuse me, miss, but may I ask where you think you are going? And may I also ask who you are? You can't just come in here and march about—"

"As you can see, Nurse, I was not marching about. I found the door unlocked and came in looking for—"

The nurse tutted irritably and Grace knew someone was about to get hauled over the coals.

"That porter . . . But tell me. Looking for who? Visitors aren't allowed to wander about wherever and whenever they feel like it. There is a strict rule."

"I am looking for my husband. Lieutenant Davenport. I would like to see him. He has been here for . . ."

The nurse's face softened and she put out her hand, placing it on Grace's arm. The place was eerily quiet, not at all like the hospital in which Grace had worked where the staff were busy in and out of wards, the men, those who could manage it, creeping about, perhaps a bit of music from the wireless, a general air of optimism and cheerfulness, even if it was forced.

A fire danced in a big grate but apart from the lively crackle of the flames and the spitting of the logs piled on it, everywhere was silent.

"My dear, I'm not sure whether that's possible just at the moment. The doctor is busy and Lieutenant Davenport is . . . is sleeping."

"When then? When may I see Charlie? It's been nine months and I have been kept away. Please, if I

can't see him now I'll wait. Or perhaps the doctor . . .
or someone . . ."

"Mrs Davenport, I have no authority."

"Then who has? I have travelled from Liverpool."

"You should have let us know then we—"

"Yes, then you could have done what?"

The nurse sighed. "Why don't you come into my
office, Mrs Davenport. I am the Matron here and—"

"Yes, I thought so. I nursed – a VAD – at a hospital
in Liverpool until my daughter was born and our
Matron was very like you."

"You mean stubborn, or perhaps officious? I have
to be to protect my . . . my patients. Now we can't
stand about here, so please, come this way and I'll get
one of the staff to bring you a cup of tea."

"Then will you let me see Charlie?"

"The doctor first . . . then we'll see."

She sat for an hour nursing a cup of tea, then
another. Matron hadn't the time to sit with her, she
said, since there were quite a few patients to attend
to, she was sure Mrs Davenport would understand.
But the doctor had been informed that she was here
and would be down to see her as soon as he could.

The hospital had evidently once been the country
home of a wealthy man, set in acres of its own grounds
around which was a high stone wall. The lawns were
like green velvet, not much walked upon, Grace was
inclined to think as she leaned against the window
frame but at this time of the year scattered thickly with
daffodils. There were clipped hedges of laurel with
spaces cut out where wooden benches were placed
and paved walks sheltered from the keen wind. There
was an arbour which, in summer, would be shrouded

with roses and all about the house was a terrace with steps that led down to all this perfect loveliness. It seemed no one was enjoying it.

At the end of the hour a tall, thin man with an intelligent face came quietly into the room, under his arm a folder on which she could see Charlie's name. He smiled, a warm, kindly smile and at once Grace felt that here was a man who understood the minds of the men he worked with, and what they had suffered, and were *still* suffering. Even before he spoke she felt a small lift to her spirits.

"Mrs Davenport, I'm Doctor Collins. Good afternoon." For by this time dusk was beginning to fall. "Please, do sit down. I believe you were enquiring after your husband."

She allowed her hand to be taken for a moment then sat down slowly, quite speechless, for the doctor was acting as though this were an ordinary hospital, or perhaps even his surgery where a wife was entitled to ask after her husband who had been taken ill with some quite basic illness, perhaps influenza or a strained back.

"It is not usual for the patient's family to turn up here without a prior appointment asking to see them, but Matron tells me you have travelled from Liverpool so I am making time to bring you up to date."

"Up to date! Doctor Collins, I have, for the past nine months, done nothing but try to get information about my husband. I nursed in a hospital and drove the doctor there mad with my enquiries as to the state of my husband's health as he was in contact with you, or so I was led to believe."

"Ah, yes." He studied a note in the folder. "Doctor Prentiss."

"Yes, but all I was told was that it would not be advisable for me to travel up here to see him."

"Yes, yes, Mrs Davenport, but you must under-stand—"

"*No*, I do *not* understand. I realise that Charlie had a horrific experience in France. They told me he had been buried" – she gulped in distress – "for fifty hours, buried alive and that when he was brought out by a brave officer he was paralysed. That though he was not physically wounded he could move no part of his body. Now surely he has improved since then? Surely he would want to know that his wife has come to see him?"

"No, Mrs Davenport, he wouldn't." The doctor's face was compassionate and his eyes looked into hers with such kindness, such sympathy, she began to feel afraid. She didn't know what of. She knew, of course, that something very serious had happened to Charlie, something that was taking a long time to put right but surely . . . Oh, God, what? Please, dear Jesus, what is this man trying to tell me? What is the matter? Charlie, my dear Charlie, give me strength to bear what . . . bring him back to me.

"My dear, there are so many like your husband. Brave young men who, as the fighting goes on and the strain under which they are forced to live weakens them, begin to show signs of mental disturbance. But Charlie lived through an experience that his mind could not cope with and so he simply shut it off. Retreated into some place where he is safe and from which, no matter how hard we try, we cannot extract him. Hypnosis, even electric shock treatment . . . you have heard of it? A new treatment which is effective in some cases but Charlie does not respond. He is . . . you could not manage him at home, if that is what you are proposing, my dear Mrs Davenport. He is . . . incontinent and has to be hand fed, changed constantly. Ah, please, my dear, don't weep. I know you want nothing more than to get him home, feed him up, surround him with the love and mercy of his family but, you see, it would do no good. The only place for him is here."

"Not for ever, please, Doctor, tell me it will not be for ever. He has a daughter he has never seen."

"I'm sorry, Mrs Davenport, that is all I can say at this moment."

Suddenly she sprang to her feet and strode towards the door, grabbing at the knob and twisting it fiercely. "I must see him. I absolutely insist on seeing him. He is my husband and I have a right."

Doctor Collins leaped up, dropping Charlie's folder and scattering papers over the carpet. He got a grasp on her arm and with the strength he had built up in years of dealing with men who were out of their minds drew her back to her chair. The moment he let go she jumped up again.

"*I will see him*," she hissed through gritted teeth. "I am a nurse and whatever his condition I will see him. I am not squeamish."

"But you love your husband, don't you, Mrs Davenport?"

"Of course I love him, you fool. Would I be here if I didn't?" The tears fell from her eyes in a wash and dripped across her cheeks to the lovely dove-grey wool of her outfit, causing dark grey drops as big as a penny.

"Oh, please, Doctor Collins, let me see him. I won't upset him."

"Indeed you won't, Mrs Davenport, for he wouldn't even know you. But you will upset yourself. I'm not even sure you would recognise *him*."

They led her through a maze of corridors, unlocking doors and locking them again behind them, Doctor Collins and the Matron, so that she was made aware of how deranged some of the men here were. She supposed behind the doors along each corridor was some poor mindless soul, for she knew that the very worst cases were brought to this place. Doctor Collins had had some success, she had been told, by Doctor Prentiss, she supposed, but some place must be found for those who could no longer live among their fellow men, for polite society would shun them and it seemed her husband, her lovable, funny, endearing young husband was one of them.

He was in a bed which was the only furniture in the room. Not even a chair, for it seemed no visitors were expected. He might have been one of the dummies she had seen in Lewis's shop window. Still, his face without expression, even his eyes, from which the lovely deep blue had faded, looking up at the ceiling. No, not looking for that implied he saw something and from their total blankness it was obvious he did not. He was tucked neatly beneath a tight sheet and there were bars on the bed, though it passed through her mind which was functioning on some level of its own that if he was paralysed, as they said he was, why should he need restraints.

His face was colourless and the crisp fair curls which had once swirled about his head were flat and lifeless.

She walked slowly across the room and placed her hand on his forehead, smoothing back his thin hair, then bent to place her lips where her hand had been. Her tears dripped on to his waxen face and she wiped them away with careful, gentle fingers.

"Oh, Charlie, my love . . . my love, " she whispered against his cheek, then turned away blindly. She fumbled for the door handle and the doctor and nurse watched her, doing their best not to be affected, for they had played this scene many times.

She didn't remember much about the journey home nor the days that followed. She was conscious of Josie and Bessie placing food in front of her and begging her to eat. She cuddled her small daughter in the firelight, her cheek against the child's fat brown curls. She watched the spring flowers bloom in her garden and the pear trees in the orchard beyond the hedge become a froth of blossom. The ditches beside the lane were massed with cranesbill and a shimmering lilac-blue carpet of bluebells came to decorate the woodland floor between her cottage and Garlands. In the depth of the wood yew and ash stood deep in wild anemones and violets and Mrs Davenport came again and again to talk of Charlie and when did the doctor think he would be fit to come home. She would go, like Grace, to Edinburgh, to see him, she declared, what did Grace think of that and was quite offended when Grace told her harshly that she must not. *Not yet!*

And in the trenches the soldiers sang with weary resignation the song that had become theirs:

> If you want to find the old battalion,
> I know where they are
> I know where they are
> If you want to find a battalion
> I know where they are,
> They're hanging on the old barbed-wire
> I've seen 'em, I've seen 'em
> Hanging on the old barbed-wire

That month the British Royal Air Force was established and Flying Officer Richard Tooley came home on leave and frightened his parents to death by his cold, mask-like expression as though he had seen things that no one else could see, nor want to. He had been flying for over three years and knew, quite positively, that he would not see the war out, for the average life expectancy for a pilot the year before had been a mere seventeen and a half flying hours! He was one of those who had survived through luck and skill and was considered to be what was known as an "ace" along with Albert Ball and William Bishop, but he knew it couldn't last.

Against the wishes and advice of Doctor Prentiss and Doctor Collins, Grace travelled three more times to Edinburgh to visit Charlie, each time sitting beside his bed and holding his hand, speaking to him of Tamsin and her puppy and her own life in Rose Cottage where, when he was recovered, he would live with them. She kissed his impassive face and stroked back his lifeless hair. She even placed her warm, living lips on his which were flaccid and unresponsive, in the hope that some memory of what they had shared might turn a key in his mind. The last time was in November.

The Germans had launched their spring offensive in March of that year but in July the Allied counter-offensive began on the Western Front, the Germans being pushed back towards their own border. In October the German government offered peace and in November the Allies and the Germans signed the Armistice.

Grace wondered why she couldn't feel more excited about it. Her brothers would be home at last. All of them, all the men who had fought and suffered for so long would be home. Ma and Pa would be themselves again and from the lovely house across the fields and woods Rupert Bradley would soon be riding his horse again, but what of Grace Davenport . . . and Charlie? Dear, damaged Charlie, what of him?

She began to cough and put her hand to her throat which felt sore, wondering if she should take Tamsin across to Bessie's for an hour or two. She felt quite dizzy for some reason and was still wondering why when she fell into a black hole, the edge of which fell in on her. She heard Tamsin laugh and the young dog barked and no more.

34

Rupert Bradley was moving, along with hundreds of other passengers just off the London train, down the wide, shallow steps of Lime Street Station, heading for the row of taxi-cabs which lined the front of the station façade overlooking the broad stretch of Lime Street. Besides the constant stream coming down the steps an equal number were going up, causing a great confusion of impatient jostling and irritation, for was not their own personal journey of far more importance than any other travellers'? It seemed the whole country was on the move.

It was November and the war was ended, though as yet the peace treaty was still to be negotiated, but the field medical officer, having recognised the symptoms of the illness which had spread through the trenches during June and July earlier in the year before dying down, had ordered Major Bradley home.

"Sir, I am perfectly able to function. Just give me a bottle of something and let me get back to my platoon. I threw it off last July and will do so again."

"I've no doubt you will, Major, but the bloody war's over so you might as well bugger off even though you have not been officially demobilised. I can provide you with the necessary papers. We'll call it leave, if you like. They can manage without you. Jesus, man, don't you think four years are long enough?" The doctor gave the drained, haggard face of the major a keen look, thanking God that at last it was done with, for he was not awfully sure this man and the hundreds of thousands of others like him could have gone on for much longer. "There isn't a man out there who wouldn't jump at the chance to get home," he went on. "Now go. Clean yourself up and go."

So he had done as he was ordered, wondering what the devil he was to do with the rest of his life. For the past four years, especially after Jessica had gone, he had literally thrown himself, in every sense of the word, into winning the next battle, into getting his men from one skirmish to the next with as little loss of life as possible, into pitting his wits, and his best sniper, against those of the enemy. He had lived in the close camaraderie of those who had fought, and died, most of them, in the trenches, aware that his frightfully mutilated face held no horrors for them. They did not shy away from him, looking anywhere but at his scars. They did not pretend there was nothing wrong with him, that he was as he had been four years ago. Like him they had seen too much that was frightful to be put off by an injury that, though it had healed, had left him with a terrible scar to one side of his face. He was a bloody good officer, so his sergeant and the men under him made him realise a dozen times a day, and he had got through the massacre with his life but now, with that life hanging about him like a heavy shroud, he must find something to do with it. The only thing he knew how to do was fight. If he had been born first he would have had the small family estate with its outlying farms to manage but Alan had beaten him to it by two years. Something in the world of ships, perhaps, since his family were connected to the shipping Bradleys who had married, generations ago, into the Hemmingway Shipping Line. Not that he knew anything about shipping but he supposed he must do something. He just felt so bloody tired. They all did. Tired in mind and body so that the news that it was all over had been met, not with cheering or excitement, but with a weary sort of relief.

He reached for the handle of the nearest cab and as he did so a small, gloved hand did the same so that for a fraction of a second his hand grasped it, and hers, pressing down the handle and pulling at the door.

At once he released it, turning courteously to the young woman who was about to get into the same cab as himself.

"I do beg your pardon," he began, for though he had plainly been there before her he was a gentleman and had been taught that a gentleman is *always* polite to a lady. He still wore his officer's uniform and his long greatcoat but he removed his cap as one did to a lady, hitching his khaki kit-bag closer to his shoulder.

"Allow me . . ." he continued, reaching once more for the door handle with the obvious intention of handing her in, but she paused, hesitating. She wore a wide, flared ankle-length skirt and a jacket with a basque and shoulder yoke. It was of a warm tweed in a flecked hyacinth blue, cinched in at her waist with a belt. Her gloves and boots were black kid and on her head was a large black hat with a turned-up brim trimmed with a wide band of hyacinth-blue ribbon. She might have been pretty with that fresh prettiness of young women had she not had a drawn look about her. She was fair, peaches and cream he had heard it described as, with blonde curls peeping from under the hat, deep blue eyes surrounded by long brown lashes, but she looked so haunted, so troubled by some inner anxiety her prettiness had drained away.

Something about her stirred a memory in his mind and, like her, he hesitated.

"Excuse me," an irate voice said at the back of them. "May one ask if you are to take that cab or not, for there are others who have somewhere to go if you do not."

Turning his scarred face in the direction of the irate man who had spoken he smiled. Not the sort of smile that expressed warmth or pleasure, a smile that twisted one side of his face and the man recoiled, muttering.

"It comes in handy sometimes," he said to no one in particular, the end of the smile returning to the young woman but this time his eyes were devoid of any wish to be alarming.

"Yes," she said but her voice was no more than cool. "And if you have no objection I will take the cab. I had no intention . . . but the trams were all full and I have to get home as soon as possible."

"Of course. Forgive me, but I seem to know you from—"

"We have met, Major Bradley." She turned her attention to the door handle, clearly dismissing him, but Rupert was intrigued. Not that he had any *male* interest in her, for his heart was given elsewhere but he would dearly like to know where they had met.

"You know me?"

"Your picture was in the newspapers. A hero who saved . . ."

At once the smile that warmed his face slipped away and his eyes cooled.

"Please, I'm not—"

"I'm sorry, Major, but I really must get home. My children are . . ."

A sudden light shone its way into his brain and illuminated a picture that had rested gently in him during the last year of mud and muck and rats and lice and the stench of putrefying bodies. A picture that he took out when the feeling came over him that if he didn't die today he would simply go off his head. He would study the picture, in his head only, of course, of a lovely laughing woman along with a small photograph of a child he kept in his wallet. Next to the photograph was a letter he had written to the mother of the child in the event of his death.

And this woman who was struggling with the door handle was connected to that woman and child.

"You were with Grace," he said stiffly, putting his hand on hers to prevent her opening the cab door.

All around them was the brisk, noisy, crawling medley of hurrying men and women, of motor cars which were increasing in number every day, of horse-drawn carriages still used by the older generation, of drays and waggons hauling goods to be loaded on to the ships in the river. There were flags everywhere, the Union Jack, brought out at the end of the war in the intense wave of patriotism and thankfulness that "their boys" were coming home at last. There were sandwichmen, their beat ended, piling their placards against the wall of the station. A couple of glossy Clydesdales moved mightily by, head chains glinting

in the pale November sunshine, feet splayed for purchase, an aproned carter at their heads. An electric
tram clattered by and the crowds surged, men in
bowlers elbowing one another aside to get a place
inside and at the bottom of the steps flower-sellers
called their wares.

"Major, I *must* get home, please." The woman's
voice was filled with desperation.

"Of course, but may I suggest we share this cab. I
will drop you off at . . . ?" He paused, waiting for her
to supply him with her address and when she ignored
him, climbing hastily into the cab, he followed her.

"Where to, Mrs . . ."

"Booth."

"Where to, Mrs Booth?"

"Spring Cottage on Derwent Road."

"Derwent Road. Grace lives on . . . on Derwent
Road." His heart was lurching against his breastbone,
beginning to beat a swift tattoo, going faster and faster.
His mouth dried up and he could not ask the question
he longed to and the woman beside him offered no
explanation, nor any answer at all.

They did not speak on the journey. She was pre-
occupied and scarcely seemed aware of him beside her
and he . . . well, what could he say, or ask, for there
seemed to be no reason for his own sudden panic.

The cab drew up at a pretty cottage. The door was
thrown open as though the cab had been watched for
and a man stepped, or rather stumbled out, his face
as grey and strained as the woman who flung herself
from the cab and ran towards him, not even waiting
to offer some payment.

Something was wrong and why, dear God, why,

did he think it was to do with Grace? This was not where *she* lived; he should know, though it was over a year since he had been in this part of the world. The autumn when he and she had . . .

He shouted after her from the doorway of the cab. "Please, Mrs Booth. What . . . ?" He didn't even know what question to ask since he had no idea what was wrong though it was obvious that something was. And was it any of his business if this woman, and the man who seemed to be her husband, an ex-soldier by the look of it, for he had what appeared to be two false legs, poor sod, had some family trouble?

They both ignored him. The man put a solicitous arm about the woman and began to lead her up the path to the front door.

"Are you all right, dearest?" Rupert heard him say. "Did Mr Hynes say he could manage? I did my best with those accounts but not knowing the business . . ." His voice died away as he bent his face against his wife's hat as though in great distress.

Rupert put his hand in his pocket and flung several notes at the cab driver who seemed delighted with them, and followed Mrs Booth and the man, stepping over the threshold and closing the door behind him as if he had every right to be there. They didn't seem to care, that's if they noticed him at all and his fear grew.

He dropped his cap and his kit-bag at the front door and followed them into the warm cosiness of a kitchen. A dog lay on a rug in front of a fire. He lifted his head, and his lip at the intruder then, deciding there was no threat to his people, put his muzzle on his paws but kept a wary eye on him nevertheless.

It was then that the man noticed him.

"Who the bloody hell are you?" he asked truculently, looking, despite his crippled state, as though
for two pins he'd knock him to the floor and when
he got up, knock him down again for good measure.
He was at the end of his tether, that was made clear
and the woman leaned heavily against him, at the end
of hers.

"Can I help in any way?" Rupert murmured, with
anything, his eyes seemed to say, though again he was
mystified as to what that might mean.

"Who *are* you?"

"Darling, it's all right, really. He's . . . Rupert
Bradley. He . . . knew Grace. We shared a cab . . ."

Knew! *Knew* Grace! The past tense. Dear sweet
Jesus, he thought he was going to go down, fall down
in a bloody faint like some girl. Grace . . . *what*? And
if he didn't faint he would surely die of a heart attack,
for inside his chest it was going at a pace no heart
should go and survive. He wanted to grab at the man
and woman, drag them towards him, glare into their
faces and demand an explanation and *at once*.

"What in hell's name is he doing here?" the man
said, running a frantic hand through his hair. "And at
a bloody time like this. We can do without visitors."

"Philip, please, darling. Major Bradley is concerned
about—"

"I don't give a shit what he's concerned about.
Haven't we enough to—"

"If someone doesn't tell me what has happened to
Grace I swear I'll knock the pair of you down. Dear
God, I'm sorry but I . . . you see, I *must know*. Where
is she? *Where is she?*"

"She's upstairs, Major, but I don't think you should go."

She might as well have directed her remark to the dog for all the notice he took of her. He lunged across the kitchen and was up the stairs two at a time. Josie Booth sighed and shrugged her shoulders, holding on to her incensed husband's arm as he would have clambered up the stairs at Rupert's back.

"Let him go, Philip. He might just . . ."

"What?" Philip glared up the stairs.

"Give her something to . . . to bring her back."

The Spanish Influenza, as it was called, came from no one knew where. Its name implied that Spain was the source of its origin but that was only because Spain, being neutral during the war, had felt no need to censor its press, as the Allies did, in order not to frighten its people. A weaker strain of the virus had occurred in the spring and Rupert himself had fallen prey to it but that was like comparing a common cold to deadly pneumonia. This strain was killing people at a frightening rate, particularly children and young adults, the very ones one would suppose it would seem certain to miss. Like a plague that must have young flesh to feed on it ignored the old or those in poor health. And it struck so quickly. A man might go to work in the best of health and would collapse in the street before he even got there. There was talk of closing theatres, cinemas, dance halls, but Grace Davenport frequented none of these places so where had she picked it up?

She lay quietly in the bed. She seemed to be asleep, though her eyes were open and he knelt beside her, eagerly taking her hand in his, but her unfocused eyes stared at the bedroom window where a slight breeze coming through the inch that was open lifted the net curtain.

"Grace . . . Gracie, darling," he whispered, touching her cheek with a hesitant, tender finger, expecting heat, as from a fever, but it was cool. She continued to lie there, not hearing him or, if she did, not caring to look into his anguished eyes.

"Grace . . . oh, my darling, what's happened to you? Dear sweet Christ, I cannot bear to see you like this. What is it?" But he knew he was talking to himself, for the woman on the bed did not seem to hear him or, if she did, had no answers for him. He could feel the pain in his heart as it surged in his chest. The blood pumped through it in such savage hurtful waves he thought it might burst open and he felt cold, a bitter cold that froze his bones and made his flesh ache, for he could not imagine his life without this woman in it. That was what was wrong with him. That was what had always been wrong with him. His refusal to accept what she offered, his fear of hurt and rejection, his horror that she might turn from his scarred face like other women, his craven cowardice, for that was what it was, that had kept him from her. Only once, the last time he was home, had he allowed himself to be wrapped in her warmth, her love, her passion, her everlasting *giving, giving, giving* and that was what it was. Her giving and himself taking. He had *allowed* her to give of herself just as though he were bestowing some honour on her. Even then, he had let his weakness get the better of him and thrown her benevolence back in her face. He had walked away from it, and from her, and from his child and now, it seemed, he was too late.

He could not bear it!

A gentle hand touched his shoulder and when he turned violently, doing his best, even now, to dash away the unmanly tears of which he was ashamed, her friend was there, on her face a look of great compassion.

"She does not hear you, Rupert. She has been like this ever since . . . She was very ill, the influenza which, they say, is rife in Liverpool. All the ports are badly hit. She had been up to Edinburgh to see Charlie only the week before. She kissed him, she said. She called it the kiss of Judas. She believes she killed him and she cannot forgive herself, for she must already have been incubating the illness. He died and then . . . her father took it; she was so ill we brought her here. I was a nurse and . . . well, her mother wasn't strong enough to . . . the babies, mine and hers . . ."

"Tamsin . . ."

"Yes, Tamsin went to Mrs Marsden at Spring Farm but . . ."

He sprang up and lurched away from her, putting up an arm as though to defend himself against whatever she was about to tell him, but it did no good. He was defenceless as she told him with great sadness, her own face wet with tears for the lovely child, that his daughter was dead and his cry could be heard by the man downstairs and the dog which sprang up in great alarm.

"No . . . oh, no. She loved that child, and so did I. Those few days we spent . . . and that poor sod. I saw him when . . . when he was brought out . . ."

"You brought him out, Rupert." He did not hear her.

". . . out of that shell-hole. What is God, if there is such a being, thinking of, to take an innocent child and a good, brave man? But then have I not seen it in France, what He made men suffer."

"No, Rupert, don't . . . don't. Men did what they did to other men."

"Don't prate to me . . ." He was crying openly now, his face awash with his devastation. He sank to his knees and put his brow against the bare arm of the woman in the bed. His tears fell on her flesh and for a long time he wept, all the tears he had stored up, for himself, for the men he had seen killed and tortured during the last four years, for the lovely laughing child who had been his daughter, for the man who had believed her to be his, and for the mindless woman on the bed who had given him so much and had asked for so little.

Josie put an arm across his shoulders and bent her head to his. Philip had climbed the stairs and hovered uneasily at the doorway and it was he who saw Grace's head turn slowly and look at the desolate figure of the man huddled at her bedside.

Quietly he took his wife's arm and when she turned, surprised, he nodded down at Grace and began to draw Josie to the door. They closed it after them.

Grace swallowed, trying to clear her throat which was still sore. She could feel the wetness on her arm and the heaviness of the head of the man who wept there, but when he raised it to look into her face, her own remained expressionless. Not empty, since she recognised him but she had nothing to express. Her

eyes were focused on him and told him that she knew
who he was but that was all.

"Grace . . . oh, my love . . . my love . . ." He could
say no more, for his own throat was clogged with tears
and his heart was in such pain, for her and for himself,
and for the child they had made and lost.

"May . . . I have a glass of water?" she whispered,
and eagerly he reached for the jug that stood on the
table beside the bed. He poured her a glassful and,
holding her head up with gentle, loving hands, put the
glass to her lips. She drank greedily. With a trembling
hand he smoothed her hair from her forehead then
gently placed her back on the pillow.

"Is that better, my darling?" he managed to murmur, looking deeply into the familiar brown of her
eyes. Once they had been a glowing tawny brown, as
glowing as a chestnut, now they were flat, set deep in
black sockets, the sockets themselves set in the ashen
flesh of her illness.

"Thank you," she whispered politely, then turned
her head away to stare once more at the small window. The movement of the net curtain seemed to
fascinate her.

Slowly he rose to his feet and removed his greatcoat,
then squatted down by the bed and took possession of
her hand, caressing the back of it with his thumb, his
eyes fastened on her face as though afraid that should
he take his eyes from her she might slip away. He sat
beside her through that afternoon and into the night,
scarcely aware of Josie who came to light the candles,
to draw the curtains, to put more wood on the small
fire that glowed in the room. He drank the drink she
put in his hand, not even aware what it might be and

when she asked him softly to leave the room since she needed to change Grace's nightgown he moved obediently and stood an inch from the bedroom door, waiting for the moment when he might be allowed to resume his watch.

"Will you not come downstairs, old chap?" Philip asked him from the foot of the stairs. "Perhaps have a bite to eat?" But he shook his head.

He watched her through the night as she slept. He himself dozed off a time or two then woke, cursing himself for leaving her, even for a minute.

How long had he loved her? he asked himself during that long, dark night, and the truth was he did not know. Probably from the first moment he had seen her at the field with her brothers, a young, shy girl, lovely and fresh as a new budding rose with eyes that told him even then that he was something special to her. He had ignored it, and her, flaunting his own handsome charm to delight other women until he met Jessica who had bowled him over. Young Grace Tooley's beauty had been ethereal, not bold and exotic like that of his wife and so he had overlooked her. But her strength, her courage, her steadfast love had not been ethereal and for the past four years – no, longer than that, for Arthur had gone in 1912 – she had dragged her family through the pain of loss, got them through and now it was she who was struck down and it was her loss, the loss of a mother for her child, that had finally broken her.

He fell to his knees as dawn was breaking, wanting to pray to the God he had reviled the night before, praying that he would not lose her again, begging for another chance to give this weakened woman the strength he had in abundance. Yes, his strength, the strength of his love which he had not known, until this moment, he possessed for this woman.

"I love you, Grace Tooley," he murmured again and again and once, for a blissful moment, she smiled in her sleep and his heart gladdened. He lifted her possessively against him and in a passion of love, kissed her cheek and her eyebrow, then rocked her back and forth in his arms.

He must have rested his exhausted body on the bed against hers in that last desperate need to let her know the breadth and depth of his love, for he woke to the sound of her voice crying out and the feel of her struggling weakly in his arms. Josie was at the door, her face creased in agitation, and behind her Philip clumsily clung to the door frame.

"Major Bradley . . . Rupert, let her go; you are distressing her."

"Make . . . him . . . go . . . Josie," his beloved woman was whimpering. "Make . . . him . . . go."

"Darling, of course. There, don't get upset. He is going, aren't you, Rupert? Please . . ."

"But . . ."

"Please . . ." Josie had her arms about Grace, holding her close, soothing her, smoothing her hair back and raining small kisses on her brow. She glared at him wordlessly then turned to Philip. "Take him," she hissed.

He allowed himself to be taken and when he was at the front door, still doing his best to argue with Philip Booth, he was almost pushed out on to the path.

"Please . . ."

"We will be in touch, Major Bradley," Philip Booth told him politely, then shut the door in his face.

35

"Nurse Davenport, I won't tell you again. If I catch you without your mask on once more I shall report you to Doctor Ryan."

"Yes, Sister, I'm sorry, but the child was frightened and . . ."

"I appreciate that, Nurse, but it makes no difference. Rules are rules and you know as well as anybody that they must not be ignored. I appreciate that you have had it but the illness is virulent as you well know and anything that can be done to reduce the risk of spreading it must be enforced. Now put on your mask and continue your work."

"Yes, Sister."

It was night-time and the ward was dark. Along each side of the long room was a line of beds set close together and in them lay women, some whimpering, some tossing and moaning, others strangely silent, one or two sleeping in what seemed some peace. The silent figures of nurses moved among them. There was a table at the other end of the ward with a low light above it and at the table sat the Night Sister, the one who had just told Grace always to wear her mask. The epidemic was tapering off now, with fewer and fewer fresh cases coming in each day and Grace was able to sit a little longer with the small girl who had been shoved into the women's ward, since the children's ward had no spare beds. She was no more than three or four years old, a scrawny little thing who bore no resemblance to the rosy-cheeked, sturdy child who had been Tamsin Davenport and Grace wondered at the mysterious ways of this disease which had killed her own beautiful healthy child and had spared this scrap who must be from the worst area of Liverpool, undernourished, neglected and yet had survived. She had been found dumped at the entrance of the hospital, unwashed, crawling with lice, her skin blotched with sores, her baby teeth rotted, her legs bowed with rickets, her breath rasping in her throat, coughing in fever and yet she had lived.

Grace soothed the child, slipping her mask down when Sister's back was turned, smiling into the terrified little face, whispering nonsense to her as she once had whispered it to her own child until she slept. They didn't even know her name since she had not spoken a word but Grace had christened her Snowdrop because she had arrived as the delicate flowers were thrusting their drooping white blooms through the soil and the other nurses had followed suit.

Snowdrops! They had been the last flowers *he* had sent to her just before she left Spring Cottage, a small basket of them, picked only hours before, she supposed, with the dew still on them, packed close together on a bed of damp green moss. Somehow the simple blooms had touched her as none of the others had done. There had been great baskets of hot-house roses, pink and crimson and white flushed with apricot. There had been African violets and even a spray of climbing hibiscus, its frilly petalled flowers hanging down like Japanese lanterns. There had been jasmine, smelling somewhat sickly in the close confines of her bedroom and all come, she was sure, from his mother's conservatory that she remembered so well. Day after day, week after week he had sent them, or delivered them to the door of Spring Cottage, pleading with Philip or Josie to allow him in to speak to her, which, politely, they promised to do when she gave the word.

He was patient at first, knowing that she was still grieving, which was only natural, prepared to wait until she was ready. He was obedient to either Philip's or Josie's request that he come again another day, turning away and climbing on the back of the old mare which still remained in the Garlands stable.

When it became evident to him that she would not see him he began to write letters. They came regularly, some by the post, some delivered by himself and others put through Josie's letter-box by the old groom who still worked at Garlands. She read none of them, leaving them unopened on the dresser at Spring Cottage, telling Josie and Philip that when the groom came again they were to be put in his hand with instructions that they were to be returned to Mr Bradley. He patiently wrote even more, or knocked loudly on the door demanding to see her, even striding round to the back of the cottage to shout under her window. But as November moved to December, then Christmas came and went, his patience turned to furious anger and, just after Christmas when he had been turned away, his Christmas present, which he had delivered previously, put in his hands still wrapped in the paper he had so painstakingly, so lovingly placed about it, he grew belligerent.

"Mrs Booth." He had never been less than courteous. "I'm afraid I must insist this time on seeing Grace, and I shan't go until I do. You must admit I have been more than patient – a bloody month and more. I beg your pardon but she must be well enough to see me. I know she is in mourning, but tell her I want nothing more than to have a word."

"She does not want a word, Major Bradley."

"It's not *Major*, just plain mister now. I was demobilised."

"Really, and what are you to do, Mr Bradley?" Josie kept a firm grip on the door, obviously determined not to let him in, though at the time Grace had already left for Sheil Road. Josie was filled with pity for this man who had haunted her house for the last five or six weeks for a chance to speak to Grace, but she could not go against her friend's absolute determination not to see Rupert Bradley, or to let him know where she was.

"I can't see *why*, Grace. The man is in love with you. He *loves* you which is what you've longed for ever since you met him years ago. He is no different."

"Perhaps not, Josie, but I am."

"And what does that mean, may I ask? No, don't say anything. I'm sorry, of course you're different after . . . after all that has happened but it's not *his* fault. You are punishing him for what has happened to you."

"Don't be bloody ridiculous, Josie. I'm punishing nobody. Can't you see, I have no feeling left in me. I'm empty. I've nothing to give him and he has nothing I want, not any more."

"Darling, things will change and—"

"Never! I don't want them to change. D'you think

I would chance my . . . myself again? I killed Charlie.
I killed my father when he came over here to help me,
and . . . and I killed my baby."

"Don't talk such blithering nonsense. You might as
well say you are to blame for the damned flu epidemic.
It was *virulent*, Gracie."

"I know, Josie, but there is nothing else I can do
except what I have been doing for the past four years.
I must go home."

"To your mother?"

"Yes. Nora is getting on and the boys will be
home soon."

"Which is all the more reason for you to make a
new life for yourself with Rupert. Dear God . . ."

"Leave him out of this, Josie. He's not been much
in evidence in my life for the past four years. Three
brothers counting Arthur, my husband, my father and
my child."

"And now you are to sacrifice a good and brave
man to—"

"Stop it, Josie, or you and I will no longer be
friends."

She began her training at the Royal Infirmary on
Brownlow Street at the end of January, but for the
first two months she did nothing but nurse influenza
cases. By the end of March the epidemic which had
swept the world and in the process killed twenty-one
million people was beginning to wane and she was to
train, not just in the work she had done as a VAD
which was with the wounded from the trenches, but
as a nurse, perhaps, one day, a Sister, in a general
hospital. She had left Rose Cottage – in fact she

never returned there – as soon as she had recovered her strength and moved back in with Ma and Nora at Sheil Road. Mr Hynes kept the shop going with the help of a young soldier who had been gassed in the early part of 1918 and whose lungs would always be at risk in the winter. The boys, her brothers, would be home as soon as they were demobilised and one of them might fancy working in the tobacconist business, so best to keep it going, Mr Hynes had said wisely. Robert, Richard and John, twenty-three, twenty-one and nineteen respectively, had faced death countless times in defence of their homes and their country and it was being said that they, and countless thousands of others, didn't want empty condolences, or charity, but jobs and perhaps one of the three of them might make a real go of it, expanding the business Pa had begun but had not been the businessman to make grow. It was all there, Mr Hynes said, and he should know, for had he not been in it more or less since Pa began it, to be grasped by someone with the gumption and the strength and the plain business acumen to work at it and perhaps the sons of Edwin Tooley might just be the men.

"Well, it's about time an' all," Nora said brusquely as Grace carried her bits and pieces through the front door. "Now, put them bags down an' get yerself by't fire. Yer look fair clemmed. 'Ere, drink this an' no argument," thrusting a cup of tea in her hand. "Yer ma's 'avin' a bit of a rest so there's no need ter wake 'er."

"I've to be at the hospital at seven in the morning, Nora, and I'd like to iron my uniform."

"Yer'll do no such thing. Edna'll be in soon an'

she'll see to it so do as yer told an' sit down. An' I've a nice 'ot-pot in th'oven so yer can get that inside yer. An empty sack'll not stand an' yer'll need yer strength ter see ter them poor souls up there." Meaning the patients who every day were choking the hospital to bursting point. The cemeteries were no longer able to cope with the bodies and new ones were being dug by soldiers in open spaces such as Salisbury Plain, on great stretches of low moorland in Lancashire and other places across the country. Cities had almost come to a stop as coal miners, tram drivers, firemen, policemen and telephone operators were struck down.

It was almost as though she'd never been away. There was only herself and Ma, until the lads were home, for Nora to fuss over, her love and natural need to nurture ready to be lavished on her two remaining "chicks". Where once it had been shared by nine of her family, now there were only the two of them, mother and daughter.

"Now stop where ya are," she scolded, just as though Grace were about to leap up and begin scouring the kitchen floor. She shook her head fiercely so that several of the pins that held back her grey hair fell on Wally who eyed them indignantly. Nora had been used all her adult life to taking command of those she loved and she loved this girl – for Grace would always be a girl to her – and this girl's family, and meant to see that no more harm befell them. Jesus, Mary and Joseph, hadn't they suffered enough, the last years decimating them, from old Mr Tooley, God love him, to that lovely babe who was up in heaven, of that she was sure, with him, with her own daddy, may the

Blessed Virgin give him peace, and with her uncles. It comforted her to know that the lovely child was with her own family. And she would work until she was in her grave for this lass, and this lass's brothers when they came home, crossing herself surreptitiously. Nora had been inclined during the last years to slide back into the protection and peace of her childhood religion, finding it gave her immense comfort.

That day he went no further than Rose Cottage where a "TO LET" sign hung askew in the garden. It was May and the hedges were green and the apple orchards on either side of the lane bursting with blossom. The oak trees which stood in at the edge of the wood through which he had just ridden were showing the first signs of golden bronze foliage and the meadows were yellow with cowslips. He had ridden across swathes of wild hyacinths which carpeted the woodland, doing his best to avoid them, and beyond them a drift of bluebells were beginning to show colour. He had heard the distinctive drumming of a woodpecker against the trunk of a tree and a pair of whitethroats chased each other across the lane, startling his mare, singing loudly. In the wet ditch that ran along each side of the lane marsh marigolds displayed their beauty. Ladies smock, all silver white . . . where had he read that, he wondered and his heart dipped in sorrow for the loveliness all around him, which had been denied to all those who were rotting in the soil of no-man's-land.

He was roused from his reverie as he stood at the gate of Rose Cottage by the sound of singing. A song that was familiar to all those who had fought, and marched, and died in the trenches. It was sung to the tune of "Mademoiselle from Armentières".

> *Three German officers crossed the Rhine, taboo,*
> *   taboo*
> *Three German officers crossed the line, taboo*
> *Three German officers crossed the Rhine*
> *To fuck the women and drink the wine*
> *Taboo, tabye, taballocky eye, taboo*

It went on, verse after verse, becoming ruder and ruder, using words which, had they heard them, would have had grown men blushing, but the three young men on their bicycles didn't seem to feel the need to moderate their language. They were riding abreast up the lane, not caring if they met a carter or a milk dray, a herd of cows or a flock of sheep. As they passed him they all three waved, then, suddenly, one stopped pedalling and came to a slithering, wobbling stop in the lane. The other two nearly went into him, both of them cursing as they clashed pedals and almost fell off their machines.

"Rupert?" the first one said hesitantly. "It *is* Rupert Bradley, isn't it?"

"Yes," he answered, perplexed, ready to be rude, for he was not much for company these days.

"Well, bugger me, lads, look who it is. Rupert Bradley. Him with the bloody motorbike we all coveted."

The young men dropped their machines and walked slowly towards him and he had no choice but to get down off his mare and stand waiting for them. Already his stupid bloody heart was beginning to race, for though it was taking his mind a few moments to recognise them, his heart did and was singing

with joy because these were *her* brothers. They had
been boys when last he saw them but now they
were men with that indescribable stamp on them
that every soldier who had been to the front recognised in another. Hardened, and yet ready to grin
at absolutely nothing, haunted about the eyes and
yet with mouths that longed to be able to laugh
again.

"It's . . . God, I can't remember your names."

"I'm Richard, this is Robert and that young fool
over there is John."

They shook hands and pummelled one another on
the back in the manner of men not much given to
demonstrations of affection and then had absolutely
nothing to say to one another, for their minds had
been concerned with things of war for so long easy,
idle conversation was beyond them, even with one
another.

"I was sorry to hear about . . . your brothers," he
said at last, his voice awkward.

"Yes, poor sods . . ." and Robert's voice trailed
away, since they had nothing to say about that either.
They looked at him steadily, studying his face but,
like all the men who had returned from the front,
making nothing of it for it was a wound honourably
received.

"Well, we must be off," Richard said at last. "We
found the bicycles where we left them at the back of
the shed. Dear old Pa . . . and decided on a last ride
before we—"

"Yes?"

"We're to try out in Pa's tobacconist's. Rob's pretty
good at selling things, especially to the ladies as those

in France could tell you . . ." They smiled nostalgic-
ally, for this peace and their own guilt at still being
alive with so many millions dead was hard to come to
terms with.

"And . . . your sister?" His breath caught in his
throat but they didn't seem to notice. Their young/old
faces at once became unutterably sad. They had never
seen their lovely little niece, but it was obvious even to
them that Grace was grieving badly for her and for her
poor beggar of a husband.

"She's nursing again."

"Oh . . . where is that?" He tried to keep his voice
casually light.

"At the Royal Infirmary. She's going in for it, getting
a proper qualification, you know,"

"I see. Well, best be off."

As they rode away, turning to wave with what they
would have him believe was a cheery hand, they
were singing another rude song brought back by the
soldiers.

No one took any notice of the rather shabby man
who leaned against a wall at the corner of Pembroke
Gardens and Brownlow Street opposite the gates of
the hospital and had they looked they would have
politely turned away for no one wishes to stare at
a horribly scarred face. It was May, spring, and the
warm weather was kind to those who had come back
from the war and were now begging on the streets.
Those come back to a land fit for heroes!

He had been there for the best part of three days –
at different times of the day – when he saw her. It was
late afternoon and beginning to drizzle, a drifting mist

off the river which laid a veil of damp over what looked like the army greatcoat he was hunched into. His head was uncovered and his wet hair lay in a heavy tumble across his forehead, dripping across his eyes. His hands were thrust deep into the pockets of his greatcoat.

She came out of the hospital with a man who bent his head to her as she spoke. She was looking up at him and smiling and the smile struck like a knife at the watching man's heart, twisting it cruelly. The man with her answered her, pointing towards the centre of town and they both hesitated at the corner where Brownlow Street ran into Pembroke Place. A tramcar rattled to a stop, heading in the direction of Newsham Park and she turned towards it but the man put a hand on her arm, evidently pleading with her. She hesitated further then, with a shrug, allowed him to take her arm and lead her back along Brownlow Street.

He followed them, the pain in him hurting quite badly and when at last they reached the Adelphi and went inside, the hurrying crowds were quite astonished when he folded in on himself, his hands on his knees, like a runner who has given his all and can go no further. They were relieved when he straightened up and began to stride off up Brownlow Hill.

John wheeled his bicycle out of the shed, leaning it against the wall while he bent down to fasten his cycle clips about his trouser cuffs. It was October and one of those days when summer, which knows it must give way to autumn, is reluctant to do so. The sun lay a brilliant but soft warmth over Ma's flower beds which were still looking their best, the colours in them, which Ma had planned so carefully, a delight to the eye. In the corner three small headstones stood among them and on each was the name of one of his brothers, those who had no known grave beyond this garden of remembrance Ma had made. He was whistling softly and as Grace stepped out of the front door she was aware that of her three brothers who had returned from the war, John was the one who had recovered the most quickly. If any of them could be considered to be *totally* recovered.

"And where are you off to, John Tooley?" she enquired lightly. "To look for a job, I hope." Knowing that Robert and Richard had settled in at Pa's shop and there was no room for the three of them. Mr Hynes had declared his intention of retiring in a year or so but in the meanwhile he was teaching the pair of them the business.

"I am, dear sister. I have been promised an interview with a local farmer and I do believe the work of a farm labourer will suit me down to the ground." His lightness turned for a moment to a deadly seriousness. "Bringing forth living things instead of killing them will do for me."

"Of course, Johnny." And she patted his shoulder understandingly, turning towards the shed to get her own bicycle. "And where is this to be?"

"Edge Bottom off the Childwall Road. Fellow we knew before the war has bought it and though he's no farmer he's going to have a shot at it. Nice chap if a bit on the quiet side. You probably remember him. We met him years ago when that flyer took off . . . what was his name? Melly, that was it."

"Mr Melly is . . . is to be a farmer?

"No, idiot, the farmer is Rupert Bradley. The farm

belonged to the family estate but his brother's sold it to . . . Grace . . . Gracie, what is it? Are you all right? God, you've gone the colour of Nora's tablecloth. Here, let me . . ." John, who had claimed his bicycle from the wall where he had propped it, dropped it with a clatter and moved to take Grace's arm, surprised when she leaned heavily on him. "What is it, old girl?"

He was badly shaken, looking round wildly for Nora, Ma, any woman would do, for this must surely be one of those things that females were struck with and he knew nothing about them.

"No, Johnny dear . . . I'm all right," she managed to gasp. A frozen mantle of paralysis seemed to have fallen about her, shrouding her eyes so that she could barely discern John's anxious face. All she could see was darkness even in the brilliance of the sunlight and all she could hear was the thundrous roar of her own heartbeat.

"Won't you sit down, Gracie?" she heard John's voice ask, longing to be rid of the burden of her, but she shook her head.

"No . . . really. I was just going to . . . to . . ." Where had she been going? And John asked the same question.

"Up to Josie's. I have a present for Elizabeth. She was three last week."

"Shall I ride with you?"

"No, of course not." She had recovered a little now. "Go . . . go for your interview. I'll be all right."

She watched him push off and begin to pedal furiously down Sheil Road towards Kensington Road, then, as though in a dream, she followed him. He was out of sight by now, for though he had been a soldier and known things many adult men did not know he was still a boy at heart and rode his bicycle like one.

There was no one about when she arrived at the gate of the farm. There was a sign neatly painted with the words "Edge Bottom Farm" and a farm track that led up to a farmyard surrounded by a sprawl of buildings. Chickens scratched and clucked in the yard, strutting in the way of their kind. Against one wall, the farmhouse, she was inclined to think, was propped John's bicycle.

She turned away, still caught fast in the dream-like state into which John's words had flung her. She opened the five-barred gate on the opposite side of the lane and pushed her own cycle through it, closed it carefully behind her and then sat with her back to the hedge, hugging her knees and blindly studying the herd of Friesian cows that grazed peacefully among the clover and daisies. They looked plump and healthy and she wondered if they belonged to the farmer at Edge Bottom. Was she sitting on his land and if so, *why*?

An hour later she heard John shouting something to somebody, something about "I won't be late . . ." then the clatter of his bicycle as he set off up the lane in the direction of home. Still she continued to sit in the long grass, then she lay back and stared into the arching blue of the autumn sky, watching as a skylark took flight going higher and higher, its rich, warbling voice liquid and silvery the further it got until it was no more than a dot.

She sighed then with a great and thankful peace and shook her head, she didn't know why, perhaps because she realised at last what it was she needed, and, right out of the blue she had found it. Or rather returned to it, and him.

When she stood up he was in the next field, walking slowly in a straight line, his arm graceful as it moved from the container he held, flowing in a fluid arc as he threw something, seeds, she supposed, first to his left then to his right. Broadcasting, she had heard it called which she would have to learn if she was to be a farmer's wife.

He did not hear her as she climbed the gate and followed him across the good, rich soil, but the dog who was ahead of him did. He turned enquiringly and began to wag his tail and she recognised him as the spaniel that had escaped him the last time she had seen him.

He whipped round to see who the dog was greeting and she thought for a moment he was about to fall. The seed container fell from his grasp, scattering the good seed in an untidy heap and she remembered thinking the birds would have a good feed this day, then she stepped into his arms.

Two hours later he lifted his head, his naked shoulders a rich amber from his long days in the summer sun, the contrast with the snow-white sheets of his bed quite startling. He brushed her hair back on the pillow, twining his fingers in it before placing his lips beneath the arched whiteness of her throat. He grinned into her dazed, bemused face, his own inclined to tremble with a strong emotion.

"What took you so bloody long?"